OX——— V/17
OX. 12/15. 11/17

FEAST OF THE INNOCENTS

Also by Evelio Rosero in English translation

The Armies (2009)

Good Offices (2011)

Evelio Rosero

FEAST OF THE
INNOCENTS

Translated from the Spanish by
Anne McLean & Anna Milsom

MacLehose Press
New York · London

MacLehose Press
An imprint of Quercus
New York · London

First published in the Spanish language as *La Carroza de Bolívar*
by Tusquets Editore, Barcelona, 2012

Esta obra ha sido publicada con una subvencíon
del Ministerio de Educación, Cultura y Deporte de España

This book has been selected to receive financial assistance from English PEN's "PEN
Translates!" programme, supported by Arts Council England. English PEN exists to
promote literature and our understanding of it, to uphold writers' freedoms around the
world, to campaign against the persecution and imprisonment of writers for stating their
views, and to promote the friendly co-operation of writers and the free exchange of ideas.
www.englishpen.org

  Supported using public funding by
ARTS COUNCIL
ENGLAND

ISBN 978-1-62365-724-6

Library of Congress Control Number: 2015950070

Distributed in the United States and Canada by
Hachette Book Group
1290 Avenue of the Americas
New York, NY 10104

Manufactured in the United States

10 9 8 7 6 5 4 3 2 1

www.quercus.com

For Gertrudis Diago

PART I

1

Help me to raise the ghost of Doctor Justo Pastor Proceso López, to unearth the memory of his daughters, from the day the youngest turned seven and the eldest was deflowered in the *finca* stables, up to the day of the doctor's death, kicked by a donkey in the middle of the street, but speak to me too of the straying of his wife, Primavera Pinzón, sing of her unsuspected love, give me strength to seek out the exact dreadful day the doctor disguised himself as an ape, by way of an inaugural joke, resolved to surprise his wife with the first fright of the Black and White Carnival. What day was it? Feast Day of the Holy Innocents, day of practical jokes, day of water and purifying baths, December 28, 1966, six in the morning, a fine mist still refusing to abandon the doors and windows of the houses, wrapping itself like white fingers around the willow trees that marked out the street corners; every soul slept, except the doctor's—pacing about his spacious consulting room, trying on a realistic ape costume he had ordered to be sent in secret from a famous shop in Canada: he had already donned the part of the ape corresponding to legs and trunk, his arms swelled with muscles and fur, coarse fur, authentic orangutan, and he had still to put on the enormous hairy head he clasped hesitantly against his heart.

Withtheapeheadinhishandshewenttolookathimselfinthemirror
oftheguestbathroom,onthegroundfloorofhisthree-storeyhouse,but
instead of confronting his yellow, fifty-year-old face once more in the
mirror he preferred to cram it straight into the velvety interior of
the black ape head, and what he encountered made him almost
happy, on perceiving a perfect ape, the reddened eyes—a ruddy gauze
covered the eyeholes, so that the doctor's eyes seemed reddened by
rage and he saw everything as if through red clouds—and he was further seduced by the ape teeth that protruded, excessively and dangerously pointed, and then the coat again, which could even be called
genuine gorilla fur; he even thought he caught a lingering whiff of
ape, and that smelly certainty, of male ape, made him sweat with all
the dejection of a male human; he said "hello," and a mechanism
in the ape's throat immediately transformed the greeting, distorted
it, made it sound guttural, a simian grumbling or threat, something
like *hom-hom*, which alarmed the doctor for a second, believing there
was perhaps a real ape in his house, or inside himself—could be, he
thought, ashamed.

He was not used to playing jokes like this. In fact, he did not joke
with anyone or about anything in that city of his which was one perpetual prank, where his forebears had lived and died laughing at
themselves, in that country of his which was yet another atrocious
joke, but a joke all the same, his city parcelled up between hundreds
of great and small pranks that inhabitants suffered on a daily basis,
whether they liked it or not, naive jokes and obscene ones, lewd jokes
and wry ones, the now-slumbering inhabitants who perhaps at this
very moment were waking in their beds dismayed to be facing not
just the joke of life, but the pranks of Innocents' Day, especially the
soakings, when everyone in Pasto was free to douse neighbour, friend
and enemy with a bucket of cold water, a hosepipe or water bombs—
the hard balloons thrown head-on or from behind, with or without the
target's consent—and the other jokes too, accepted with resignation,

the tricks and awful pranks to which they all would be subjected, from the wisest to the most ingenuous, young and old, as prelude to the Black and White Carnival.

One December 28, Alcira Sarasti, wife of his neighbour Arcángel de los Ríos, invited him to an Innocents' Day feast at her house and served some *surprise empanaditas*, filled with cotton wool, which he ate, the only innocent fool, greedily gullible, unlike the rest of the guests, later suffering from an excruciating stomach ache the entire night, what poison was that cotton wool soaked in? An emetic? An astringent? Homemade cyanide? The pious Alcira Sarasti had dreamed up that mockery made to measure and just for him—he was a tall and dignified man, but podgy and self-important as a piglet, his prominent belly betraying what could otherwise very well be an attractive fifty-year-old body; no doubt about it, that pious woman has hated me ever since I said God was another of man's bad inventions, he thought.

Frankly, he loathed pranks and pranksters, or was he afraid of them? He considered them peculiar beings who came along to disturb the peace; in general they were men and women who displayed some perfidious facial tic: a half-closed eye, for example, at the precise moment of the prank—or the jeer, which is the same thing, there is no prank without jeering for these unimaginative people, he thought— they were men and women who must have undergone some trauma in childhood, marked out by a certain savage furrowing of the brow, that narrowing of the eyes, the tongue moistening the sibylline lips, the suitably malign voice, because pranks fly close to slander, the wind laden with accusatory lies, a prank—or the jeering in it—could turn out to be more merciless than a shock, any shock was preferable to any prank, he thought. Yet, nevertheless, months earlier he too had started to plot his prank, the ape joke, just like everyone else in Pasto, because each person planned their prank during the year to put into practice on December 28, and then to perform in all its variations over the days of the carnival, January 4, 5 and 6, to keep it up, show it off, recreate it in the frenzy of fun, talcum powder and streamers, monumental floats, rivers of *aguardiente* and loves, both known and unknown, of the Black and White Carnival.

The simple prank of the simple ape exalted him to the point of freeing him to imagine himself an authentic, terrifying ape, in the early hours of that December 28, waking his wife and two daughters with his black presence and enraged eyes and simian leaps, frightening them out of bed one after another, ending up chasing them all over the house, trampling furniture and toppling ornaments and throwing the order of things into chaos as only an ape can do, exactly as he would never have done had he not found himself disguised as one, scaring the two girls possibly to the point of tears—I couldn't help it, Floridita and Luz de Luna, forgive me—and then, in the intimacy of the master bedroom, when everything signals the end of the prank and he makes as if to remove his costume, taking his wife, but taking her by force, the sweetest force, something that had not happened in years; standing before the mirror, Doctor Proceso was once again startled at himself, at the idea, the spectacle of envisaging himself on top of his own wife, disguised as an ape, struggling to subdue her by sweet force—what sweet force?—that sweet force had long since disappeared and he wondered whether it might have been better to have drunk a double shot of *aguardiente* well beforehand, in order to embark on this absurd, truly idiotic prank, which even included conjugal rape, he was out of his mind—what was the matter with him?—he and his wife had nothing to do with one another, either in bed or out of it, on earth or in heaven: the most excruciating boredom, heavy with hatred, had hovered over them for ages. Thinking of that, in front of the mirror, he beat his chest as apes tend to do out of aggression, but he did it so slowly and pitifully that the ape in the mirror looked funny and then sad, he thought, a shit-scared ape.

But the ape rallied, now imagining leaving his house to ingratiate himself with the world, via the shock of his joke, embracing people he did not usually acknowledge, not through silly pride, but because he had forgotten about the world since—recently graduated from medical school, at twenty-five years of age—he had resolved to use his spare time to write the definitive and genuine biography of the never-so-misnamed, so-called Liberator Simón Bolívar.

He had already turned fifty and the biography was not finished, would he die in the attempt? This ingenious prank that would make him friends with the world was indispensable—and, in passing, it would fire him with the enthusiasm to complete *The Great Lie: Bolívar or the So-Called Liberator*—he would go, for example, dressed as an ape to say hello to Arcángel de los Ríos, his neighbour and chess rival, prosperous dairy producer, one of the richest men in Pasto, "Don Furibundo Pita" they nicknamed him for his furious honking of his car horn, a quarrelsome drunk, but a good man when in his right mind—weren't they close friends in their youth?—he would walk into houses with open doors and knock on closed doors and poke his ape's face in through windows, chase women and girls and old ladies, make cats bristle, confront dogs, definitively concoct the story of an impeccable prank in Pasto, a city whose very history was forged from pranks, military or political or social pranks, bedroom or street pranks, as light as feathers or as thumping as elephants, his own would pass through, intimidating martyrs for just a fleeting moment, but a moment of particular shivery fright—is it really an ape escaped from some circus and might it kill me, they would think, didn't a lorry full of bulls overturn one day and the angriest one charge forward, all set to gouge a notary's door, which opened at that precise moment with Jesús Vaca right in the way, the old secretary who used to wear a hat and would have retired in three days' time and of whom nothing was left, not even the hat? Yes, like the furious bull, a gorilla was possible in this life, just around the corner, more than one person would be terrified, sorrowful like a child facing a bloody end at the hands of an older ancestral brother.

And thus, terrorizing citizens in the streets, he would trace his famous route to the chilly centre of Pasto, to the lofty doors of the cathedral, and kneel down and pray before them as only a trained ape is in the habit of doing, convinced by the word of God, repentant, astonishing the faithful, shocking the priests, because not even the Bishop of Pasto—Monsignor Pedro Nel Montúfar, better known as "Obispo Avispa" or "the Wasp," friend and fellow pupil from childhood—would be excluded from the joke, he would visit him in his palace, pester him, assault him and, if they let him get inside the Governor's Palace dressed as an ape, he would annoy Governor Nino Cántaro too, another fellow pupil from primary school, but never a friend, top of the class, "the Toad," it would be splendid to chase him down the corridors of power, but the soldiers who guard the governor's residence would not allow it, quite likely one of those idiots would take the fact of a crazed ape on the streets of Pasto at face value and shoot not once, but three or five times, to be sure the church-going ape who dared to kneel would not be left alive.

No: a rebel ape would be unsafe; it was risky to attack the government in fancy dress.

He would settle for just being the immortal ape kneeling before the cathedral doors, and that is where the high point, the crowning moment of the prank, would take place: he would remove the ape head, revealing himself to posterity with his real face, Doctor Justo Pastor Proceso López, eminent gynaecologist, receiver of life, secret historian; "It's Doctor Proceso," eyewitnesses would cry, "disguised as a gorilla," and they would say, "the worthy gynaecologist frightened almost everyone, his humour's not just black, it's multicoloured, he has a gift for it, he scandalized Monsignor Montúfar, he's one of our own," and as in a fairy tale, his prank would turn him into a beloved citizen for ever, the unforgettable ape praying on its knees at the cathedral doors, a parable with many possible interpretations, he thought, the docility of the wild beast before God's goodness, the violent creature bowing down before celestial authority, the ape, ancestor of the human race, prostrated at God's doors, an example for that same human race, ever more idiotic, to follow, God, God.

God.

But such a prostration—the doctor foresaw—a chimp praying at God's doors, would be considered a serious case of ungodliness by many, a blow to Catholicism, a despicable joke that had to be penalized not only with an impossibly high fine, but also excommunication and a dressing-down from a committee of the representatives of decency—no matter, he concluded, the wisdom of the prank would ultimately prevail over the boorishness of the tricked, the news of his disguise would appear on the front page of Pasto's only newspaper, skilfully interpreted under the byline of the wise Arcaín Chivo, philologist, sociologist and palaeontologist—another of his old friends— better known as "the Philanthropist," former holder of a professorship in history at the university and holder of another in a subject which he himself dubbed "Animal Philosophy," with fundamental irony. A photograph of the doctor dressed up as an ape, or one of the ape kneeling at the cathedral doors would give an explicit idea of the historic deed, his wife and daughters would be sure to take him seriously for the first time in their lives, he would exist for them, they would be reconciled, everyone would bring him up in their daily chit-chat, it was possible the Mayor of Pasto, Matías Serrano, "the One-Armed Man of Pasto"—who was not actually one-armed, but a friend of his, unlike the governor—would issue a decree that he replay his practical joke for the fancy-dress parade, and not a single band, troupe or float would be more memorable than his disguise of a kneeling chimp praying at the Black and White Carnival.

Doctor Proceso fled from the mirror as though fleeing a cage.

He went into the living room, where the fireplace was still warm and from the golden walls, in the same photograph, the puzzled eyes of his grandparents judged him, seated around a piano in the sepia-toned atmosphere of an old house. He too sat down, in his easy chair, a sort of throne in the middle of the room, and intended to cross his legs, but the bulky costume prevented him so he remembered again he was an ape, and was reminded once more by his own reflection in the glass protecting a watercolour painted *en plein air* of his wife, Primavera Pinzón, represented as the country maid with the pitcher of milk, the famous story of "The Milkmaid" down to the last detail, the thoughtful, vigorous girl building castles in the air, barefoot, rosy rounded calves, threadbare skirt ripped at random by the thorns of a bush, in reality shredded by the knowing hand of the watercolourist, who had slashed it almost to the crotch, up to the curve of a buttock, close by the magnificent hips; thus was the beautiful Primavera portrayed, petite rather than tall, with golden plaits, two cherries joined at the stalk over her ear as an earring, artful mouth, shoulder bent under the weight of the jar, fleeting shadows about to obscure the magical road that would lead her to the village to sell the milk and buy the chicks and sell them and buy the hen and then the piglet and sell them and get a shed with two cows and earn more money than she ever dreamed of—before the breaking of the milk jug.

The watercolour of "The Milkmaid Primavera"—or the glass that protected it—reflected his actual appearance, a flesh-and-blood ape sprawled in the easy chair, a pensive beast with its head resting on one hand like "The Thinker," whatever am I doing as an orangutan?— he said to himself in alarm, and sat up, experiencing a premonition of disaster, his future absurdity in the eyes of his family: his fifteen-year-old Luz de Luna and his seven-year-old Floridita and above all his wife, who would take advantage of the ape joke to remind him of it for the ensuing year, to rub it in day and night, and not as a celebration but pure derision, stressing how much she detested him; it is quite possible I am ill-prepared for an ape costume, better to take off the body and head as soon as possible and chuck this feeble attempt at conquest in the bin, although better still to burn it so not a scrap remains, how to explain a brand-new gorilla suit in the bin? Who brought this nonsense in? What were they thinking? Questions his wife and little Floridita would ask out loud, Floridita who was already beginning to hate him; the last time he tried to give her a paternal goodnight kiss she had turned her face to one side and said, "yuck, mummy's right when she tells us you smell of pregnant women's undies," but what did that little girl know about the smell of pregnant women's underwear? What kind of language was this? For God's sake, Justo Pastor—he said to himself—he needed to burn the rubbish, get into his pyjamas on the double and get back into bed with Primavera, who would no doubt get angry at being woken in the middle of the night but who, nonetheless, would be hotter than ever under the covers, her moist crotch almost open, and would fall back into a deep sleep, allowing the gynaecologist's expert finger to softly graze the tip of each pubic hair and then after an hour of gentle flight to land on one labia and check it over and then straight on to the other, affecting nonchalance, and after another hour of valiant and almost painful effort begin to sink itself into that font and fountain of molten lava that his wife became when she slept, his beloved—beloved in such a way, one thing in real life and another in dreams—until the final climax, hers and his, the never more alone Doctor Justo Pastor Proceso López, silently masturbating beside his wife's blazing body, the woman who, were she to wake at such liberties would surely scream, he thought, *what have we come to?*

He went up the stairs, a thoughtful, irresolute ape, one hand on his chin, the other scratching the shaggy head, more surprised at himself now than when he saw himself in the mirror, he went up as if he were on the point of collapse, to the first floor where the guest bedroom was, along with the laundry room, the toy room and, furthest away, his library, which was also the chess nook, with its rosewood table, marble pieces and two solitary chairs.

He went in there and stopped by the chessboard, where he had last played years before with his neighbour Arcángel de los Ríos, Don Furibundo Pita, winning a bet he could no longer recall. He remembered, yes, they started another game straight away, but did not finish it because they were interrupted by a tremor, the brief but worrying tremor that traversed the city, a terrestrial shudder that made lamps swing and the foundations of the houses creak; tremors were frequent in Pasto, a city wisely wary of its fiery volcano—the age-old Galeras, which poked its nose from under your sheets at the most unexpected moments—they were disturbed by this tremor, which on other occasions lasted a long time, too long, and left its mark by demolishing poorly constructed houses, but God knows how He distributes his earthquakes, he thought, how He metes them out, assigns their victims, how He ends the ones that must end and how He leaves alone the ones yet to begin, but, he wondered, is God really fair? God, God, the tremor—like the heart of the volcano—it would gnaw away at you in the most intimate hours of the soul, it was an unsuspected, unexpected, ill-timed and always-unwanted guest who was dreaded as the city's worst joke, or worst fright—*from Pasto, with love to my children: a volcano is my heart*—the city's immemorial joke, fright and joke simultaneously, it froze hearts while it lasted, thoughts were fractured for the duration of the rocking, hairs rose on the nape of your neck, you went grey, on one occasion, the last, he had had to curtail the climactic embrace with Primavera, the almost-sweet finish in unison, through the singular fault of a a tremor, the fear of dying was that strong, stronger than the culminating embrace, it tore them apart at the peak of the restorative embrace and did not fit itself to the desperate rhythm of their bodies—as the most innocent would think it might—but dangled them from the all-encompassing fear of death, which is stronger than any love.

It had been his last attempt to love and fall in love again.

Finally the ape resolved to tackle the third storey of the house, the octagonal floor with wood-panelled walls, large paintings of Christs and Madonnas hanging here and there, intimate and familiar, where his daughters' rooms and his own marital bedroom were to be found, all three doors open wide.

He had promised himself he would burn the disguise right away, embark on another session of sleep-love in bed with Primavera Pinzón, but he paused, lost in thought, before the bedroom of the elder of his daughters, Luz de Luna—the name insisted upon by his wife, who had still considered herself a poet on entering into marriage and decreed that if she gave birth to a girl she would be called after the poem she wrote on her wedding night, "Luz de Luna: *This day the pure moonlight arrives at my wedding bed / And frees my soul from the dark circus where it wanders / It illuminates and redeems it from the onslaught of the donkey who / With his brutish conquering lance / Pierces my maidenhood.*" Doctor Proceso knew it by heart; it was his wife's last poem because, according to her, she lost not only her virginity on her wedding night, but also her poetic talent, a misfortune not only for her family but for humanity—you were to blame Doctor Donkey, said his wife, who never called him by his name, but only "Doctor Donkey," with feigned affection, unlike the women who visited the doctor's consulting room, his utterly faithful patients of all ages who, as a courtesy, and in feminine retaliation, called him "Doctor Gentle."

Before the charming but everyday scene of Luz de Luna sleeping, the inert ape, slack-mouthed, ran a hand over his jaw, it really was an ape in the doorway, reflecting; he went back over the fifteen years that had gone by since that highly unusual wedding night, the night that had surely engendered Luz de Luna, because many nights would pass before he tangled with Primavera Pinzón in bed again. When they got married, the doctor was thirty-five and his wife twenty: now she was a woman of thirty-five and he was a fifty-year-old. He remembered that first night as if it were this one: as soon as he finished, his wife got free of him with a cry that could have been disgust or defiance and leapt from the bed to the table to write that poem by the light of the moon—and, in fact, moonlight was shining through the window—that poem, he thought, where he ended up, in such a roundabout way, likened to a donkey.

So, his Luz de Luna was fifteen.

The bedroom window was open; it looked onto the garden, where the glossy boughs of the Capulin cherry tree reached upwards; the ape went to the window and closed it. Then, leaning over his daughter, who slept face down—long dark hair, pale profile—he saw her for what she was: already a young woman, her mouth tinged a blueish hue, open, as if she were speaking voicelessly. Stretched over the side of the bed, one of her feet stuck out from under the covers, dangling like something pink and formless, not exactly a foot, he thought, but a piece of something separate from his daughter. He thought the sight of the horrible ape would be a nasty awakening for Luz de Luna, and moved away on tiptoe: it was better to go back to his room, take off the costume and consign the joke to oblivion, the joke he had thought over to the point of exhaustion during nights of insomnia and which exalted him more every day. No. He was no good for jokes—or jokes were no good for him? What sort of man was he? Really, a normal man or a defenceless spirit exposed to the universal waywardness that makes the weak its victims? Then, cautiously, he withdrew, alarmed because his daughter spoke a word in her sleep, a word he could not understand: "stables?"

He was already heading for his bedroom when he discovered, by the half-light of a lamp, that a boy was asleep in the room belonging to his younger daughter, Floridita, in the same bed, what was the world coming to? Who could it be? That December 28, Floridita turned seven, and the boy, that boy—who was it?—seemed a little younger, around six—wasn't it the son of Matilde Pinzón, Primavera's sister? Primavera already knew he did not approve of the excessive camaraderie between the boy and his daughter, that constant coming and going together around the house. And now he had to find them sleeping in the same bed. For years now Primavera had utterly tormented him, and the torments he recalled were more serious than two children cuddled up in bed; Primavera, Primavera, he yelled to himself, who would not one day wish to become your murderer?

And at last he entered the marital bedroom. He forgot about the ape he found himself inside, and seeing an ape in the mirror made him swear and jump backwards: he had frightened himself, there he still was, dressed as an ape.

He carried on, hurriedly, so as not to see himself any longer. His bulky silhouette was afloat in the blue light of dawn. In the doorway he had already started to remove the ape head, determined to make it disappear, when he heard the sleeping woman moan, the humid moan of Primavera Pinzón that issued softly from the centre of the bed, her velvety tone, her indecipherable song and, instantly, he forgot about the costume, observing Primavera with delight. Was she dreaming she was making love? Dreaming of love? Or did she not love? And, from his own experience, hearing her murmur "here, here," he opted for love, and leant over the bed, over his own bed in which this time his wife alone slept, or his wife slept alone with her dream of love: the alpaca mattress moulded itself around her supine position, one arm bent beneath her head, her face, eyes closed, pointed at the ceiling, lips parted, moist, reddened, legs splayed, the inherent scent of heat which could only emanate from her neck, from the blonde hair spread over the pillow, now Doctor Proceso López was not yelling Primavera, Primavera, who would not one day wish to become your murderer, but he promised himself solely to make her fall in love again for a minute, or die, God, God.

God.

He swore he would give his life just for one embrace and an exuberant caress from Primavera at that exact moment of desolation, or to at least get into bed with her and never mind that she would wake against her will and in a bad mood, he thought, he would have her there anyway, all of her, and when she turned over, exasperated, to sleep far away from him—her face towards the other side of the bed, her soul much further off—the light of the dawn would help him appraise at leisure the marvellous rear of the unapproachable Primavera, the rounded whiteness with pinkish sheen, and perhaps later on his medic's hand—his medicinal hand, his hand well-versed in desperation—would caress her with that lightness of touch akin to fearfulness, persistent in the end, advancing from hair to hair towards Primavera's most hidden ones, the doctor was just imagining this ritual of sleep-love when Primavera Pinzón woke up, unfortunately for them both, she opened her eyes and first of all saw the ghastly shadow, the shadow in flesh and blood of an ape in her room, both hairy arms raised over her, ready to go for her throat, Primavera screamed noiselessly, her hands shielded her face, she tried to get to her knees under the heavy bedspread but did not manage it, her legs were turned to butter, now she saw that the immense ape was grabbing its head, gripping it as though it were hurting him, Primavera's eyes goggled, she could not believe it but had to, there was an ape in her bedroom, and in a whirl of panic she was able to remember that apes carried off native girls and took them to their dens in the trees and there they possessed them like female apes, surely this one would be no exception, he would carry her to the garden, take her up to the top of the cherry tree and once there—not only in front of her daughters, but the servants and a neighbour or two—convert her into a female ape crying out, but in terror or pleasure, she was able to wonder, regretting her very question; who knows whether he

would take her from the front or behind, Primavera was able to wonder that too in her swoon, now still more horrified to see, incredulous, that the ape was taking off its head and out came the head of,
who could it be, my God, my husband, she cried.

With the ape head in his hands the doctor only dared to smile at
his wife's astonished face as if expecting a kiss and begged "forgive
me, I'm going to explain" when she interrupted him, stammering
"God, but what a beast you are," and now she could neither stammer nor breathe—out of fear or indignation, the doctor wondered—
because Primavera's mouth gaped open, searching for air, her chest
was contracting inside, the vein in her neck was throbbing, her staring eyes finally closed and her head lolled to one side in defeat. Doctor Proceso hurled the ape head onto the pillow and stretched his
arms towards his wife; he tried to take her pulse but the ape's great
mitts hindered him.

With considerable effort he took off the ape hands, threw them on
the floor as if they were burning, pressed his fingers to his wife's neck
and gave a start; it was necessary to ask for help—he realized—fetch
a heart doctor, and he ran from the bedroom as if he were escaping,
hurled himself at the staircase and, between the second and first floors,
while shouting "Primavera could die of shock" to himself, stopped in
his tracks remembering that *he* was the doctor, so he headed once more
for the bedroom to give Primavera mouth-to-mouth resuscitation:
cruel sarcasm to kiss his wife in such a manner, he thought, an urgent
and desperate kiss, it's quite possible Primavera is already dead, to
think we will have to hold the wake right on Innocents' Day, and it was
during this very brief trajectory, while he painfully ascended the stairs,
that he convinced himself his wife would, in fact, die, it was true, Primavera Pinzón would vanish from the earth, innocent victim of a joke
more innocent yet, and the news of his joke would not only fly around
the city, but take hold of the entire country and maybe the world, it is
not very often a man kills his wife with an ape costume the moment
she wakes up.

And after that unlucky death, through which, of course, life's cruelty, its fatality, its irony would be corroborated, a man wants to make his wife laugh and kills her, he would be "overwhelmed by grief" and attend the burial "dressed in black" although he should go dressed as an ape, he thought, suddenly considering, in the brief time spent going back up the stairs, the other possibility: that Primavera's death would free him to marry another woman, lusty and warm, more willing than Primavera when it came to caressing, more lenient and generous than Primavera Pinzón—cold, bitter, perpetually unfaithful, and that was the hardest thing to bear, he thought, her ugliness is the terrifying type, the ugliness which hides behind beauty is much more shocking—he cried out imagining another woman in his bed, but it seemed unwise to desire another woman at this juncture, he told himself with remorse, and preferred to consider another possibility, imagining that after so much pain, in the middle of the funeral, right there in the cemetery, his two daughters and the other relatives would unexpectedly begin to laugh, pointing to him as the victim of his own invention; Primavera Pinzón's death had been a joke on the back of his own unsuccessful prank; the coffin lid would open, Primavera would emerge with a sprightly leap attired as a bride—as she wished to be when she died—a balletic leap, looking tastier than ever—thought the doctor, who used to liken his wife's beauty to the sampling of an exquisite dish—and meanwhile he, the victim, would be congratulated by the Bishop of Pasto, also an effective partaker in the joke, and his friends, the professor Arcaín Chivo and the mayor Matías Serrano, would greet him, and even the gravediggers and the rest of the mourners, half the city would surround him, because after all was said and done how magnificent that joke was, begun by him, cleverly carried on by his wife and then by the city, the joke would last a thousand years, he said to himself, and now he fervently wished his wife would live, that he would not find her lifeless—as he had left her.

He entered the room, fearful, swallowed up by anxiety—it was quite possible Primavera would be dead from an attack of indignation—he entered at a run, half dressed as an ape, and lurched to a standstill: there, sitting on the edge of the bed that Wednesday, December 28, 1966, Innocents' Day, happy prelude to the Black and White Carnival, Primavera Pinzón, her mouth open, the tip of her tongue passing over her lips, was contemplating with enormous curiosity the black ape head resting on her knees, she turned it round and round, discovering the seams, tracing the red film over the eyes with trembling fingertips, testing the consistency of the fangs, stroking the wiry fur and then, expressionless, getting to her feet, depositing the hairy head extraordinarily carefully on the bed, in the very place where the doctor used to sleep, *his place*, and pointing to the great ape head as she breezed past, she said:

"I prefer him."

2

He woke alone, what time did he succumb to sleep? He did not hear his younger daughter's shrieking, as was the norm, a delight of childish pandemonium all over the place, but he remembered as if in a fog that Floridita and Luz de Luna, along with their mother, were travelling that morning to the *finca* to finalize details for the birthday party, what time would they celebrate it? He had forgotten, hordes of children would turn up, the clown company, the puppets, the trio of musicians. He had bought Floridita a Shetland pony as a present, which was being kept hidden in the stables, with a great yellow bow around its neck.

There was no-one in the house, or yes, there was someone: very close beside him, in the bed, looking almost like he was breathing, lay the ape, split in half, the hairy suit stretched out lengthways, the feet and hands; the great black head seemed to sniff at him, what time did he take off the disguise? Or had Primavera Pinzón removed it, taking pity on him? Doctor Proceso gave such a heart-rending sigh that he felt sorry for himself, as only an ape could be, he thought, and let out an incongruous laugh, bitterly sorrowful and strangely joyous, a desolate celebration; he remembered Primavera that morning when she discovered the ape peering into her face, how well she faked her mortal fright, what a great Innocents' prank had been thrown together in an instant—on the back of his practical joke—what dizzying imagination! She had even seized the chance to say "God, but what a beast you are," and convinced him, a doctor, of the possibility of a death from heart failure; yes, she had mocked him majestically, as only a woman can: his woman. His wife was enough to make you laugh and cry and die and be born again, never another woman like Primavera, he thought, but where had their love ended, if it ever existed? What had become of their love? A foolish word, among the most foolish of all, an infantile deception, just a physical, carnal attraction that lasted as long as the sowing and harvesting of the corn, no longer.

From the kitchen, the cook Genoveva Sinfín, the old woman who had been with him for years, called him with a yell: "Doctor, are you awake? Can you come down?" An unusual cry in the history of the house: something serious must have happened. He put on his dressing gown and opened the window overlooking the garden. "What's wrong?" he shouted.

"Come down, for God's sake."

He ran to the stairs carrying the ape's head and the rest of the costume; he meant to have them get rid of that nonsense, and forget about it for ever.

Sinfín was waiting for him in the kitchen, hands on hips, face more wrinkled than ever, pinched mouth turned down at the corners, a great grimace of tribulation. Furious—or did she just look it?—Sinfín perspired, eyes brimming with tears, behind the table upon which a sumptuous roast pig reposed, face down on a serving dish; blue flies were circling its broad ears.

The cook brandished a wooden spoon and buried it in one side of the pig; she took it out, steaming, and held it towards him; the doctor

saw the stuffing of toasted rice, the pork meat shredded among peas
and kidney beans. Then he heard the cook wail:

"Ground glass, *señor*."

Yes. Blue streaks of glass glittered along the edges of the spoon.

"It was Floridita. She ruined my week's work. And to think this pig
was for her very own birthday."

"She couldn't have," the doctor said.

He examined the inside of the pig, digging about with the wooden
spoon; now he detected big pieces of glass from a broken bottle. The
sausage smell made him feel nauseous. Nearby, there was another serving dish, piled high with roast guinea pigs, corncobs and boiled cassava.

"The guinea pigs too," Sinfín said. "They stuffed them with pins.
I don't know when I let down my guard. I felt them hanging around me,
over here, over there; they lay in wait for me, laughing: it was Floridita
and her cousin, that little devil Chanchán. God forgive me, but you had
to know about it."

"Order roast chickens for the party," the doctor said. "Chorizo,
chips, pork crackling. And don't worry about it any more, Genoveva."

"And what are you going to do about the prank, if you don't mind
me asking, Doctor? It's not my place to say, but things can't end here,
or aren't you going to protest?"

"Of course I am, Genoveva. I'll speak to Primavera: if Floridita and
her cousin are to blame they'll get their proper punishment, don't you
worry. Now, if you'll excuse me . . ."

"Doctor, that's not all. Follow me, please."

He followed her, displeased, out into the garden. They passed in
silence through a large peeling gate. There, sitting on a wooden bench
that leant against the trunk of the Capulin cherry tree, where turkeys
and hens roamed about, was the gardener, bare chested and with a
white shirt tied around his head as a bandage. Even from far away, the
doctor could make out the bloody shirt.

"Homero, what's the matter?" he asked.

"Nothing, *señor*," the gardener answered, blushing. He was a pale, sickly man, around forty years of age, famous for his perpetual silence and because he had long lived in a lonely hut on the edge of the Pasto cemetery. Some said he had killed his wife, burying her under the laundry sink; others that his wife had killed him, even while he lived, because she ran off with the gravedigger, provoking this near muteness in him, that sort of lethargy towards life that was reflected, exactly, in his way of being, just like a corpse, they said: dead to speech, dead to walking about, dead simply to existing at all.

"Nothing?" the cook grew indignant. "Somebody balanced a jug on the top edge of the gate, where Homero comes in every morning. He opened the gate and the jug fell down and cut his head open."

The doctor walked over to him. "Why didn't you tell me about this first, Genoveva?"

"Because it had already stopped bleeding," the cook said.

The doctor untied the shirt carefully. He looked at the wound, touched it.

"Not bad," he said. "It's already clotted. No need for stitches, Homero."

"Of course not, *señor*. You didn't have to come," replied the gardener, bewildered, not losing sight of Sinfín.

A strong smell of human shit, issuing from the gardener's head, then repulsed the doctor: he took a step backwards.

"The jug was full of it," Sinfín explained. "Another joke played by Floridita and her Chanchán, celebrating Innocents' Day in their own fine way, *patrón*."

The doctor remembered the ape head he was carrying under his arm, and the rest of the costume: he had noticed his servants' questioning gaze earlier on.

"Floridita turns seven today," he said, without looking at anyone. "I won't say anything today. Tomorrow. Sorry, Homero, I'll compensate you for that injury, you'll see. For now, I'm going to ask you a favour."

And he held out the expensive ape costume he had ordered from Canada.

"Burn this," he said. "Don't give it away. I don't mean hide it, either. Burn it immediately."

The gardener received the costume without saying a word. He left the garden by the back gate, which led to the garage. He looked strange, weaving his way through pots of geraniums and azaleas with the hairy suit over his shoulder and that enormous gorilla head dangling from his hand: he had half hidden it with the shirt that previously covered his wound, so now the gorilla looked like a hunter's bloody booty.

Starting to shave, in front of his en-suite bathroom mirror, the doctor was in a position to observe another prank: hanging from the wall behind him, reflected in the mirror, was the scorched body of a black cat spying on him for evermore. It seemed preposterous to him that his younger daughter—just turned seven—should involve herself in such ghastly matters.

He breakfasted, more alone than ever, served by Sinfín, who studied him in silence. And, still overwhelmed by the cat prank, he put on the raincoat hanging from the umbrella stand. He headed for the door, which opened on to the street, feeling sunk in dark presentiments.

"Aren't we going out in your jeep, Doctor?" Sinfín asked, about to go and open the garage.

"No," he said. "I'm going to walk."

"Walk where? They're expecting you at the *finca* for the birthday party. It's getting late, you have to take me, who's going to cook for them? That's what we arranged with the *señora*. Remember Floridita and her Chanchán poisoned the pig: we need to buy some chickens, *señor*, and the sweet maize dumplings, egg whips, toffee sticks, crumbly *alfajores* and meringues for the children."

"I'm just going out to walk. For a bit."

"You'll get soaked, Doctor. Remember it's Innocents' Day. The ones playing out there have no respect for anybody, can't you hear them chucking water about? You'll catch a cold."

But he closed the door behind him.

He remained lost in thought—as though he did not recognize the world—facing the lonely square block occupied by his house, in that residential neighbourhood known as "Las Cuadras," its houses as large as they were faded, each with a terrace and front garden.

Then a blue pickup truck flew past him: it was carrying a gang of sprites in the back who were flinging waves of water to left and right with their pointed hats; no wave caught him but, in one second, a girl dancing in the middle of the sprites suddenly shot at him, from her red open mouth, from her throat—as if it were a narrow fountain—shot at his mouth, which was open in astonishment, a blue jet of water, a tiny wave against his face; he felt the droplets, more than warm, splash over his eyelashes and nose and then dash between his lips—he recognized the bittersweet water, its intimacy, drawn from who knows what female depths, he thought, he managed to think.

The pickup disappeared around the corner, with a screeching of tyres.

He asked himself, too late, if it would not have been better to heed Sinfín's advice. He was revived by Pasto's wind, whistling icily around. There was no-one else on the street, apart from the heads—the eyes and smiles of those who peeped from terraces to spy on him, innocent victim of Holy Innocents' Day. But he walked in any old direction, as if it did not matter to him.

Disturbing his tranquillity, on the corner he ran smack into a Pasto pedestrian who was taking, leading or moving himself along by pulling his own nose; at least that is what he saw, or understood: that there was a man hauling himself along by the nose, one of his hands gripping the end, and he was dragging himself who knows where. It must be another Innocents' prank, he thought, as he watched the passer-by disappear off down the pavement. "Or maybe," he said aloud, "it's some idiot who knows me and decided to make fun of me." Just then he heard a honk, and another: it was his neighbour Arcángel de los Ríos, Don Furibundo Pita, who had just pulled out of the garage in his Willys, and honked at him three, four times. Furibundo Pita's jeep, with its two-man cab, was carrying six trussed hens and a milk churn in the back that morning.

"Get in, Pastor," he heard him shout. "Get in quick or they'll soak you."

The doctor wondered whether he should jump and hurl himself into the back, among the hens. The hesitation cost him dear: the door of a neighbouring house suddenly opened and a group of monks appeared, each with a bucket of water, who surrounded the doctor and doused him. In spite of having his raincoat on, he felt the water enter under his collar and shiver its way down his back. Don Furibundo had already opened the passenger door and the doctor got in the cab, pursued by further lashings of water at the nape of his neck.

"Get back, you bastards," came Furibundo Pita's formidable bellow. Small-framed, but his voice, though shrill, was that of three men. As if by magic, the monks retreated: Don Furibundo Pita was the only person in Pasto capable of crossing the city on foot on a December 28 without anyone daring to soak him, throw a pinch of flour at him, sing him a ditty or dance around him.

Out of danger, soaked to the marrow, Doctor Proceso thanked his neighbour.

"The worst thing about that lot," Furibundo said, "is that they use dirty water. They are Martínez's sons, well disguised, they may have soaked you in their urine, the wretches. Did they pee on you, Justo Pastor? Poor Doctor Justo."

And he laughed, gunning his Willys through the streets, honking left and right for no reason.

"No," the doctor replied, recalling the gardener's head. "It's clean water."

At least that is what he wanted to believe, without much conviction.

Furibundo Pita was one of the richest men in Pasto. He did not keep his money in the bank; he had it buried under the courtyard of his house, where he raised his guinea pigs. He attributed the origin of his fortune to horse racing: he had bet all his savings on the speedy Cincomil, and won. He did not bet again, and increased the capital. He was the owner of a trucking company and four cheese-producing farms, and had not lost the habit of escaping to relax each morning in the humblest of his *fincas*, in Genoy. But that morning he was not going to Genoy, and this was the first thing he told the doctor:

"I'm not going to Genoy today. I'm going to defend my honour."

The doctor did not reply, what was that about defending honour? He was quite familiar with his neighbour's eccentric way of thinking, his quarrelsome character, especially when he succumbed to his weekly drinking spree.

"If you want me to give you a lift anywhere," Don Furibundo went on, "I don't mind delaying the salvation of my honour."

"I'm not going anywhere," the doctor said.

"You went out so they could soak you, and they soaked you, Doctor."

The cab seat, covered in calfskin, was sopping wet all over.

"I forgot what day it was today," the doctor said.

"Shall we go? Will you come with me?"

"Where to?"

"To defend my honour. I'm going to Tulio Abril's—the maestro. Do you know him?"

Maestro Tulio Abril was one of the most famous craftsmen in Pasto, who devoted his energy every year to the construction of a carnival float that would compete in the competitions on January 6. Doctor Proceso remembered him: a short, robust man who must be going on seventy and who, one midnight ten years ago, turned up at his house to request his services; he'd brought his wife, Zulia Iscuandé, lying on a handcart: her ninth labour had become complicated in the hands of a midwife. Doctor Proceso managed to save Zulia and the baby. Out of gratitude, Zulia Iscuandé baptised the newborn with the doctor's names: "Justo Pastor," adding a third—"Salvador."

"Let's go," the doctor said. He wanted to know how honour was saved.

Now on Avenida de los Estudiantes they saw the truck belonging to Pasto's firefighters go by like a reddish meteorite, firemen aloft like drunken acrobats, not off to put out fires and dam floods but taking part in the fiesta: they shot great jets of water from the hose, straight at a dense knot of revellers dancing up on the sloping parapet around the Obelisk, the jets denser still, like blows, pushing them to the ground, sweeping them along amid shrieks of delight; one of these white jets, worse than a clout, hit the back of Furibundo Pita's jeep, instantly drowning the six hens he was carrying; Don Furibundo wanted to brake, but thought better of it. "I'll charge my hens to the firefighters," he said. "They'll pay me for every last feather, dammit," and he roared with colossal laughter and accelerated, honking at all and sundry.

They left the avenue heading for Chachagüí, near the airport, but soon abandoned the main highway and went up a dirt road, bordered by large brick houses, submerged in mist, facing into the void. Half-dressed children were playing in the mud, celebrating Innocents' Day in their own way: they threw lumps of sludge in each other's faces, ran off, returned to the fray. Furibundo Pita's jeep did not escape the onslaught: it was hard to make out the track through the filthy windscreen; Don Furibundo hurled curses out the window; honked incessantly; on one of the bends he had to get out to clean the windscreen: that was when the children, a dozen or more, surrounded them, perplexed. "It's him," they shouted, "it's really him." No-one threw any more mud; they looked at Don Furibundo in panicked silence. And when Furibundo set off again they ran behind, escorting them; they managed to catch up to the driver's window, pointing at him and shouting: "It's him, it's really him."

The doctor looked over at Furibundo enquiringly, but he pretended not to see him. Who does this man remind me of?—the doctor wondered, intrigued, and it was in that instant that Furibundo Pita, with his sharp face, dark sunken eyes, prominent cheekbones, heavy brows, curly hair, slight body—sharp, narrow shoulders and bony knees—reminded him of someone or of the likeness of someone very close to him, very well known, but who? He could not guess.

It began to drizzle.

Sticking his narrow head far out of his window, Don Furibundo asked a peasant approaching on his donkey the whereabouts of Maestro Abril's workshop. "It's possible Tulio's still there behind the church," the peasant answered, open-mouthed in surprise at encountering Furibundo Pita's unmistakeable face before him. The peasant's eyes, his voice, seemed wreathed in unfathomable cunning. Don Furibundo accelerated without saying thank you, leaving behind the leathery, smiling face that scoffed covertly, who knows about whom, or why, the doctor mused.

They went up the muddy track until they reached the top of the hill, the children who had followed them now outdistanced, and began to descend, slipping in the mire, honking loudly at every bend. And thus they burst, hooting, onto a lane as slippery as glass, with dilapidated houses set around a circular plaza, where a tiny church stood.

"I won't believe it till I see it," Don Furibundo said.

Doctor Proceso was beginning to regret the riotous outing. He no longer felt any curiosity to discover his neighbour's disputes over honour. How did I end up here, he wondered, shouldn't I be celebrating Floridita's birthday?

Beneath the increasingly heavy drizzle, which seemed never-ending there, on one side of the church, they could just make out Maestro Abril's workshop, looking as though it was huddled in a nest of fog on the narrow street. Don Furibundo stopped the jeep beside the large metal door, slick with rain, almost a mirror; through a hole in the middle, where a chain and an old padlock stuck out, they thought a face peeped for a moment, an almost wooden-looking face that saw them and vanished. Don Furibundo gave two, three, four honks on his horn, but everything remained as it was, no-one came.

In that brief time, the children caught up with them, running, but without shouting, without a sound.

The doctor and Furibundo got out.

On either side of the door was a long, crumbling wall that surrounded the workshop where Maestro Abril worked. And protruding above the wall, jagged against the sky, the formidable shrouded skeleton of a carnival float could be made out, its vague silhouette, the mystery Maestro Abril had been assembling, step by step, for months, in order to compete in the procession of floats on January 6. Only the monumental proportions of the form could be seen, not its spirit, it was covered with huge tarpaulins that protected it from rain and curious glances. Every so often, from inside, they could hear the hammering of labourers hard at work, occasional voices or laughter, a woman's complaints. Maestro Abril worked alongside his inseparable comrade Martín Umbría—also a master craftsman—and was helped by Zulia Iscuandé, their sons, daughters in-law and grandchildren, and others from the neighbourhood, sporadic apprentices who put their faith in the maestro's imagination year after year. Many years earlier, Tulio Abril had won, and this was a matter of sufficient pride to encourage him to build floats every subsequent year of his life. He invested all his time and savings in the construction of the yearly float, and went on building it in sickness and in health, with unassailable determination; from time to time Zulia Iscuandé threatened to leave him—because the paltry and rigged prizes handed out by the government did not repay even half the investment—nevertheless, after the annual arguments, the domestic setbacks, no-one was interested in anything but the contest on January 6, and went on every year underpinning what they had dreamed up: another carnival float. It was the same for the rest of the artisans, alone or in company, alive or dead—the doctor mused—because for time immemorial, even from beyond the grave, they would go on competing, making floats for a carnival of the dead—he thought, as he observed the bare bones of the half-built float, bandaged in coloured cloths.

He regained his curiosity when he heard Furibundo Pita using the padlock to pound on the door.

The voices inside stopped talking.

"It's Arcángel de los Ríos," Don Furibundo said. "I need to see Maestro Abril."

The silence continued, then came more pounding with the padlock.

"Get Maestro Abril," Don Furibundo reiterated.

The drizzle got heavier. At the summit of Galeras a band of fog, rough with grainy sleet, seemed to start to fall.

"Open up, you pricks, it's Don Furibundo Pita himself," Don Furibundo Pita himself shouted in the end.

"It *is* him," the children confirmed, in unison. "It really is."

Don Furibundo rounded on the children, who retreated, startled; even so, like the peasant on his donkey, they harboured a dark, biting mockery. Clearly—the doctor realized—that underlying jeer reminded Furibundo Pita of something that had reached his ears, some gossip: news about the spirit of the float Maestro Abril was preparing. Don Furibundo was about to knock again when a strong hand poked out through the hole in the door, grabbed the chain and padlock and opened up without hesitation; the door creaked on its hinges; on the other side, Maestro Tulio Abril appeared, bushy-moustached, as short as Don Furibundo, but feisty and holding himself erect. He was wearing overalls, had a dark scarf around his head, and held what looked like the door of a jeep, six times larger than life, made from papier mâché.

Behind him, like shadows scattered under the zinc roof, craftsmen young and old were working away, Zulia Iscuandé too, all seated on tree stumps and rocks, polishing the components of a colossal jeep: one had a tyre, another the rearview mirror, over here a lit headlamp made of sheet aluminium, over there the exhaust pipe, the bumper, the mudguards, the enormous windows.

The maestro and Furibundo Pita contemplated one another for what must have seemed to them a never-ending moment, for they both appeared painfully overwhelmed; it was as if they were meeting face to face for the first time—after thinking about it day and night for years.

And both, ultimately, seemed disappointed.

"Let us in," Don Furibundo said.

"By all means," Maestro Abril replied.

He put the papier-mâché jeep door to one side and held out his calloused hand to the two men. He did not recognize downcast Doctor Proceso, sunk inside his raincoat, but he greeted him deferentially.

But before the men could follow him, the children, of one accord, and without anyone inviting them, darted into the workshop and dispersed to every corner like watchful birds.

In the murky drizzle, they saw Furibundo Pita suddenly run off, go up to the skirts of the float and pull urgently on one of the tarpaulins as if someone were trying to stop him, and no-one did stop him, but he could not get the cloth off: after several tugs he was just able to tweak apart a fold. What did he discover? Only a papier-mâché woman's calf, voluminous and white, not yet painted. The next tarpaulin was tangled around one of the protrusions. The impossibility of exposing the float with a single jerk made Don Furibundo turn pale: he dithered painfully, working out the best way to uncover it, then seemed about to attack it tooth and nail on a grand scale when, at a signal from the maestro, the children scrambled up and with a "one, two, three" laid it bare, revealed its vast outline, white as frost, exposed to everyone the spirit of the float, which Don Furibundo contemplated open-mouthed, eyes goggling, as did his companion Doctor Proceso and the rest of those present—as if they too were seeing it for the first time.

Way up high, whiter and a hundred times more massive, was Furibundo Pita himself, seated at the wheel of his still-unfinished jeep—a jeep with a spectacular flatbed, crammed not only with pigs and hens, but tigers biting polystyrene arms and legs; there were dragons breathing fire between overflowing cardboard milk churns—it was a contraption imbued with life that leapt forward rather than rolled along on four monstrous wheels, Furibundo's vast hand steering it, the other hand bearing down on the horn or klaxon or hooter, which was like a giant trumpet reaching up to the sky and, fleeing terrified in front of Furibundo and his Willys jeep—desperation on her face, flamboyant skirt flying above her waist, exaggerated buttocks—was Furibundo Pita's own wife, the pious Alcira Sarasti, the kind-hearted, languid woman who went to Mass at the Franciscan church every evening and who, any day of the week, on leaving the church, had to face her husband, the brawling Arcángel de los Ríos, "father of my children" as she called him, who stalked her, chased her in his jeep, caught up with her, overtook her, came back at her and confronted her, fenced her in, and honked and accelerated and slowed down and honked and harassed until he had her cornered, after along and shameful pursuit, up against the front door of their house.

There was no-one in the whole of Pasto who had not seen this happen at some point.

Tulio Abril and Zulia Iscuandé knew the devout Sarasti very well, and not only felt sorry for her, but complained—as did many others—about this weekly abuse, and they also visited the grounds of the Franciscan church from time to time, as Mass was ending, just in case they should come across the pursued woman, suffering the Stations of her Calvary at a trot, across the twelve ill-fated and scandalous blocks that separated her from salvation.

"So you wanted to surprise me, Tulio," Furibundo Pita said slowly, his gaze now fixed on the dirt floor while he shook his head, "and not just me, but Pasto too, the whole of Pasto, but at my expense, no?"

He gave the mud a kick.

No-one said anything. Martín Umbría and the oldest craftsmen positioned themselves around the maestro, as though they were protecting him. Only Zulia Iscuandé had opened her mouth and she was approaching him with a silent smile when Don Furibundo cut her off: "I didn't come here to speak to women."

And he stood firm in front of the maestro.

"You can't do this to me," he said. "Not to me, not to my wife. Who gives you the right to make fun of others, Tulio? Who do you think you are—God?"

The maestro did not answer.

"You succumbed to temptation. I know they call me Furibundo Pita because I like honking the horn too much, but so what? Who am I hurting? Have I ever run over my wife?"

He looked again at each and every one of them around him, as if scolding them all. Now he shouted: "Who's to say she doesn't like it? Who's to say that the fact I chase her isn't a game for her? It is a game, gentlemen, a game between me and her, between the two of us, so mind your own business, you utter bastards, you swine."

Doctor Proceso was astonished by the words, and Don Furibundo confronted him too, as if railing against *him*.

"What would become of carnival," he asked, "if we devoted ourselves to airing the sins of others? Or their humiliations? Or their embarrassments?"

The doctor immediately thought of Primavera. Don Furibundo kicked the ground again.

"I came here as a friend," he said. "I brought half a dozen hens in the Willys, Tulio. The firemen drowned them with a hosing down, but there's nothing wrong with them: they'll make a good stew. Let's eat and drink as friends."

He looked at the float again out of the corner of his eye.

"But first," he said, stressing his words, "first I want you to destroy this travesty with your own hammer, by God, Tulio, or I'll get drunk right here, right now, Tulio."

These last words, uttered as a terrible threat, made everyone freeze. Don Furibundo was getting hoarse, no more air in his lungs.

"You can be sure that if I'm drunk things will go rather differently," he managed to say. "Who knows what I might take it into my head to do."

He took a deep breath, let it out:

"So? Friends?"

"Friends," the maestro said, with a sigh.

And he looked up at the foggy grey sky, and put his hands in his pockets and lowered his head.

"But I will finish my float," he said.

Don Furibundo sagged. The maestro went on unperturbed: "I'm nobody's enemy. I show what this year has seen, what we've all seen in Pasto for ages. That's why we make floats, to remember the years, *señor*."

Don Furibundo moved still closer to the maestro.

"You haven't understood me," he said. And he ordered the children to fetch the chickens. In no time at all, six appeared at the maestro's feet.

"Those are not even worth the float's hooter," Zulia Iscuandé said.

"Very good, Señora Zulia," Don Furibundo replied. "I should have let you have your say from the beginning. You're right. I didn't come here to offer these chickens in exchange for your goodwill. These are for you to cook and for us to sit down to eat and talk like friends and negotiate. Now," he said, scratching his head, "if you are not decent enough to negotiate like this, I'm going to stop wasting your time:

either you take the float apart or I'll get drunk and tear it apart with my bare hands and then I'll shoot the lot of you. I'm only too aware you've worked all year on this mockery, but is it my fault I only just found out about it? Just yesterday a little bird came to my window and asked me to please pop in to Maestro Abril's workshop, as they were preparing a nice carnival surprise for me. I didn't believe it at first, but I came along, and what do I see? I see that anything's possible in Pasto when it comes to making fun of your fellow man and that it's me who's the victim. No, Tulio. I won't allow it. I'll blow you to bits, float and all, right now, all by myself, unaided."

"No-one, not you, not anybody will make me take this float apart," Maestro Abril said, unmoved.

And then:

"Fire as many bullets as you like."

It was as if he considered the conversation over.

"Your wife has more common sense," Don Furibundo replied. "She said six chickens aren't worth the hooter. And she's right."

Zulia Iscuandé opened her mouth, but did not say a word.

"How much is first prize?" Don Furibundo asked everyone.

No-one answered.

"How much did the winning float get this past January?" he asked again, encouraging them. And as they still did not answer he added: "I'm playing my last card here, gentlemen, how much?"

"Lots of pesos," came the sudden voice of one of the men who worked with Maestro Abril.

"Lots of pesos?" Don Furibundo laughed. "Well, find out how many there are in *lots* and I'll sign you a promissory note for the same amount right now, and Bob's your uncle, we all live happily ever after."

Tulio Abril looked reproachfully at the artisan who had spoken. Then he sought out his wife, and, lastly, Don Furibundo. With great sadness in his voice, he said: "It can't be done, *señor*, forgive me."

"It can be done, Tulio. It can. Everything in this life can be done. In the next life, I don't know. In this one, it can. Remember what our grandmas used to say: *Yesterday came the dressmaker, tomorrow comes the undertaker.* That means, in pure Pasto-ese: *eat, drink and be merry.* Think again, Tulio. Here, in front of my friend Doctor Justo Pastor Proceso Lopéz, I give my word of honour that you will get the same amount of money as the winning float in the carnival. Isn't that enough for you? This is the money I pay for the work you have put into mocking me this year, it's me that comes out the loser, dammit, don't you get it? Where has this been seen before? Paying so as not to be made fun of? In Pasto, of course. You're the one who should be paying me, you great prick, for mocking me."

He did not manage to say any more. He could not. But he left the workshop unhurriedly, like someone going for a walk, and got into his Willys. Doctor Proceso wondered if he should accompany him, speak to him, calm him down, leave with him, but Don Furibundo did not start the engine: he simply sat behind the steering wheel, sighed, scratched one cheek, smoothed down his hair, leant towards the glove compartment.

"He's taken out a bottle of *aguardiente,*" one of the smallest boys reported, perched on top of the wall, right at the corner by the doorway. "He's drinking it, he's still drinking it, he's drinking it all up, he's started to get drunk."

"Are you Doctor Justo Pastor?" Maestro Abril asked meanwhile. His wife and the artisans had already gathered around the doctor.

"God bless you again," his wife said, "forgive us for not recognizing you, would you like a nice cup of coffee?"

"Salvador, Salvador, where's Salvador?" Maestro Abril asked all around.

One of the children came forward; he was just like all the others: ragged, face black with mud.

"Say how do you do to Doctor Justo Pastor, who helped you come into the world," the maestro said, and Salvador held out his hand. At that same moment they heard from the boy up on the wall. A sort of delighted astonishment was apparent in his voice.

"Now he's drinking another bottle. He'll get even drunker."

They all turned to look at the Willys: Furibundo Pita was slugging down what was left of a second bottle of *aguardiente*, as if it were water.

"If he carries on drinking at that rate he's going to die," Zulia Iscuandé said.

"And now what are we going to do?" the maestro asked his wife. "What are we going to do with that bastard? By God, I'm not about to wreck my float, Zulia, not for all the money in the world."

"You should consider it," his wife said.

Her husband's steadfast gaze dissuaded her.

They heard the shattering of a bottle against the pavement: it was Don Furibundo, who had just smashed the bottle and got out of the Willys. His budding drunkenness clouded his eyes, he came straight towards the maestro, faced him once more:

"So?"

After an encouraging silence, came the maestro's voice:

"No."

And, very earnestly:

"Go back where you came from, *señor*. If you don't want to see the float, don't see it: don't go out that day, pretend you don't exist. Sooner or later everyone will forget all about it."

"Dammit!" Don Furibundo was stunned. "I'm offering you what you'd win for first prize, and all because you're making fun of me. What more do you want, Tulio, tell me what more you could possibly want? Tell me!"

Zulia Iscuandé sighed deeply.

The other artisans were also noticeably rattled: the thing was, hand on heart, during that whole year working on "Don Furibundo Chasing his Wife"—that was what the float was called—they had never imagined getting first prize. Maybe third, if God was on their side. So the offer unsettled them to the point of exasperation.

"Convince this pig-headed fool," Don Furibundo urged them.

"No," the maestro replied, "Nobody here is going to convince me of anything, and nobody comes here to shout at me either."

"Well I won't shout any more then," Don Furibundo shouted. His voice had changed. He had become someone else.

And again they saw him run off towards his car.

Instinctively, they all took a step backwards.

This man is truly insane, the doctor thought, witnessing Furibundo Pita dash off, get in the jeep and poke about in the glove compartment again. They thought he might be looking for another bottle. He was not.

"He's got out a gun," the watchboy exclaimed, his delight now running over.

And so he had: Furibundo Pita came at them flat out, brandishing the weapon, his face ablaze. Maestro Abril set off at a run too, and could think of no better direction to head in than where the float was being built: he disappeared behind the monumental shape, closely followed by Furibundo.

And it was while watching Furibundo Pita pelt past that Doctor Justo Pastor Proceso Lopéz suddenly realized who it was he looked like.

"Simón Bolívar," he said out loud. "He's identical." He was able to confirm this by lifting his eyes to the colossal figure on the float—"It's Simón Bolívar himself"—because, in fact, the Furibundo Pita on the float looked even more like Simón Bolívar, but a hundred times bigger, he really was just as portrayed by the artists of the time, the selfsame so-called Liberator, Simón Bolívar, he thought.

But that amazement was to be surpassed by what followed, when the critical moments took place, the fleeting seconds while the two men were invisible behind the float; just as Zulia Iscuandé started to cry out "protect him, Our Lady of Perpetual Help" they heard a shot, then a second, and a third. It was as if the silence that followed made everything go cold.

"My God, he's killed him," the woman shouted now, raising her arms to heaven.

Don Furibundo emerged then from the bowels of the float, ran past the doctor, got into the jeep quick as a flash, pulled away and went honking off down the track.

Everyone ran to peer behind the float.

There was Tulio Abril, more alive than dead, without a scratch on him.

3

The vision of Simón Bolívar riding high on the float was just what Doctor Proceso needed as a better reason for living than his wife's indifference and the raising of two contrary daughters. Before him lay the extraordinary possibility of showing, with a puff in papier mâché, what he had unsuccessfully planned to reveal twenty-five years ago, when he started writing *The Great Lie: Bolívar or the So-Called Liberator, a Human Biography*.

He based his own work on the foundations laid by Nariño historian José Rafael Sañudo, who was born in Pasto in 1872 and died in the same city in 1943. Sañudo had been the first historian in Colombia and practically the first on the continent—as Doctor Proceso used to stress enthusiastically—who dared irrefutably to unpick Bolívar's historic image, without the false patriotic sentiment or the exaggerated style of flattery (ears deaf and eyes blind) that the great majority of historians have traditionally bestowed upon Bolívar since his death.

"A courageous biography," the doctor wrote on the subject of José Rafael Sañudo. "Published in 1925, *Estudios sobre la vida de Bolívar* provoked the contempt and condemnation of his supporters, not just in the country at large, but in Pasto, among his fellow Pastusos, who professed 'profound surprise and indignation at his abominable lampoon.' In Manizales they hollered for him to be hanged, in Bogotá he was declared a traitor, the Colombian Academy of History called him an ungrateful son, the Bolívar Society also called him a son, but one unworthy of Colombia, and if on publication his book found one or two moderately serious commentators, all of them, without exception, discussed it in tones of sheer panic, and one, despite acknowledging that Sañudo committed no slander and each of his assertions was well founded, did not hesitate to label him a retrograde Pastuso, hirsute theologian, convoluted prose stylist and old casuist. These labels did nothing to dampen the spirits of the Pasto historian, a man who was also a mathematician and philosopher, a reader of authors in Greek and Latin, and who stirred up the storm in advance by giving his book the words of Lucian of Samosata—in Greek—as an epigraph: 'do not write merely with an eye to the present, that those now living may commend and honour you; aim at eternity, compose for posterity, and from it ask your reward; and that reward?—that it be said of you, *This was a man indeed, free and free-spoken; flattery and servility were not in him; he was truth all through.*'"

"Lamentably," Doctor Proceso wrote, "the statue of José Rafael Sañ-udo does not preside, as it should, over the portico of the Nariño Academy of History, which he founded: the statue of José Rafael Sañudo does not even exist." But he added: "What do statues matter? The work endures."

The only thing Doctor Proceso granted Sañudo's detractors was that his style really was convoluted—amalgam of philosopher, mathematician and polyglot that he was—regrettably more suitable for consumption by other historians than by the general public. And for this very reason Doctor Proceso had proposed a volume that would describe, with crystal-clear clarity, not just the political, economic and military deeds of the so-called Liberator, but his other deeds of more human aspect, which would end up shedding light on the monumental historical mistake of conferring upon Bolívar a noble leading role in the independence of the Latin American peoples, a leading role which he did, of course, play, thought the doctor, but of the most atrocious kind.

This objective, however, this book he had spent half his life struggling to write, had turned out to be beyond his powers. Doctor Justo Pastor Proceso López, whose work (running his practice, the two or three women who were his occasional lovers as well as being his patients, the management of his *finca* in Sandoná, his considerable reading, various obligations at home or to do with his two daughters, and his genuine concerns about Primavera Pinzón, who did not cease to plague him with excessive expenses and assail him with other worse tribulations) took up the majority of his time, Doctor Justo Pastor Proceso López admitted to himself that he would never really perfect his *Great Lie* of Bolívar, that a Sañudo is born but once every hundred years, and that he himself was no writer, no historian, no musician, no poet by any stretch of the imagination.

But he held on to certain expectations concerning what he called "Human Investigations," interviews he had obtained over the years, with people from all walks of life in Pasto and in various towns in Nariño province, about the so-called Liberator's shameful passage across southern Colombia. Of those interviews, some on paper, some recorded, his hopes were centred on the ones he carried out, on tape, with two direct descendants of people who had suffered Bolívar's rage: a woman, Polina Agrado, recently deceased in Pasto at ninety-three years of age, and Belencito Jojoa, still alive, an old man of eighty-six who lived in the Obrero neighbourhood with his third wife and numerous children and grandchildren.

Something which piqued the doctor's curiosity, and troubled him, was that both testimonies had to do with the so-called Liberator's lust rather than with any of the other passions—anger, cowardice, ambition, vanity—he had possessed in such abundance. But testimonies as truthful as these did not grow on trees, so he transcribed them just as he recorded them, even though they seemed like discordant voices in the work he had planned, a work which would wipe the dust and lies from the face of history—or historians, he said—and guide the youth of the day through the Latin American wars of independence under the banner of truth.

And now, eager as a child, in front of Maestro Tulio Abril's shot-up float, "Don Furibundo Chasing his Wife," Doctor Proceso threw himself into imagining, represented over three or four carnival floats—or on a single, huge one—each and every one of Bolívar's most troubling exploits: troubling because they were false and because, even being so, they continued to circulate in schools and colleges as if flowing from the fountain of truth. With this float, he thought, Simón Bolívar would plainly and simply be exposed as a myth, an utter myth, each of his most infamous and obvious manoeuvrings woven together—Simón Bolívar, he said to himself, revealed at last, Simón Bolívar just as he was: his extraordinary capacity to convince his contemporaries and, in passing, generations to come (with letters and proclamations that were bombastic, scheming, raving and wily, pompous and pedantic, passionately wordy, pastiches of Alexander the Great and Napoleon) that he was someone he was not, that he had achieved things he had not, and that he should pass into history as the hero he was not.

Maestro Tulio Abril's teeth were still chattering, not so much from the cold as from what he had just been through. Seated on a bench, he was drinking a cup of hot *aguapanela*; Doctor Proceso was doing the same beside him, while Zulia Iscuandé handed out more *aguapanela* to the workers.

"Not a scratch," the doctor said. "It seems the avenging Arcángel shot more at heaven than at you."

"At heaven?" The maestro became angry. "He shot at me, I felt a bullet warm my ear."

"Well, thanks be to Our Lady of Perpetual Help he only warmed your ear," Zulia Iscuandé said. "Drunk as he was he could have shot us too, not just you, or shot himself, all with the same damned rotten nerve."

"Check the float," the maestro ordered. He trembled with anger and shock. "Check it over inch by inch to see what damage that devil did. Salvador, check the float."

Salvador ran to the float, followed by the rest of the children.

"I'm never going to destroy it," the maestro said, "even if they offer me paradise on earth."

"You're not going to destroy it," Doctor Proceso responded, and added, after an expectant pause: "You're going to convert it."

They looked at him without understanding, without recognizing him. And it was because the doctor looked like someone else, very different from the man who first arrived (soaked through, in a bad mood and longing to leave); now he shivered, not with cold, but emotion, he was constantly raising his eyes to "Don Furibundo Chasing his Wife" and going off into raptures: had he gone mad? He was jabbering and whispering, blurting out exclamations and biting them back, like someone prey to the most profound illusions.

"And how do you want me to convert it?" the maestro asked. He asked out of politeness, because he was still grateful for the help he had received from the doctor ten years before, but his pride was hurt: he never liked anyone to come along and suggest changes to his floats. Had it not been the doctor he would have thrown him out of the workshop long ago: after all, he had arrived in the company of the drunken devil.

The doctor steadied his voice. Now or never, he thought. He was well aware they were waiting for his answer. He had to tread carefully.

"Maestro Abril," he began, "we'll make Arcángel de los Ríos pay what he promised, but three times over. We were witnesses here: attempted homicide, wasn't it? Tomorrow, when he wakes up after his binge, the avenging Arcángel will be like putty in our hands. I'll speak to him, I'll tell him I will use my good offices so that none of the artisans file a suit against him, but I'll warn him, on your behalf, that he'll have to pay triple what he promised, I mean three times the prize money for the winning float."

There was an eerie silence.

And a piercing whistle was heard from Iscuandé.

"Sounds good," she said.

"Many a slip . . ." Martín Umbría said. He was the master crafts-man who had been working with Tulio Abril the longest, and they listened to him respectfully. "The main thing is that the drunkard pays up and doesn't come here again, plastered, and shooting every which way."

"I'll take care of it," the doctor said. "I'll tell him he won't be on the float chasing his wife any more, but that he'll have to pay triple not to end up accused."

"There's something that doesn't convince me," Maestro Abril said. "How come he's not going to be on my float?"

Zulia Iscuandé grew exasperated by her husband's words. She pre-ferred to listen only to the doctor.

"Tell us what you're suggesting," she said. And even so it seemed to Tulio Abril that Doctor Justo Pastor Proceso López really had gone mad, or just about: he looked at them without blinking, his hands were shaking.

Now or never, the doctor said to himself again, meanwhile. It was the opportunity of his life. His face was all lit up, as it had been when he made his first communion, when he received his medical degree, when he went to church to marry the woman he was in love with, when he saw her naked, at last. And his face was so full of wonder because he was looking and looking again at the huge figure while he said:

"Furibundo Pita is identical to Simón Bolívar."

No-one said anything. The children stopped searching for the places where Furibundo's bullets had left their mark on the float and for the first time attentively regarded the immense figure towering over them, now provided with an alternative identity.

"It's just like him," the boy who had been the lookout said at last. "It's the Liberator himself from the books at school."

"Simón Bolívar can stay up there just as he is," the doctor went on. "Furibundo's wife might come in handy later on, we'll see how and where; with that terrified expression and fleeing the way she is, she's like our country."

No-one seemed to understand, or would admit to understanding, the comparison.

"The only thing up there that can't be used is the jeep," the doctor continued, all in a rush. "Luckily, it's not finished, we'll transform it. We'll put a victor's chariot in its place, a sort of nineteenth-century carriage, where that selfsame Bolívar will go, but in uniform and with a laurel wreath on his head, sitting on his velvet cushion; and the cart will be pulled by twelve girls—I said girls, not young women—with garlands around their hair and skimpy tunics on, like nymphs. That's how Bolívar liked them."

He lowered his vision-filled gaze and met the astonished eyes of the artisans for the first time.

"Which Simón Bolívar are you talking about?" Maestro Abril finally asked. "The one from Independence?"

"The very same," the doctor replied.

It was too late to backtrack now.

But how to explain history in just a single moment and to such an audience?

This carriage the doctor proposed existed just as he described it, in Caracas, on August 6, 1813, when the same people who had celebrated the entry of the Spaniard Monteverde months earlier were now celebrating the entry of Bolívar, giving him a hero's welcome for accomplishing victories that were not his—the real heroes of those early days had been Piar, Mariño and Girardot—Bolívar's "victories" were just skirmishes, but the villagers in his path eagerly swelled his ranks, and Bolívar made the most of this and entered Caracas, and he was the one to call himself "the Liberator."

The Liberator: a title the Caracas city council would later confer on him.

The little fellow had lost no time, the doctor thought. That's what he used to call Bolívar, when he brooded over him and immersed himself in the man's historic past as if in a bad dream that became more nightmarish because it was impossible to wake up from.

The little fellow, who ended up betraying General Francisco de Miranda, commander-in-chief of Venezuela's insurgent forces, personally handing him over to the Spanish in La Guaira, after cunningly persuading him to postpone his journey to England, taking him captive at three in the morning, ordering him to be placed in irons and shackles and offering him up to Monteverde in order to get safe conduct and the approval of the Spanish authorities in exchange; the little fellow who had been the real reason for General Miranda's fall after abandoning the fortress at Puerto Cabello—the best equipped of the insurgent strongholds—abandoning it despite having more than sufficient forces to thwart a spontaneous uprising by unarmed Spanish prisoners, the little fellow who fled in the night to his San Mateo estate with eight of his officers, without warning his troops who ended up without a leader, let alone any orders to follow; that same little fellow was now received in Caracas as if he were a Napoleon.

Yes, the doctor said to himself, it was the surrender of Puerto Cabello that forced Miranda to sign a treaty that would re-establish Spanish control in Venezuela, and Bolívar was the cause of the defeat: a great deal of shamelessness was required in order for Bolívar to seize Miranda, accusing him of betrayal, the very betrayal that Bolívar did commit by handing his commander over to the Spanish.

No-one will ever be able to understand, he mused, shaking his head in agitation, why they believed in him, how he managed to impose his lie. What to blame this on—ignorance? The uncouthness of the rebel leaders of the day? Why did they send him to negotiate with the English for protection, with such poor results? Why was he named colonel, why was he chosen as commander of the Puerto Cabello fortress? Because of his wealth. Why else? Francisco de Miranda, like any other military leader, gave the buying of arms and munitions and the upkeep of the troops the importance it merited; that was why he had to enrol that bourgeois, who was incompetent by any reckoning, into his army.

And the doctor's bitter incredulity was sincere: he saw Bolívar as a make-believe strategist, faker of victories that were not victories, or worse—victories that were not his.

He tried, then, not to let his own agitation show in his voice.

"The carriage I'm telling you about," he explained, "existed, just as I described, one hundred and fifty-three years ago, in Venezuela."

Once again, an astonished silence surrounded him.

Doctor Proceso was suddenly hit by the hard truth: no-one there knew anything about Bolívar other than the official lies learned at school.

"What do you know about Bolívar?" he dared to ask, and felt his own uncertainty, like a great wall of encircling ice.

"He was the Liberator," the lookout boy said.

"Father of the nation," Maestro Abril said, as if adding a full stop; he would not lend himself to mocking Bolívar's memory.

Doctor Proceso thought his vision—of the Liberator's carriage—already lay in pieces. It would be superhuman, he thought, to overcome people's fundamental ignorance of Bolívar's true face in just one minute. What am I doing here? What am I proposing? Isn't this futile—more than futile, humiliating?

The artisans withdrew; that morning's interruptions had been unusual—first a drunk, then a lunatic—best get on with some work. Then they heard Zulia Iscuandé, who had not said a word that whole time.

"My grandfather always talked about Bolívar," she said.

She half closed her eyes, as if remembering.

"He talked to me about Bolívar," she said.

And then, resolutely, finding the memory, seizing upon it:

"He was always talking about Bolívar, but he said Bolívar had been a complete son of a bitch."

The workshop shook with an explosive guffaw. Doctor Justo Pastor Proceso López's eyes were watering.

My God, he thought, there is still memory among us.

"And not just in Pasto, but right across the country," Iscuandé continued, spurred on. "Grandfather told us Bolívar was always a complete son of a bitch, wherever he set foot."

The doctor, who was usually temperate and controlled, asked for a glass of *aguardiente*, not to celebrate Zulia Iscuandé's scorn, but her words. That was when Salvador and the rest of the children descended from the float. They had finished checking it over inch by inch.

"The three bullets hit the lady," the watchboy gabbled. "One on the forehead, one on the bum and the other on one of her tits."

Another guffaw. With a whistle, Maestro Umbría remembered it was Innocents' Day, "Here's to life!" he roared. Doctor Proceso did not want to interrupt the hullabaloo. All he saw, in front of him, was the colossal figure of the Liberator.

"Just like here today," he said to himself, astounded, "Bolívar was never injured either, not once in his soldiering life, he always knew how to hide, he never showed his face."

Well into the evening, the artisans took him home. They loaded him onto Martín Umbría's truck—the one Bolívar was later to be fixed to for his procession. Even the children accompanied the doctor: Innocents' Day overexcited them from the start. The adults proposed toasts at every corner and people out celebrating clambered up to soak them all, not just leaping into the back but also onto the running board beside the cab in which Zulia Iscuandé, Tulio Abril, the doctor in the middle and Martín Umbría—who was driving—were all drinking. Behind, on the open flatbed, the artisans and apprentices were fooling around, along with the horde of children who responded to each water attack with more water: they had a big earthenware jar full of bombs, which they hurled by the handful into the crowd. The clamour of the festivities swept over them from all sides: you could hear the din of water bombs exploding, crashing like boiling waves against the windscreen, the water like white lashes from a whip shooting over them, shouts like whistles—was that laughter or wailing? Heavy sighs, band music pulsing in the background, the traditional cries of "Viva Pasto, dammit!" from the revellers.

Right in the middle of the Avenida de los Estudiantes, at risk of being run over, a white-haired old man popped up, sitting astride a pregnant, squealing sow; delighted children urged them on at a run, and a fat woman, probably the pig's owner, gave chase trying to catch them. A cow, completely soaked, was grazing terrified on one side of the Obelisk. Also soaked through like the cow, but happy, much more so than when he was a child and had joined in, Doctor Proceso got out of the vehicle at his lonely house, happy because he carried with him the maestros' promise: they would create the Bolívar carnival float.

Long before the *aguardiente*, to prove their word as master craftsmen, the two maestros had climbed up onto the float and pulled down the devout Alcira, they toppled her bulk to the ground without hesitation; in her place they would put up the twelve girls pulling a victor's chariot in which Bolívar would be seated with his Roman wreath on his head. And they themselves decided—to the doctor's surprise—that around this carriage, on carved wooden panels, would go the key scenes of the War of Independence, which the doctor was to select: he would have to talk to Cangrejito Arbeláez about that, they suggested, one of Pasto's best-known sculptors, who carved men and women and trees and animals as if breathing them into being. He was the only one who could triumph over the time left until the parade on January 6: exactly nine days.

*

With the maestros' promise, Doctor Justo Pastor Proceso López said goodbye, reeling outside his house, drunk for the first time in years; it was some thirty since he had imbibed to the point of swaying about in such a fashion, but the cause was well worth the trouble, he thought, and he would not skimp: he would pay the artisans three times the float prize; he would not waste his time denouncing Furibundo, who was as rich as he was miserly—hadn't he heard him swear he would charge the firemen for the six hens they drowned? Furibundo's offer was a fabrication: he had wanted to trick and then startle the artisans, a ruse. The doctor would have to finance Bolívar's carriage by himself. He was disheartened to recognize the fact that if the artisans agreed to support his idea it was purely and simply for money, three times the prize money of the winning float: why else would they work?—he said to himself—no other reason, don't be naive, let's not get carried away.

Because, when all's said and done, who was he to set himself up as an expert on the true story of the Independence, and among artisans? There were nine days to go. Wouldn't it be prudent to look for other allies? A float like the one in the offing could provoke resentment; it was Bolívar's carriage, with his whole history on its back. He had to turn to his friends—to people who were his friends, years ago—but which ones? Doctor Proceso began to reflect on this, genuinely alarmed.

For now, he said to himself, finish the float, exhibit it on January 6, and more than that, let it exist in the world, as though memory were preserved on any corner of Pasto's streets, the first bastion of the truth, of the real past. Something must come out of this float, something crucial, something definitive. Ah, he said to himself, if it could be exhibited permanently right in the middle of the children's park, for the edification of infants and grandparents alike, but how would it be installed? What nook of the city would permit its permanent presence? For now, pay the craftsmen for its construction, guide the work; he would have to choose the scenes carefully—from among the many macabre events with which Bolívar's life was full to overflowing.

He would sell his *finca*. He had been ready to do this for a long time: sell off those several, poorly managed acres of wheat, the ancestral but collapsing house, the abandoned sugar mill, the swimming pool with its missing tiles, the stables empty of livestock, the gardens empty of flowers—Primavera must be the only woman in the world, and poet to boot, who did not know flowers existed. One thing's for sure, he thought, the frustrated poet would be delighted to get half the *finca* sale price in cash; she would not complain, she would immediately plan what clothes to buy, which shoes, where she would travel. But he would not stint on paying Maestro Abril what he deserved, nor Martín Umbría and the sculptor Cangrejito Arbeláez, and each and every one of the makers. They would understand later on what work they had created. Zulia Iscuandé had shown that sufficient memory still survived in Pasto. Bolívar's carriage, the carriage of history, of legitimate rage, was imminent. No-one was going to stop it, no-one.

Then he sneezed.

"Provided I don't die of a cold first," he said, because he was dripping water, leaving a wet trail as he walked through his lonely house, empty of voices—not just the voices of his family, but his employees too: Sinfín was nowhere to be seen. He found her hurried note, written in a childish hand: *We bought the chickins already Im going with the señora its midday now docter dont be long.*

In the margin he discovered Primavera's rounded writing and it scared away his drunkenness: *I hope you'll come to the birthday party and stay with your daughters at the finca, that's if you remember, you ape.*

Ape.

It was still not too late.

He drank a mug of black coffee and put on dry clothes. A one-hour journey to the *finca*, near Sandoná, lay before him; the hot weather there would cure his cold: he was not going to die.

But before setting off he made up his mind and telephoned the philosopher and professor Arcaín Chivo, a fifty-year-old like himself and a childhood friend, who asked, rather taken aback, whether the fact that he was calling meant the world was coming to an end. They had not spoken for years, not since their mutual interest in Simón Bolívar used to drive them to meet at the Guadalquivir café on Nariño Square and reconstruct the details, the bickering and backbiting, setbacks and apathies of Colombian independence. That was years ago now, when Arcaín Chivo was Professor of History; these days they just recognized one another every so often, from a distance: in Pasto's only bookshop, or in the queue for one of the three cinemas, or on some corner—life slipping past as quickly as crossing the street.

"See you at my house this Friday, seven o'clock," Doctor Proceso said, rounding off his invitation.

"The day after tomorrow, December thirtieth? Let's wait one more day and we can bring in New Year together on the thirty-first."

"Our New Year hug can be brought forward."

So he fixed a meeting with Arcaín Chivo, better known as "the Philanthropist" thanks to his notorious stinginess, emeritus educator at the University of Nariño—friend or acquaintance? Whichever he was, the doctor needed a deputy he could count on for the whole fast-approaching carnival firestorm.

And he also considered the involvement of Monsignor Pedro Nel Montúfar, Bishop of Pasto, the "Wasp," who despite being a priest was—he thought—an intelligent one at least, representative of ecclesiastical power, plus the involvement of Mayor Matías Serrano, the "One-Armed Man of Pasto"—not actually missing either arm—representative of civil power; both acquaintances of his since school—although that might not mean much, but he could rely on them, unlike Governor Nino Cántaro, the "Toad," who had also been at the same school but might yet turn out to be an enemy, he thought, due not so much to his intelligence, but his irrational idiocy.

He called the mayor and the bishop and they accepted the invitation, more intrigued than happy about it: it was unusual that Doctor

Justo Pastor Proceso López, gynaecologist-historian, should remember a living soul—what was he up to?

And he arrived at his *finca* in Sandoná after a tortuous journey along the unpaved road; he arrived after nightfall, making plans like dreams are made, battling with himself. He parked the Land Rover beside the other vehicles belonging to the guests; he could not see Primavera's Volks-wagen, and this bothered him. He smelled the damp earth, the wet bark of the trees. As he approached the house, hands in pockets, absorbed expression, his shadow stooping between bushes and sheaves of wheat, hearing dogs barking without really listening to them, he seemed like a sombre stranger.

Primavera was not at the *finca*.

Genoveva Sinfín told him so, surrounded by a tumult of clowns and kids, among whom his daughter Floridita stood out, riding her Shetland pony.

"The *señora* went back to Pasto," Sinfín explained. "She left word that she wanted to be alone and that you would look after things here till tomorrow."

They were talking about fifty metres from the main entrance to the house, in the middle of a wood of eucalyptus trees. The windows were shining with a yellow light. Floridita did not even acknowledge him: when he wanted to say hello, she turned her head, irritated. He did not try going up to her, sensing only too keenly that she would run from him—but why? He did not know. What had he done? His seven-year-old daughter loathed him, possibly instructed by her mother; she was going back and forth on her pony, followed the whole time by the boy Chanchán and the gang of admiring children; when all was said and done, it was her birthday: she could do and not do whatever she liked.

"And Luz de Luna?" he asked.

"I haven't seen her for ages," answered the cook, after a guarded silence. "She must be around somewhere."

She scratched her greying head; did she want to change the subject?

"I'm here, obliged to serve, as is right and proper," she said. "I've got six girls helping me, but they're on their knees. And to think this goes on till tomorrow, *señor*."

The doctor greeted the steward, old and aloof, who was no doubt waiting his turn to put in his complaints. The strumming of various guitars could be heard in the house: twelve-string *tiples*, a mandolin. A woman was singing off key. Applause. Stamping on the wooden floor. It was Primavera's family, the Pinzóns—the doctor sighed—who never missed a christening or wake in Pasto.

He paused halfway between the eucalyptus wood and the front door. More parked cars warned of a sizable gathering. He asked Sinfín to bring him a cup of coffee and headed for the opposite side of the house, where the swimming pool was, closely followed by the steward. He did not listen in detail to his complaints: he was asking for money to pay the farm labourers; the tractor needed a spare part that was impossible to get in Pasto, they would have to order it from Bogotá; somebody was stealing the fence posts; the sheep pen was empty of sheep one morning; some-one set fire to the pine trees, *señor.*

"Never mind, Seráfico, we're going to sell all this," the doctor said, coming to a halt. The old steward studied him in astonishment and stalked off to his cabin without saying goodbye: he was not just cursing, but also seemed to be sobbing—however, the doctor did not think it had anything to do with him.

He went to the swimming pool because the water liberated him; the pool was missing tiles and the water looked black: it was a black mirror he would lean out over before splintering it with his naked body. He wanted to take a dip, and then think about life. But now near the pool he heard voices and laughter. He drew back, hiding himself in the shrubbery, and saw how Matilde Pinzón, her husband, and various unknown couples amused themselves, lounging around the pool in bathing suits. They were smoking and drinking by the flickering glow of the fireflies. One of them dropped a bottle of *aguardiente* into the water. The doctor went back the way he came.

This business of the birthday party was a turnaround, he thought. He and Primavera agreed that just he and his daughters would sleep at the *finca* after the party. Had they really agreed that? And now, by the look of things, the party guests would stay the night, people he could not stand. Primavera should take care of her family, he thought, but he tried to understand her: perhaps she could not bear them either, and had fled to Pasto. He was the one who would have to look after them, by rights. No, no, he could not. He would go back to Pasto too, and make the most of it to get down on paper the relevant scenarios from the Independence, which the sculptor Arbeláez would have to bring to life in wood. The prospect of a peaceful night, working on his own interests, cheered Doctor Proceso up. He took his coffee from Sinfín.

"I'm going back to Pasto too," he said. "Look after the girls, see they get to bed early, and you along with them. And if you want to throw these people out, do so, you have my permission, tell them I ordered you to."

"What, Doctor? You're not going in to greet the guests? You're leaving just like that? Aren't you taking the girls?"

"You know very well they won't want to come with me."

Sinfín's mouth twisted in annoyance, but she quickly resigned herself: it was not the first time the doctor and his wife had let the responsibility for a party fall on her shoulders.

The doctor finished his coffee in one gulp. He turned down the steaming cuts of roast pork Sinfín offered him on a tray, and repeated that he would not go in to greet the guests. The starry sky glowed above their heads. While they were walking along the winding path, amidst the chirring of crickets and the leafy darkness of the *finca*, Sinfín advised the doctor to come back early the next day to pick up the girls, thus avoiding the guests staying right through until lunch.

"They've eaten the lot," she confided. "And they're good and drunk: they sent for Don Seráfico's three piglets to be killed, and then when they'd been roasted and eaten, nobody wanted to pay up. That's why Don Seráfico got angry."

The doctor no longer wanted to respond.

He was about to get into his jeep when Sinfín interjected again:

"Your daughter," she said.

"My daughter?"

"Your daughter."

"Which one? Floridita didn't want to say hello to me."

"Luz de Luna."

"Where is she, Genoveva? I already asked you, don't you remember?"

"I think she's in the stables, Doctor. It hasn't occurred to her to leave the stables all afternoon."

He strode off towards the stables.

But the cook did not want to follow him there.

"Whenever you see the stars, I'll be seeing them too, Luz de Luna, and we'll go on seeing like that for ever and ever, wherever we are, you in Pasto and me in Bogotá."

That is what the doctor heard on entering the stables: through the high, unglazed window, the world's stars were peeping in. Who was talking? He did not recognize the boy in the gloom, but he saw him trying to sit up and then stop, embarrassed, and he also heard him call him "uncle." It was another of Matilde Pinzón's sons.

The two cousins were sitting on the dirt floor, lying back against a mound of chaff, shoulder to shoulder, hands entwined. His fifteen-year-old daughter's long black hair was tangled, strewn with bits of straw, and there was dirt on her blouse. The doctor took all this in at a glance, along with her shining eyes, and heard her trembling voice, as frightened as it was resolute:

"Papá. You made it."

"And now I'm leaving," the doctor said. "I've got things to do in Pasto."

"Yes, Papá."

"Your mother has gone to Pasto, in case you didn't know. You'll have to take charge, stay with Genoveva, look after your little sister."

"Yes, Papá."

"I don't want you hanging around in the stables any longer, okay?"

"Yes, Papá."

"Did you hear me?"

"Yes, Papá."

The two cousins got up without letting go of one another's hands, like it was some kind of shared challenge: it seemed they wanted to shout to the world that they were a couple. Proud of themselves, they ascertained that the doctor was not making a fuss, quite the reverse; he followed them in silence, at a distance. The doctor wondered what he should do. He suffered over the way things were, or the way the world was—what had things come to with his daughters, this tremendous distance between them in which he, alone, was the outsider, the intruder? Oh, if only he had not had them, he thought, if only he were not tied to Primavera, if he lived alone, could do his own thing: he would be free, he would have stayed with the artisans all night, celebrating the future as it should be celebrated. It's too late now, he thought, too late for this family man.

"Goodbye, dear. Come and say goodbye to me."

Luz de Luna gave him a kiss on the cheek.

"Bye, Papá."

The boy said goodbye too, from a distance:

"Bye, Uncle."

And the doctor was on the point of explaining to him, "I'm not your uncle, I'm your aunt Primavera's husband, I've got nothing to do with your family," but he stopped himself. He remembered that years ago he had thought the boy showed signs of learning difficulties, and he had been on the point of alerting Primavera to the fact, so she could tell her sister.

Well, no, he said to himself, as he drove the Land Rover along the highway, he's no retard, he's another poet talking about stars and he's already deflowered Luz de Luna—"dammit!" he yelled into the night—I hope her mother has at least given her some good advice about how not to end up pregnant. Primavera Pinzón, who would not one day wish to become your murderer?

4

Just seconds before opening the door to his house he realized Primavera was not expecting him: really not expecting him, he thought. He was going to surprise her, then. In fact, it had seemed odd to him that the Volkswagen was parked on the street, why hadn't she put it in the garage? Primavera would be going out that night, and where to? He did not open up the garage either, and parked the jeep on the other side of the road.

He was already pushing open the door when a woman's voice in the street waylaid him—"Doctor"—this startled him: he had not noticed how close she was. "Who's that?" he asked, as he did not recognize the woman with a dark veil over her head—the veil of the churchgoing faithful, half covering her face. "It's Alcira Sarasti," she said.

It was the wife of Arcángel de los Ríos.

The doctor greeted her impatiently; he did not want to know anything about anything anymore, and much less about Furibundo Pita and his revolver.

"He's told me everything," she said.

She sounded on the verge of tears. The doctor remembered her: she had been the very shy, skinny, mixed-race girl who used to keep herself to herself and read her Bible on a bench in the children's park; and she's still beautiful, he thought, an innate beauty, who knows what penance cast her into Furibundo Pita's jaws, but didn't she try to kill me one Innocents' Day with those poisoned *empanaditas*? And hadn't he been in love with her when they were children? Wasn't she the same girl leaning over a balcony, a black Bible in her pale hands? The same Bible she was always reading as a youngster? It was her.

She swallowed air, as though it would give her courage to speak.

"He told me he fired at a man, and that he doesn't know how."

She waited a few seconds for the doctor to answer but he was so surprised that he could not. He just thought: I don't know how either.

"He told me he fired at Maestro Abril and he doesn't know how; he's sorry."

The doctor remained mute.

"Arcángel's not like they say. He drinks, it's true, but that's all; he's done me harm, but he's a good man, when all's said and done."

Doctor Proceso looked at her in amazement: there was Alcira Sarasti, sticking up for Furibundo Pita.

"He told me about the float, about what that float represents. I myself . . ." she said, stifling a sob and raising her voice, "I'd be the first to be insulted; how could such a float occur to a man like Maestro Abril, someone I know? How many times did I go to his house with the Day of the Poor ladies to comfort his children, to leave shopping, pencils and exercise books, clothes, medicines; why does he repay us in such a mean-spirited way? How could he think of goading my husband? He knows my husband well; the whole of Pasto knows my husband when he drinks. Don Tulio Abril knew perfectly well what he was taking on."

And she made up her mind to ask, terrified:

"Tell me, Doctor, for goodness' sake, just tell me he didn't kill him."

She had started to cry.

"He didn't kill him," the doctor said.

She crossed herself.

"Thanks be to the Blessed Virgin of La Playa," she said, and lifted the veil from her face; her shining eyes appeared, her voice recovered:

"I knew God would protect us, how could Arcángel think of firing at so good a man as Maestro Abril?"

The doctor looked at her, yet more astonished.

"I don't know," he said.

And he was about to go in, but she stopped him; she placed her gloved hand on the doctor's arm.

"Wait," she whispered, "are you in a hurry? Are you sure Señora Primavera's expecting you? Come over to ours, just one minute, Arcángel needs you. He sent me to beg you to listen to him, one minute."

"Tell him he didn't hurt anyone. The float won't be seen. Tell him to forget the whole thing."

And once more, he made as if to go inside.

"No," she said, "don't go in, please."

Did she really want to stop him entering his own home? It seemed so: her hand bore down on the doctor's arm. And, all of a sudden, she began to stroke it, really began to stroke it, she was stroking it: the doctor found that Alcira Sarasti was stroking his arm without realizing it, as if she were caressing him.

"Don't worry," he said. "No-one got hurt, this whole misunderstanding's going to be cleared up: neither you nor Arcángel will have anything to do with what the float says."

"Dear God," she fretted. "It would be my biggest sorrow."

Her eyes roamed across the starry sky; was she going to cry again? She recovered:

"Listen," she said, "I understand Maestro Abril, I know why he did it, I know him better than I know myself. He's a good man."

"Another good man," the doctor said.

But the pious Alcira did not hear him.

"One afternoon, coming out of church, after Benediction, I bumped into Maestro Abril. He didn't just say hello, but walked along with me. I don't know if he already knew, like everyone else, what was in store for him: Arcángel appeared, as he always does, hooting in the Willys, accelerating and slowing down, making all his usual racket when he finds me in the street after Benediction. He came up behind us, Hell itself on our heels. I said to the maestro: 'Señor Tulio, you don't need to come with me,' and he said: 'Don't you worry, I'll stay with you.' Arcángel caught us up: he hooted more than ever, shouted at the maestro to leave me on my own, he said some things to his face it would be a sin to repeat, Doctor; the whole of Pasto heard them, what an insult, and me so sorry to be the centre of attention. The maestro took my arm, because I tripped and nearly fell over with fright, can you imagine? He didn't let me go and stayed with me and told my husband that he should get out of the car, to see if he was big enough to make him leave my side, he said that to him, my God, and thank heavens Arcángel didn't get out: somebody turned up, one of his secretaries, a good angel who tempted him with a meal of guinea pig in Catambuco and took him away, that angel saved us, because Maestro Abril remained stubborn, determined to accompany me, taking my arm: Arcángel would surely have run us both over, he was capable of driving over us a hundred times, out of fury. But the maestro's bravery was something to see: he wasn't scared, although he was trembling as much as I was or more, and he was crying like me, from pure courage, God bless his strength of purpose. How rotten I feel, my shame shaming others. I put a good man like Maestro Abril's life in danger, do you understand? That's why the maestro got his own back with the float, he was saving my honour, what an upright man. Thank him for me in any case, because it's the thought that counts at least."

"Goodbye, Señora Alcira."

"No," she said, with an expression the doctor thought was pity for him. "You shouldn't go in."

"And why not?" he asked.

She smiled, undecided. He thought she would insist, in order to convince him to go to her husband, for a minute. She gave up, her voice a whisper:

"My regards to your wife."

And she disappeared down the street: slowly, light-footed, as though afraid of making a noise, she seemed to float. The doctor grasped the door handle again and pushed, at last, as if it were a heavy sheet of lead.

He made the door click audibly as he closed it: best let his presence be known, although it was possible Primavera had already heard his conversation—that depended where she was, he thought.

And straight away he saw her emerging, from the depths of the corridor leading to the guest bathroom, a shadow barely illuminated by the single light bulb switched on, was she still unaware of his presence? She approached with her leather skirt hitched up almost to the waist, bending down—in the middle of the infinitely complex manoeuvre of pulling down the skirt stuck around her thighs—and at the same time he heard her voice. It was hard to make it out.

"I heard the door," she said, "who was it?"

"Me," he said.

Primavera Pinzón stopped in astonishment, open-mouthed, just like him.

"A fish bone," she said.

And despite everything, he discovered, her voice was unchanged, unruffled by the slightest emotion.

Bewildered, he heard her persevere:

"A fish bone got stuck in his throat. I was seeing that he drank some water, in the bathroom."

The doctor had already moved towards her. They looked at one another numbly.

"A fish bone," he repeated, and nodded.

In the shadows of the corridor it seemed as though they were trying to work out whether it really was the two of them. As though Primavera were making an effort to remember him: he looked taller and stouter to her, but a chilly aura made him different from her memory, and, for that very reason, at that moment, a stranger, someone truly unknown and dangerous and much stronger than her, alien to the house.

She felt her daughters' absence made her vulnerable.

But she shook off the fear: it was just her husband, Doctor Donkey, hadn't he surprised her early that morning dressed as an ape, giving her a preview of his pathetic prank from beginning to end? And wasn't he even more pathetic now, so hesitant and ultimately deferential towards convention, as expected?

By then, with that almost magical, invisible speed of movement with which every woman dresses and conceals herself, she had finished fixing the skirt and straightened up, slightly flushed, as though with a final scrap of strength.

They both turned to look towards the door of the bathroom where early that morning Doctor Justo Pastor Proceso López had dressed up as an ape: there, through the same doorway, a head stuck out—a different head, a head with moustache and sideburns, that dithered without making up its mind to say hello.

Who can it be?—the doctor wondered.

The truth was, he expected to find a *boy*—an adolescent, which was the same thing as far as the doctor was concerned—given that he already knew his wife's secret tastes, her unsuspected love, her outrageous, perpetual desire: boys. With good reason he once heard a whispered conversation between two of his lady patients, who referred to Primavera as "the Cradle Snatcher," a nickname the doctor found very amusing.

Years before, one afternoon at the *finca*, he had surprised her at a bend in the river with one of the young labourers, a recently weaned colt—the doctor had thought—a prize yokel, a country boy who must have been for her, with all her respectable reasons, the most wonderful thing in the world; he discovered her right in the middle of the preliminary persuasion while they were each eating a guava, sitting very close to one another on top of a large, white boulder at the river's edge: the foaming current chattered, swallowing up the laughter, the words. Primavera was wearing that long summer dress he knew so well, grey and frothy with a large flower embroidered on it in gold thread, a dress sprinkled with river spray, here and there, on the shoulders, on the back, wet and sticking between her open legs, where her hands were resting, and she had one foot bared, rosy and small in the grass; the sandal, not far off, lay upside down, as if the foot had freed itself by kicking it off in annoyance. Primavera's head remained bent downwards; she seemed to be contemplating the tips of her breasts; from time to time her teeth bit into the guava, her lips sucked at it, while one of her hands ran over her long blonde hair as if untangling it; in reality she was sweeping it in shining strands across the boy's bare shoulder, grazing his skin like real, wounding darts. Primavera never displayed such furious and mute mortification as she did that afternoon, when the doctor disturbed them, saying hello. Primavera loathed him, smiling at him; and the colt fled, stammering.

But tonight was different. This was no strapping youth who leaned out from the doorway. It was General Lorenzo Aipe, a fact that not only amazed the doctor, but disconcerted him: he hardly knew the general, they had been introduced at the governor's house—when was that? This was not a boy: the general must have reached his half-century, just like him; together they totalled a hundred years. That made all the difference.

"General Aipe," Doctor Proceso said.

"He can't speak," Primavera interrupted, "didn't I say he'd got a fish bone stuck in his throat?"

"You did," the doctor said.

"That fish from Tumaco that Yolandita, Gerardo's niece, sent."

"Yes."

The doctor headed for the bathroom, while the moustached head remained sticking out, waiting for him without saying a word, unable to say a word, according to what Primavera herself had decreed—the doctor thought—the general must be furious, unable to speak, Primavera let slip something about a fish bone, isn't that ingenious? Ah, bountiful Primavera—he carried on talking to himself as he made his way very slowly down the corridor, too slowly, gloomy and chill, like a ghost ship.

And how repulsive, how absurd this General Aipe seemed to him compared to the graceful savages at the *finca*, what a sorry, unfortunate transformation Primavera's taste had undergone, he thought.

Primavera managed to flash her blue eyes at the doctor, dark with bitterness, as though saying to him: "If you already know what's going on here, why don't you leave? I've left you in peace plenty of times, now you leave me in peace."

With your boy?—the doctor said to himself, and he seemed to hear Primavera reply: "With my boy."

But *that* isn't a boy—the doctor went on thoughtfully—it's General Lorenzo Aipe.

"Let me see," he said out loud, clapping one of his hands on the general's shoulder, gently pushing him into the bathroom. "Supposedly, I'm a doctor."

The general spluttered something.

"Don't speak," the doctor said, "it's not a good idea for you to talk."

General Aipe sought Primavera's eyes, but she had lowered her head, in a confusing gesture, which could signify anger or resignation. The general was a bald man, robust and very tall, though not as tall as the doctor, and gave off a strong whiff of armpit. The doctor wondered whether Primavera, like other women, was fond of that smell. The general, embarrassed at having to submit to Primavera's extraordinary inventiveness, the fish bone, decided to accept the situation and allowed his tongue and throat to be examined in front of the large mirror in the guest bathroom; the room was dark when the doctor approached: they had to turn the light on as they went in; all that time, the only weak light came from the bulb that illuminated the corridor, so that it seemed impossible to the general that this giant of a doctor should suspect nothing untoward, or was he pretending? The general and Primavera had been in the kitchen first, and after concluding the whirlwind of an inopportune embrace—standing up, semi-naked against the wobbling fridge—they went to the bathroom simply to adjust their clothing in front of the mirror, as they would be going off in Primavera's Volkswagen to eat guinea pig in Catambuco; and they had just entered the bathroom, without yet switching on the light, when Primavera heard the front door open and went to have a look.

Now the general heard, inexplicably, the unbelievable doctor's earnest voice:

"Yes, yes," he said.

And he felt him place one of his great big fingers, overly confidently, on the top of his tongue, at the back.

"I can feel something here, General. Luckily, the bone hasn't gone into the throat, good, very good, it's buried itself almost completely; the tongue is a fleshy organ, making it very difficult to find a fish bone, but never fear, General, we'll extract it, if it turns out there is, in the end, a bone there, because the body itself is capable of assimilating it, do you see? It's quite possible your system has already absorbed it. Come with me to the consulting room, General, just for five minutes."

The general seemed to assent with a sigh.

And this time he did exchange a reassuring look with Primavera Pinzón.

"Alright," the general agreed unexpectedly, in his normal voice, "it's best you help me." And he enunciated it perfectly, the doctor discovered—a grave mistake for a general well versed in strategy, he thought, to speak so clearly with a fish bone stuck in his throat.

"Best not make the effort to talk," the doctor said to him, affably. "Stay calm and come with me. If you had that bone in your actual throat I'd have to give you a few hard thumps on the back, or compress your thorax; I'd have to get behind you and hug and squeeze you, squeeze to fainting point. Fortunately, there's no need. The procedure is different for a fish bone in the tongue, if you still have the fish bone in your tongue. It'll be a simple, yet delicate matter: the fish bone can splinter and go into the jaw, and then take up residency beside the carotid artery on its way to the heart, no less. But we're going to check it out."

And they headed for the private consulting room, right there, on the ground floor, through a discreet oak door on one side of the living room. Primavera followed behind, bewildered: she had thought the matter would not go on for long, that they would all, formally, say goodbye to one another, and that her husband would go on being the man she knew. But to see him so composed and obliging, leading General Aipe along, intrigued her as much as it irritated her. Her Doctor Donkey was so naive—she calmed down at last—he really must believe the general was suffering from a stuck fish bone. Then, going along behind her husband's tall figure, glancing at his affable profile, she suddenly wondered, very surprised at herself, why she was not in love with him, or why she did not accept, after all, that this was her husband and she loved him; there are so many ways to love with resignation, she told herself, why, simply, did she not love him or try to love him and stop, frankly, fucking about? Primavera Pinzón asked herself this, engrossed in her own moment of truth, and now—she suddenly cried out—what will happen? Why did I think of a fish bone? All this is through my fault, through my fault, through my most grievous fault, amen, and for a second she believed, unable to credit it, that she was laughing, that she was roaring with laughter at herself and the two men by her side.

Had he made a mistake in returning home, the doctor wondered, meanwhile.

For years a sort of tacit agreement had been established between him and his wife regarding their private wishes to be "alone." The doctor himself sometimes went out to the *finca* "alone," for a weekend, and Primavera did not object. No doubt about it—the doctor thought—he had neglected to remember the agreement in time or, remembering it too keenly, he had found himself there, *besieging* Primavera. The fact was, they both knew what to expect from one other: the reckless female patients, for example, who from time to time, and so thriftily, became the doctor's lovers, did not pass unnoticed by Primavera, who smiled patronizingly—stronger than he was. As for him, why did he resort to these affairs? Simple repayment—he told himself—generosity towards the generosity of certain women exhausted with their husbands, women who were starting to grow old, like him, who admired their doctor and found an occasional diversion in him. The doctor did not feel one iota of tenderness for these tormented patients who invented a whole range of illnesses in order to visit his practice; he just proved to himself that he was alive, and that he was more alive if he managed to make them happy, but—he recognized—while the hospitable embrace occurred, his memory took refuge in the flesh and eyes of Primavera Pinzón: he did not succeed in ridding himself of her.

And now—he wondered—what was he doing leading the general towards his consulting room? If it were only a matter of another of Primavera's boys, he thought, he would let him go, unscathed, but it was this horrible General Aipe. And something at the doctor's core inflamed and—conversely—pleased him: the irritation on Primavera's face pleased him to the point of anguish.

"Eleven o'clock at night," he said, consulting the clock on the consulting room wall, "Innocents' Day isn't over yet."

He seemed genuinely eager to assist, bent over the little table of medical instruments, searching here, searching there; an unassailable force was at work in him which froze his wife and the general, a force that sprang above all from an inspiring serenity. For that reason, lying back on the leather couch, more of a divan than a couch, General Lorenzo Aipe listened drowsily to the medic's calming voice. The general had his mouth open, lit by a small torch the doctor was holding in his hand. Then the general saw him pick up a tongue depressor and, almost immediately, a syringe; the needle went in, clean and painless. For a moment, the general's hand seized the doctor's.

"Steady, General," Doctor Proceso said. "It's preferable to anaesthetize the tongue to avoid any pain: we'll find the fish bone, if there is one."

"*Is* there a fish bone?" Primavera asked, fixing her darkened eyes on her husband.

"It's the likeliest thing," he said, without altering his expression. His voice was uninflected, neutral, professional: a medical practitioner carrying out his duty. "That's what the colouration of the tongue here suggests. I'll need to palpate it. Patience, General."

General Lorenzo Aipe wished to speak; he gave a sort of prolonged sigh, and wanted to add something with his hands: signals of astonishment and dissent, incredulity at what he was going through, that well-aimed jab he had been the object of. He started to get up, but the doctor's hand spread open on his chest and pushed him gently but firmly back onto the couch's leather pillow.

"General," he said, "don't try to speak. At this moment, your tongue is a dead one—like Latin."

The general and Primavera exchanged another look, full of misgiving, urgently apprehensive. But the doctor's voice went impassively on and was of a candour that persuaded them.

"Let me do it, General, it won't hurt, it's a case of finding the end of the bone, taking hold of it and pulling it out, or breaking it off and destroying it," and while saying this he already had in his hand, as if by magic, a slender scalpel, like a glinting streak, that he quickly used on who knows which of the seventeen striated muscles of the tongue, as he explained while he did it, "the tongue is a fleshy organ possessing seventeen striated muscles," he said, concentrating, "that's done it, general, I'll apply this little bit of gauze for a few seconds to stop it bleeding, like so, good, the bone has been absorbed into your tongue, from there it'll dissolve into the intestinal flora and cease to be a danger; it'll become just like you and me and everyone else: pure shit."

The horrified silence which followed his words was the decisive push that helped the general to finish getting up, Primavera to finish getting out of the consulting room, the two of them to finish crossing the living room as if fleeing from a lunatic.

The doctor followed them unhurriedly to the front door: he saw how they got into the Volkswagen and left—Primavera at the wheel, the general just a panic-stricken face, goggle-eyed, his hand at his lips.

Afterwards the doctor returned to the living room and sat in the easy chair—"bad job," he said to himself, "bad job."

He did not know when Primavera got back. He felt her pass by him, vaguely, like a draught, heard her go upstairs and slam the bedroom door with all her might.

She came back to him much later, by the light of the dawn tinting the windows. He sensed her pass him again, go to the kitchen, head slowly back up the stairs to the first landing: there, Primavera rested her elbows on the handrail.

"And you're happy," she said.

The doctor heard her, frozen in his easy chair, but understood absolutely nothing: he was thinking about that episode in Bolívar's life that Belencito Jojoa had recounted to him one rainy afternoon.

Then he felt her go past again, towards the front door.

"Where are you going?" he said, just for the sake of it, because he thought that was what he ought to ask, or rather, what anyone would ask, and he did not want to disappoint her, he wanted her to leave for wherever she was heading, calmly, at peace.

"The girls," she snapped, "remember them?"

She clenched her fists. She trembled beside the door.

"You abandoned them to the mercy of those drunks; doesn't it ever occur to you to worry about your daughters?"

Those drunks are your brothers and sisters, your family, he was on the point of retorting, but contained himself.

"Don't you ever think that some pervert might just rape them?" Primavera asked, without expecting an answer. "I'm off to the *finca*, if you really care."

And then:

"That's if I'm not too late. And please don't follow me, don't even think about it."

Motionless, he saw her open and close the door and disappear.

*

He did not know how much time went by, but he was disturbed by the telephone, which dragged him away from Belencito Jojoa telling tales of Bolívar that rainy afternoon, pulled him from his dreams—although not sleeping—in that same easy chair where he was still sitting from the night before. The morning advanced across the windows: now the light hurt his eyes, and yet—he thought, wiping away a tear—for him it was as if the night was still going on. Are my eyes watering because of the brightness of the light or because I'm crying? The telephone persisted, beside him. He stretched out an arm and answered it. Even before putting the receiver to his ear he heard a voice that sounded like it was coming from the other side of a storm. Not only did the interfering noise resemble that of a storm, but the quiet voice itself could be heard breaking up into crackling sounds. It was the voice of General Lorenzo Aipe, or rather, a sort of guttural groaning he was making—more words, fewer words, and always fragmented:

"Doctor, if I'm damaged for life, you're dead, do you hear me, you sonofabitch doctor? You're dead if you injured my tongue."

Doctor Proceso let the morning advance over him, let the sun touch the edge of his shoes, his knees, his waist, his chest, and on up to his eyes. He had resolved to go out to the *finca* after Primavera, for his daughters— but no, he said to himself. "No," he repeated out loud, "I won't go."

He would visit the sculptor Cangrejito Arbeláez, as agreed with the maestros: renew his enthusiasm for Bolívar's carriage. From that moment on, his pain of a love for Primavera, that absurd uncertainty of love, would be left behind. From now on he would think only of himself and the float, with no backing down, unlike what he had been permitted his entire life, his whole life condemned to the suffering caused by a single name: Primavera.

But when he crossed Pasto's sleeping streets in his jeep, that Thursday, December 29, 1966, he was still remembering the scalpel that had seemed to have had a life of its own, the pink and white tongue, Primavera's astonished eyes, the blood, General Aipe's tortured voice threatening him.

"Bad job," he said to himself again. "Very bad job."

5

Without yet having exchanged a word with the doctor about the float, the sculptor Cangrejito Arbeláez had already chiselled reliefs of the early events of Bolívar's life onto wooden panels. At that moment, he was marking out the betrayal of Miranda, and Doctor Proceso was observing, fascinated, the gradual appearance of Simón Bolívar and the other conspirators, beneath the rapid chisel blows, Bolívar with Miranda's sword and pistol—Miranda who waited, sitting up in bed, hands and feet in chains—the Spanish soldiers approaching and, underneath, running the full length of the panel, in carved lettering: *SIMÓN BOLÍVAR BETRAYS HIS GENERAL, FRANCISCO DE MIRANDA.*

"How many men went there with Bolívar?" Doctor Proceso asked.

"Five: Miguel Peña, Juan Paz del Castillo, Carabaño, Mires, Casas. As you can see, you're not Sañudo's only reader. Surprised?"

The doctor leaned over one of the panels that was already completed: Simón Bolívar and eight of his officers abandoning the square inside Puerto Cabello—with its three thousand guns and four hundred quintals of gunpowder—to the mercy of an uprising by unarmed Spaniards; they fled flat out, the nine faces showing disproportionate fear;

even the galloping horses had expressions of terror, and, if you looked more closely, there was something extraordinary about them: the gaping faces of the nine horses were faces of petrified virgins, about to be sacrificed. The wooden lettering stated: *BOLÍVAR FLEES FROM PUERTO CABELLO AS IF THE DEVIL WERE ON HIS HEELS.*

"But I want to show you something I made, long before reading Sañ-udo," Maestro Arbeláez said.

He left his tools on the table and stood for a moment in thought, wiping his hands on his leather apron. He came from Tumaco originally: a burly black man, with bloodshot eyes, and—the doctor thought—the unwavering sullenness of an abandoned child. He marvelled at this apparition of a giant, who carved wood as if breathing life into it, and he allowed himself to be led along a pathway of shrouded statues.

The studio was in a large, damp, rented house, and was so dark that it was surprising a visual artist could create his work in there. The maestro had to labour by electric light: beneath the pale bulbs his shadow seemed to float as if among age-old torches. He stopped in front of one of the sculptures and became thoughtful once more. Before uncovering it, he turned to the doctor.

"I didn't make this because I'm black," he said. "But almost."

And he smiled, without losing his sullen expression.

"I have to admit," he went on, "that the fact General Manuel Piar was black aroused my curiosity, in the beginning, and later on, more than anything, Bolívar's reasons for ordering him to be shot: he said Piar wanted to establish pardocracy, and used this to frighten the upper-class patriots, who feared being under the command of a black man, how about that? Bolívar assumed just the right kind of ingenuity for his day and age."

"They left Piar unprotected," the doctor said. "Piar, who up to that point had acted impeccably, unlike Bolívar and his flawed imaginings. That was how Bolívar managed to disguise the real reasons for the execution."

"Bolívar was afraid of Piar's intelligence, his independence of thought, not just his military qualities," Maestro Arbeláez picked up the thread, "Piar wasn't a toady, like the others. Faced with Bolívar's campaigns, all of them useless up to that point, Piar had nicknamed Bolívar the 'Napoleon of withdrawals,' no less. I don't know if the name reached Bolívar's ears, but Piar had already warned the others about his idiotic and pretentious Napoleonism, and about his main strategy, which seemed to consist of retreating at the slightest sign of danger."

Here the maestro's smile put in another appearance, and now his sullenness ceased to be unwavering; the more he talked, the closer he came to roaring with laughter.

"Remember the Battle of Junín," he said, "which wasn't a 'battle,' according to the technical terminology of warfare. Sañudo initially says it was a 'skirmish,' subsequently he says 'fight'; in his *History of America* Estébanez says it was really an 'engagement'; Cortés Vargas goes further and calls it a 'gamble.' Skirmish, engagement or gamble, Bolívar fled the field when he thought his cavalry was defeated; he didn't stick around long enough to observe that a squadron of lancers took the royalists by surprise; he alone fled to behind the cover of his infantry, galloping at the double, and withdrew to a hill 'until the evening shadows covered the field' . . . Colonel Carvajal finally managed to find him to inform him that while the general was retreating, the enemy was put to flight. He said: 'Fear not, Liberator, victory is yours.'"

The maestro finished off his speech with a great guffaw but the doctor was unable to join in, too astonished by the pearly splendour of the laughter, its immoderate booming. And yet he heard the maestro say, with the last gasps of mirth:

"Gamble or engagement, historians used Junín to build another pillar of glory for Bolívar to stand on, another crowning moment made from what was only a brief skirmish in which two thousand Peruvians deserted the royalist ranks, a fight that wasn't even suggested by Bolívar but by the Frenchman Canterac, who led the royalist forces; Bolívar wasn't even there for the clash, he ran away."

With a tug the maestro pulled the dust sheet from the sculpture—a realistic figure, in reddish bronze—and waited in silence; it was General Manuel Piar's execution by firing squad: no blindfold, looking at the sky, barefoot, his shirt torn, legs slightly bent, it looked like he had just been hit and was starting to fall without ever reaching the ground.

"We must put the shooting of Piar up on the float," Doctor Proceso said. "Poor Piar, a great strategist: he waited for death calmly and said it was not being a traitor but a patriot that led him to the firing squad. His end was terribly ironic: they were not shooting him because he interfered with Bolívar's plans, but because he was black and wanted to establish pardocracy."

"Piar had been born in Curaçao, of a white Venezuelan father and a mixed-race mother from the island," the sculptor responded. "He was a combination of races, like Bolívar: Bolívar's paternal great-great-grandfather had a relationship with a black woman in his household called Josefa, who gave birth to María Josefa: *her* daughter Petronella married Bolívar's grandfather, and this doesn't matter to us, not to you, not to me," he suddenly shouted, "we don't give a damn, but go and say that to Bolívar, were he alive: one more execution."

"Who doesn't have black blood mixed with indigenous and white in these beleaguered countries?" the doctor asked.

The maestro was exhilarated by this.

"We're not black, white, indigenous or yellow," he said, "but we've all got black, white, indigenous, yellow and who knows what blood running in our veins. Best we don't find out." And again, an explosive laugh that barely let him speak contorted his face. "In fact, Bolívar didn't care about blacks: the abolition of slavery was just a signature on a document for him, he didn't do anything concrete for the blacks; the first time he mentioned the need for abolition was because of the request from President Pétion, a black Haitian, who made him formally promise the emancipation of the slaves in return for money and munitions. Pétion effectively supported him when Bolívar fled to Haiti in order not to face up to the responsibility that was his due as leader. Bolívar would only go back once the wind was blowing in the patriots' favour; he was a wily parasite, taking every opportunity afforded him by the other generals' victories."

Another guffaw burst out and rang all around.

"He didn't just hold a grudge against Piar," he managed to resume, close to choking, "but against Mariño and Páez too. He could not run any risks with his presidency for life, his monarchy of the Andes. And what about Admiral Padilla's execution by firing squad?" he asked, laughter bubbling up inside him. "Another black man, another of Bolívar's innocent victims, I don't know how I'll represent it, but I'll definitely do it, Doctor, don't you worry."

And he had just finished saying that when a mighty crash was heard at the studio door. The din froze his laughter. The door had jumped off its hinges. Three men in carnival masks—a frog and two goblins—burst in and rushed at the burly maestro. They pushed his back up against the wall. In the throes of shock Doctor Proceso surprised himself: he became indignant they were paying him no attention, as if he posed no danger to anyone. He hurled himself towards the masked men who were grappling with the maestro, seized the frog by the shoulders, shook him, and had already made him turn around when a blow to the head left him unconscious.

He came to, stretched out on a sofa, Maestro Cangrejito looming over him.

"What happened?" he managed to ask.

"They took 'The Battle of Bombona' and 'Time of the Rifles,'" Maestro Cangrejito said.

They were two of the best reliefs of the War of Independence in Pasto.

"It's not the first time my work's been stolen. Last time they took some carvings, I didn't know how or when, and I discovered by chance they were selling them in Cali. I bought them myself: I asked where I might find the artist of such good carvings and they told me he'd already died, that *I* had died; and another time I found a lost statue in the parish church of a priest I know: he told me quite shamelessly that he'd fallen in love with it like with a statue of the Virgin; it was of a black woman in the act of taking her dress off over her head: the good priest had her well hidden away among the plaster angels in the sacristy. But I must admit, Doctor, this is the first time they've robbed me like this: with violence, as if they hated me as well as stealing from me—did they hurt you? There were five of them, it wasn't easy to stop them, they wanted to set fire to the studio, they'd brought a can of petrol with them; I don't know what would have happened if the other tenants of the house hadn't come to my aid—good people, firm friends: the two Chepes, Jaime, Franco, Nene, Marco, Pacho and Muñeco—the party's over, Doctor, look how they left the place."

The studio was turned upside down, sculptures scattered about, broken in half. At least the one of General Piar was still in one piece, the doctor noticed. The large table, where the tools were, seemed to have been destroyed.

"That's where I threw one of those goblins," Cangrejito said, "I must have broken at least six of his ribs."

Doctor Proceso began to worry. It was possible the attack was something more than a simple robbery: Cangrejito Arbeláez had heard about the float from maestros Tulio Abril and Martín Umbría; no-one else in the whole of Pasto could know about it, so what had happened? Common robbery? A veiled threat? Was the governor, were the authorities, involved? Impossible, he told himself, it would be too soon.

"Let's imagine it was a coincidence," the doctor said as he left, "but send whatever you make to my house, and at my expense, as you go along. I want to see it all, check it before putting it up on the float. What are we going to do now, for example, about the stolen reliefs?"

"Out with the old and in with the new," the sculptor said. "I'll make them again, and even better."

"I congratulate you," the doctor said. "It's not often you find such enthusiasm among artists. Generally speaking, they kill themselves, one is led to believe."

They both smiled, looking at each other steadfastly: was that a challenge?

"I'm not the suicidal type, but who knows, one of these days," the maestro responded. "Who hasn't thought about it, at some time or other?"

"Several times, in my case, and without being an artist," the doctor said. I hope I can go on chatting with this man in the future, he thought, he laughs and his face says the opposite. Then he said goodbye: "Send every piece to my house, you'll be better protected."

Why did I say that—he asked himself later on—how can I guarantee it? Could his house really be considered *safe*, with Primavera and General Aipe hanging around? The things he said. Why did he promise these people the earth?

His head hurt, but he plucked up courage from where he did not have it and, disillusioned, negotiated Pasto's chilly streets, cluttered with debris from the fiesta. He was going to Maestro Abril's workshop, in the far-flung hamlet.

There, in the midst of labouring artisans throwing jokes back and forth, among jugs of *chicha* and platters of roast pork, by shelfloads of tools, surrounded by the din of children, barking dogs fighting, shouting, banging, hammer blows, by the smell of varnish, amid the onslaught of clouds of sawdust, Bolívar's carriage was beginning to take shape.

The promised payment was already a fiesta in advance.

For a moment the doctor was overcome with the fear that no-one would complete it after all, that a mob of drunks would end up sleeping around the unfinished float. But he cheered up when he noticed that the former Furibundo Pita was every inch the Liberator Simón Bolívar, enthroned on the float, dressed in his blue-and-red uniform from head to toe, the gold and medals, the crown on his temples. Of the twelve girls dressed as nymphs who rose up, immense, hauling the chariot, three were perfect in every detail: the blue faces, innocent laughter playing on their lips, their delicate arms reddened by the leather straps, their backs bent from the effort of pulling the carriage on which Bolívar lounged. They were like flesh-and-blood girls, lively and happy beneath the swags of paper roses around their wavy hair—the roses the people rained over them.

Maestro Abril and Martín Umbría, up aloft on a pile of building materials, were directing the positioning of a huge polystyrene dove that would fly around the float, a snowy dove with a stain on its breast like a drop of blood in the shape of a heart. The two maestros toasted and conversed in shouts with the doctor, without deigning to descend from the summit; they calmed him down—the robbery was not as serious as it seemed, they said, pure coincidence.

"Nobody here has talked, nor will they until you wish it," Umbría said.

Doctor Proceso was watching the women, the children—likely reckless mouthpieces for the embryonic float. He wanted his float to be made public, fearlessly, in the parade on January 6, and then let the sky fall in; he would know what to do by then. But a sticky situation in advance, without the float having seen the light of day, made him nervous.

Zulia Iscuandé was even more distrustful, approaching the doctor to ask if he had yet put in a claim with Furibundo Pita concerning the payment. The maestros did come down from their peak then, and even the children fell silent.

"You'll get that money," Doctor Proceso said. "You can work without risking a thing. If the drunk doesn't pay up for the float, I will, with all my heart."

The answer surprised the artisans, but also reassured them, for the doctor spoke in all seriousness; he was, what's more, a doctor: he had his *finca*, he had money, he had rich patients who paid him.

And, just like on Innocents' Day, they filled him with roast pork, cheese and sweetcorn, and above all with *chicha*, and once again they sent him off at eleven o'clock at night, smelling of varnish and glue, tripping over himself, they waved goodbye with the roar of a general cheer and toasted his health; they did not seem hopeless drunks and, what was certain, the float was still there, growing in front of them all.

6

On the night of Friday, December 30, Doctor Justo Pastor Proceso López was more worried than ever; it was no coincidence, the whole of Pasto was in the know, he confirmed this when the guests arrived at his house, at seven on the dot: Professor Arcaín Chivo, or "the Philanthropist," famous for his miserliness, Mayor Matías Serrano, called "the One-Armed Man of Pasto"—though missing no limbs—and Monsignor Mon-túfar, the bishop, better known as "the Wasp," all very well informed about the float under construction.

"You're going to get into trouble," they warned him, each in their own way.

The doctor felt put out. He had anticipated telling them things from the beginning, with his motives well backed up, in order to win unconditional support. Now all he saw, looking back at him from the armchairs in the living room, were sceptical faces, expressing a sorrowful irony.

"Governor Cántaro and General Aipe will waste no time in taking measures," Matías Serrano was arguing. "They're not going to let Simón Bolívar dance to your tune, Justo Pastor, especially not up on a carnival float. It'd be different in a book: nobody reads books; on a public float there's a name for this: disrespect towards the founding father, and that, as far as those animals are concerned, is worse than insulting the flag, coat of arms and national anthem all at once, three distinct entities in a single true God. It'll be wretched. They'll have the whole weight of the law on their side to smash your float, imprison you, if you insist, and give you a few warning wallops."

"That's if they don't mangle your fingers, like happened to that Vicente Azuero, who published articles against Bolívar's dictatorship in his newspaper. A colonel by the name of Bolívar, perhaps another grateful descendent, sought him out and smashed the fingers he'd written his truths with. It was a straightforward threat: break the fingers of anyone who writes against Bolívar. I've suffered similar experiences myself, and I can describe them, if asked."

It was Professor Arcaín Chivo who had spoken.

He was the first to arrive, breathless in the cold: he made his journey on foot, to save the taxi fare from his house, which was on the other side of town—behind Canchala church, where they worshipped the Lord of the Good Death. He'd come all that way, and there he stood, perspiring, with arms outstretched, when Doctor Proceso opened the door. It was exactly seven o'clock in the evening.

"My dearest Justo Pastor," Chivo began, still with his arms spread wide like a crucifix, but without taking a step forward, without yet coming in for the clinch, by which Doctor Proceso understood that he must wait for the professor's salutation, a greeting possibly rehearsed in advance.

"The only redeeming feature of old age is that one ages alongside one's friends," Chivo said, jubilantly.

Tall but stooping, he had the bloodshot eyes of a hardened drinker, bushy grey hair and a leathery, yellow face. He held back a few more seconds before concluding:

"To each of us comes the same slice of sorrow, or ugliness, that the years bring with them, isn't that right, my dear Doctor Justo Pastor Proceso López, you hermit crab, sage in solitude, one more of Pasto's shades?"

"Must I thank you for this greeting?" the doctor asked, still without embracing the professor. "I just hope that your communal old age, with sorrow and ugliness to boot, will be a bit happier tonight, in my house."

And they embraced.

They clapped each another heartily on the back, still inspecting one another; laughingly, they said they were going to give death the brush-off.

"Each passing year brings us closer to death, it's true, but also closer to God," came a sudden voice of ecclesiastical solemnity. It was the Wasp, or the Bishop of Pasto, who was in the habit of popping up like a wraith, unexpectedly. Neither the doctor nor the professor had noticed the long black Ford parking; the driver opened the door, promised to wait for His Excellency without moving from the spot, but neither the doctor nor the professor heard him, and they did not see the bishop either—who, what's more, was not wearing the characteristic vestments of his office, just a black cassock with a small cross at the collar. Had he heard them, or did he speak of death and the passing years by chance? Hard to say: the three of them had their little tricks and their little ways, they were childhood friends, they had been through primary education together at the same school, San Francisco Javier.

And just then the Mayor of Pasto—another one from the same school—arrived, with more pomp than his predecessors: he was guarded by a policeman on a motorbike. He got out of the official car, spotted the three of them and hailed them at the top of his voice:

"By God, Bolívar is on trial today."

By which Doctor Proceso understood once and for all that Bolívar's carriage was common knowledge, or at least known about by the authorities.

"Let it be in God's hands and the Devil's," he said quietly, but not so quietly that the bishop did not hear him.

"What's that, Justo Pastor?"

"Let's go inside at once, *señores*. Pasto is cold."

7

In the living room, when all they had done was exchange those few warning words about the Bolívar float, Primavera Pinzón appeared before the learned invited friends, appeared, because you had to appear—he thought, gazing at her as if for the first time—my wife, he thought, you had to appear when I least needed you, showing up as if absolutely nothing had happened between the two of us (no scalpel, no tongue of any General Aipe), waltzing in, what's more, as if the Bishop of Pasto were not among them; her appearance dazzled them, her blonde hair in two plaits, hands on hips, her hatred and vengeance well concealed—the doctor thought—Primavera Pinzón appeared wearing her costume for the Pasto carnival, and said:

"I was just trying on my *ñapanga* costume, *señores*, which will have its debut on the sixth of January. What do you think?"

And she gave a twirl.

Like a flame, thought Arcaín Chivo, recovering from the surprise. He was the first to approve.

"And God created woman," he said, "the only thing in the world capable of coming between two brothers."

"Or two peoples," noted mayor Matías Serrano, "if we look to the *Iliad*."

The professor ignored the reference. He had said what he said after taking a gulp of air, and without knowing whether it was appropriate to say it. He pulled himself together:

"It's been ages, Primavera, since you've graced us with the pleasure of your company. That costume does wonders for you, but you do far more for it."

"It'll be a controversial costume," the mayor said. "The *ñapanga*, the traditional dress of the Nariño countrywoman, comes down somewhat further below the knees."

"This has been the year of the miniskirt," Primavera reminded them. "At last they invented the miniskirt for us, *señores*."

"Glorious invention by men for men," Arcaín Chivo said. "Marvellous gift." And bowing his head slightly in the bishop's direction, he added: "Begging the pardon of those present."

"There's no need to beg the pardon of anyone present," the Bishop of Pasto seemed benignly put out. "The discussion is worthy of interest. One might just ask oneself whether a real *ñapanga*, our countrywoman, would ever adopt this last word in fashion: the miniskirt."

"Usurper of men's peace," the professor added quickly.

"I don't think she would," the bishop answered himself, ignoring the professor. "The Vatican has already expressed its disapproval— yes, allow me to continue, Arcaín—these days nobody cares about the Pope's disapproval—you're a living example of that—but it's a matter of the Pope's reflection, which we should consider from time to time, as Christians."

"No *ñapanga* would wear a skirt that short," the mayor said. "You're taking a risk, Primavera: I read in the newspaper that a man was arrested for biting the thighs of a woman in a miniskirt; he claimed to the judges that she had provoked him."

"A flimsy excuse," Arcaín Chivo said. "It is provocative, but that doesn't give us the right to go so far as to bite."

"Quite so," the mayor said. "We should ask permission first."

"Not even if they do ask my permission, *señores*." Primavera smiled fleetingly. "My thighs are not flesh for anyone's nibbles."

"I can't believe that," snorted Chivo, and confronted the doctor with a wicked look.

"Come to think of it," the doctor said, straight-faced, not looking at Primavera, but watching her, "I can't remember having bitten you in such a distant place."

Discreet chuckles were heard coming from the mayor and the professor. The bishop did not join in.

"I shall rectify that mistake," the doctor went on coolly.

Primavera struck a capricious pose, which might have meant pity or defiance.

Primavera Pinzón, stood with arms akimbo, one leg slightly out in front of the other, irremediably beautiful, turned yellow by the firelight, then suddenly red, a standing sphinx, the doctor thought, inflamed by men, unseasonably shivery in the midst of all those eyes, not knowing what to do or say—you allowed yourself to be adored dressed as a *ñapanga*: the skirt of coloured, woollen cloth, trimmed with a velvet border; velvet too around the edges of the huge pocket; again the skirt, pleated from the waist, somewhat shorter than the petticoat, of which they could see the crocheted edging; the white, shiny satin blouse revealing her pert, medium-sized breasts, deliberately badly covered up with a fringed, embroidered black shawl; on her head she wore a tortoiseshell comb, and ribbon bows finished off the plaits; against the whiteness of her throat the glass beads, the necklaces virtually tinkled, a gold filigree crucifix glittered; she wore large earrings; both hands played nervously with a felt hat that she remained undecided about putting on; her rope-soled *alpargatas* showed off her tiny feet, the toenails of which she had not neglected to paint a vivid pink: it was that detail Professor Arcaín Chivo observantly fixed upon:

"My dear *señora*," he said, "like a good *ñapanga* you did not forget to paint your nails pink; I bet you don't know why *ñapangas* do that."

Primavera looked at him for a moment with genuine curiosity. She tossed her head as she said:

"So you don't bite us, *señor*."

The mayor congratulated her:

"So you did know," he said. "Painting the toes pink wards off bites from snakes and academics. You are farsighted, Primavera."

Chivo opened his arms.

"You've beaten me," he said.

And he turned back to Primavera; he could not take his eyes off her.

"Nonetheless," he advised, "wearing *alpargatas* is incorrect; *ñapanga*, my lovely lady, is a corruption of the original word *llapanga*, which is Quechua for 'barefoot.'"

"Come off it, Arcaín," the mayor continued. "You're not suggesting our Primavera go through the streets barefoot on January the sixth."

"Heaven forbid," Arcaín Chivo protested hammily. "I just want . . ."

But Primavera was no longer paying him any attention.

"Your Grace," she said, making for the bishop, and seeming frankly astonished, almost shocked at herself, but only for a second, "forgive my intrusion. I did not know you were among my husband's guests. You'll understand my delight in the carnival—which is why you see me in my costume," she said, gesturing at herself from head to foot.

"I understand, Primavera, I understand. Don't worry," the bishop said, and allowed the radiant woman to kiss the episcopal ring on his finger.

"I've brought you *empanadas de pipián* and anisette," she went on, once more in control of her words. "Genoveva, Conchita, what's taking so long?"

Genoveva Sinfín and the maid emerged from the shadows, both holding vast trays, over the tops of which peeped the dainty peanut and potato *empanadas* and endless glasses of *aguardiente*.

"Do the *señores* need us, or can we go?" Sinfín asked unceremoni-
ously, while setting down the trays in a bad mood.

The bishop felt embarrassed, and took pity on them.

"Go in peace, ladies," he said. "We'll look after ourselves."

Sinfín and the girl recognized him. They both crossed themselves;
it looked as though they were going to fall to their knees.

"Most Reverend Father, we didn't see you," Sinfín said.

"Go in peace," the bishop repeated, blessing them.

Genoveva Sinfín and the girl needed no persuading. They vanished
as if they were fleeing.

"I'll be back in two minutes," Primavera said. "But without this
ñapanga costume, so as not to cause a stir. I just want to sit with you,
señores, and listen."

So Primavera left the living room, taking the party with her, and
the guests took a further, long minute to recover themselves; no-one
looked at anyone else, there were no words; all converged on the trace
of perfumed air that the costumed Primavera had left in her wake.

"You should feel proud of a woman like that," the professor said.
"She's left us stunned. Who was expecting her? I wasn't."

And he began tucking in to the steaming *empanadas*. They all followed suit. No-one drank the *aguardiente*.

Doctor Proceso did not respond straight away. He came round with
difficulty.

Yes, he said to himself, why would one not feel proud of an unpre-
dictable woman.

Matías Serrano extracted him from the sticky situation:

"Confess that all this business with the *ñapanga* costume is designed
to draw attention to Nariño's history, to your Bolívar float, isn't that
so? I admit you've got us on tenterhooks: maybe we're being hasty to
criticize it without first hearing your motives."

"That's right," the doctor exhaled. "That was just the beginning."

"A magnificent beginning," the professor ribbed him. "Worthy of you, Justo Pastor."

"I don't know whether to wait for Primavera to come back," the doctor said.

"So, she really is coming?" Chivo said in surprise.

"She should hear this," the doctor replied. And he called to her: "Shall we wait for you, Primavera?"

There was silence.

"Coming!" They heard her voice clearly, and immediately saw her arrive, no longer in her *ñapanga* costume—just the rope-soled *alpargatas*—but in a comfortable outfit—wool sweater, mid-length print skirt—she arrived as though walking on tiptoe, bathing them all in her habitual splendour, all the more splendid as she sat on the sofa, letting herself fall onto the cushions like a great flower opening and closing, stirring a breeze from her own self, from deep in her bones, next to the Bishop of Pasto no less—who shifted uneasily, as if afraid of her.

8

"Tell them, Doctor Donkey," Primavera said, and met the doctor's eyes just for an instant, because afterwards she just looked into space, "tell them about your float for January: you'll give them a lot more to talk about than my *ñapanga* costume."

There was a silence no-one wanted to break, because they could not. Did Primavera just say *Doctor Donkey*? Did we hear right? Doctor Proceso ignored the nickname. His voice sounded beyond natural: indifferent.

"That's the mystery," he said, "how you came to hear about the float, when it was only yesterday the artisans started working on it. What to put that down to? The city I live in? Little town, living hell; walls have ears in Pasto. But I'm not going to give you each the third degree to find out how you heard about it. I want to get people talking about the float, let's hope much more than about my wife's *ñapanga* miniskirt; I want to display snippets of our memory, on a carnival float."

And he described as best he could, summoning strength from where he had none, the carriage in which the so-called Liberator would ride, the emperor's crown on his head, the twelve girls like stooping nymphs, and Cangrejito's reliefs around the edges—Bolívar fleeing as if the Devil were on his heels, the sculptures, the models, the masks, the history of the south in fragments.

Following his words, a silence mightier than a wall rose up in the midst of them all. They could do nothing but raise their glasses—with a stifled reticence.

"I'm listening," the doctor told his friends. "That's why I spoke."

No-one responded.

"Propose the key events, *señores*, the ones to show on the float."

The silence continued, but the invitation exerted a powerful influence over the guests: their eyes moved uneasily.

"What do you think?" the doctor coached them, opening his arms.

"More bad business," Arcaín Chivo said.

The bishop's meditative voice was heard:

"They're not going to let you do that to Bolívar, Justo Pastor, in any city in the country, or in any town, or any village."

"In Pasto they will," the doctor said.

"Maybe so," Matías Serrano said. "Maybe in Pasto, if Pastusos remembered. But nobody in Pasto remembers anymore, Justo Pastor. They've been efficiently incorporated into the fine history of Colombia, with its whole host of heroes and angels."

"Don't you believe it," the doctor said. And he told them of Zulia Iscuandé and her grandfather's words: "Bolívar was always a complete son of a bitch." While repeating the sentence he could do no less than excuse himself in the bishop's direction, as Arcaín Chivo had done earlier: "Begging the pardon of those present."

"Do let's stop asking for the pardon of those present," the bishop said.

"Yes," the professor said, "let the people speak how they speak."

"But how," the mayor continued, "how will the governor judge the float? What will he decide? He's a Pasto man, but, like many others, at the front of the queue when it comes to not knowing who Agualongo was, who our hero Agustín Agualongo really was, and he won't have read Sañudo, and he doesn't think, he brays; it's unbelievable the amount of rot a human being can hold inside, not in the gut but in the mind. He'll confiscate your carriage like he'd confiscate a gun at a party: he'll return the gun when the party's over, if he returns it at all, and that's what he'll do with your float, he'll return it after carnival, if he doesn't destroy it first, along with all the artisans' good intentions. Don't make them work in vain, Justo Pastor. Don't be naive."

"Naive?" Doctor Proceso asked no-one in particular, his tone pouring scorn on the word, then he got up and walked over to a large piece of pine furniture, to one side of the crackling fire. The watercolour of Primavera Pinzón *en plein air* presided over the cabinet, and the doctor fretted, bent over the compartments and drawers: he kept part of his research into Simón Bolívar's life in there. So many years pursuing dates and facts and events, without ever settling down to organize them, he thought, surprised at himself: he felt the presence of the tattered exercise books with their green covers like an accusatory chaos.

He started to look in one of the drawers while he was speaking.

"Years before publishing his *Estudios*," he declared, "Sañudo recognized the need to write about other aspects of Bolívar—not the public ones, but the private. He said the private aspects were a way of getting to know the public, that family life resembles a tracing of public life: the leader is always the same, with the same passions, in the family arena as in that of the state."

Here Doctor Proceso cleared his throat and cast an uneasy glance around him; Primavera seemed to laugh imperceptibly at his words.

The doctor ignored her.

"Someone wrote that history must treat the great as God treats us all," he said, "impartially and truthfully; those who want their private life respected must limit themselves to living privately, but those who raise themselves on high are very visible and their vices teach those lower down how to commit them. What did Bolívar teach the whole host of politicians who would succeed him throughout Colombia's history? Firstly, to think only of themselves: of power. Next, to think only of themselves, of power, and then, power again—and so on and so on to infinity. Never to think of the real needs of the people."

"How very true," the mayor said.

Primavera's fleeting laughter was heard at last. The doctor continued, unaffected:

"If Sañudo covered the political and military sides of the so-called Liberator in his *Estudios*, he never touched upon other intimate facets, and that was out of pure decorum. Besides, those were not the facets he was interested in. But the polemic his *Estudios* unleashed in the 'cultured' corners of the country tempted him to embark upon Bolívar's other face, his other dimension, the human one. But, nevertheless, he never did take on the work he talked about."

"Sañudo didn't write it," the professor said, "but he did make ironic comments at times. He alleged that little could be said about Bolívar's education, because he was packed off to study in Spain when he was seventeen years old and still didn't even know how to spell; that he was only in school there a year, as he opted to marry his cousin and tour around Europe enjoying himself like the Creole dandy he was."

The professor laughed at his own wit; no-one joined him.

The mayor chipped in. He picked up with Sañudo again, too:

"Bolívar used to say he benefitted from many teachers—does that prove his learning? When young he had Don Andrés Bello, who had no experience and was not much older than he was himself, and after that Don Simón Rodíguez, a conceited and eccentric fellow, whose real surname was Carreño, which he dropped because of a disagreement with a brother; Rodíguez came from Europe, where he had been immersed in the ideas of the French *encyclopédistes*, and made a show of his religious indifference to the extreme of giving his children the names of fruits and vegetables."

"Is that true?" Primavera was constantly being surprised, and let out another yelp of laughter, short, frank, of pure amazement. "I'd like to have known a man like that, father to artichokes and beetroots—what if they'd called me 'apple?'"

With that hair of yours, golden delicious, thought the professor, going off into a reverie, and he raised his glass and forced the others to do the same.

"To Primavera," he said, "for her presence, saving grace of the evening."

Mayor Matías Serrano toasted unenthusiastically, and immediately returned to Sañudo:

"In one of his letters to Bolívar," he said, "General Sucre told him that Simón Rodríguez (who Bolívar named Director for Public Education) made a lot of silly mistakes and messed up the instruction in schools in Cochabamba, where he'd spent ten or twelve thousand pesos on non-sense in six months. 'I have asked,' Sucre wrote to Bolívar, 'that he bring me in writing the system he wants to adopt, and in eight months he has been unable to present me with it. But in conversation he says one thing one day and the following day another.'"

"He was Bolívar's tutor," the doctor said, "Simón Rodríguez, who endeavoured to apply the theories of Rousseau's *Émile* to the little Simón, which consisted of not teaching his pupil anything, so that he should remain in a 'natural' state and learn what he could on his own account; this meant Bolívar's early instruction must have been utterly useless."

The bishop, who had barely spoken, joined in impatiently, as if he wanted to clear the matter up once and for all: "Sañudo pointed out conclusively that Bolívar was made into a myth, such that the common conception of him bears no relation to reality. But so what, Justo Pastor? The people need their hero—what reason is there to topple Bolívar now?"

"True, why screw Bolívar?" the professor agreed, to ingratiate himself with the bishop.

"'Screw,' what an ugly word," the bishop said, put out. He wanted to go on talking, but just the sight of the professor's smile dissuaded him.

"No-one here is trying to screw anyone," the doctor countered. "And what vile injustice towards Sañudo: I still see his ghost passing along Pasto's streets, always alone, and why wouldn't he be? In 1925 he dared do no less than the worst thing you can do in this country: tell the truth. It's the memory of the truth, which struggles to prevail sooner or later. By correcting the error of the past, speaking out against it, you correct the absence of memory, which is one of the main causes of our social and political present, founded on lies and murder. It's not a whim, Arcaín; it's our duty to dot the i's if we don't want to sin by omission. I'm surprised at you, we've talked about this. You share my views more than anyone."

"Of course," the professor replied, offended. "And what's more I speak from personal experience. Remember what happened to me at the university. I'll remind you if you ask—may I remind you all?"

"While we're on the subject of truth," Matías Serrano said, scorning the professor's own experiences, "I want to let you in on something I'm convinced of, after carrying it around with me for years: Simón Bolívar, the long-winded author of proclamations and ravings, could not have written the Jamaica Letter, the famous one."

"And if Bolívar didn't write it, who did?" Primavera asked, just for the sake of it.

All eyes turned towards her. Primavera was entranced by herself; she found she liked the sound of her own voice. She recalled that famous letter, read and reread to the point of tedium at school: Franciscan Sisters, Father Muñoz, history class.

"Some wise little fellow," the professor said, happy to be exchanging views once more with the only woman at the gathering. "A disinterested foreigner?" he wondered. "An idealistic friend of Bolívar's? It's possible; in any case, the Jamaica Letter is nothing out of this world, for goodness' sake. But I agree: nobody knows who wrote it."

"Some little 'philanthropist' of the day?" Primavera responded.

Chivo hung onto her words, like one begging for mercy.

"Bolívar did not want for power or gold," the mayor said, "to procure good services. He had no end of amanuenses, ranging from the most well-informed to the most uncouth. The truth is, it's hard to believe in his authorship; the Jamaica Letter is no big deal, true, but it's a sensible analysis, and it's not in Bolívar's style, if we think of his other writings, those from before and after that 'Delirium on Chimborazo,' including the 'Cartagena Manifesto,' the 'Angostura Address' and the 'Message to the Congress of Bolivia.'"

That "Delirium" was another of Bolívar's writings, Primavera remembered, almost a poem, that she and two fellow students recited as girls, one July 20, day of the Cry of Independence: "*I came, wrapped in the mantle of Iris . . . A feverish delirium seized my mind. I felt inflamed by a strange superior fire. It was the God of Colombia who possessed me . . .*"

"And even if he did write the Jamaica Letter?" Doctor Proceso said. "What is written with the hand is wiped out with the feet. How about him talking of freedoms while planning to crown himself monarch of the Andes? He urged on the advances of the republic, but behind the scenes tore down everything he constructed in public; he schemed, deceived, dissembled, so that once again those around him echoed his real objective: dictatorship, which they proposed as if it would never have occurred to him. There were innumerable occasions. He was engaged only in this, while the crucial priorities of the new republic were held in abeyance: education, industry, those things that make for the real independence of a country—not the independence of one master being replaced by another. Oh, the soldier: he prolonged the war to suit himself. For years. Chaos fascinated him. The most naive now say that he aspired to monarchy because he found it necessary in order to combat the fickleness and brutalities of the politicians of his day; nothing could be further from the truth: he led the way in fickle brutality, he was the prototype himself. If there was killing to be done on a whim, he killed on a whim. The dream of Gran Colombia was his own dream, of his own power. He delegated authority and public wealth to rough squaddies and unrefined thinkers, to the toadies who did not trouble his ambition, the same men who ruined Colombia at his fall, imitating him like little mirrors from which destiny called them. Upon the living flesh of Gran Colombia (a beautiful dream if you look at it like a child, but a dream for us, the millions of us, not for Bolívar), upon Gran Colombia's young body, his minions carved out larcenies of their own: *if he did it, so can I.* All those treacherous men are epitomized, explicitly, by one of the most unpleasant sycophants: Vidaurre, a character from Peru, Bolívar's plenipotentiary for the Panama congress, who got down on all fours in meetings so that Bolívar might mount him: and Bolívar did; Bolívar provided the disastrous model that would turn itself over time into Colombia's political culture."

All the while, Doctor Proceso was rifling about in the cabinet drawers. What was he looking for? A book, a letter, a document? He could not find what he was after and this fact seemed to weigh down not just upon him, but on his audience too.

"Well, *señores,*" he said, "I have human records, which might clarify certain hidden aspects of Bolívar, those aspects repudiated by historians. To be precise I've called them 'Human Investigations.' I'd like to share two of the most important testimonies with you: two tapes, two recordings."

And from a drawer he took a white tape recorder, and placed it beside the trays, which encouraged the guests to eat *empanadas* and drink more *aguardiente.*

"Belencito Jojoa, Polina Agrado," the doctor said. "Do those names mean anything to you?"

"I knew Polina Agrado, may she rest in peace," the Bishop of Pasto said. "An upright woman. God bless her soul."

"And we're all familiar with Belencito Jojoa, of course," Chivo, the professor, added. "They say he's very sick."

"Two of Pasto's old folk," Matías Serrano sighed heavily. "How could we forget them? And we know their stories, too."

"But not in their own words," the doctor replied.

He carried on opening and closing drawers, showing his irritation for the first time. He did not find what he was looking for. Finally he opened and searched the last drawer, which he thought would be the end of it, but still he found nothing. His voice trembled: was he muttering? Talking to himself? He looked anew in the drawers he had already been through: it seemed he had found the recorder, but not the tapes.

"Which of the two tapes shall we start with?" the mayor asked. "Doña Polina or Belencito?"

"Justo Pastor has to find them first," the professor replied, unruffled. "Couldn't we run through my own Bolivarian experience at the university in the meantime?"

"Patience, Justo Pastor," the bishop said, paying no heed to the professor's request. "You could have put the tapes in another cupboard."

"When the tapes appear, we'll start with whichever one you choose, *señora*," the professor said. "Polina or Belencito?"

He awaited the answer eagerly: unable to prise his eyes from Primavera, as she lounged beside the bishop, legs crossed; one of her sandals, half falling off, showed her delicate toes, tiny and pink; above, her pearly face was hidden behind the smoke from a cigarette.

"Let fate decide," she replied. "My husband can choose with his eyes closed." And she smiled wearily.

"It's very simple," the doctor said, turning to Primavera. "I can't find the tapes."

She held his gaze steadily:

"Are you sure?"

The doctor returned the tape recorder to its drawer. He closed the rest one by one, unhurriedly; he went back to his chair and sat down, breathing heavily, without a word—Polina Agrado had already died, he thought, Belencito Jojoa did not leave his bed; he would die soon; it was impossible to get those voices again. He had the recordings transcribed onto paper, but paper was not the same as the voices, the recording of their sufferings, their real turmoil, their bitterness and jokes, their weaving in and out through memory.

Amid the uneasiness, they heard him clear his throat.

"I'll soon find them," he said. "Whatever happens, I've got them in my notebooks."

But it pained him to see—was he sure that he saw?—a cruel smile on Primavera's red mouth. It's perfectly possible, he thought. And also perfectly possible that the paper transcripts no longer existed either, that they had made them disappear. Was it really likely, he asked himself, and asked again, aghast. He did not believe Primavera had any regard what-soever for Simón Bolívar, nothing would be falser; this was all against him, against his nights of work, his zeal, it was against him alone that Primavera conspired.

But, he wondered, disconcerted, what about General Lorenzo Aipe?

He remembered the robbery the sculptor Arbeláez had undergone. He remembered that the night before, on Thursday, December 29, he had been out of the house until midnight, first with Cangrejito, then with the maestros Abril and Umbría, and that he had not slept with Primavera: he found the bedroom door locked; he had to resort to the couch in his consulting room, the same one where he had 'operated' on General Aipe. He carried on sleeping on the divan that Friday morning, and breakfasted there alone, as Primavera and the girls disappeared without saying goodbye, and there in the afternoon he treated an older woman with a tricky pregnancy, and there too he lay to reread the poems of Aurelio Arturo, which had the power to calm him, while his guests were arriving.

He felt panicky.

Was it possible they had stolen the recordings, his documents?

He pulled himself together as well as he could. He showed not one iota of fear as he said:

"I also have the conversations memorized, from beginning to end, with expressions and everything. If you like, I'll recite them."

But, notwithstanding, to his surprise, the guests were already beginning to get to their feet and say goodbye. Did no-one want to listen?

"Another day," the bishop said.

They were leaving, apparently scandalized. They were leaving.

Why?

None of the company could imagine what Doctor Proceso went through in that moment, trailing behind them.

"What's the matter?" they heard him say.

Polina Agrado and Belencito Jojoa's testimonies amounted to the most valuable part of his research, how come they were not paying any attention? This is what he was asking himself as he followed them to the front door. At last he caught up with them:

"I'm not going to let you leave, *señores*."

His wife stayed behind; she had not got up from her seat of honour in the living room.

In fact, she was the sole cause of the stampede: inadvertently, or on purpose, she had for one implausible moment rearranged her bosoms beneath her sweater, and she did it in such a way that one flawless breast seemed to light up the audience for a second, starting with the bishop, who was the first to get up, blinded, like one who sees hell and flees at the very sight, and then the other guests, who were also dazzled, but accompanied the bishop in his flight—as a moral duty—going against their innermost desire to stay and find out whether it was the natural gesture of a woman who carelessly rearranges her bosom beneath her sweater in public, or a red-hot gesture, fascinatingly frivolous, but deliberate which mocked not just her husband, but all the men in the world, including the Bishop of Pasto.

9

Like everyone else in Pasto, Doctor Proceso knew that Belencito Jojoa, elderly resident of the San José Obrero neighbourhood, was in possession of a Bolívar memory—a memory that touched the old man's soul because it had to do with his family.

The doctor knew the memory, all of Pasto knew it, but he needed to hear it from the lips of Belencito Jojoa himself: for months he tried to get an interview and finally Belencito received him, sitting up in the cedar bed he himself had made—he was a carpenter—a large bed, and larger still for Belencito, shrivelled and yellow and creased like parchment, a bed he had not left in three years, he said, because of illness, without specifying which illness it was, and when the doctor asked, in case he could help, Belencito answered that it was the worst, *señor*, boredom:

"Hell is boredom, *señor*."

He belched and, as if to make amends, crossed himself.

"I'm bored while dying, don't you think that's depressing? Somebody should distract me, a woman, there are plenty of them out there in the world, but they won't let me look for one, or even shout out the window to call one over."

He said his third wife did not sleep with him:

"She's just a helper, a helper who sleeps elsewhere."

And then—in spite of his self-absorption—he let out an almighty fart while saying:

"That's the problem. If she slept with me like she did years ago as well as helping me, a different cock would crow: one can be very old, but still fancy a tickle, or to be tickled."

And he began to laugh, horribly toothless:

"Before, she used to help me so much. Suffice to say we had six children, which added to the eleven and the ten from my other two wives makes twenty-seven. I've buried seven of them, and I have forty-six grandchildren and how many great-grandchildren? I no longer know, and I don't care either. Why bother to find out? What if I were to set about summoning up all the women I've had who disappeared as soon as they appeared? It would be a century of children, *señor*, but one thing's for sure: my women wanted to sleep with me, I didn't make them; grown women, not little girls still wet behind the ears, I never forced them to embrace me. But who are you? You should bring me a little quarter-bottle of *aguardiente* next time you visit, *señor*."

He closed his eyes and fell asleep. Or was he pretending?

On his second visit the doctor took with him, hidden away, the small bottle of *aguardiente* that Belencito Jojoa had suggested. Facing the bed, seated on a chilly wooden chair, the doctor waited for three or five children, morose and famished-looking, to leave them; they were some of Belencito's grandchildren and seemed older than their grandfather; only once they left did he proffer the bottle.

"Thank you," Belencito said in surprise. "Did I ask for this in a dream? Must have done."

He drank shakily: much of the mouthful ran down his chest onto the covers.

"Your wife's going to notice," the doctor said. "This will smell of *aguardiente*—what if you die on us, Don Belencito?"

"There isn't a man alive, no matter how old, who doesn't believe he'll live to see another day: I heard that here, in Pasto, long before the one who said it told me. I'll make the effort not to die and tell you what you're after. You've been a friend to bring me this elixir of life, God's blood; if I got past eighty and am on my way to ninety it's thanks to this stuff, my secret for putting up with the stupidity of men, the pain of toothache and the woman who suddenly stopped loving, without warning."

And he drank another long swig: half for him, half for the covers.

"You already know what I've come for, Don Belencito, you know what I want you to tell me. You couldn't do it last week because you fell asleep and also because the nurse arrived to wake you up. I took it all in, how could I not? It so happens I am a doctor; as far as I can see, you are not just suffering from boredom, Don Belencito, but why tell you what you're suffering from again? I'm a contrary doctor: I think the worst thing is to go around repeating such things to patients. But don't forget, please, what I'm asking you to tell me."

"I remember, I remember, and you should bring me another little bottle for that, there's not much of a kick in this one, poor wee thing. Smoke a cigarette, and pass it to me every so often."

"I don't smoke, I don't have any cigarettes."

"I do. Inside that black shoe, there behind the door, you'll find cigarettes. Get one out, light it with the candle by the Christ statue, and give me a puff when I tip you the wink, okay?"

Doctor Proceso did as he was told. The shoe was at least fifty years old, full of filterless cigarettes, dried out like the shoe, almost fossilized. And he had not yet finished lighting the cigarette when in came Belencito Jojoa's third wife, Doña Benigna Villota, fat and spry at her seventy years of age:

"Is that cigarette for you, Doctor? Don't let him smoke, or he'll die on us. You'll see. Aren't you supposed to be a doctor?"

Had she been eavesdropping on their conversation? Whether she had or not, she left them, after flinging open the window of that shadowy room: a narrow window, which gave onto the front garden; birds could be heard singing in the street. Ever since he was a child, the doctor had been familiar with that single-storey corner house, with a dark garden full of Capulin cherry trees, which reputedly harboured the wailing of ghosts. They also said it was the wailing of Belencito, when he was drunk—whatever the case, he thought, no wailing had been heard for a long time.

It was six o'clock, getting dark.

He passed the cigarette to Belencito, who was madly winking a bright eye: he inhaled vigorously, two, three, six times. The doctor was afraid he would choke, so he sat on the edge of the bed and stretched out his arms as if the old man were already starting to fall and he alone, with a providential lunge, could save him. Nothing happened: Belencito gave back the cigarette and he bent down to put it out on the floor; a guitar lay under the bed, still golden and with all its strings. At last Belencito finished the *aguardiente*. The last swig was uproarious.

"Who are you?" he said next. "What are you doing sitting on my bed?"

And he fell fast asleep again.

"An opportunistic Belencito," Matías Serrano interrupted, helping himself to another shot of *aguardiente*.

They were once again seated in the living room, with Primavera. She had gone to the front door herself to help convince them to come back. What's more, while she was pleading with the men, she repeated the movement of arranging her bosom beneath her sweater, and did it so fleetingly it seemed to support the conclusion that her earlier gesture had been entirely innocent; and was it really?—the professor wondered, thanking Heaven the bishop had agreed to return to the sofa, followed by the mayor. That would be all we needed, he thought, that we should abandon you, you delicious creature, unruly Primavera, what a face, what a cloud-like breast, oh, what inescapable beauty.

He did not hear Proceso's talk, he did not manage to pay attention to it: Primavera Pinzón's every move, position, imposition, sign
of approval, grand gesture and display of indifference made it impossible, bedazzling him. It is, he thought, as if I were hearing her and her
alone singing me Nariño's unofficial anthem, "La Guaneña."

Primavera Pinzón, however, was paying avid attention to the talk.
Flushed in the cigar smoke, damp with the heat of the men's glances,
she knew—she felt—that it was not only the professor who was swiftly
examining her face, her neck, the erect nipples under her sweater, her
rounded knees crossed one over the other, but that all eyes, even the
bishop's, prostrated themselves in suffering at the centre of her, her
oracle, in the ardour of the *aguardiente*.

And, nonetheless, Primavera could only marvel at her husband's
conversation, not recognizing him—and she did not recognize him
simply because he had seduced her. She was seduced hearing
him recall the details of his visits to Belencito Jojoa, above all that third
visit, when even before saying hello the doctor had solemnly warned
that he would hand over *aguardiente* and cigarettes only to the extent
that Don Belencito remembered what he had to remember.

"You're a crafty one," Belencito had said. "But you're right. If I
drink and smoke I'll forget about you and sleep. Those are the best
dreams when you sleep after drinking, when you go off into a dream
right there, just after, you're a boat floating free, and you dream the
strangest things, but it's lovely, try it, you'll remember me."

"Remember about Simón Bolívar, about what you've told everyone
so many times," the doctor said.

"Everyone? I don't remember having told it to everyone, dammit.
The thing is that everyone knows everything in Pasto. But me, tell all
of them?"

"Alright then, nearly all."

"In that case why tell it again, if you already know it?"

"I want to hear it from you yourself, Don Belencito, and after that
I'll come back and visit you, just for fun. We'll talk about whatever we

like. I won't fail to bring you your *aguardiente*, light your cigarette, and, if you really want, I'll smuggle in the woman they won't let you call from the window, really I will, Don Belencito."

"Really?"

"Really."

Doctor Proceso hurried to admit to his audience that he never did keep his promise.

"A dreadful oversight, an unpardonable mistake," Primavera said unexpectedly.

"Which I'll take care to put right one of these days," the doctor declared immediately. "Begging the pardon of those present."

This time the bishop did not respond.

That rainy afternoon, Belencito Jojoa, spurred on by the promise, ignoring the recording equipment that was humming on top of the bedside table, asked a question into the air, into space, into the murmur of dark rain among the trees, asked as if asking for forgiveness, and without the doctor understanding the reason he asked it:

"Why bother them?"

And he took up the bottle and drank:

"Anyone from Pasto could talk about the disgracing of Chepita del Carmen, an ancestor of my family, when Bolívar passed through here," he said, and drank. "Walk over every inch of Nariño province—do it on foot, if you can, if you've got the strength to crack the mountains— there are signs all over the place: 'Bolívar was here,' 'Bolívar slept here,' 'he woke up here,' 'he took a step here,' 'he retreated here,' 'he retreated some more here,' 'he carried on retreating here.' If there's a stone that says 'Bolívar wept here' there must also be one in every place where we remember he lay down here, he got up here, he spoke here, he shut up here, he shat here, he pissed here, but with fright, he was here and he was not here, what a goddamned prick, on our house they could also put Simón Bolívar stole Chepita del Carmen Santacruz here, and he brought her back here, pregnant."

He drank some more.

"That bastard ended up victorious, right? It was tough for him, it seems, but he won; he entered Pasto, where the family of the man you see before you, a very humble carpenter, was then among the most powerful, they were people who read more than you do, *señor*, and you're a doctor, one of those clever doctors who helps people live longer; it's very obvious that you're interested in my story, not all doctors are contrary, as you say you are, and give their patients *aguardiente*, cigarettes and a woman, do they? That's why you deserve to hear me tell it, for being like the Devil. Why not bring a full bottle instead of a quarter? Oh, but you're going to get me a woman, aren't you? Past eighty, the only beautiful woman we'll be able to get will be a whore; make her dress up as a nurse, that's the only way they'll let her in, and we three will have to shut ourselves in, Doctor, nurse and future corpse, and double-lock the door and shut the window and swear to me on your mother's grave that you'll shut your eyes too."

"A sorry tale," Matías Serrano chipped in, "people around here are not very well informed. What Belencito's talking about must have happened the first time Bolívar entered Pasto, in 1822, and he didn't exactly enter victoriously, as Belencito believes: it was a capitulation imposed from afar by General Sucre, who had just won the Battle of Pichincha, a stone's throw from Los Pastos province, and the people of Pasto, who had no provisions, lacked arms and ammunition, found themselves obliged to sign the surrender, which allowed big-headed Bolívar in, the very man they'd already crushed at Bomboná. And who was it who'd humiliated him? A smaller army, an army made up not just of men, but of women and children armed with sticks: the Pasto militias were formed primarily of highlanders; Bolívar retreated 'in the most painful disgust and almost humbled,' in his own words."

Matías Serrano drank, alone.

"Such ignorance as Belencito's is sad and breaks your heart," he went on, "but how to avoid it, when there's not a single school in the country that doesn't insist on the world revolving around Bolívar at Bomboná? Not just the battles he was actually involved in, while he was squandering things away, but also great battles he was nowhere near. Upon this dreadful error the building of our nations began: a lie is worth more than the truth; a gimmick, a stab in the back: the end justifies the crimes. Simón Bolívar said to Perú de Lacroix: 'The people love most those who do them most harm; it is all a matter of how it is done. Jesuitism, hypocrisy, bad faith, the arts of deceit and duplicity, which are called vices in society, are virtues in politics, and the best diplomat, the best statesman, is he who best knows how to conceal and make use of them.' This, Sañudo concludes, was how Bolívar made his own ideas on public morality known. But why don't you remind us, Arcaín, Justo Pastor, about that Battle of Bomboná, which Bolívar *won* and which allowed him to enter Pasto? You two, more than anyone, could help us to remember what we have forgotten for a hundred and forty-four years, a people without memory."

"Why don't you please let Belencito Jojoa speak, Mr. Mayor?" Primavera said, irritated, rekindling the guests' surprise at her.

"Belencito will speak," the doctor said, "and we'll all speak, all of us. Don't get worked up."

"Why don't you let me recall my experience at the university first? It would serve as an introduction," the professor persisted, vehemently, "and also as a warning to you, Justo Pastor. All these things happening around the Bolívar float oblige me to refresh your memory."

He had noted Primavera's blossoming interest in the discussion, and wanted to assert himself now, over the doctor and Belencito. And no-one could hold out against him any longer, his plea was so stubborn, but the woman lit another cigarette, with undeniable annoyance.

"I'll just pop into the kitchen for a moment," she said, and deserted them.

She seemed happy to make them all sad.

PART II

1

Arcaín Chivo himself used the word "catastrophic" to refer to the first course he taught at the university, in the early 1960s, that a well-supported student petition had forced him to give up. At least that subject, "The History of Colombia," had served to strengthen his friendship with Doctor Proceso, revolving as it did around the menacing figure who shared their lives, the so-called Liberator, as they called him, and above all it had served to teach him a lesson. He remembered the catastrophe with visible dread and distress. The moral of the story, he said, was not to go plunging into the dark waters of Colombian independence with your students, because not just your career but your very life would be endangered.

So it was that from the post in history he moved on to one in philosophy, and only there did he manage to remain in peace, without anyone bothering about his existence. But, he wondered, what had actually happened with the history post? He didn't have an answer, or rather he had a whole host.

It all began when the students complained to the vice-chancellor about the peculiar way Chivo sometimes delivered his classes: he lay on his side on the large desk, his head propped on one hand, face turned towards the class, like someone speaking lazily from bed, and, according to his detractors, curled up still further, head sunk onto his chest, observing a sombre silence, completely motionless, then suddenly raised his ruddy, smiling face and asked his students whether his pose reminded them of a young thought in its foetal stage. He did and said bizarre things like this (his students complained) without anyone being able to explain why or what for—a reproach? a provocation?— and then he jumped down off the desk and carried on with his class as if absolutely nothing had happened.

But it was not for this alone that the most fervent students got rid of him: to start with, he called Karl Marx "Saint Karl Marx." He said that he did it knowing full well he was "surrounded" by Marxists. He had nothing against Saint Marx, he explained: on the contrary, Saint Karl was the basis for his interpretation of labour and the eternally unjust relationships between men—which is the same thing as saying life itself, he said—but then he'd go on to argue with Marx afresh and against the use made of his doctrine by totalitarian regimes, and he called him "Saint" again, as an element of irony, which nonetheless infuriated the potential Marxists who beset him. Doctor Proceso wondered why they were also incapable of tolerating a bit of sarcasm, when he found out about it.

The intolerance spilled over when Arcaín Chivo—who pained his students every morning by chalking a pun up on the board: *Arcaín arts = insanity*—started to study a text written by Karl Marx on Simón Bolívar:

"This is an article Saint Marx was commissioned to write by the worthy gentlemen of *The New American Cyclopaedia*. His study contains certain errors and inaccuracies that are not serious and do not damage the overall picture. For example, he confers upon foreign legions, above all the British, a decisive role in the independence struggles; but Sañudo can better explain what the role of the 'foreign legions' was: usually mercenaries who came only in search of gold, in the style of the Spanish conquistadors, and served the highest bidder; they changed sides depending which way the wind was blowing. The thing is, historians never agree on the details, kids. It's impossible to expect such agreement. They agree, it is to be hoped, on the essence of events, if they are truthful historians. In the case at hand, Saint Karl Marx and José Rafael Sañudo are very much in agreement on the biographical picture they paint of this inimitable leader, Saint Simón Bolívar. They concur with the unavoidable truth, so suppressed by historians of various periods. What truth? That Bolívar is a lie, nothing more than that. And why? That's the question to answer, my young friends. That's the reason *The New American Cyclopaedia* proposed the study. Saint Karl had to think hard about our hero and research him even harder, and why not? This is Saint Karl Marx, *señores*. He wasn't going to write for the sake of writing. Among his sources he had the testimonies of European officers who fought alongside Bolívar. Saint Karl did his utmost, no doubt; he was conscientious in what he did. And it doesn't matter that he might have done it with the object of getting a few pennies so he could eat, because that great saint, who must have suffered hunger (so much unproductive time, I mean, spent sitting writing, without getting the smallest cash in return), also had to waste his time, otherwise devoted to philosophy and sociology, on the shadowy figure of a dictator of the Andes, thanks to an American encyclopaedia, the one which paid the best for the thought of the age, I suppose."

"Dictator of the Andes": the students stirred; a wave of dissenting voices ran around the lecture theatre for a moment.

The essay was included in a collection of the *Selected Writings of Karl Marx*, in English, but the professor had already translated and typed it up "with great affection," as he would say in his defence, "for my enlightened students," and he would explain that at the time he was not worried that none of the "enlightened" asked him for a copy.

"We're going to read, boys and girls," he had said to them, "we're going to read in turn. That's my way of making everyone do it; you are all free to think 'my voice is better than yours.' Appreciate the drastic summary, readable because it's convincing, don't be put off by the few pages to come, you're not going to get worn out reading them."

And he started to read, and had to carry on alone, because in open rebellion none of his students agreed to take over from him, to read how Marx describes Bolívar, from his birth in Caracas in 1783 to his death in Santa Marta forty-seven years later.

With the voice of a budding actor Arcaín Chivo took a firm, booming stand at certain points, and from time to time offered the pages, with a sweeping gesture, to his listeners, but no-one consented to go up on the stage.

"Señor Rodolfo Puelles, please read."

"I don't read, Professor."

"Señor Zarama, read."

"I don't read either, Professor."

"Señor Ortiz."

"No thank you, Professor."

"Señor Trujillo."

"Me neither, Professor."

"Señorita Antonia Noria, come and read."

"Me?"

"Enrique Quiroz."

"You read, Professor. Your voice is better than mine."

Chivo persevered, brazening it out. But, nonetheless, the students' absence of enthusiasm or even their simple attention affected him; he did not stumble over his words, but he did omit certain pages and radically reduce his comments. He felt as if he were reading to a gathering of stones.

He read that Bolívar, who had belonged to the Venezuelan Creole aristocracy, visited Europe, attending Napoleon's coronation as emperor in 1804 and his assumption of the Iron Crown of Lombardy in 1805. That in 1809 he returned to his country, refused to join in the revolution that broke out in Caracas, on April 19, 1810, but once the uprising was over, accepted a mission to London with the objective of buy-ing arms and soliciting the protection of the British government. He obtained nothing beyond the authorization to export arms for ready cash, and hefty taxes on top.

He read that the betrayal of Miranda procured for Bolívar the spe-cial favour of the Spaniard Monteverde, to the extent that when he applied for a passport, Monteverde declared that "Colonel Bolivar's request should be complied with, as a reward for his having served the king of Spain by delivering up Miranda."

He read, pages further on, that Bolívar proclaimed himself "dicta-tor and liberator of the western provinces of Venezuela" thanks to the victories of other patriot generals. He read that he established the order of the "liberator," created a choice corps of troops under the name of his "body-guard," and surrounded himself with a sort of court, but that (like the majority of his countrymen) he was incapable of sustained effort, and it was not long before his dictatorship became a military anarchy, in which the most important matters lay in the hands of favou-rites who squandered public funds and then resorted to foul means in order to restore them.

"The same thing happens today," Chivo said. "Identical."

None of his students responded. Some of them were leaving.

But it was later—on reading about some of Bolívar's other deeds—that Professor Chivo incited the wrath of his listeners: he read that Bolívar, while advancing in the direction of Valencia with eight hundred men, met the Spanish General Morales not far from Ocumare, at the head of a troop of about two hundred soldiers and one hundred militia-men. According to an eyewitness, on seeing that the initial skirmishes with Morales' troops had scattered his advance guard, Bolívar "lost all presence of mind, spoke not a word, turned his horse quickly round, and fled in full speed toward Ocumare, passed the village at full gal-lop, arrived at the neighbouring bay, jumped from his horse, got into a boat, and embarked on the *Diana*, ordering the whole squadron to

follow him to the little island of Buen Ayre, and leaving all his companions without any means of assistance."

"Tell that to your granny," he heard an anonymous male voice mut-
ter somewhere in the lecture theatre.

Well, he had managed to get their attention, Chivo thought.

"Did I hear something?" he asked, lifting his eyes from the sheaf of
papers. "Does somebody want to say something? It's still possible to
talk like civilized people."

Enrique Quiroz raised his hand:

"You're just confirming with your reading what Simón Bolívar himself feared to the end of his days. He said he ploughed the wind and
sowed the sea."

"I believe he said he ploughed the sea. It's possible he also said he
sowed the wind, nobody knows."

"At the end of his life," the student Quiroz continued, unperturbed,
"Bolívar pointed out, quite rightly, that there had been three great
madmen in humanity: Jesus Christ, Don Quixote and himself."

"He didn't say madmen. He said 'greatest fools.' He said this to
Doctor Révérend: 'Do you not know, Doctor, who the three greatest
fools in history have been?' The doctor replied that he did not, and
Bolívar said in his ear: 'The three greatest fools in history have been
Jesus Christ, Don Quixote, and myself.'"

"Madmen or fools, for our purposes it's the same thing."

"Well, no, it isn't. A madman is not the same as a fool."

"They were the words of a visionary."

"Quite," the professor replied. "A visionary. It's true that he
ploughed the sea, in the sense that he did not get what he wanted, his
cherished dream right from the beginning of his political career, that
lifelong presidency, or dictatorship or monarchy or whatever you want
to call it, the absolute power over the new republics: yes, he ploughed
the sea. His influence over the fate of the nations was so disruptive that
in the end nobody wanted anything more to do with him, and he was
asked to leave Colombia. So, the fact that he compared himself to Jesus

Christ and Don Quixote is simply further proof of his infinite vanity. In the case of Jesus Christ, I don't need to explain why. In the case of Don Quixote, even lovers compare themselves to him, but Bolívar? Poor Don Quixote."

"He died in absolute poverty. Where's the vanity in that?" Enrique Quiroz insisted. Pale, bolt upright at his desk, not a single muscle moved in his face.

Professor Chivo approached him.

"Everything about Bolívar's life has become the stuff of legend," he said, "Sañudo warns us of that. Legend goes so far as to tell us he died destitute, to the extent that they had to ask the indigenous leader— the '*cacique*' of Mamatoco—for a shirt to bury him in; a puerile myth: didn't it occur to its inventor that those attending the funeral were wearing shirts, even if Bolívar wasn't, so there was no need for the embellishment of a semi-savage chieftain? According to the inventory that his nephew Fernando Bolívar and steward José Palacio took five days after his death, he left great wealth behind him. Not just dozens of linen shirts, but six hundred and seventy-seven ounces of gold in coins; three dinner services: one ninety-five-piece set of solid gold; another thirty-eight-piece platinum one; and the third, two hundred pieces of beaten silver—aside from sixteen chests of his clothes and other personal effects, another chest containing gold and silver medals, and one full of jewellery set with precious stones plus gold and silver swords, the most noteworthy of which was the solid gold weapon given to him by the Municipality of Lima on his saint's day, encrusted with one thousand, four hundred and thirty-three diamonds, with a very ornate scabbard and a magnificent sword belt. This gift, according to Ricardo Palma, cost twelve thousand, eight hundred and seventy-nine pesos and five reales in total. As a curious aside, Bolívar owned around twenty tablecloths. In the inventory, bejewelled insignia, thirty-five gold medals and four hundred and seventy-one silver ones, and ninety-five gold knives and forks also appear: he had cutlery for his own exclusive use, he did not take his meals with his soldiers; in fact, he did not eat meat, which was the dish *par excellence* for the troops, and more than anything he enjoyed the salads he prepared himself, according to recipes learned from the ladies of France. He spent ten thousand pesos of the day on perfumes, and they lasted him no time at all, so unhealthy was his fondness for splashing them on, morning, noon and night: he never took the scented handkerchief from his nose. A division of body-guards surrounded him, protecting him from the world. He had no need for ready cash because he could avail himself of the public purse whenever he liked, and he got through hundreds of pesos a week, as well as the pension of thirty thousand pesos a year for life they gave him shortly before his departure from Bogotá for Santa Marta—that is to say, shortly before his death 'in the most abject poverty,' as so many historians so foolishly maintain."

Chivo returned to the stage.

The students were leaving in increasing numbers.

Without taking his eyes off the page, Professor Chivo said to them: "I can hear you rushing off, *señores*. Rush off and read Sañudo and check the inventory. I'm sure I forgot something."

In spite of having so few listeners left, he took up reading again. His voice and face seemed steady; in fact he felt saddened, not just by his students but by himself, by his apparent inability to stimulate dis-cussion and capture attention. A sudden drowsiness came over him: he would have liked to be at home, sleeping alongside his cat.

But he carried on.

The more he read, the more desertions there were on the part of the students.

From time to time, Chivo raised his eyes for a few seconds to observe the young faces still watching him, and perceived that several of them were afraid to show interest in what they were hearing, as if they were committing a sin—but what, or who, was causing this fear?

2

According to the students, then, it was not just Karl Marx, but also the Liberator Simón Bolívar who was being horribly maligned in the madman's classes.

Chivo said it never occurred to the angriest students—the very ones who should have carried out the most careful analysis—to check the veracity of the article. They accepted only their own ideas. And he was not mistaken: the students concluded that the Marx text was spurious, that it must have been written by Chivo, the imperialist puppet, spy and retrograde, terms that were all the rage at the time, only a few years on from the Cuban Revolution. Young people across a number of faculties were considering abandoning their degrees and heading off into the mountains of Colombia, to the guerrilla war, which had not yet officially begun but was already a great hope that guaranteed the taking of power, as Cuba demonstrated, they said: in less than five years a new revolution will shake Latin America, a Colombian revolution.

And when, in the company of Karl Marx and José Rafael Sañudo, they came to the War of Independence in Pasto, the capital of Nariño province, southern Colombia, beginning with the Battle of Bomboná, things for Professor Arcaín Chivo took—as he himself would say—a turn for the worse. Because it was following those last, surreptitiously defiant classes (in which the Battle of Bomboná defined Bolívar's ignominy, no more no less, and Pasto's Black Christmas made Bolívar's name synonymous with barbarism) that Arcaín Chivo had to leave the post in history, after a very discreet kick from the vice chancellor at first, and then a very real kicking from hooded heavies who frightened off, once and for all, an already frightened Arcaín Chivo. He lost his irreverence and mischievousness, his speculative daring, and accepted his thoroughly humiliating situation; he never imagined that the university's board of governors and the academics of Pasto University themselves, most of them Pastusos, hailing from various Nariño villages, precisely where Bolívar had surpassed himself in vengeance and brutality, would actually disagree with historical truth and not support even a single one of his arguments—or the claims of Karl Marx, or those of José Rafael Sañudo—and, worse still, would be scandalized, would throw him out.

"Professor Chivo," Enrique Quiroz had said to him—known as "Enriquito" to his friends, he was one of the famous Quiroz brothers, and was the president of the student committee—speaking right at the critical moment of one of Chivo's classes, "bear in mind that Pasto, our city, was royalist, monarchist, opposed to the republic, to the call for independence from the American people. Pasto was a Spanish stronghold, nobody can deny it, and in that and that alone lies the cause of Bolívar's justified aversion."

"Let's consider first that call for independence from the people of the Americas," Chivo replied. "Then we'll move on to Pasto being a royalist stronghold, and then to what you call Bolívar's justified aversion."

He was on his feet, leaning back against the desk, fingers spread around the wooden edges. It was the first teaching period of the morning: the room smelt of soap and cologne. Before him were thirty-two heads: the boys bearded, the girls with bare legs; Chivo did not look at the girls, not a bit, he would lose his grip, he had to finish his lecture (although he used to publicly admit in the canteen that he was one of those lecturers happily aroused by the blur of his fashion-conscious female students, who looked as if they were nude from the waist down; he said this quite openly). The bearded faces got him worked up in a different way, they made him laugh indulgently: they are just twenty-year-old faces, he used to say, but hairy ones, and he said it with a gesture that seemed scathing, but was in fact only quasi-paternal irony; he never imagined they would hate him for that too.

Through the large windows, the volcano Galeras darkened.

"No people," he said, "achieved independence then, and it's possible none has done so yet. The cry for independence was less than half a cry: it was a yelp from the Creole elite, the bourgeoisie who wanted to make the most of the carve-up at any price. None were thinking of their fellow Americans or other such moony dreams, but about their own property, ladies and gents. That's why they were yelping." Here the professor started to yap like some strange caged animal, and was delighted to observe the smiling admiration of the girls, his blurry female students, and gladdened by the indignation of the bearded ones.

"Not all the Creoles behaved as you say," Enrique Quiroz interrupted.

"They did," Chivo countered, "every last one of them. But their yelp got away from them; they only wanted the powers of the monarchy so they could rule as they pleased and enjoy more of the spoils, and what happened was that the wretched of the Americas, the valiant Indians and even more valiant *campesinos*, who really had suffered the perennial lash on their own backs ever since the conquest, got worked up over the yelp, cried out with manly might, the powder keg was lit and, just like Bolívar, the little rich kids set off to command a war without knowing a thing about military strategy, but the nigh-on suicidal fearlessness of the Indians and peasants supported them, and they gained independence from Spain and then didn't know what to do. Perhaps it would have been better to wait fifty years, or a hundred? Nobody was prepared. And the oh-so-great example of their first leader was an atrocious one: from Bolívar stem dictatorships large and small, and all these shoddy, corrupt entities that the most cynical commentators have taken to calling 'developing countries'; the Indians and peasants are in the same situation as ever, and into their proverbial poverty are now added workers in the cities. It's as if the girl sitting at the furthest desk—yes, you—were to decide to swap one inadequate, temperamental boyfriend who sometimes exasperates her, swap him not for one, but two brutal boyfriends, two eternal rivals who never tire of stripping her naked, who slap her, torture her, bleed her, prostitute her, sell her in the marketplace, spit on her; Colombia had very bad luck with this whole climax of independence, *señores.*"

Here Professor Chivo could not avoid the blushing young woman who smiled at him from behind her desk. He had to hurry the class along, because composure was no longer possible for him.

"Forgive me," he said to the girl later, as he shut his book with a thump, signalling the end, "forgive me for using you in my feeble allegory."

Her thin voice was heard over the racket of scraping desks:

"Forgiven."

That's how Professor Chivo was.

He lived alone, or lived with his cat, and this seemed to him "happiness enough," as he used to say. The daily company of his students, their "vigorous normality," made him "die less quickly," he asserted. He did not predict the black storm fast approaching; he did not foresee himself becoming a whirlwind of emotions.

"Tomorrow we'll start on the Battle of Bomboná," he said to his students, "tomorrow we'll look into whether Pasto was a royalist stronghold, and the matter of the great and justified aversion of little Bolívar." He shouted this at his students, who were hastily abandoning the lecture theatre.

Little Bolívar: no-one could tolerate it any longer, for quite a while a letter to the vice-chancellor's office had been doing the rounds asking for his head, the head of the crazy Chivo, a forceful letter because lecturers from other departments also signed it, indignant about the insults to Karl Marx and Simón Bolívar.

3

"Hold on to your hats, kids, youth of the Sixties, future of Colombia, we're off to witness the Battle of Bomboná, considered 'strange' by writers of school history books, who want to make excuses for Bolívar's defeat with that 'strange'; another great big lie, but a heroic battle, and the cause of General Bolívar's visceral hatred towards Pasto and the Pastusos of the day, his bottomless resentment, his innermost bitterness. For once in your lives pay attention to the details, kids, to the before and the after: judge for yourselves, read between the lines, don't just trail along the track others want you to follow, like sheep, seek out and snatch the truth from the immense mountains of muck that official history has accustomed us to."

So began Professor Arcaín Chivo's lecture that early morning, while his impassive students watched him, still half asleep.

"Bolívar wanted to make all the victories his own. It's not me saying that, Sañudo reconfirms it in his *Estudios*: he tells us Bolívar wrote to General Santander on the twenty-third of August, 1821 to say he was thinking of going to liberate the province of Quito, so Santander should command Sucre and Torres (who were already there) to stand *only on the defensive*.

"He wanted to make all the victories his own.

"He wrote to José de San Martín that he was marching with his army 'to shatter as many chains as he should encounter binding the enslaved peoples who cry out across South America,' and that he would go to Peru 'with four thousand men to embrace the Children of the Sun.' Bolívar set out for the south from Bogotá on December thirteenth, and arrived in Cali on the first of January, 1822, and as he wished to make Quito independent he wanted to go on to Guayaquil by sea, but on hearing there were enemy ships in the Pacific he decided to go overland on the seventh, after attacking Pasto, and he authorized commanders to send the new recruits to their barracks heavily restrained, so they should not escape, with any offenders to be shot.

"Here another shameful strategy Bolívar used should be pointed out, one that nevertheless a Colombian writer has lauded and praised as a brilliant idea, despite it being within the grasp of any swindler; well, it's nothing other than a falsification of official public instruments, international ones. It's an order given to General Santander to send forged communications to certain foreign diplomats; it was written on the nineteenth of January, and dated in Popayán, albeit Bolívar was actually absent from that city at the time, as he only left Cali for the south on the twenty-third, and arrived in Popayán on the twenty-sixth of that month."

4

When Professor Chivo finished reading and commenting on Bolívar's letter to Santander and the appalling events and repercussions in Pasto, he paused, scanning the lecture theatre to confirm what he'd imagined: hardly anyone was still there. The Quiroz brothers had already arranged to desert the room, and behind them disappeared the vast majority of the students; there remained on the horizon the bodies of just two, fast asleep: a girl with her head resting on her arm, long hair sweeping the dirty wooden floor, a boy sprawling, mouth agape as though recently arrived from a party and still drunk; this pair of sleeping students in another class was unthinkable, but judgement had already been passed on Chivo and his History of Colombia.

And, yet, also still in the room, still conscious, was the young woman who'd served as an allegory, who did not dare leave and make the absence complete; she was the last fully conscious student in the lecture theatre: she herself could not explain why she stayed or what for, in front of this man who talked alone and read alone in a room that was lonelier still. Did she feel sorry for him? He looked so lonely, she thought, so absolutely and utterly alone with his discourse on Bolívar, his reading of Sañudo, his indignation and his battles, poor madman, she thought.

"I've finished, you can go," the professor said, so she could make her escape.

The girl stood up and seemed to be about to say something, but thought better of it and headed very slowly for the door. Behind her, the last two students carried on sleeping. It began to drizzle against the large windowpanes: cloud alone filled the sky; the Galeras volcano had disappeared. Suddenly the girl stopped in the doorway: a round, pale face, surprisingly pale, as if lacking mouth and eyes; she turned to the professor and said she had a question:

"Señor, I've listened all this time and I'd like to ask something."

"Go ahead," the professor responded without curiosity. They're still trying to comfort me here with a question, he thought, little imagining how disconcerted he was about to become.

"Why make yourself hated?"

5

So, it was due to his own experience that Professor Chivo could not understand the suicidal decision of his friend Justo Pastor to show everyone a carnival float on January 6 featuring Bolívar's deeds and misdeeds. Listening to the doctor, observing him, he seemed as if he were from another world, so fired up, almost sanctified, recalling the plight of Chepita del Carmen Santacruz. Chivo did not share his audacity, but for that reason he also envied him: Justo Pastor seemed immune to fear.

And the fact was that the doctor had witnessed Chivo's final mortification, when not only had the vice chancellor backed the students, but the students themselves went to his house at midnight, masked (he recognized their voices, they were led by the Quiroz brothers), knocked down the door, and knocked him down too, kicking him upright again, shattering his ribs, forcing him to drag himself through the streets to the door of the University Hospital, where by a miracle he was treated; voices from the shadows went with him, shouting "keep dragging yourself along, snake, that's what you were born for."

They had killed his cat, a ginger Persian called "Mambrú," hanging him, and they left a note tied to the animal's tail: *Puppet*. Pasto's only newspaper did not report the attack. Not a single one of his colleagues from the university visited him, only Doctor Justo Pastor Proceso López, whom he would nevertheless stop seeing after that incident, as if the sacrifice Arcaín Chivo had made also meant sacrificing the friendship between the only two men in Pasto united in denouncing Bolívar.

Perhaps it was the professor's fear that repelled the doctor and made him decide not to see him anymore, or perhaps it was his warning when they were alone, in the hospital itself, at the end of his visit, when the nurses were no longer listening. "Best we keep quiet about the so-called Liberator, Justo Pastor, they're going to hurt you like they did me; give up your book, Sañudo already made a better job of it; live your life, keep it to yourself, or they'll chop your balls off."

They did not touch on the subject again for years, not until that Friday, December 30, 1966 when Chivo turned up at the doctor's invitation, opening his arms and declaring that the only redeeming feature of old age is that one ages alongside one's friends.

"As our mayor points out," the doctor said, "the business with Chepita Santacruz must have taken place during Bolívar's initial entry into Pasto, on the eighth of June, 1822.

"Sañudo states: 'He entered the city at five in the afternoon, entered the city surrounded by royalist troops who had formed up in his honour, proceeded to the parish church where the bishop and clerics were waiting to lead him, as Bolívar had arranged, in the manner of a royal tribute, under a canopy, up to the altar where the "Te Deum" was sung. The same day the surrender was ratified and Bolívar issued a proclamation full of promises to the people of Pasto.'"

It was after this proclamation that the Liberator was invited over to drink chocolate, as was the tradition, by one of the most powerful men in Pasto: Joaquín Santacruz himself, Belencito's ancestor, who had very good reasons for making a fuss over Bolívar and ingratiating himself, at least for the duration of his stay in Pasto. The gold coins Santacruz kept in his house were famous, buried in a secret corner— under his bed, as was the tradition—and Bolívar's aide-de-camp had already informed him, as he had the rest of Pasto's merchants, that a contribution towards the cause of freedom would be required, as was Bolívar's tradition. But Santacruz did not fear so much for his property as for the fate of his daughters, still very young, any one of whom Bolívar might take a fancy to, quite devoid of responsibility—as was also the tradition. Handing over the gold, Santacruz believed, would mean he could expect his daughters' honour to remain intact in return.

"That's how simple solutions were back then," the doctor said, "very simple indeed, as they are now, with certain variations, in order to defend honour against the passing whim of a powerful man."

And Primavera let out a ringing laugh as she was returning from the kitchen, where up to that moment she had been listening to everything, curious and entertained by the conversation; then she, who had resolved to go straight up to bed and sleep, without saying goodnight to anyone, decided to go back in to the living room and sit down next to the bishop, brash and happy. Hearing the stuff about honour on the point of dishonour gave her renewed energy, although she would have preferred to hear it from Belencito Jojoa himself—via her Doctor Donkey, who was seducing her with stories of independence in those moments, much to her surprise.

Belencito drank some more, and spoke:

"My grandfather Pedro Pablo was still living in the house belonging to his father, Joaquín. My grandfather was one of three sons, along with José and Jesús. There were seven daughters: Redentora, Prudencia, Severa, Digna, Cirila, Metodia—pretty names, eh?—and the youngest of all: Josefa del Carmen, better known as Chepita, thirteen years old.

"At that age her disgrace arrived, with the arrival of the Liberator. And her disgrace came at night, when the Liberator came to be there."

Before the evening got properly underway, Joaquín Santacruz and the Liberator, escorted by a lieutenant who pretended not to take any interest, shut themselves up in the smoking room. They did not smoke in there because the Liberator loathed tobacco, but the master of the house presented his offering: sixteen chests of gold coins for the cause of freedom. Without a word, with just a gesture, Bolívar indicated to his lieutenant that he should take charge of the chests. And then he let himself be led back to the main part of the house. "The only thing I ask in return, Your Excellency," Joaquín Santacruz dared whisper in his ear, "is my daughters' integrity." Bolívar still did not say a word, behaviour his host interpreted as tacit agreement, and he proceeded to introduce him to his wife, Lucrecia Burbano, as conservative a woman as ever lived, pale and dressed in black, who ceremoniously observed the customary greeting, surrounded by her children—more waxworks in the icy silence.

Lucrecia Burbano suffered, she suffered over the fate of her daughters; with great reluctance she had acquiesced to Joaquín Santacruz's scheme, which seemed absurd to her: make overtures to Bolívar, invite him for chocolate and hold him to his word with gold. But her husband had already warned her: "He doesn't just know about the gold, he knows about our daughters too." Lucrecia Burbano would have preferred to flee with her daughters and the gold into the fiery entrails of Galeras itself, or at least into one of its caves, but it was already too late, the little fellow was there in the flesh, he was opening and closing his hands, small like a woman's; his feet must be smaller still, she thought, inside those riding boots that seemed made for a child. Lucrecia Burbano observed before her the excessive mobility of the Liberator's body, the overly large head, the curly black hair; she endured his startling proximity to the point of exasperation. At this meeting, the

Liberator alarmed her with his shrill voice, but appeased her with his perfect bow. He really was a proper little gentleman, whom she knew they nicknamed "Manikin," "Zambo" and "Chipolata," but who she also knew could very well send them "to the other side" with a word, if he had a mind to.

Bolívar greeted the sons, and then set about complimenting the seven Santacruz daughters, the cream of the city with their beauty and good manners, the seven Santacruz sisters who, according to the ribald remarks of the first drunken liberators, could satisfy, on their own, the whole column of eight hundred mounted *cazadores* that Bolívar had brought with him for his entry into Pasto.

The eldest was twenty-six.

The musicians had already taken up their instruments, bolt upright on their little cane chairs, beneath a porcelain clock; the snare drum could be heard, a clarinet, a flute and a trombone were announcing the *contradanza*, the guests drew themselves up straight, observing themselves in the mirrors, under the glittering bronze chandeliers, and in the ballroom with its decorative urns, around the piano, Bolívar greeted the seven Santacruz sisters one by one: he would have to open the dancing with one of them, and then his officers would follow his lead. The wooden floor trembled. The house looked aflame, illuminated by torches on all four sides, the double rows of windows glowing behind the ever-present geraniums on the balconies; it was one of Pasto's main houses, right on Santiago Square, opposite the Church of the Apostle, and, from its far-off kitchen, near the stables, came the delicate aroma of chocolate being prepared over a low heat: pastilles of fine chocolate brought from Lima and kept in cedar chests for years, for whenever an occasion might arise. And what an occasion it was, Lucrecia Burbano lamented: the entire ballroom seemed to her to smell of horse droppings, leather and sweat. A heady perfume came from the little fellow—she was later to recall—but he also smelt of blood—she would say—it was a sorry hour, a thousand times over, when that scented scoundrel appeared.

Bolívar did not dance with any of the sisters, but to many, who would later remark upon the fact, it seemed that "he spent longer than was customary over his compliments to Chepita del Carmen Santacruz."

In spite of being just thirteen, Chepita noticed her father's disturbing anxiety, and she found it odd that her mother should demand she carry her favourite doll in her arms for the official presentation. She complied without understanding why. How could she comprehend the maternal tactic, both childish and desperate, to signal her innocence? Chepita cradled the doll, although "the mistake had been made"—Lucrecia Burbano would confess, and confess that she thought of it too late—"of dressing Chepita like a young woman."

For Chepita, at any rate, the whole display of dancing and chocolate was fun, just another game. The Liberator not only failed to dance that night, he did not try the chocolate either; he left his officials to head the table and withdrew. His hosts never dreamed of such indifference, and, of course, were not at all offended: they thought the gold coins had been sufficient.

"That was not how things turned out." The doctor drank, just as Belencito Jojoa had, and everyone else in the room drank too, including the Bishop of Pasto.

"What happened," Doctor Proceso told them, "was that on the tenth of June, Bolívar left Pasto for Quito, and barely two hours after he set out a detachment of riders deliberately returned to Joaquín Santacruz's house. They got in through the back, through the stables, killed two pigs and a donkey, nobody knows why, then murdered one of the servants who was going to help them dismount, and carried off Chepita del Carmen Santacruz. Less than a league away, Bolívar was waiting for her. He used her straight away, and carried on using her out in the open during that whole forced march up to the gates of Quito, six days later. Only then did he return her to Pasto."

"Pregnant," Belencito had said, and drank some more. "That was the sad thing: she was thirteen, but it happened; it can and does happen; marked for life, not so much as far as the city was concerned, that was the least of it, but in the eyes of her own family, my ancestors. Bolívar's fault, of course, but also my people's. Her pregnancy set her apart like a scar on the soul, just as soon as it was confirmed. With a different father, it would have been a different story. But a child of Bolívar's was a child of hate. Who knows which was worse, the Liberator's breach of good faith or Lucrecia Burbano's terrible and insane decision: she shut Chepita away for life in her bedroom on the first floor, in that old Santiago house."

"Didn't she ever see anyone again?" Primavera asked, heatedly. "Didn't anyone ever see her again? And her child? What became of her child?"

"It was a daughter," the mayor ventured, "at least, as far as I know. Some say they sent her to a convent in Popayán when she was old enough; others that she stayed with her mother in confinement and that, after the mother's death, the daughter went the same way."

"So sad," the bishop concluded. "Something is known of that calamity."

The doctor let them talk.

"What convent in Popayán? No convent took her in," Belencito had recalled. "At least the two locked-up women had their room looking out on the Church of the Apostle: there was a little square, they could see the world through the window, and the world could see them too, but only through the window, because their window was the only one in the house that didn't have a balcony, they didn't give them the privilege of a balcony. Lots of people from Pasto, all dead now, could remember them looking out of the window; first it was the girl holding her little daughter, then the woman and the little girl, then it was the old lady and the woman, and finally the two old ladies, they were the ones I knew through the window: I saw them disappear like dust on the wind."

"It seems," Primavera said, "that Don Joaquín and Doña Lucrecia did not mind sharing their double tragedy with everyone else, the
tragedy of their daughter and granddaughter in the window. Didn't it
occur to them that people might have fun, spying on them? Wouldn't
it have been better to keep them somewhere else . . . ?"

"Bury them, so nobody should see them?" The professor regretted
jumping in with such bleak humour, too late, because Primavera was
already blushing, embarrassed.

6

"Polina Agrado's ancestors had a worse time with Bolívar," Doctor Proceso said.

The elderly Polina Agrado had received him at her house, which must have been the oldest in Pasto, with three rows of windows, thirty-six unoccupied rooms, empty barns, abandoned kitchens, dark hallways, phantasmal whinnying and phantom riders, and a large kitchen garden full of tangled rose bushes: such was the house in 1966, grey and white, looming up opposite Santiago church.

To his surprise, Doctor Proceso was announced in the old-fashioned way, by a manservant as ancient as Polina Agrado. The old lady received him dressed as though for a funeral, more than surrounded—protected—by three of her nine daughters. He thought he was in Paris, at a marquise's salon. The old lady's head was covered by a Franciscan veil. She held out a gloved hand, which the doctor kissed—as her daughters had demanded when he made the appointment by telephone: "Greet her with a kiss on the hand and sit on the stool you'll see in front of her. Don't say a word. Just listen. She knows what you're after."

"I like to talk looking out at Santiago church," Polina Agrado had said, "and especially when I have to speak about things I no longer want to. It is even sadder to talk to someone who asks, without a drop of pity, that I tell the tale of my family's misfortune. But I knew your parents, Doctor, honest folk, and that's why I'm speaking, out of respect for them. I know nothing at all about you, but, at the very least, I expect your discretion. I do not know what you are going to do with my truth, I cannot imagine what you have in mind, and I prefer not to find out. I leave it in God's hands; that's the only reason I agree to talk about things one cannot forget, even at my age. If I keep my eyes on the window, do not think I am ignoring you: I just look at the church so God, who resides within, may give me strength."

The daughters served coffee. In utter silence they settled themselves down to stay. "Leave," Polina Agrado told them, "you do not need to hear what I'm going to say again, because then you would have to go to Confession again." So the daughters went out, and the door was closed. The whole place smelled of old age. The doctor distracted himself by contemplating the arabesques in the cracked ceiling: there were pink and blue landscapes, angels and swords, suns.

"Now I'll begin," Polina Agrado said.

But she did not.

Silence.

Sighs.

Was she crying?

Primavera poured more *aguardiente* into the glasses. The professor did not take his eyes off her hands. Mayor Serrano was speaking; Doctor Proceso was speaking, heatedly. The bishop was deep in thought. Professor Chivo contributed, but switched his attention painfully back and forth between the story of Polina Agrado and Primavera's hands, her indifferent eyes.

"Polina Agrado's ancestors were a grandmother and her granddaughter."

"And both suffered their own calamities in the tragedy. A lot of people think it's beyond belief, but it happened," Chivo interjected.

"It's been passed down by word of mouth like the tale of an unlucky Little Red Riding Hood, but it's a true tale, and that makes all the difference. 'In order to understand my ancestor's gesture,' Polina Agrado had said, 'to understand the gesture made by Hilaria Ocampo—better known as the widow Hilaria, because she lost her husband very young and raised her children alone—you have to understand the predicament she and her granddaughter faced.'"

"In order to understand the 'gesture?' Is that what you're saying she said, Justo Pastor?" the professor marvelled. "If you can call that a gesture . . . I know all about the gesture, although I'd prefer to call it a 'desperate measure,' and sweeten it a bit, and even so it would still be appalling."

Everyone drank.

"Five months after the surrender of Pasto the rebellion broke out again, on the twenty-eighth of October, 1822, this time at the hands of Benito Boves and Agustín Agualongo. They escaped from prison in Quito, at a point when a good many people in Pasto already seemed reluctant to see further uprisings; those with something to lose, the well-off, could not afford to run the risk of remaining royalist, at least not until a reorganization of Spanish forces came into effect, which looked more than unlikely. It was the same for the middle class: they too had something to lose if they continued to oppose the republic. The common people, the soldiers who had sworn loyalty, the highlanders, the indigenous population stayed under clerical control—king and God, or the other way around: God and king, which amounted to the same thing. Curates and priests, for or against the republic, exchanged vehement edicts, sermons and letters in Latin; they excommunicated left and right, de-excommunicated when it suited them; it was a brawl among scholars who discredited themselves, bandying bits of Latin about: 'The excommunication imposed upon all those who *directe vel indirecte* have cooperated with the republicans is not only unjust but illegal and reckless because it has not taken the pronouncement of the sacred Council of Trent into account and does not proceed from three canonical monitions.' But ultimately, curates and priests were all encouraging the same thing: war, and I say this begging the pardon of those present."

"You don't need to beg my pardon," the bishop broke in, "I agree with you."

"The indigenous people remained subject to fate, and were soon fighting not for king or God, but for themselves, for survival. The war had left enough poverty for everyone, while they'd been out defending the idea of a king who did not protect them, an insubstantial king. That was the general feeling of resignation when the cry of rebellion broke from the mouths of Boves and Agualongo."

"But who were Boves and Agualongo? Forgive me for forgetting, *señores.*"

"Forgiven; lovely, elegant Primavera."

"Your adjectives are lovely and elegant too," Primavera replied to the professor, mortified.

"No-one can remember it all," the mayor butted in. He contributed very infrequently, but he did contribute. Now he tried to catch the bishop's eye, as if urging him to pick up the topic. The Bishop of Pasto was just listening. He had wanted to air his views when curates and priests were mentioned, and was thankful no-one noticed his desire. He simply said, in a conciliatory manner: "Go on, Arcaín, Justo Pastor, stop interrupting each other."

"Benito Boves was a nephew of the bloodthirsty Asturian general Tomás Boves, who had already confronted Bolívar, defeating him in Venezuela, at the head of a division he himself called 'the Legion of Hell.' He was, nonetheless, considerably less bloodthirsty than a number of patriots Bolívar surrounded himself with, above all those from his own country, the Venezuelans Salom, Flórez and Cruz Paredes, who would in turn take charge of Pasto, following strict orders from

Bolívar, obeying his mandate of death and his suffocating decrees to the letter, much to Pasto's misfortune."

"And Boves the uncle and Boves the nephew came to very different ends: while uncle Boves died in battle, nephew Boves fled—right in the thick of the fighting, when he was most needed—ran off with the Spanish soldiers, his army curate and two other clergymen 'at breakneck speed' to the village of La Laguna, from there down the Putumayo River, then to Brazil, and no more was heard of him."

"But let's not get ahead of ourselves," Arcaín interrupted, "don't make them flee when the October uprising has barely begun. The Spanish ran off at Christmas. Besides, Primavera was asking us about Agustín Agualongo."

"He was," the doctor began, "the man who would take charge of the resistance, alongside his own people, his compatriots: Estanislao Merchancano, who was also a learned man, Colonel Jerónimo Toro, famous warrior from Patía, Juan José Polo and Joaquín Enríquez, both reputedly invincible, José Canchala, indigenous *cacique* of Catambuco, the Benavides brothers, the formidable negro Angulo, leader of the Barbacoas blacks, Captain Ramón Astorquiza, Francisco Terán, Manuel Insuasti, Lucas Soberón and Juan Bucheli, among others. It was Agualongo who brought about the participation of the people, precisely because he was of the people, a noble and war-hardened Indian, nobler than any Creole, a strategist who stood out by virtue of his talent for command and his intelligence."

"He was not the ignoramus official historians have made him out to be, even going so far as to make fun of his name, nor was he a 'humble servant.' He knew how to read and write, he painted in oils and, like many others, he joined the royalist ranks early on. He'd been born in Pasto, in August 1780, and was not a pure-blooded Indian, but mixed-race. If only he had been completely Indian, he would have been even more estimable."

"He too ended up fighting, no longer for the king, but for his own people. The tricking of the Pastusos and later the barbarity unleashed upon them would ultimately become the sole motivation for his struggle, the banner he would defend until his death by firing squad. It was after his flight from Quito, in the company of Benito Boves, that he entered Pasto in order to organize the resistance. In the convent of the Sisters of the Immaculate Conception he gathered his armaments together. And, to the surprise of those in Pasto who were indisposed towards the idea—the civil authorities and certain ecclesiastical ones—his army of four hundred militiamen assembled, to which around five hundred highlanders, drawn from neighbouring villages, were added; they crossed the Guáitara River, took the garrison held by Antonio Obando—the military chief Bolívar had left behind—and reconquered territory for the royalists as far as Tulcán, no less."

"It wasn't long before the Liberator heard what had happened; the news found him celebrating in Quito, at the beginning of a banquet in his honour, and when his aide spoke of events into his ear he erupted into profanities, as usual, and, as those around him witnessed, 'leapt onto the table with a single bound and began kicking cutlery and crockery from one end to the other.' In a state of shock, quite beside himself, he must have remembered fearsome men like the Pastusos only too well: men who had already made him suffer, the same ones who, almost unarmed, had defeated him at Bomboná; he had seen them fight and decimate the Vargas and Bogotá battalions."

"So he mustered a division of more than two thousand men, made up of the Rifles, squadrons of *guías*, mounted *cazadores* and Dragoon Guards, who were the most experienced troops in the southern army, and put at their head none other than Sucre, the victor of Pichincha."

"But Sucre was driven back too, in Taindala on the twenty-fourth of November, by Agualongo's army, which relied on only seven hundred fusiliers, a few lances, and palm sticks and *guayacán* clubs for the rest."

"In reality, these were people armed solely with courage: they made up for the lack of rifles with sticks and stones, and sheer obstinacy. Without arms or munitions the order given before each battle was straight-forward: *A club for the rider and another for the horse; the spear to the stomach.*"

"Sucre withdrew to await reinforcements, which an infuriated Bolívar sent without delay."

"And this was how the army of veterans, boosted by the Vargas and Bogotá battalions and the Quito militias, took Taindala on the twenty-third of December, descended on Pasto on the twenty-fourth, and, following isolated bloody affrays, went out onto the city's streets to kill."

"It was not a victory of patriots over royalists: it was a hideous misunderstanding that Bolívar, who should have resolved it, brought about; he was unable to pluck the thorn of Bomboná from his ludicrous, wounded pride."

"This is the point at which Benito Boves flees with his posse of priests and Spaniards to the Putumayo, never to return. Agualongo, who was from Pasto, would fall back to the mountains with his captains, to draw strength from the craggy landscape. He little suspected that the people of Pasto, without militiamen to defend them anymore (the last fell before incoming forces that were ever more numerous), would end up burned alive; he never imagined the mercy that he did grant the defeated would not be granted to women, children and the elderly."

"It would be the first major example of barbarism in the history of Colombia: the first major massacre of many that would follow."

"The stuff of every day," the bishop said. He spoke for the first time.

"This is also where we hear for the first time about Hilaria Ocampo and Fátima Hurtado, ancestors of Polina Agrado, may she rest in peace. It's here we begin to learn of her tragedy, passed down like a fable from one teller to the next, here 'in the horrid butchery that followed, in which soldiers and civilians, men and women were promiscuously slaughtered,' as O'Leary points out. But is it right to say 'soldiers?' Only the defenceless—women and children—remained in the city. Sucre continued the assault on them, and followed Bolívar's orders."

"Historians who speak of Sucre, his thinking, the dazzling clarity of his actions, doubt he participated in the massacre. No doubt he closed his eyes and carried out orders, because this business of 'carrying out orders' was and remains the universal excuse when it comes to butchery. Even if Sucre did not enter the city during the slaughter, he did send in the chief of assassins, a certain Sanders. Bolívar's orders were irrevocable, and the Rifles and Dragoons must have turned themselves into animals to carry them out."

"Polina Agrado's forebears were not in the least bit wealthy, unlike Belencito Jojoa's, isn't that ironic? Here's Belencito, a carpenter: there stands his Santacruz ancestor, rich and influential. Here's Polina Agrado, a fine lady with a three-storey house on Santiago Square: there are her ancestors, obscure, battle-hardened mountain people, and above all that forthright and resourceful grandmother, the widow Hilaria Ocampo. Her own loved ones had already gone off to fight and she had heard no news of them for weeks; only she and her granddaughter were still in Pasto. If she had not been ill, she would surely have gone to fight too, but she also had to look after Fátima, her fourteen-year-old granddaughter who 'struggled with words,' as the family put it: it was hard for her to get them out, and, when she did, she directed them to her grandmother alone. What language was she speaking? It was a muttered gibberish that only grandma could decipher; her grandmother was the one person Fátima trusted: she laughed with her; they slept in the same bed; they went to Mass together every morning; the grandmother herself used to say: 'She has faith only in me.' But she also said that sooner or later Fátima would come to believe in others too, for good or for ill, and that she must be given time."

"For a long time Fátima's beauty had been startling; it was just that her loveliness, paired with the mental fog that shut her in ('She seems an odd girl,' 'She's virtually dead'), meant it was no sooner noticed than forgotten; it was something everybody had got used to, the extraordinary beauty that blazed just for an instant, because it was immediately overwhelmed by the certainty of a gentle, absent madness."

"They stayed inside their house, on the outskirts of Pasto, at the mercy of fate and war. The River Chapalito ran nearby, crossed by a stone bridge where granddaughter and grandmother sometimes went, and waited. The grandmother despaired of the time spent without news: months before her illness (her right arm was paralyzed, they said it was bewitched) she took an active part in the fighting, and for this very reason the tale that's been passed down commemorates her. From his pulpit, the vicar of Pasto had already given her just cause: to defend the king was to defend God. With this holy blessing behind her, the widow not only took charge of cooking for the militia but at times, in the clamour of the fight, abandoned the stove and ran to help, body and soul, wherever she might be most needed. When she was forced to resign herself to the paralysis in her arm, she symbolically handed in her kitchen knife to Estanislao Merchancano, colonel of the Invincible Squadron. And now, instead of a knife she carried a sharpened eucalyptus stick, hidden in her bodice, which she surely used more than once, with her one good arm, the day Bolívar's Rifles entered Pasto: one Liberator or another could have fallen to its point, but the fable passed down by word of mouth records its use just one single time."

"A single time?"

"Hilaria Ocampo was a redoubtable lady: a giant of a woman around six feet tall, but with the face of a kindly grandma, the face old women have who were once beautiful. She was not Fátima Hurtado's grandmother for nothing: 'As lovely as she is sick,' the soldiers would say of Fátima when they discovered and chose her for Bolívar, 'but lovely still.'"

"The widow had fought against Bolívar at Bomboná, that Sunday, the seventh of April, Feast of Flowers; she found herself shoulder to shoulder with the six hundred Pasto militiamen who crossed the Cari-aco ravine not fearing enemy bullets, climbed the steep sides, entered the encampment of the Vargas and Bogotá battalions, stripped them of flags, arms and munitions, and after leaving most of the troops in a bad way and the principal patriot commanders injured, returned to their own camp taking many prisoners with them: she took along four herself and kept them safe until it was decided to return them unharmed, with the others, to Bolívar. The Pastusos in the Invincible Squadron called for her; their leader, Estanislao Merchancano, said she brought them luck. Now, with such perfidious paralysis, she could not fight against Zambo, and stayed in Pasto, with Fátima, waiting. That December twenty-fourth, during Black Christmas, she had not managed to find any of her loved ones in the confusion of the slaughter, and she felt afraid: they might be dead already, dead beneath the dead."

"When Agualongo's men left the city, she believed, like most people, that since the resistance had faltered, the killing would also stop, that Pasto had been captured and peace would once more ensue: restrictive, but peace after all, settling for whatever was to come—the republic?—so be it, this was something she and everyone else were already resigning themselves to. What she did not anticipate was the subsequent actions of murderers in the Rifles on the undefended city: 'the killing of men, women and children went on even though they took refuge in the churches, and the streets ended up filled with corpses; so that *the time of the Rifles* is an expression which has stuck in Pasto to mean this gory catastrophe,' Sañudo tells us."

"That battalion had a very bad name even among Bolívar's own troops. Under the command of that man Sanders, the Rifles foretold days of bloodshed that were coming not just for Pasto but for the whole of Colombia, from that time onwards, for years and years that are still without end."

"After that Black Christmas, four hundred civilian corpses of all ages lay in the streets of Pasto, not counting the militiamen lost in combat, and the carnage would continue for three more days, with the acquiescence of General Sucre, who 'was carrying out orders.'"

"But what became of the widow Hilaria and her granddaughter?"

"They were two of the 'Hidden Thirty' underneath Our Blessed Lady of Mercy's cloak, when the bloodbath began, at dusk."

"The slaughter had started at dawn, actually, once the last militias in the city were defeated, but let's say the killing got properly underway at midday: it was pure butchery, not one official stepped in to halt it; quite the contrary, the orders were precisely that, to incite cruelty."

"They hid under the Virgin's cloak? Did they survive?"

"The statue of the Virgin was in the middle of a large wooden platform, from which twelve poles stuck out, six on each side, that the privileged Dozen Devout, chosen from among the sturdiest and most respected women, carried on their shoulders to transport it through the streets of Pasto, shouting prayers to her while the men fought. The cloak was draped from the Virgin's crowned head and it came down at the back to the two furthest corners of the platform, so there was a sizeable concealed space underneath it."

"Hilaria Ocampo had dodged death at every turn. The only thing that mattered to her was keeping her granddaughter away from the devastation: at first they had stayed shut up in their house on the outskirts, the night of December twenty-third and the early morning of the twenty-fourth, but they had to flee without delay because this was the place, near the Caracha river, where isolated troops of invaders began to appear, from the early hours of that day. The widow thought they would be more protected on the streets of Pasto, but it was worse: the liberators went into the San Miguel and El Regadío neighbourhoods too. Fire began to light up many places; would they burn Pasto down? Knowledgeable about war, Hilaria saw with dismay that few of the militiamen put up a fight, compared to the hundreds of liberators who continued to arrive in double rows of infantrymen; these were detachments with well-assigned orders, furious cavalry troops who burst into the terrified city."

"Right in the middle of Calle Real the widow wanted to go back home, but hesitated: there was death on all sides; enemies on foot and on horseback were multiplying; she didn't know which would turn out to be for the best: to go on, to go back, to stay still; nowhere seemed like a good place; the only thing on their side was anonymity: the fact that amid all that random death, nobody noticed them, it was as if they did not exist; by lucky chance none of the eyes looking for people to kill saw them; those many eyes, reddened and hasty, passed right over them, without noticing; in the blur of victims they did not spot them, did not make them out, despite the light, because it was still light, dusk had not yet fallen."

"They had fled up Calle Angosta, skirting bodies that were scattered like stains, in the most unlikely poses, and they had to go along jumping over these stains, deliberately ignoring them, because stepping on them occasionally was unavoidable, and they didn't stop until they reached one side of the cemetery, where the widow imagined they would find the best place to hide; she thought it would not occur to anyone to kill in a cemetery, so what she saw appalled her all the more: plenty of people had the same idea, and they were killing them there too, in the cemetery; she could not make out whether it was men or children or women, she only saw red-coloured stains, and above all she heard them, each identical cry, unearthly, drawn out like a river."

"She fled once more, pulling her granddaughter through the streets: at her passing front doors splintered to bits; the liberators entered on horseback, spearing and shooting anything that moved. Unable to avoid the destruction, they ran aimlessly on; they came out at the doors of the former cathedral and there encountered a group of parishioners craning forwards, into the church, paralysed in a stone-like silence. Were they pretending not to notice? As if the war were not going on around them, the rigid faces were watching something happening inside; not only did they not dare go in (as the grandmother would have liked, in order to hide), they did not dare flee either: they stayed riveted before the doors, fatally frozen, their faces fixed. Hilaria and Fátima peered in too and at that exact moment witnessed how Old Galvis got his head smashed in, at eighty years of age, right on the altar. 'Galvis,' the widow shouted, 'Galvis.' They lived near Galvis; she chatted to him at times, and now he was dead, just as they would be if God did not protect them. A stampede of soldiers dispersed the group; the widow felt the shadow of a bayonet just graze her back. She grabbed Fátima and they ran off again, because death was still circling around them, death which still did not look them in the eye, death not looking at them, still not looking at them."

"The doors to the Sisters of Mercy's convent were on fire. Inside, behind the smoke, tongues of flame showed glimpses of the unbridled shadows of Rifles on top of the naked shadows of screaming girls: at the same moment they raped them, they killed them, the widow observed. Fátima saw, her arm tightly gripped by her grandmother. Then she spoke in her murmuring gibberish, spoke for the first time since the catastrophe began: she asked if they were all playing in there; her grandmother did not reply, she was tormented by what the question foreshadowed. Would it be a game for Fátima, if it happened?"

"They went up to the Santiago neighbourhood, where the Church of the Apostle stood, and it was worse; the fight was still going on there, in its death throes: three or four militiamen were holding out against at least a hundred liberators, the grandmother calculated, well-versed in war. She could not help: she was in charge of her granddaughter; she had a bad arm; she was only good for running away. And the demise of these cornered men made her cry at last; they were attacking without achieving anything, barely defending themselves, they tottered weakly from here to there until they fell, hidden in a forest of lances, without a sound, as if they were grateful; it made her weep silently, and another pile of dead men made her cry some more. Dead men? Women, she discovered, it was a corner full of dead women, acquaintances of hers she recognized in horror: the seamstress Otoniela, Zenaida Montúfar the hat maker, the two Patoja sisters, Cándida Iriarte, Facunda Bucheli, Terencia and Tila Moncayo, Cirila Cruz, the deaf Castillo woman, all she had to do was look at a face to know the name straight off, it pained her, and so she stopped looking for more names and more dead, but she was shaken to her core to discover the women were carrying white flags, flags made from white cloths, which had done them no good."

"In the midst of the dead women, Fátima inexplicably burst out laughing. And her laughter appalled her grandmother, who was leading her blindly, without a destination in mind, along the horrific street, no hope left: she thought her granddaughter had finally gone completely mad. In Taminango, one of the most traditional neighbourhoods, overflowing with the injured, the cries of those dying and the cries of those killing, they could not run any further; where would they run to? 'God help us,' the grandmother heard someone below her shout, 'they're going to murder the city.' She was the one shouting, and it was the first time she had. Fátima did not hear her: she had felt something warm stroke the top of her head, and raised her eyes; wings grazed her forehead; it was a dark bird that escaped, soaring into the sky, and now Fátima laughed harder still, the great delirious laugh crossing her face."

"On the banks of the River Pasto the carnage intensified: on the skyline, figures up on the bridges, figures dying, figures killing, dying and killing beneath and on top of the bridges; the rays of a curiously ruddy sun cloaked them both; where was fear leading them? In the blink of an eye they appeared in the middle of the San Andrés neighbourhood, and it was there the grandmother ran headlong into her friend Isaura Olarte, who was crying. She was fleeing with her daughter, a girl younger than Fátima; after staying hidden in the entrance to a granary, they had to leave when the main door started to burn. Just two steps away from the burning door, and perhaps protected for this very reason, the two friends tried to make themselves understood amid the explosion of whistles and gun-fire, the moans and screams, and the terrifying gallop of horses. Isaura Olarte spoke of her dead, of her house razed to the ground; she cried out, in a hoarse voice, that 'all she asked for was a white soldier for her daughter, that she not fall into the hands of a black one, that no black man get her pregnant,' and she cast about her in desperation as if summoning up a white soldier to save her. 'Black or white, it makes no difference,' the grandmother told her, and suggested they run to the Church of Jesús del Río where the statue of Our Blessed Lady of Mercy was. 'There,' she said, 'the miracle will happen.' Isaura Olarte refused with a shake of the head: 'They kill more in the churches; it's like going up to them and saying *here we are, kill us*.' The grandmother remained stock-still, her eyes trained on the inferno; the faces of the horsemen who directed the slaughter were all soot-streaked. She pulled herself together. 'Come with me,' she shouted again, but already her friend and the daughter were moving off into the swirling mass, pressed like bundles up against the bloody walls. Now the grandmother shook with fury, she grabbed Fátima roughly. 'Get a move on, you idiot,' she told her, and it was the first time she ever spoke to her that way. 'Why don't you get going?'"

"They came to the Church of Jesús del Río."

"And that's where their troubles began."

7

"Eight years before calamity struck Hilaria Ocampo, in 1814 (when Pasto was besieged by General Nariño, whom the Pastusos defeated), the Dozen Devout carried the statue of Our Blessed Lady of Mercy out of the church for the first time, accompanied by the rest of the women from Pasto, paraded her on high through the thick of the fighting, and took her fearlessly into the fiercest clashes, shouting to her 'don't ignore us, don't wash your hands of us,' entreating her with prayers and even insults to take their side, tugging at her cloak, her rosary, slapping her knees, tickling her plaster feet as if to wake her, pleading that she too should fight, that it was high time, *come down on our side, Most Holy Mother of Mercy, be true and be strong like us*."

"And she did come down on their side."

"But things didn't happen quite like that: General Antonio Nariño, that authentic independence leader, later betrayed not just by his men but by destiny, saw through his spyglass a long line of soldiers advancing on him from the very heart of the city; they weren't soldiers, but a horde of women: it was a procession from San Agustín to the Church of Mercy, headed up by the statue of the Virgin, but the Virgin never went round the most intense areas of fighting, like they say she did."

"But eight years after Nariño, when Black Christmas happened, the widow Hilaria and her granddaughter found the statue of Our Blessed Lady of Mercy in the Church of Jesús del Río, at rest on her platform, facing the doors, as if about to go out by herself but never leaving: the Dozen Devout lay strangled around her, and there was no-one else in the church."

"Or so it seemed."

"The murderers had tried to set the church on fire, and had given up. If the killers were gone, the grandmother reasoned, that would be the best place to hide, among the twelve dead women, at Our Blessed Lady's discretion: to go back out onto the street would be tempting fate. A few candles still flickered from the walls, all was devastating silence, the silence of ruins, but at length they heard a whimper. No-one could be seen in the half-light, among the charred confession boxes; it smelt of smouldering. But they heard the whimper again, and discovered its source: someone had to be concealed under Our Lady's cloak. They heard several horsemen pass the doors at a gallop without slowing down, and were just about to get under the cloak themselves when sudden footsteps rang out behind them: it was one of the murderous Rifles. By the dim light of the candles, in the warm glow of confessionals, like red-hot coals, the grandmother saw that the soldier was very young, that he was alone, and that he was coming towards them bent on killing; they heard him shout, calling out to his companions: 'There are some here.' The grandmother intercepted the murderer, confronted him, took Fátima by the arm and handed her over, purposefully, with a gentle shove: 'Here,' she said, 'for you. For the love of God, protect this child, she is yours alone.' The soldier opened his reddened, shining eyes very wide. His shirt was stained with blood, the sleeve torn, and he had a straw hat tied around his neck. He looked at Fátima in disbelief; it seemed to him the beautiful but peculiar girl was yawning in his direction, as if she were going to swallow him up, so he stopped pointing his bayonet, received the yawning Fátima, and clasped her to him; she felt his mouth glued to her neck, smelled gun-powder and sweat, and saw the face streaked with soot in which his eyes shone with an almost atrocious innocence, but in a flash she also saw her grandmother, behind the soldier, heard her say with absolute calm: 'Close your eyes tight, Fátima.' She opened them again when her grandmother was pushing her towards the Virgin, after she heard the scream like a stuck pig; the one who had been taken by surprise was on his back, arms and legs flailing, one hand clutching at his throat, which was gushing blood; the grandmother was putting the eucalyptus spear away in her bodice."

"And they got in under the Virgin's blue cloak, with the rest of the Hidden Thirty, those elderly women who used to accompany the Devout."

"And they weren't quite thirty women, as the story has it: the priest Elías Trujillo was in there too and Ninfo Zambrano's four children, all boys."

"But they were discovered because of that same recurring whimper: it was one of the boys. The liberators pulled the hidden out one by one, and one by one slit their throats. Fátima felt as though she were under a stone: her grandmother would not let her move. Purely by the grace of Our Blessed Lady of Mercy the killers did not realize that there were still two survivors, squashed up together, in a corner of the platform, beneath the Virgin's violet cape. It was not altogether a blessing: the massacre lasted three days. They had to eat candlewax and drink holy water from the baptismal font. It was not a blessing: at the end of the third day Hilaria Ocampo and Fátima Hurtado emerged to join in the universal grief, to inhabit the phantasmal city like phantoms themselves and to accept, like the rest of the survivors, the new order established by Bolívar."

"That's to say, to accept another barbaric act: the decrees."

"The decrees and Bolívar's trap."

"Bolívar had arrived in Pasto on the second of January, 1823, nine days after his Christmas of Death, and immediately began: he issued a decree confiscating goods, and imposed a contribution of thirty thousand pesos and three thousand head of cattle and two and a half thousand horses, which the sacked city of Pasto could not pay. Property belonging to Pastusos was parcelled out to republican officers. In addition, contravening the constitution itself, which abolished the exacting of tribute-money from Indians, he commanded the Indians in Pasto to pay it (with taxes backdated), just as they had been previously paying the Spanish king. How was the rebellion not going to continue, starting with the Indians? What kind of Liberator was this, who only gave orders for ruination?"

"Bolívar would leave Pasto on the fourteenth of January. But he was still in the city when he set up his trap and gave his grand last order to General Salom. And what did Salom do? Carried it out to the letter. O'Leary sums it up: 'Salom carried out his assignment in a manner that did little honour to him or to the government, albeit they were dealing with men who ignored the most basic rules of honour. Feigning compassion for the fate of the vanquished Pastusos, he issued an edict calling them to assemble in the city's public square, to swear loyalty to the Constitution and to receive assurances of the government's protection from that moment on. Hundreds of Pastusos, obeying the call, or perhaps fearing a worse punishment, converged on the designated place, where they had read to them the law stating the duties of the magistrates and the rights of the citizens. Under the law, both property and person were amply protected and the responsibility of the magistrates was clearly defined. The law was read, in the presence of all those in attendance, and documents of guarantee were distributed as evidence of the government's good faith. But in direct violation of the agreement, a picket of soldiers was stationed in the square and took one thousand Pastusos as prisoners, who were immediately sent to Quito. Many of them perished on the journey or at a later date, refusing to take food and declaring in unmistakeable terms their hatred for the laws and the name of Colombia. Many, on arrival in Guayaquil, ended their lives by throwing themselves into the river;

others mutinied aboard the ships conveying them to Peru and suffered the death penalty.'"

"Part of Hilaria Ocampo's family fell into this Bolivarian trap, and
the rest would be finished off later, on the plains of Ibarra, on the six-
teenth of July, 1823, when Agustín Agualongo's men, greatly outnumbered, once again confronted Bolívar's army of veterans."

"Bolívar pitted an army against a band of highlanders."

"Before the fight, Bolívar's aide, Demarquet, wrote: 'His Excellency plans to operate according to all the rules that the art of war
provides . . . His Excellency's intention is to defeat the Pastusos out
on the open plain and far away from Pasto so that not a single one is
able to return . . . and that once defeated, villagers should be advised
that they may harry them, killing them or taking them prisoner . . . and
in addition he offers a reward of ten thousand pesos to the corps which
is first to break them.'"

"In Ibarra—without arms, without logistical support, when they
were resting—the Pastusos were surprised by a devastating cavalry
attack. Agualongo's men hurled themselves at the horses' necks, trying to bring them down. They fought without surrendering: they had
no trust. How could they believe in the word of the liberators, when
the Liberator himself so conspicuously failed to abide by his word, just
as his successors in Colombia would be conspicuous from then on, for
ever and ever?"

"It was an appalling battle, if it can even be called a battle when it
was so unequal. And as is traditional, historians shut their eyes when
faced with it."

"At a certain point in the fighting, being apprised of the death of
more than five hundred Pastusos and only eight republicans, Bolívar—
rather than halting the action, calling upon his good judgement, or at
least showing the indulgence of the victor once things were already
way past victory—did the exact opposite: he overcame his legendary
cowardice, or displayed it all the more clearly, and rode off to fire on

the unarmed, instructing his lancers to run through body after body without mercy, until night fell."

"The final tally gives an idea of his ruthlessness: according to official sources, more than eight hundred Pastusos lay scattered on the battlefield, and only thirteen republicans. Wounded Pastusos were shown no quarter; they were finished off. The bodies were not buried, as the most fundamental human right demands: Bolívar made them into a pyre."

"And what about the widow Hilaria and her Fátima, after Black Christmas?"

"Fátima was on the bridge over the River Chapalito when Bolívar returned to Pasto, on the morning of January the second. From that bridge, enveloped in the cold, she saw Bolívar cross the other: the bridge over the River Pasto, far off, though visible; she saw him almost without being able to make him out, but how could you not spot him on his white horse, at the head of an endless column of armed men?"

"Men without mercy."

"Bolívar didn't need to see her to find her; they used to take the Liberator the spoils of the hunt, and he would choose."

"He had his 'fixer' for these errands: a discreet subordinate with name and surnames, but so out in the open that no historian ever showed any interest in mentioning him. Some simply acknowledged his task, and gave it their blessing, applauding it: 'And then he enabled that magnificent leader, that invincible man, a latter-day Alexander, to put aside his role as hero for a minute; he sought him out and showed him the little doe.'"

"That's how the Liberator got his bit on the side."

"The fixer took him to the first assignation of the night, encouraging him: 'Liberator,' he said, 'woman was made for the warrior's repose.'"

"But in Bolívar's case you shouldn't really say woman, but little girl, child, maid, kid, infant, innocent, babe, pure flesh."

"Very pure appreciation, a very pure list," Primavera said to the professor, and he deliberately ignored her, secretly thrilled by her interest.

"The fixer was a religious and sober man too, just the type employed for the dressing and undressing of a general in those days, doing his hair and shaving him, putting him to bed and waking him; a man who inspired a certain spiteful respect among the soldiery because of this. He was cunning, just as he was discreet. He knew how to tell the Liberator things without saying them. He arranged everything, from the time of the assignation to the bedclothes. He preferred to take charge of things personally, as he knew His Excellency's likes and dislikes very well."

"Three days after the Liberator's arrival in Pasto, the fixer and his men 'discovered' Fátima Hurtado. They found her at a gloomy bend of the River Chapalito and, when they observed her contemplating herself in the water, in the words of the story passed down by word of mouth, they knew straight away she was another of the 'Liberator's doves,' as they called them."

"Like they were secretly jealous."

"It wasn't unusual for the soldiers themselves to present these offerings to Bolívar, or else they did it via his officers. Everyone, just like the fixer, knew of His Excellency's most pressing needs."

"Fátima Hurtado was like Our Lady of Fátima," Fabricio Urdaneta reportedly said; "he was native of Riohacha, a barber-soldier under the fixer's orders, one of those who discovered Fátima, according to the story passed down by word of mouth."

"Marvelling at the apparition, and observing the due caution these exercises demanded on pain of death, the soldiers and the fixer followed her through the outskirts of Pasto, without the apparition noticing. The soldiers seemed quite unhinged by so much beauty concentrated in one girl: the fixer discovered them plotting as they followed her, but a single reprimand from him, invoking the name of Bolívar, was enough to discourage them."

"And they saw her shut herself up in the rural quiet of a tumble-down cottage, with a little path of carefully swept stone leading to the door, this was the house where Fátima lived with her grandmother, sole survivors, given that they knew nothing of their relatives."

"There the soldiers knocked at the door, with the fixer in their midst: he waited prudently, mindful of convention but, nevertheless, authoritarian; there was an uneasiness that came over him whenever a mission of this type drew towards its conclusion; he knocked on the door again himself."

"And the widow Hilaria Ocampo answered it—the giantess."

"From this point on, the inexplicable story, passed down by word of mouth, unfolds. Doña Polina told it very well, with its back and forth, its body blows, eh, Justo Pastor? I heard it too. Now I should pass it on."

"If you wish."

"I'd rather hear it from Polina Agrado," Primavera said.

The professor pretended not to hear.

"The fixer was intimidated by the brawniness of the old woman who came to open the door. But he regained his composure and explained, with the restraint typical of him in such situations, that he would have to take her daughter to the Liberator, Simón Bolívar. That these were his orders.

"'She's not my daughter, she's my granddaughter,' the widow clarified."

My ancestor Hilaria Ocampo already knew what was afoot—Polina Agrado related—*sooner or later the time had to come. Sooner or later they were going to discover her—not her, but her Fátima—sooner or later.*

She had avoided being corralled by death during Black Christmas, dodged the monster's ambush, its claws, and now she saw it at the door, inescapable, in the summoning of her Fátima. This time it was not the young murderer who had harried them in the church, and whom she dispatched as was only right and proper, but Bolívar, for God's sake, it was Zambo.

And it grieved her that that very morning she had considered hiding Fátima out near La Laguna, far away from Pasto, but she had let the premonition pass and remembered it too late, when they were hammering at the door: that was what distressed her most, forgetting to hide her granddaughter when so many eyes were already menacing her; not hiding her in time. Why, she lamented, didn't I do it? Why didn't I tie her to my apron strings? At what point did I let her out of my sight? She was confounded by the fact that her granddaughter had not ended up being claimed by some murderer, whom she might very well take on and defeat, but by a well-dressed agent who was almost pleasant, and a few open-mouthed soldiers—four in all, she counted them, preparing herself—Bolívar's emissaries. It distressed her, and finally she understood: it was Bolívar; behind that whole calamity stood Zambo.

Thinking about it today, I imagine my ancestor did not know whether precisely that fact—that it was Bolívar and not some other chance assassin—was better for them or worse. "Worse," she should have yelled, "it's worse." Or would it help them? In spite of herself, she would still wonder that, and hate herself for thinking it. "Worse, worse," she had to tell herself, "everything's worse with this horrible Zambo son-of-a-bitch."

"Tell him, by God, tell him to come for her himself," Hilaria Ocampo said to the fixer, with a sort of happy amazement. Would she kneel down? She spoke as if she were in church, the fixer thought, and rightly so: anyone would think Hilaria Ocampo had waited for that proposition her whole life and had anticipated having to answer "tell him to come for her himself."

"That cannot be," the fixer said.

He was unnerved by that peculiar hindrance, this request which was not really an impediment: you could even interpret it as a genuine entreaty, an invitation. What to do? He smiled for the first time in years. After all, they were asking an elegant favour of him. Not gold. Not offices. Not passports. Not recommendations. This woman was simply requesting the pleasure of the Liberator's presence. Was this for real? He must tread carefully. It was true that he had a sweet-voiced old lady in front of him, but she was a dark horse, he thought. Her stature, her conviction, the intensity of her gaze—these things disconcerted him, and not just him, his soldiers too, who still, he was embarrassed to see, pointed their rifles at her chest, the idiots, but immediately he felt sorry for them: they were bewildered like him, and not one of them knew why. The smell? There was something about this gigantic old woman: the penetrating eyes, lips clamped shut, the two enormous hands hanging open, as if she would be prepared to kill and die at any moment.

With a gesture, the fixer made the soldiers lower their rifles:

"Do you know what you're asking of me?"

"That the Liberator come and get her."

"Impossible."

"I will have to bathe her and dress her," the grandmother said, "I will have to fix her up as she should be fixed up." And then, harshly: "I will have to instruct her, as is right and proper. Go, and bring him back with you."

No-one responded.

She raised her hands in the air:

"We're talking about His Excellency the Liberator here. He deserves every consideration."

The four soldiers exchanged a look of alarm. The fixer retreated, almost overpowered.

"Tell him, by God, tell him to come. It will be an honour for this humble woman to receive him and personally hand over her only granddaughter; he's doing me a kindness, I know His Excellency will look after her, help her."

Of course he was not going to come back with His Excellency, thought the fixer. But he acquiesced. Now he knew what the old lady was after. He had uncovered it at last among her final words: "look after" and "help." He would return with the offering, the payment, the gold: that was all the old woman was asking, what her good common sense was demanding. He had been wrong about her.

"Yes," he said, "the Liberator will come, why not?"

And he left two watchmen posted on the door.

"What is certain, definitively so, was that news of Fátima had also reached the Liberator's ears."

"That's never been proved."

"It has."

"It's never been proved that Bolívar had heard from anyone but the fixer."

"He did hear, and long before the fixer told him. He knew about Fátima's extraordinary beauty when he dismounted in the middle of the main square, and got straight back on his horse again. 'Where is she?' they say he said."

"You're kidding."

"I'm not."

"There is some discussion over whether or not the Liberator knew, from earlier on, about the dove living in Pasto, the dove his diligent fixer was already preparing for him. How can any of the possibilities be proved? Maybe the Liberator didn't know. Maybe he did, and later, extremely gratified to hear about the grandmother's impassioned plea, went along with the fixer."

"According to Doña Polina, the Liberator arrived minutes after the fixer. First came the fixer, with a little chest of gold, white robes and food. Then the Liberator, Simón Bolívar. Nobody knows if they reached an agreement between them."

"When the fixer got back to Hilaria Ocampo's house, the reports the watchmen gave him were almost normal: they'd seen the old woman leave the house with the girl, and followed them. The two women went to the wash house, at the back of the dwelling, and they'd followed. They'd seen the old woman undress the girl, soap her, scrub her, and rinse her over and over in front of them, as if they did not exist, and as if that would never matter to them, nor to the old woman or to the girl. The fixer could not get over his astonishment: *you saw the girl naked? We saw her*, señor: *fit for His Excellency.*

"And they saw them enter the house and bolt the door: *that's where they were, señor, inside, there was no way they could escape.*

"They waited another moment in the dreadful silence, because all of a sudden nobody dared bang on the door. But time, for the women, ran out, and they knocked. The door did not open. Their eyes ached, glued to the door; the door did not open. The frightening thing was that they felt other eyes, the old woman's eyes, coming at them from deep inside the walls of the house, spying on them. Then the gallop of approaching horses was heard. The Liberator dismounted."

"It's not known for sure whether Bolívar dismounted. They say he waited on horseback, and that what happened there took place with the Liberator up on his white horse."

"He dismounted: 'Let them bring her out,' the Liberator said."

"That voice, like a bird's, could only be Bolívar's.

"There was the Liberator, halfway up the stone path that led to the door: hands on hips; chin up; eyes 'like a hawk,' as his chroniclers describe him. The fixer stepped aside, discreet but wary. Bolívar's voice was enough; it was not necessary to knock on the door again, it opened in an instant. And the burly widow Hilaria Ocampo appeared before the Liberator, the same woman who had crossed the Cariaco ravine under enemy fire on the Sunday of Bomboná and had climbed the hill, defeating him—the same woman. Only now she carried no weapon other than a girl. She held her up in just one arm: dressed in white, Fátima's long black hair dripped water over her shoulders."

"Here you are, Liberator," Hilaria Ocampo said, and she offered her up.

It's not me, Polina Agrado, telling you this. The soldier Fabricio Urdaneta tells it, the barber-soldier who was actually there, born in Riohacha and raised in Ocaña; he would stay on to live in Pasto, with the passing of the years; in Pasto he would have children; in Pasto he would die, of old age; I heard him tell the tale myself, as a girl. He told it, the first record of the story passed by word of mouth, and you, Doctor, you tell me whether or not it's true, he told us that the Liberator came up to receive Fátima "without a doubt in his mind," and that he held out both arms "without hesitation," he went to receive her "even rather impatiently," and they saw him lean in and then take a sudden step backwards and stride rapidly in the direction of his horse, ashen-faced: "Christ," they were able to hear him say, "she's dead."

And he told us that Bolívar set upon a tree, kicking it, and that afterwards he knelt behind that same tree and started to vomit. Fabricio Urdaneta, barber-soldier, says he does not know how it was he didn't have them shot. The whole lot of them.

8

Gales of laughter united them like a colossal embrace—in the living room, which was all ashake.

"If it didn't happen that way," the professor said, "it should have done."

"Impossible to check whether the story is completely accurate, but it did happen," the doctor said with great difficulty, and laughed along with the rest, including the Bishop of Pasto.

And the fact was, Fátima and her grandmother's end, their tragedy, had strangely overexcited them, to the point of hysteria. Once again, they drank *aguardiente*—as they had been doing during the whole unfolding of the tale. Once again, Primavera offered it generously around to each of them—with genuine affection?—the professor wondered. She offered it right on the back of the guffawing which boomed out, a manly sound; that's how Primavera heard it, from all sides, like the laughter of hairy hunters around the fireplace applauding a joke, she thought, and I'm the only woman here: the fire.

Arcaín Chivo, slumped in his easy chair, was adoring her. And he suffered, sighing over her, when she leaned towards him, offering *aguardiente.* He snatched up a glass and drank it down in one, stole another straight away, and slurped from it noisily.

"When it comes to drinking," he said, "I drink like a poet, and if a woman like you is pouring the booze, Primavera, what other hope is there but to drink? You are the unattainable woman, the impossible dream."

Doctor Proceso heard him too. At that point the mayor spoke into his ear:

"Wouldn't it be best, Justo Pastor, to wind up the evening now? Our dear Chivo is starting to flirt with your wife."

"Ah, Chivo," the doctor replied in a whisper. "Chivo the wise, Chivo the temperate, his intelligence overwhelmed by a good pair of legs, my wife's legs."

"What are you laughing about?" the bishop asked, swapping to a nearby seat. "Are you going to let me in on the joke?"

Doctor Proceso felt a little tipsy; he had thought the mayor and bishop were not far behind him, but as the story unfolded he had discovered quite the opposite: Primavera's presence did not captivate them, and they were not even drunk. They're pretending to drink, he realized, and in the last exchange he detected their eagerness to find any excuse and disappear. Worse still, as far as Bolívar's carriage was concerned, they had not confirmed whether they approved of it or not. They'll wash their hands of it and go, he thought.

"And the music?" Chivo said, "Shouldn't we round off the sad tale we brought back to life with some music?"

"It's a bit late for music," Primavera said, taking them by surprise, given that not long before she had been offering around the *aguardiente* and laughing. "My daughters are sleeping. I think it'd be best to make coffee, would you like some?"

The Bishop of Pasto thanked her by quickly clapping his hands.

"It'll be coffee for the road," he said. "We really must go, it won't be long till dawn."

"We need coffee," said the mayor, and threw the professor a sardonic look.

Arcaín Chivo took another glass, in a hurry. He set off behind Primavera, who was already on her way down the corridor:

"Allow me to keep you company while you make that coffee, *señora*. Let me tell you another story about independence, one worthy of your ears."

Primavera neither consented nor refused. She headed silently for the kitchen; she felt pursued by the professor as if by a dog, she thought, a dog sniffing about. The others had already picked up their conversation again, but, nonetheless, the professor did not go straight into the kitchen: he seemed to hesitate at the bend in the corridor, as if an inopportune moment of lucidity were going to prevent him committing his indiscretion. Then he went back to the living room, but no-one there paid him any attention now, they were once again embroiled in plans for the carnival float, the bishop insisting on scrapping the spectacle: "You'll run into serious problems, Justo Pastor, nobody's going to allow it." Matías Serrano described the idea as picturesque, but pointless: he said the world would go on as ever.

Chivo sank down into his chair, panting. For a few minutes he felt sorry for the doctor, with his obvious efforts to get his influential friends to commit to the undertaking. Efforts the bishop and the mayor repaid with little conviction. "Count on us in any case," the mayor said, "to the extent that we're permitted." The bishop fretted: "We need to arrange another get-together; we could meet on the second of January." Chivo was watching them—how ugly they looked, he thought, how horrible, how old, how skeletal; cheerio, corpses, I'm out of here with the beauty, he yelled in his head. The bishop's indifference encouraged him to drink more *aguardiente*, and to run stealthily in pursuit of the fleeing Primavera.

Primavera was in front of the stove, about to filter the coffee, when Professor Chivo came in, hot on her trail. Dishevelled, his face shiny with sweat, he threw himself without thinking at Primavera's tiny feet—more naked than ever in the rope-soled *alpargatas*—he knelt before them as if in ecstasy and kissed her toes rapidly, silently, many times.

"What are you doing?" Primavera asked. And then provided the answer herself, unable to credit it: *he's kissing my feet.*

She tried moving her feet away, but the professor's hands were gripping her ankles. The voices of the bishop and mayor could be heard in the living room. Chivo, on his knees, raised his intoxicated, inflamed face; it was as if he was catching a glimpse of Primavera in Heaven and he was much further away, in Hell.

"You are to be adored," he said, as if crying.

"Get up from there," Primavera urged, in an anxious whisper that sounded like a warning but also a celebration. In response, the professor simply crouched down again and redoubled his kisses, this time around her ankles, and then he moved lower down and started to plant kisses between Primavera's toes, while she opened her mouth, incredulous, bowled over by a wave of heat. And he's still kissing my feet, she cried inwardly, paralysed: now she could not even *attempt* to move her feet backwards. My feet?—she asked herself—not just my feet, because the kneeling professor was kissing her calves and had suddenly lifted a burning hand and was sliding it over her knee towards Primavera's thighs, underneath her skirt.

"My dear Don Arcaín," Primavera managed to blurt in surprise—with pleasure or annoyance?—and she thought that having said "My dear Don" to him, which she never said to anyone, and saying it in such a tone, she was calling him to order, "I could scream, they could hear me."

And yet, in spite of everything, an immeasurable delight took hold of her, against her will; the presentiment that they could be discovered at any moment: that was what worried her most, that her husband and the bishop and the mayor might come into the kitchen at any time—above all the bishop, she thought—but she felt the professor's hands moving even higher up her thighs, like dizzying, burning wings, pushing her legs apart; will I faint?—she wondered, leaning over the professor, who trembled on his knees as if praying—I will faint; and she opened her mouth to gulp down air because she could not breathe and it looked as though she were going to scream so the professor stopped his marauding: he lowered his scalding hands to encircle just one calf and left them there, as though shackling her.

"You," he said at once, not giving her time to react, "you are the remote Virgin of my childhood, surely it was for a kiss from your lips that my great-grandfather killed himself, or that he was killed, or that there was that war between two peoples, each of their kings wanting to abduct you and throw you on the marriage bed and gulp you down thirstily, Primavera, like a drop of water in the desert," and meanwhile he was looking fleetingly at her knees, and raised his gaze, fleetingly, to the place where her sex must be underneath her skirt, and from there he moved up fleetingly to her eyes, nothing daunted, and held her shocked, liquid blue gaze, held it without wavering while she stretched her mouth wide and exposed her teeth as though laughing silently, and yet it seemed she did it out loud, he thought, a torrent of feminine mirth cascading over him, encouraging him to keep talking, to provoke another silent, obliging laugh, she was challenging him to make her laugh more, or lose the game and see the laughter turn to contempt.

"I live in the hope of your love, the hope that one day you will open up for me like a flower, mistress of my pain," he said and recited "*sweet and sacred little light within my heart*," and chided her: "You'll never imagine what you're missing out on, not letting me adore you."

"God, what are you saying? Do you know what you're saying to me?"

Astonishment made her voice crack; another wave of heat washed over her; Arcaín Chivo renewed his wandering, his hand high inside her skirt.

"Don't do that," Primavera seemed to beg with a groan, mute laughter playing across her flushed face the whole time, and she lifted her free leg slightly and rested her foot on the kneeling professor's shoulder (so that for a blazing moment Arcaín Chivo could see she was entirely naked beneath her skirt); oh unattainable sex, he thought, and was able to stammer "unattainable Primavera," incredulous at such joy, and as Primavera moved he believed he managed to detect, on the air that wafted from inside her skirt, her most intimate scent, a sort of bitter sweetness, he thought, and now in a trance he was straining his neck head face mouth much further in to her when she pushed her foot against him with all her might and the professor collapsed backwards against a cabinet amid a clatter of saucepans and spoons, which simultaneously crashed down on his head.

"Arcaín's just fallen over," came Primavera's nervous announcement. "Something happened. He's hurt himself."

The others arrived: three long, grey shadows leaned in through the doorway. The professor had hit the base of his skull, hard.

"I think I've had too much to drink," he said, half getting up. The doctor himself held out his hand and helped him.

"I think I'd better go, *señores*," Arcaín Chivo continued, and it was impossible to tell whether he felt angry or overwhelmed with delight—he did not know himself.

"Us too," responded the bishop. "I'll drop you home, Arcaín. It's all been quite enough, if not too much. There are holidays on the horizon, but that doesn't make the days any easier to get through, eh, Justo Pastor? Promise me we'll meet again before carnival."

"I promise," the doctor replied. He could not take his eyes from his wife's flushed face, the face that was looking right back at him, happy.

But the joy on Primavera's face drained away as soon as they were alone, as the guests' voices on the other side of the front door grew fainter; she crossed the living room at once and started to go up the stairs, with the doctor behind her, neither of them hurrying, but escaping and in pursuit.

When they got to the first-floor landing the doctor took her by the arm and made her stop. "We need to talk," he said. "I'm going to see if the girls are asleep," she responded. With a brisk jerk she shook off her husband's hand, and carried on going upstairs. He hesitated over following her: in the end he headed for the study on the first floor, still hoping to find the recordings, or at least the paper transcriptions. He spent a long time there, in the office, rummaging through files, all to no avail: he had already lost the urge to ask Primavera about the tapes and start another row. He went up to the second floor with the intention of going to bed and putting the world out of his mind, but saw Primavera in Luz de Luna's bedroom, leaning over her sleeping daughter, and to see Primavera so calm, in peaceful silence, reawakened his impotent rage and the misery of depending on—or not depending on, more like it—a woman like her. Would he ask her about the tapes, without worrying about the row? He remembered his daughters were sleeping. My God, he said to himself, was it possible Primavera had stolen the tapes?

He chose to go back down to the first floor: he turned on all the lights, went in to the guest room, the laundry room, the room with the ping-pong table in it—all lined with further bookshelves—and in each room he continued his search, for endless minutes. Absolutely nothing. How long ago did he lose track of the recordings? He could not remember. Didn't he keep the tapes in a Cuban cigar box? Where did he hide that box? Why was his work—the only thing he had going for him—in such a muddle? The final room on the first floor was the toy room, and that was where he headed. He switched on the light: wooden Pinocchios, cuddly bears, lizards and whales, giant mice, penguins, plastic dolls and wind-up ones, puppets, wooden horses, electric trains, rubber ducks, tin soldiers, ballerinas, fairies and elves on strings all seemed to greet him at once with the most monstrous guffaw—that's what he heard—a freakish laugh issuing from deep within the toys as they lay piled in heaps against the walls, like multiplied versions of his own daughters.

In the middle of the room there was a table for playing Chinese chequers, with a huge bouquet of red roses in a vase and four chairs set round about. He tried to remember the last time he had sat at this table with his daughters: it was years ago. But he could not recall them putting bunches of roses on the games table. What kind of game was this?

There was a card stuck to the vase. He read, *From an undying admirer*, and, almost immediately, felt the presence of his wife, who had just come in, noiselessly, behind him.

"What?" she said. "Now you're going to play with dolls?"

He did not answer. Nor did he turn around. But he detected the apprehension in Primavera's voice, the doubt: had he read the card?

"I need the tapes," he said in the end.

"Well of course I haven't got them," she replied. Her voice had gone back to normal, the same old steady mockery. "I expect the toys have them, to play with."

He turned to look at her: she was coming towards him from the door, without hesitation. The games table stood between them. The bright light in the room shone into their faces and made them blink.

"What do you know about the float, what have they told you, what are they telling you to do about it?" the doctor asked.

"Something to do with Simón Bolívar," she said, "the father of the nation, I believe. I know the governor has taken steps. You're getting into a mess, and it doesn't matter to me. I don't care if you get yourself in all the damn messes in the world, but do it on your own. Seráfico told me you want to sell the *finca*. You're dragging me and the girls into your insanity, don't you see?"

"You never know what you're talking about," the doctor said. He sighed resignedly. He was about to leave when Primavera made him pause with a bitter, muffled cry.

"Idiot," she said.

And then:

"They can even put you in prison for mocking Bolívar, the father of the nation.""Did your General Aipe tell you that? Was he able to speak?"

"Luckily for you, he *can* speak now. He had to go to Bogotá, to specialists. It wasn't serious, fortunately for you."

He spun around, possessed; knocking two of the chairs out of the way with a sweep of his hand, he reached her in two strides and grabbed her by the hips; he was behind her, pushing her forward against the edge of the table. The vase overturned; water splashed out among the blazing roses.

"What father of what nation?" he yelled. "Father of your General Aipe, more like." And he loomed still further over her, and, holding her around the waist with one arm, yanked up her skirt in one go with the other; her naked backside glowed, very white. "So, nobody's ever nibbled your thighs?" he asked, as though he were choking. He did not recognize himself.

"You sod!" she shouted. "Run back to your pregnant women!"

"The father of the nation is the sod."

And as Primavera's skirt, which he was forcing up, had fallen back down like a curtain, he ripped it open at the seams; Primavera bellowed, wounded, she on the verge of passing out with rage, breathing hoarsely, twisting about furiously within the imprisoning arm, but he clasped her furiously and did not let her go, furious with himself, above all, because he desired her. He desired her with all his might, against his will, and it was impossible for him to kill the desire; he pulled down the zip of his trousers. There was a moment's pause in which they both seemed to make one single body: Primavera's rage spilled over on realizing that he intended to sink himself where none of the sixteen lovers in her life—she had them counted out—had ever dared to. She defended herself more fiercely than ever: bent her head, sinking her teeth into the hairy arm that encircled her. In answer, the doctor arched his body—he looked like a colossal, curved maggot—caught up the bunch of wet roses, grasped them by the stalks and whipped Primavera's rosy rear, just once, smashing blooms and thorns to bits, the roses shed their petals all over the place, she felt the multiple wounding of the thorns like tiny bites and the wet petals graze her skin; if, immediately after this peculiar botanical lashing, he had kissed her, offered any caress, an entreaty of love—Primavera thought, she managed to think—she would have gladly surrendered, but right at that moment he pushed her face down on the table, her luxuriant hair fanning out, the nape of her neck offering itself, and he bit her there, bruised her, parted her buttocks and surged towards the middle of her being, while Primavera twisted about in vain; in vain she cursed him without, it's true, failing to notice the particulars, the strange sensations linked to an ambivalence it was still impossible for him to pick up on, then she bawled "Pig! They're watching us! Your daughters!" and turned her head in the direction of the door, and he let go and looked to the door and now could not avoid her twisting around, slippery, and she leapt and ran, letting out a laugh of loathing and mockery—because there was no-one in the doorway. No-one at all. Just Primavera's extraordinary laughter as she fled, free of him.

He let himself fall weakly into a chair, alone again, and lonelier still because peeping from his open trousers he saw his sex, trembling and wet, more solitary than he was—tonight we'll sleep by ourselves, he thought—and in the middle of it all, and in spite of it all, Doctor Justo Pastor Proceso López laughed, he laughed, surrounded by toys on every side.

9

The morning of Saturday, December 31, Primavera sent a message with the old cook that she would be spending New Year's Eve at her sister's house and would be taking the girls. The doctor, who was in his consulting room, where he slept badly and with no hope, did not have time to say goodbye to his daughters; when he went to look for them, they left: he heard them dash off. A New Year's Eve apart, he thought, but did not think they'd mind—they won't even think of me.

And, on top of that, he received an invitation from the wife of Arcángel de los Ríos, Alcira Sarasti, written in her own hand, to come and see out the last night of 1966 together; the New Year's Eve parties at Furibundo Pita's house were famous—as were all Pasto's New Year's Eve parties—at midnight on the dot they burned the *años viejos*: large dolls, which looked identical to the people setting them alight, dolls made of cloth, rope, true to life, one-eyed and toothless, drinking *chicha*, smoking pipes, seated on rocking chairs, legs crossed, a rotten banana for a penis; you saw them dangling from blasted trees, hanged lovers with a poem pinned to the heart, or leaning against doorways like ill-fated visitors, each with his respective will and testament around his neck, or asleep in ramshackle cots, all bloated with explosive surprises:

sparklers, whistling bangers, volcanoes, firecrackers, rockets. At Furibundo Pito's New Year's Eve celebrations, shots were fired into the air, horses turned up in the living room, and there were *chumbos*—black turkeys with red coxcombs—they pumped them full of aniseed-flavoured *aguardiente* to sweeten the meat, inflated them; the turkeys danced drunkenly among the dancing guests and were later decapitated in the same room—even without heads, they carried on dancing—before being taken out to the kitchen, amid shouts and applause and live music. The doctor did not remember having been invited to such revelry before, only for those *surprise empanaditas* one Innocents' Day years before. Maybe Furibundo Pito wanted to redeem himself? Was he afraid of being prosecuted for being trigger-happy?

One of his patients also telephoned him, Chila Chávez; a woman beset by misfortune, she had married and been widowed that very December, and now suspected she was pregnant, when could he attend her? "Next year, *señora*, when all this miserable partying is over," he said circumstantially, and added: "Let me remind you, next year starts tomorrow." With the woman's laughter over the telephone, the air turned feminine, captivating, and the doctor wavered, befuddled. Before hanging up, Chila Chávez asked him where he would be spending New Year's Eve, just for something to say, out of politeness, and the doctor did not know how to disguise the hurt in his voice: he said he did not know. She did not hesitate to invite him to her house, as if she sensed his sorrow straight-away, "I'll be on my own," she said, "but in good company with you."

And she certainly lived alone, in one of those devastatingly huge Pasto mansions, set on the top of the Bethlemites' hill, a glass house resembling a cage that her husband had had built for her before his accidental death: the brakes failed on his truck and he hurtled into the Guáitara. The doctor wondered whether he would go, whether he was capable of it, while the widow's still-ardent voice told him over the telephone to think about it. Like a stroke of fate, what claimed to be a consultation might turn into a party for two. But the doctor would not go, he checked it against his conscience; the only thing in this world or the next he was concerned about was the Bolívar float: he wanted to know what had befallen Cangrejito Arbeláez and his sculptures. Had the robbers come back?

At midday he said goodbye to Genoveva Sinfín, not without informing her that they should expect him, he would spend New Year's Eve with her and the rest of the staff, "with each and every one of you," he said, brimming with bogus bonhomie, and he gave her carte blanche to prepare the dinner. "We'll eat in the garden," he said, "whatever the weather." And he remembered the gardener, his day labourers: "Tell Homero he's invited, tell Seráfico, tell the plumber, that Cabrera fellow and Chamorro that we'll eat guinea pig today like they've never tasted in their lives, tell them to bring their girlfriends or their grandmothers, I'll expect them here." Sinfín could not hide her astonishment, and the doctor thought she seemed pleased. He was to be disappointed: Sinfín asked permission on behalf of herself and the staff to celebrate the last day of the year with their respective families. He could do nothing but spread his arms open wide, in suffering: "Do what you like," he said. He would have to spend it alone, if he did not decide to go to Furibundo Pita's party, or to the widow Chila Chávez— dear God, he said to himself, why such panic over being alone?

So he drove his Land Rover to Cangrejito Arbeláez's house: with low expectations, feeling resigned. In Galerías, the marketplace, while he was waiting for the lights to change, he thought for a split second he saw an ape come stumbling out of a bar, with a gourd full of *chicha* in his hand. "It can't be," he thought, "Homero?" The ape immediately disappeared back inside the bar and the doctor decided not to check for himself which ape it was. It had to be Homero, he thought, there could not be another costume like that in the whole of Pasto. But they would see each other soon enough, he thought, he would explain soon enough.

Following that apparition, when the light changed to green and the jeep was starting to pick up speed, a shadow stepped out in front of him. He had to slam on the brakes: it was a very pale, tall young man, who stood looking at him fixedly after the sudden halt, and even came towards him, up to the driver's window, when he set off again, as if he wanted to ask him something; the doctor braked again and wound down the window to hear him, but the young man kept on going, without so much as a gesture. That young man was Enrique Quiroz, the eldest of the Quiroz brothers, Enriquito, the instigator—according to Professor Chivo—of the beating he had received at the hands of masked thugs. The doctor knew about the incident, but he did not know Quiroz.

And very soon he forgot about the passer-by who almost got himself run over at a traffic light.

PART III

1

They pretended to be a theatre group, in order not to arouse suspicion, as they put it. Every Saturday morning they met at the parish church of Nuestro Señor de los Despojos, in the community hall, to "rehearse": they were putting on a theatrical version of *The Imitation of Christ*, the idea of Rodolfo Puelles, poet of the group, but a secret poet to boot, as no-one knew—nor could they know—about his poems.

Puelles himself hid them: if his comrades discovered what they were about—which had nothing to do with the social emancipation of the people—they would not only brand him bourgeois, but a pervert. Because he wrote erotic verse, which he described as "about humorous love." His work in progress was titled *Nineteen Sugar Bums and an Enchanted Vagina*, and the "First Bum" began: "*Teresa into whose bum the dick begins/To vanish . . .*"

There were twelve of them, all men. The only woman, Toña Noria, a lanky black girl from Barbacoas, who studied agriculture, had been expelled from the group by common consent because "her natural lubricity disrupts the activity of members." She did not care: from the left-wing group she moved on to the university choir and then the women's chess team. Her absence was lamented solely and secretly by Rodolfo Puelles, who had already immortalized her in the most torrid of his poems, "The Enchanted Vagina," which he wrote without yet having exchanged more than a word with Toña Noria, as all he could do was idealize her during lengthy study sessions. Rodolfo Puelles tried to make up for such things with his poems of humorous love and by mocking the world and the poetry of his country, but more than anything mocking his own solitude, because at the age of twenty-two he had never known a woman, let alone love.

The group was a completely anonymous band of students, which sought to link itself to the National Liberation Army, with none of its members knowing whether the likelihood of that link was real or pure fantasy. They talked of "urban nuclei," "urban networks" and "cells" within the student body; they were marked by a clear "pro-China orientation"; they attacked not just "the system" but the traditional Communist party, the "fascistization" of the university, "proverbial obscurantism," "McCarthyism," "anarchist tendencies within the student body," "revolutionary spontaneity," "verbal ultra-radicalism," "divisive factions."

And the sole "contact" with the "forces of the revolution" was Enrique Quiroz, who claimed to know leaders and was in constant communication with them about what steps to follow, but did not give out further information on the imminent link-up for reasons of "revolutionary security." Be that as it may, the journeys Quiroz had been making to Bogotá and other cities, for months, guaranteed some truth to it all. His efforts were anxiously followed by everyone; there was even talk of representatives of the guerrilla war visiting Pasto in a few weeks: they would interview members of the group personally and "baptise" the chosen ones. The group, in spite of not belonging to any real political force, deemed itself radical, along Marxist-Leninist-Maoist lines, and had not yet identified the name of the armed wing it intended to support, whether it be independent or in the service of the organized revolution. In Pasto there were twelve members. At least as many again were waiting for them in Bogotá, plus two or three sympathizers in other major cities around the country. The Pasto twelve went to a lot of trouble over their cover as actors and assured everyone they would be presenting their *Imitation of Christ* to Pasto and the whole wide world in 1967—on March 19, Saint Joseph's Day—it being a work of reflection and devotion never before seen on the stage. At least, that is what the parish priest, Joseph Bunch, said about it; a closet homosexual—clandestine, like the poet—Bunch gave them his support and also spied on them from time to time, ogling them when gym was part of their rehearsals; but neither the Quiroz brothers nor anyone else from the group, the poet included, had read a single page of *The Imitation*, and quite possibly Father Bunch never had either, they joked. With a theatrical enterprise like this, designed to extol the priest's good Catholic deeds, they felt safe from the enemy: *camouflaged*.

Enrique and Patricio were the eldest sons of Sebastián Quiroz Carvajal, the architect; there were eight sisters behind them. Neither of the brothers had yet finished his university studies, and they were getting ready to go to Bogotá to continue them. The others in the group were working hard to do the same. They would all go: things "happened" in Bogotá; Pasto was "asleep." What is more, it was not possible for them to use their *noms de guerre* in the small city because people knew who they were, had done since they were children. It was different in Bogotá: there, Enrique Quiroz was "Vladimir," and at twenty-seven years of age had, not one, but two families of his own. One with "Tania" and the other with "Simona." With the former he had three children: Lenin, Miguel Mao and Lenina, and with the latter, two: Simón Ernesto and little Stalin, just six months old. In Pasto, his third family was on the way, secretly, with his pregnant cousin Inés Bravo. No-one at home knew anything about all these households—three women and six children—but it was the architect Sebastián Quiroz Carvajal who, never dreaming it, supported them all. This did not stop Enrique

Quiroz, after receiving his generous monthly allowance, referring to his father as an "old retrograde," "iniquitous bourgeois" and "petty oligarch." Enrique did not worry about his families' straitened circumstances, circumstances he did not share with them, or worry about bringing further children into the world. He talked of "more soldiers for the revolution" and it was precisely for this reason that his brother Patricio, "Boris," admired him. Patricio already had his first soldier on order, with a pure-blooded indigenous woman from the Sibundoy Valley, and he was euphoric about it: this presaged the incorporation of indigenous peoples into "the cause"; there was a new race on the horizon. Patricio Quiroz was the only member of the group not studying law and political sciences: he was doing economics, but considered himself an artist, and for years had been saying he was composing the great anthem of the Colombian Revolution. A heavy drinker, he played the accordion and crooned serenades.

The members of the theatre group appeared so committed that they even "rehearsed" on Saturday, December 31, the last day of the year, despite the sounds of celebration drifting through the streets. That morning they were settling how to bid the year and Pasto farewell, as once carnival was over they would travel to Bogotá, all of them already enrolled in the National University of Colombia. The plan was to shape an urban guerrilla war, in Bogotá, an idea they had been working on for months. While in Pasto, the city of their birth (although three of the twelve were not Pastusos: one came from Cali, another from Chocó, the third from the plains), they planned to put an end to the dangerous treachery of a multimillionaire gynaecologist, Doctor Justo Pastor Proceso López, close friend of the madman Chivo, who meant to mock the Liberator Simón Bolívar, father of the revolution, with a carnival float.

"He's got it coming to him."

Enrique Quiroz, chief instigator of the action against Doctor Proceso, had spoken.

"That doctor is boss and ringleader for the idiot Chivo. Both of them are barmier than billy goats, but poisonous ones."

The church bell tolled ten o'clock, ringing for morning Mass. Three of the group members gave an account of their military action:

"Yesterday we managed to seize two sculptures from that sell-out Cangrejito, the black piece of shit, artist of the enemy."

"They're wooden. Huge."

"The shooting of the twenty Capuchin missionaries of Caroní, on Bolívar's orders."

"And of the La Guaira eight hundred, on Bolívar's orders."

"The captions were: *Bolívar shoots the twenty Capuchin friars, 1817* and *Bolívar shoots the La Guaira eight hundred, 1814*, with dates and everything. Some balls, those bastards."

"They looked very nice, really well made, for what it's worth. In the one of the twenty Capuchins there was a Bolívar figure on horseback; a soldier was telling him about the capture of the twenty friars; Bolívar was asking, in wooden lettering: *And you haven't killed them yet?* In the one about the eight hundred there were some old folk tied to their chairs, and that's how they were carried and put up against the wall, because they couldn't walk anymore. How about that? The captions also said: *Gunpowder was expensive so they used sabres and pikes* and *The executions began on February 13 and finished on 16.* Where did they get that from, those oafs?"

"What is to be done with history?" Puelles asked. "We don't know who these people were, or who they were not either."

"We didn't know about these executions, at least. Did you?"

There was a silence, sharp as a guillotine, that Enrique Quiroz rushed to diffuse.

"If Bolívar shot them or used sabres or pikes on them, it was because they deserved it," he said. "Bolívar cannot be called into question."

"Those planks burned well on the bonfire we made."

"Was that big black guy there, in the workshop? Did he put up a fight again?"

"He'd gone out. His apprentices were there, a bunch of yobs."

"Watch what you say," Quiroz said. "The apprentices are the people. Workers and *campesinos* add up to the future of the revolution. In this particular case, ignorance makes them innocent."

"Perhaps the black guy hasn't come back; he saw the way the wind was blowing. He took most of his work with him: he wants to show it all together on the float. That's what he thinks."

"Shitty reactionary. We're going to blow his carriage sky high, along with everyone putting it together."

"We don't know where he went," the apprentices told the doctor. "He disappeared in secret."

They were in Cangrejito's studio, empty of work. Despite it being mid-day, it seemed like night-time in there. There were three apprentices, big simple lads, propped against the walls, having their lunch of steamed corn parcels and cold oat milk.

"He took his sculptures with him yesterday, Friday, in a truck: imagine a truck full of carnival. And the thieves came last night; they didn't find anything; they could only take two 'Executions,' which Cangrejito left behind because he hadn't finished them."

They did not seem frightened to the doctor, more like intrigued.

"They swore they'd give us a pounding if we carried on with the carriage," the oldest apprentice said, chubby and smiling. "They were armed, that's how they got away with stealing what they stole, they didn't look very tough."

"Police or military?"

"They were masked up, Doctor. I don't think they were soldiers. You could see their hair, lots of it, underneath. Long-haired guys. They were just robbers, that's all, and scared."

The doctor was disconcerted. He could not imagine who they were up against. Was General Aipe behind all this? Now he doubted it.

"They said," added another apprentice, fair, almost albino, "that in any case they were going to boot us all up in the air, one by one."

"Like we were lying around to start with," the fat one said, laughing. But the fair boy spoke again, very grave:

"They especially mentioned you, Doctor. They said: 'We're going to boot that so-and-so sky high.'"

"As if I were lying around too," the doctor said.

"And if you carry on being a nuisance, they will shoot you, not boot you, Doctor."

The fat boy burst out laughing; only then did the rest join in.

"Lucky none of us is lying around," the doctor said in parting.

He drove through the muddy streets, unable to guess Cangrejito Arbeláez's destination. The midday chill dampened his spirits. Who was he fighting against? Was it possible the mayor and bishop's warnings would come true? He was worried about the sculptor's fate—where would he have gone? Maestro Abril was the only person who could bring him up to date with events.

The secret poet Rodolfo Puelles was not convinced by the direction things were heading in. He had, above all within himself, serious reasons for this—or, better put, one single and terrible reason, although he admitted, inwardly, that things had begun with the best of intentions. But why, he yelled inside, are we messing them up?

Two years earlier, the group's founding members had participated in one of Colombia's historic student marches, which brought together more than five hundred thousand citizens in the capital. It was during this encounter that the group gained in numbers and enthusiasm: one of its members had even been given a grant by Fidel Castro's government and travelled to Cuba to complete his studies. He sent passionate and inspiring letters from the island, which were seen by the group as triumphant war reports. When the student wrote that he was to go to Russia to specialize, and in addition receive political training, maybe military, the group was divided: some argued the student should return to Colombia immediately to take up the struggle again and occupy the position allotted to him, while others felt his sojourn in Russia was an "essential" experience, which would be to everyone's advantage. So the hours had flown past until the early morning, and the wasting of energy on similar controversies, and other even more trivial matters (should you read or not read Count Leo Tolstoy: decadent writer, retrograde, symbol of Russian aristocracy?), undermined the poet's morale, all the more so when the "polemic" about Tolstoy originated not from a sensible study of his work, but in a chance occurrence: the book had fallen out of his knapsack onto the table, and in spite of the covers being carefully wrapped in newsprint, the paper came adrift and title and author appeared before them all: *The Devil, Leo Tolstoy.* Enrique Quiroz picked up the book, showed it around as if showing them the actual devil, and did so with a disparaging smile, the same one spreading across the others' faces: incredulous eyes scrutinized the poet Puelles as if they would unmask him. What was he up to, this Puelles, who was he, really? Puelles prepared himself for the fight, more apathetic than resolved: he gave up before he started—and with all the more reason, he thought, when Tolstoy was the namesake of the dissident Trotsky.

Was it so important to finish your degree, or better to take up arms, go into the mountains and educate the rural masses?

The recent death of Father Camilo Torres—founder of the sociology faculty at the National University, principal representative of liberation theology, leader of the people—which took place in February 1966, when he was cut down during his first combat, had been the trigger for Enrique Quiroz's group to seriously consider the creation of an urban guerrilla front. The poet Puelles backed the initiative: he would prefer to fight in the city (he could not imagine himself firing a gun in the depths of the jungle), finish his degree and, above all, pursue his secret occupation, poetry, his poetry, the humorous love that sprang from his pores, as he put it. That is why he devoted himself to supporting the urban front and making it a reality. Up to that point, everything had gone well for Rodolfo Puelles, but formulating urban guerrilla war in Bogotá, with the Quiroz brothers plus three others from the Pasto front, and four from the capital, got off to an unanticipated start.

The secret poet Rodolfo Puelles had returned to Pasto after that whole venture in a state of shock, his life for ever divided into a "Before" and "After."

As a "trial by fire," the members of the group (without anyone knowing who came up with the idea, nor how or when) had decided to "eliminate an enemy": kill a policeman, the secret poet repeated to himself, still incredulous; a policeman they had already had under surveillance and who did nothing but earn his wages chasing pickpockets in Bogotá; a policeman, what's more, who was in civilian clothing at the moment of his "execution"; they killed him when he went to buy milk at a shop, one block from his house, in a working-class neighbourhood. He was the enemy. The enemy, the secret poet thought, what enemy? He was not in the least convinced.

Although the revolution should give no respite, a trial like that never seemed necessary to him, and he had not managed to get a decent night's sleep since, but the reason he could not sleep in peace—over and above everything else in the world—was because it was him, in short, Rodolfo Puelles, secret poet, who had shot the policeman, an "indigenous-looking man in a poncho who turned out to be a police officer"—as reporters for the gutter press would later describe him—"He went out to buy milk, and never came home," "Killed for a bottle of milk," "Policeman, out of uniform, was buying milk," "Thieves unaware he was carrying service revolver."

It happened at seven o'clock at night.

Enrique Quiroz was in charge of the strike: when the big moment arrived, he froze. The other Quiroz got drunk the night before, and had stayed that way. There were three more from the Pasto front with Puelles and Quiroz—"Ilyich" from Cali, "Catiri" from the plains, and "Ulyanov" from Chocó—and four from Bogotá, scattered at strategic points around the objective: all frozen. Only the secret poet fired once, at the head. Yet he was the most frightened and the one who least supported the action. He fired out of pure, physical fright, he thought; he remembered he'd wet himself as he did it. The policeman crumpled instantly and they all fled, every man for himself; they did not seize the police weapon. Did anyone take the bottle of milk? No, that was an invention of the bourgeois press, they said, it must have been filched by the homeless guy who was looking on.

They returned to Pasto by separate routes, and only met up again after several nightmarish days.

Enrique Quiroz could not forgive the fact that no-one had taken the victim's gun, that no-one retrieved it as a trophy, that they did not leave a written note, that they did not shout a defiant warning, a challenge, advance notice of the new revolutionary force. "What utter retards," he bawled, "and we haven't even got a name."

Quiroz, better than anyone, understood the radicalism of guerrilla war, and applauded it. The year before, a commander in the People's Army had executed a deserter. That was something else, he thought, that was betrayal, and fully deserved execution. The death of the policeman was a mistake that Enrique Quiroz, the real originator of the idea, did not want to, nor could ever, admit to in front of his men— "Bolívar made big mistakes," he said to himself, "the mistakes of a great man: necessary errors, but he didn't go around confessing them"—and when the group was back together again, in the safety of the parish church of Nuestro Señor de los Despojos, he told them the elimination of anyone in uniform was one more victory for the revolution, and that the death of a policeman must not be "sentimentalized," because even if he was a plain and simple officer, he was someone who, although an authentic son of the people, was still in the service of imperialism, the master's dog, the guardian of the oppressor, dammit, this is a war to the death, like the one Bolívar waged against the Spaniards. And he banged his fist on the table:

"Don't mention the matter again, you bastards, nobody cry over it."

Several of Enrique Quiroz's acquaintances, active supporters of the revolution, had already gone into the mountains of Colombia to support the insurgents and follow in the footsteps of Che and Fidel, fine examples of manhood, Quiroz said to the group.

Rodolfo Puelles disagreed. In Bogotá, in the cafeteria at the National University, he had heard about another "execution" in the mountains, of two young members of the guerrilla forces: driven by hunger, they stole a block of cane sugar from the command stores. They were killed. The deaths of these hungry young men—were they an invention by the enemy oligarchy to discredit the insurgence, or was it all true? And he had heard, without being able to verify it, about the mistreatment of recently recruited university students, about the contempt they were treated with if they were seen reading, writing or—worse still— if they expressed their desire to educate the *campesinos*, or stumbled in training exercises, or tired during the terrible forced marches and collapsed. Revolutionary enthusiasm was a powerful force, the elation was immense, but the muffled messages issuing from the mountains gave rise to doubt: something bad could be going on, Puelles thought, something harmful about the way things were advancing, in how devotion and effort were being used or abused.

Puelles, who stayed with his uncle—a taxi driver by profession— when he went to Bogotá, had disappointing experiences. One of his earliest contributions to the cause was handing over the keys for his uncle's taxi to three comrades who would carry out an "act of expropriation" on a small neighbourhood fruit and vegetable market. The night the keys were handed over, when the three revolutionaries (Ilyich from Cali among them) went off in his uncle's taxi, they crashed straight into the lamp post on the corner. None of them knew how to drive: were they really intending to carry out a revolutionary act, or were they just planning to go out on the town? One Saturday at "rehearsal" in the church, Puelles ironically brought up that particular failure, the lack of preparation. Ilyich from Cali stood up for himself at the top of his voice, like he was barking. He had an extraordinary face: one eye blue, the other black. Sallow and skinny, it was Toña Noria who had given him a nickname that stuck: she said he was thin as a plate and from then on they called him "Platter," although alongside his *nom de guerre*, Ilyich, of which he was so proud. He launched himself at Puelles to shut him up. Enrique Quiroz and the comrade from the plains pulled them apart. "That's just what imperialism wants," Quiroz said, "for us to kill each other. Are we going to oblige them?"

A meek silence followed his words.

Enrique Quiroz was not just the leader of the group, he was also the oldest: twenty-seven. And he saw, or felt as though he saw, the people surrounding him for the first time: they were very young, he thought, maybe too young, and he concluded that so much youth is a double-edged sword.

They studied Lenin, Engels and Mao together, carrying *What is to be Done?*, *The Part Played by Labour in the Transition from Ape to Man* and *Five Essays on Philosophy* in their pockets as standard issue, prepared to "triumph or die"—as they used to chant in emphatic voices at the beginning of each rehearsal. "Actually, to triumph," Quiroz told them, "the 'transformation' is a matter of months away—two years, at most." That is what he told them the morning of Saturday, December 31, because he was utterly convinced not only that they would still be young men when the revolution triumphed, but that they themselves would make it happen.

Nineteen sixty-six was over.

2

"Starting from today, we'll be keeping Doctor Justo Pastor Proceso López under surveillance," Quiroz told them. He said it slowly; it was more than an order. And, directing himself towards the poet Puelles, as if confirming who would carry it out: "You know where the doctor lives, don't you? The doctor will lead you to the carriage. Here are the keys for the Vespa: follow him over the next few days leading up to Black Day, which falls on Thursday, January 5. Follow him until Thursday, but, listen, before White Friday, the day of the parade, we need to know the whereabouts of that reactionary float and destroy it to justly make amends to Bolívar's memory."

"And the artisans?" Platter Ilyich asked.

"Nobody mess with the artisans," Quiroz replied. "A clout or two, at most, nothing major. As Christ put it, forgive them for they know not what they do."

But why surveillance?—Rodolfo Puelles wondered. He did not hide his dismay. After the categorical "chat" about the policeman, which was not even a critical investigation, and in which only Quiroz's judgement on sentimentalism was heard, the secret poet Rodolfo Puelles had realized he did not so much inspire respect among his comrades for his resolve on the night of the action in Bogotá, as exactly the opposite: rejection.

Rejection, he jeered himself, and rejection of the worst kind: revulsion.

It was hard to admit, but that was the way it was; he had thought his leading role was going to set him up as a man of action, at least earn him some credit. But, no. Revulsion. This was the conclusion he reached after examining the faces of his comrades, one by one, and their behaviour. Maybe—he thought—they saw I pissed myself when I fired the gun; but at least I fired it, chickenshits, he bawled at them, inwardly. And he already knew that shouting inwardly meant no-one would ever hear him, no-one would ever know of his troubles.

But, nevertheless, there was one person who did not feel revulsion towards him, and he knew who it was, of course: Quiroz. And for that very reason, Quiroz charging him with a job such as surveillance seemed to him an insult. Why not give the task to that halfwit brother of his? And the fact was, in any case, the secret poet Rodolfo Puelles, twenty-two years of age, could not care less about Simón Bolívar and Doctor Proceso and his reactionary carnival float; the only thing he wanted to do was get himself into a brothel during the Black and White Carnival without any of his comrades finding out, without anyone subsequently accusing him of involvement in crimes against humanity, in capitalism's most characteristic blot on society: prostitution. Thinking about it, Rodolfo Puelles smiled in anguish; he had really determined to make the most of the Black and White Days to finally plunge into the brothel, to discover and smell and celebrate the sex of a flesh-and-blood woman, a real face, real breath, at last, to touch the moon, kiss her inside, deeper inside, much deeper. Now he would have to tail and trail a grumpy gynaecologist who, clearly, was not even a millionaire, as Enrique Quiroz had made out, and he had to tail him and trail him during the January celebrations no less, and follow the mission through to completion: to find out where a stupid carnival float was hidden. What a country. What was I born into? He would have preferred prehistoric times.

Enrique Quiroz was looking at him fixedly.

Rodolfo Puelles picked up the keys for the scooter, without arguing.

And yes, it was glaringly obvious: it was not revulsion on Quiroz's face, but resentment, envy, Puelles shouted to himself—worse than revulsion, he must be suffering more.

That certainty astonished Puelles: Enrique Quiroz loathed him for being the one who fired the gun, for being the one who had *dared*, but he loathed him above all for being the one and only witness to his cowardice, the intimidation of Vladimir, hesitant little Enrique, utterly spineless, weren't the two of them shoulder to shoulder the night of the action? That certainty, rather than making Puelles proud, scared him. His resolve had won him an enemy: Vladimir no less. Was it possible little Enrique believed his leadership under threat? Why not? Stupidity is infinite, he thought.

But after the group said goodbye and dispersed, a worse fear occurred to the secret poet, a real one: perhaps Enrique Quiroz wanted to repeat the exploit with the policeman, but this time with a gynaecologist? "Not that," he said out loud; such colossal imbecility would not be possible, or would it? Stupidity, he thought again, and then regretted everything and everyone and his own self; "fuck," he bawled; a terrible desolation seized him: he thought of the mass of youth who were struggling frantically during these years, in every one of the universities in the country, in the schools and colleges, where students and teachers stood by the same ideal. What would happen? Where would it all lead? Wasn't this energy being wasted? Wasn't it being sacrificed at the hands of stupidity?

As for him, he would have liked the earth to swallow him up.

Doctor Proceso was overwhelmed too. Once again rain greeted him in Maestro Abril's neighbourhood, once again the volcano was blowing out ice, again the narrow street, just the same, was engulfed in fog; but the carriage did not loom over the wall as before: they had "disappeared" the float, and no-one came to the gates, no child materialized, no woman came with news, he thought, as if the world had gone to another world. Was it because it was the thirty-first, the last day of the year, a hiatus?

He got back in the jeep: a black hen was pecking about in the rain; a dog ran off avoiding streams of yellow water, banana skins, dismembered plastic dolls.

He drove through empty streets. He parked on a corner; he did not know how long he lingered there, peering into nothingness. Then he drove across Pasto to the other side, got onto the sodden highway, which led to Lake Cocha. It was late afternoon. At the top of a lonely rise he got out and ran into the squall, to contemplate the lake; he could not see it; fog covered the vast expanse with lead. So he returned to Pasto, no destination in mind. And in the first street he ventured into, he felt the accumulated hunger of the day for the first time, and for that very reason believed he was alive, with something to live for: food. He had not even had breakfast; he deserved lunch, he thought, even if it *was* the last day of the year.

He stopped at a basic-looking restaurant, with covered terrace, lettering badly painted across the canvas: *LA ESPERANZA'S FRITOS.*

Beneath the big circus awning, solitary tables were set around a hazy platform: he caught a glimpse of very slow shadows that passed from one side of it to the other. A thin, ageless woman put a plate of *frito* on his table: chunks of roast pork, popped corn, boiled potatoes and, with a celebratory thump, although the doctor had not ordered it, a half-bottle of *aguardiente* and a tall, metal cup—like a chalice.

As he ate, amid the fog that swathed the place, straining his eyes, he was better able to make out the stage. There was a band of musicians, he discovered, and he learned more: they were all blind. The sightless were playing guitar, *quena* pipes and ten-stringed *charangos*, bass drums and a violin, they were ancient and decrepit, undeniably blind, they must be—he checked, incredulous—they wore those thick green glasses, the ones for blind people—those not wearing glasses exposed their eyes like sores—the youngest of them must have been seventy.

What kind of place have I fallen into? On one of the drums he deciphered the white lettering: *MUNICIPALITY OF LA LAGUNA, BLIND ORCHESTRA.*

No doubt his arrival—the appearance of the first diner, the only one—prompted them to start playing: they began with "La Guaneña." Behind the blind men a chorus of hundred-year-old women, nine or ten of them, trilled weakly, and it seemed more like a death rattle than "La Guaneña." "This is how they bid the year farewell," he said to himself, "and how they'll greet the new one," and on one side of the platform he spotted an old couple dancing; it was a listless dance, little clouds of dust were scuffed up by their shoes. It disheartened him to hear "La Guaneña"—war anthem from the days of Agualongo—transformed into a requiem. He drank more *aguardiente*, and that did nothing to lift his spirits either. He sensed something like bad news in the fog: a presentiment. Luckily the world is a long way off, he thought, I'll go to bed. He wanted to get up, but his legs felt like someone else's: he found that during the time that "La Guaneña" lasted he had drunk three half-litres of aniseed *aguardiente*, plus the first one, which meant that, without knowing it, he had consumed two whole bottles of *aguardiente* to the lonely strains of that "Guaneña" for the blind. "Right then," he said to himself, "either I stand up, or I'm dead."

And he stood up.

He paid the woman. One of the old dears in the choir called out to him, in her faraway, tremulous voice:

"Happy New Year, Doctor Justo Pastor, may God be with you, today as yesterday, tomorrow as today."

Was she an old patient, or a patient from the other side? The doctor waved goodbye: he could not even manage to reply—it was as if he had forgotten how to talk.

Night was falling. At the Land Rover's slow passing the city centre began to light up; he wound down the window: the smell of dust and fried food oppressed him; furtive shadows crossed at corners; the first drunks came out onto the street, music swelled, isn't that Mandarina's house? The first "visit" of his adolescence had happened there: he had trembled from head to foot; black Mandarina was not only the madam of the establishment, she also initiated the babes, she initiated him, she must be an old lady by now, he thought, why did they call her Mandarina? He remembered her large sex, round and smooth like a split orange, and shivered. Now, in the wide doorway of the big old townhouse, illuminated by a red glow, two girls wearing miniscule skirts, backs hunched over, were lighting cigarettes; they stood scrutinizing him, to see what would happen; one of them came over: lascivious, she offered ancient, unfamiliar words in his ear, and the other, with thick dark hair falling to the back of her knees, carried on staring at him with the constancy of a happy moment, as if she had known him for centuries. "Happy New Year," the doctor said through the window, and neither girl could understand him, so spellbound did his voice come across. "Not so very long ago," he carried on, as if telling a joke, "December in Pasto was the month of the dead, but you've got to sing and dance, carnival is on its way, nobody cries here, or do they?"

They did not understand him. He was babbling. The girls turned their backs.

When he got home he saw a Vespa parked on the other side of the road and, sitting on the little wall, a boy reading by the scant light of the street lamp, frowning, looking worn out; he was wearing a beret. The poet Rodolfo Puelles did not seem to notice the doctor's arrival, the noise of the jeep parking, so immersed did he appear to be in his reading. The doctor entered his house hoping to find Sinfín, and did not; he would have liked to ask her whether Maestro Arbelaéz came to look for him the day before, or that very morning.

And only then did it occur to him—Primavera, he thought, Primavera went to open the door to the maestro, she dealt with him and dismissed him, without telling me, Primavera, Primavera, who would not one day wish to become your murderer? This certainty upset him like a betrayal: Primavera had told Cangrejito he was not at home; the sculptor had to go elsewhere with his truck. And it was more than likely, too, that Primavera was not with their daughters: no doubt she had left them at her sister's house and gone off to meet General Aipe. That possibility revolted him; "Primavera," he said, and, for a moment, involuntarily, painfully, he imagined her amorously entwined with General Aipe, or with any other body on earth, and his drunkenness aggravated his suspicions: he imagined her spreadeagled on a squeaky hotel bed, suffocated, and an intimate thrill ran through him, in spite of himself. He was alone in his house, a house even lonelier than he was.

"Damn you, world," he said.

And he repeated this to himself while back in his jeep driving around streets that were getting busier all the time with the New Year: eyes like invitations, shouts, entreaties, explosive music that shattered windows.

He was going to the widow's house, as if to the castle of an irreproachable maiden.

But he was more excited by Primavera Pinzón than by Chila Chávez. He could not even remember the widow's face. Was she beautiful? Less beautiful than Primavera? Much more so? She was not an older woman, but not a girl either; her voice redeemed her, it revealed her utterly.

It was a struggle for him to park the jeep without crashing it. Walking to the front door he felt like a thief about to commit a robbery: a dead man stood behind this woman, he thought, and would be no less present for being dead; not a month had passed since his disappearance, who knows what other shapes he would take, is he that willow tree guarding the door? The willow calls me, keeps calling me, or is it the wind moving the branches? He chivvied himself along.

He raised his hand to the doorbell and did not ring it.

There was no light in the windows. He was sure the widow was not going to be expecting him. And what if he found her waiting for him? After so many tribulations, the widow was a shoulder to cry on, he thought, but to cry with too.

The living room curtains opened and Chila Chávez's face appeared behind it, pale above her black dress, astonished. When she discovered it was him, she seemed more astonished still, but happily so, letting out a great silent laugh. Straight away, she opened the door. She appeared barefoot, her curly hair swept back:

"Come in, my dear doctor," she said, "but what an old-year face you've got on you, I'm going to make it new."

She was utterly drunk.

Her voice was slurred, as if in rapture—fine Pasto girl of my heart, he thought. She said she had slept and just woken up.

"Come in, come in, my dear doctor," she said. She indicated a peaceful room where a black radiogram took pride of place and an Agustín Lara record was playing. A local girl, drunk, he said to himself, a disaster waiting to happen? She'll fall asleep. No, he thought, in spite of her widowhood, or because of it, he was the cause of her small happiness: it's me that's exalting her. But the next moment he found out it was not so, in that very instant it is not me embracing her but her immortal deceased, he thought, or managed to think, buried in the widow's perfumed hair, and he heard her whispers, almost without understanding her, but he did understand her, aghast, *little doctor of mine, I was waiting for you here, my mouth and my legs wide open, little husband of my soul, why did you go and die on me?*

Opposite the widow's house, to one side of the lamp post, Puelles the poet settled down to read, back against the wall: "I'll keep an eye on you from here, Doctor, but only until eleven, I've got my New Year's Eve too."

An only child, he lived with his parents and his grandfather, Capusigra the cobbler. His parents hated him—or so he believed. Things were different with his grandfather: they played dominoes, read aloud from the newspaper, or from his grandfather's favourite book—*Don Quixote*—whatever page it fell open at. His grandfather was an ancient old man, but lucid, and was expecting him—he'll definitely want to have a drink with me and see out the year, he thought. He looked at his watch: nine o'clock. He had left the Vespa in the shadow of an elm tree so the doctor would not see it. What am I doing here? What is my body doing in this street? He thought it shameful and even more idiotic to find himself there, spying on the gynaecologist, carrying out the orders of a lunatic. Wouldn't it be preferable to jump this ship as soon as possible, to forget the tragedy of the policeman and start life afresh? In a city where no-one knew him. Singapore? Change his name, change his face, be reborn? One thing was certain—he swore—he would never give up his poetry.

He had read in a Sunday paper about a movement of young poets in which the latest ideas were brought together with the positions and impositions of established national poetry. The journalist explained that this was a crowd of young people "mad with a different joy," and although the poet Puelles did not consider himself mad with joy of any kind, he would have given a leg to find himself among crazed poets reading any of his *Nineteen Sugar Bums and an Enchanted Vagina*, or simply atoning for or celebrating the poetry of any century, from the first to the last. Poets from every country who were proclaimed by the demented youngsters, philosophers and novelists whom they revered, all of them were already old friends of Puelles—he had read them backwards—and this comforted him, he was not so far off track, in spite of everything, he thought. The *in spite of everything* was that street, that doctor, that absurd persecution, that dead man hanging around his neck for ever. Puelles looked off in a different direction and scared away the apparition.

From the little hill on which the widow's house was built you could glimpse a strip of the city, lit up by New Year's Eve fire: rockets shot straight up into the black sky, and their multicoloured explosions seemed to lightly touch every peak, but "Father Galeras" was unmoved, a great impassive shadow, fleetingly crowned with fireworks—*I can do better*, Puelles imagined it meant to say.

Occasional cars went up and down the winding road; the festive December noises barely reached this elevated neighbourhood of large, spread-out houses; the road was a narrow carriageway heading down, each curve leaning out over the one below, and there were exactly three bends; on the summit, the concrete smudge of the Bethlemite Sisters' college stood out, a big empty mass. Below, oblivious Pasto, Puelles thought, lights upon lights.

The book he was reading, *The Black Heralds*, made him suffer, not so much for the lines he read, but because he had to read with only half his mind; with the other half he had to keep watch on the house into which a certain Doctor Proceso had disappeared. Who was that guy really? A quack, he thought, a distinguished insect. He could not read any more: it felt like he was sitting on ice, his buttocks were numb, his legs asleep. He put the *Heralds* away in his knapsack and walked down the road, where the night was a distant rumble. On the first and highest of the bends he pushed his way into a dark hollow, between bushes, to pee. From there he observed the continuation of the road, the curve immediately below, flanked with other houses, and then he saw him, sitting on the pavement: Platter Ilyich.

Platter was not reading, he was smoking; not far away from him, in the grass, lay Patricio Quiroz's orange scooter—the Quiroz brothers were the only "motorized" ones in the group. What was Ilyich doing there? Coincidence? Logistical support? For a second, Puelles was buoyed up: whatever the case, now he had someone to chat with to pass the time, even if it was the loathsome Ilyich, but then something like a light flicked on in his brain. "He's following me," he said to himself, "he's been following me all this time, while I follow the doctor." And he put two and two together, still incredulous: "He's following us. He checked how far we went up, and dug himself in down there, where the doctor and I will have to go past sooner or later. What morons, why do they have to tail me? Do they doubt me? Well, when eleven o'clock comes, Platter will have to follow me home: I'm off then, and Vladimir can kiss my ass."

And while he peed he remembered things about Ilyich from Cali.

He had known him since the first week at university: Ilyich announced to the world that he wrote poems; then that he painted and made sculptures; months later he played the sax; finally, he was an expert on film and photography. For ages they had kept their distance from one another, but they met again—and were both surprised—when they joined the leftist group led by Quiroz: surely that was Ilyich's true destiny.

And Puelles called him to mind more vividly, suffering over the memory: he had a sharp face, perpetually morose; his eyes and mouth were marked by an unfathomable mistrust, grounded in malice, suspicious of everything, everyone, maybe even himself; his extraordinary, different-coloured eyes were small, a bird of prey's; his mouth was large, purplish, always wet; his voice was deep, but phoney; everything about him, from top to toe, added up to something repulsive, he thought. Platter was a born traitor, quick to mock and bad-mouth people, he had the habit—which Puelles hated—of speaking ill of whoever had just left the room: he resorted to scathing invention, subtle lies—which the rest, who were afraid of him, applauded as a display of intelligence, how about that? He found it astonishing.

And he remembered him in Bogotá—the two of them active members of the group by then—the day Ilyich introduced him to his friend "Comrade Rosaura." The pride with which he presented this friend—a mature woman, very short, almost a dwarf, who worked as a domestic servant "in the guts of bourgeois society"—disconcerted Puelles; they met in Rosaura's room, in a stripped-out tenement building in south Bogotá: the place consisted of a bed, table and chair, a small spirit stove on the floor, an empty little saucepan; mice scampered quickly across the floor, mosquitos attacked, but it was precisely this pitiful narrowness that exalted Ilyich. Resting on the table, open almost at the middle, lay Marx's hefty tome, *Das Kapital*, which Rosaura had pointed to, "I'm reading it," she said. And with cheerful sincerity added: "I don't understand a word of it, but I'm going to finish it, like I promised Ilyich." A questioning look escaped Puelles, which he shot—regretting it too late—at Platter Ilyich, believing he would share in it: what was this about reading *Das Kapital* to the end without understanding it? But the blue and black look he found on Platter's wan face was fully accepting, a look of triumphant pride. This ended up discouraging him for ever—he would never again expect anything of such an ass, he thought.

And now Platter was brooding down there, a few metres below him, no doubt more bored than he was. Puelles did up his fly; he preferred to go back to thinking about the Medellín poets—there was a light on in those great minds, he thought, and he could at least yell out his poems of humorous love without fear of crucifixion. And he continued with the image of light: us poets are light years away from those pigs, he thought. And he had just thought this when a chilly wind, inopportune like a gust against his skin, that seemed to come from deep inside himself rather than from out there, knocked him flat: could he consider himself "a poet light years away from those pigs?" He asked it in spite of himself. A profound despair welled up inside him; he was overwhelmed by the fear of himself; he was, above all, a murderer: he had killed, and not in self-defence, he thought. I killed him in an underhanded way, I killed him idiotically, yes, but I killed him. He very rarely forgot about the event, and when he did it was always an ephemeral forgetting, sooner or later, and sooner rather than later, sleeping or waking, the mild figure of the policeman appeared to him, leaving the shop with a bottle of milk in his hand.

As if invoking otherworldly forces, Rodolfo Puelles took refuge in poetry and from the whole of his memory chose the words of William Blake, clung to them as if they were a plank floating on the ocean: "*Drive your cart and your plow over the bones of the dead.*" What's more, hadn't he read in some great Russian novel that you can kill and rob and, nevertheless, be happy? Where had he read that? And he repeated to himself over and over that he was a poet, above all and in spite of it all, and that no matter what, he was light years away from those pigs, I'm a poet, that's what I am, come what may.

And when he understood, yes, that Platter Ilyich was following him, a pure peal of laughter burst from him, ringing in the night. Platter heard laughter above his head, but he did not know who it was.

3

"Floridita, we're going to cover you in flour."

"But today's not January the sixth."

"We're going to flour you anyway."

They were on one side of the children's park. She did not know the three boys blocking her way. She could not remember them from anywhere but, somehow, they knew her name, and had said they were going to flour her—on the first of January, no less, when the carnival had not yet begun. She could not understand it: people painted their faces on the fifth, because it was Black Day, and they threw talc at each other's faces on the sixth, because it was White Day. Why were these boys all around her on the first? What's more, they did not even have the little bottles of scented talc she was familiar with, only grubby bags of flour. And they really were going to flour her, she thought, and if that flour went in her eyes she might go blind.

"If today was January the sixth, I would let you," she told them. "But it isn't. That's why you can't flour me either. Don't you know what day it is? It's Sunday, January the first."

Above Pasto's rooftops, crystal clear—pure, clear blue—the volcano Galeras rose up so close that it seemed to be listening.

Floridita walked off, and the three boys let her through, but they followed her, their hands in the tops of the open bags. She stopped again and faced them. The boys retreated, very slightly, not as she was hoping. She set off again, blushing, taking faster steps, and with faster steps the boys followed her. She checked there was no-one around who might help her. Then she confronted them one by one, her eyes glinting, lips compressed. For the first time in her life she had decided to go out of the house by herself, without her sister Luz de Luna, and this happened. For a moment she stood looking at the imposing silhouette of Galeras without really seeing it, and, when she did, it felt to her like it was coming down on top of them, that it would flatten them all; in the ruddy evening light it looked like a mountain of blood.

She set off. Her indifference cleared the way for her. But once more she heard:

"We're going to flour you, don't run away."

"Who's running?" she asked. And she paused again.

"Don't cry now, Floridita," the same boy said. Who was he? Did they know one another?

"Me, cry?" she asked, laughing, and her face immediately took on a scornful sneer: "Cry?"

Actually, yes. On the verge of it. And that boy had guessed it. She felt her legs trembling, but more than anything she felt unbounded rage that they might notice. What if they did flour her? With that flour in her hair, with it all over her face, how not to cry, she wondered.

And she broke into a run, heading further into the park. Her speedy dash left the boys standing; they were not expecting it; they thought she would give in, and they were wrong. Without thinking twice, they belted after Floridita. She had a good head start, but they managed to catch up with her by some tall eucalyptus trees; that is where they cornered her.

The boy who had spoken caught hold of her by the sleeve, at the same time as the others threw handfuls of flour—not just at Floridita, but at her captor.

"Not me, you idiots," he yelled.

They seemed submerged in a dense fog, in clouds of fog, it was the flour smacking against her hair, her face; she closed her eyes and felt one of the boys—the one who had spoken?—no, it was all the boys, all their hands lifting her dress up to her neck; now she felt great lashings of flour under her clothes like mild stings. She began to cry and only then did the boy who had spoken let go of her. The others stopped throwing flour.

She was already moving away when she was halted by a tremendous clatter of wings in the sky, like applause. She and the boys raised their eyes: above, gliding over their heads, a flock of carrier pigeons was surging up, like the tip of a spear, then wheeling down like a circle, in dizzying hieroglyphics; now the flock seemed to brush against their heads, and swam up into the sky again, vertically, ascending; suddenly, it hung motionless for a few seconds, and, in a whirl of distress, with no order whatsoever, the birds tore off to seek out their pigeon lofts, or any protective niche in the walls. And all because, at the very instant the pigeons fled, there was a harsh, hungry cry of a hawk not far off; the children spotted it—a fast-moving smudge in the sky—and soon they could make it out above them: its broad, blunt wings, predatory beak, yellow eyes scanning for prey. The instant it shrieked, the pigeons scattered, to any roof, any roost, and the hawk's cry cornered them again, terrifying them with its deadly raucousness. In a second, the sky was left empty of pigeons and the hawk kept on going, high in the sky, flying to the volcano; the volcano looked completely black now against the evening blue, a dark triangle silhouetted against the sky; the children remained looking at it as though it dazzled them; into the middle of its blackness the hawk vanished, swallowed up, just as the boy who had spoken appeared in Floridita's memory: he was the steward Seráfico's son, and those were his friends. What were they doing here? Shouldn't they be watching the sheep? It was Toño, little Toñito, the boy she always saw around without really seeing him: at her birthday party he followed her all over the place, but only now was she able to see him.

"Now I know who you are," she said, pointing at him. "You're Toño, Seráfico's son."

"She's recognized you," the other boys chorused, terrified. Toño turned pale. Floridita ran away from them. But her voice was vengeful:

"I'll get you back, you'll see."

Zulia Iscuandé saw her arrive home: she was a girl with the hair of an old woman, bright white, and she must have been floured all over because she ran along as if floating on white clouds. For some minutes Maestro Abril's wife had been on the doorstep, without making up her mind to ring the bell. She wanted to speak to Doctor Proceso. The girl's arrival brought her wavering to an end: when the door opened she would ask for the doctor.

Zulia Iscuandé took a step backwards; the girl, enveloped in the cloud of flour, which billowed around her at every step, not only pressed the bell without let-up, but gave the door a kick; the cloud got bigger, whiter still. Genoveva Sinfín opened the door. The girl went in like a wave, but when she heard her father being asked for she turned around, fuming.

"Papá isn't here," she shouted. "Doctor Donkey is never here."

And she disappeared.

"How odd, my dear Zulia: the girl has told the truth this time," Sinfín said. "Her father isn't here. But wait for him, come in and have a coffee, just in case."

The two women walked over the trail of flour Floridita had left, right through the house.

4

Doctor Justo Pastor Proceso López did not manage to get back home until January 4, in the early hours of the morning. Zulia Iscuandé was waiting for him at the front door, a persistent visitor for the past three days.

The doctor was returning from slaking a thirst that had lasted years: the widow had revived him. "You've turned me inside out, Chila," he said on parting, "now I believe in another world." They had entwined amorously in the most unexpected corners of the vast house—to occupy it, they said—and in truth they took the place apart with passion on a grand scale: upstairs and down, out the back, in every nook and cranny, on the roof terrace, with half of Pasto spying on them, including the secret poet.

They were seen dancing *bambucos* in the streets, their madness anticipating carnival, with no respect for the departed, witnesses said; they were seen glittered over with cold, right at the top of Las Lajas cathedral; and on the shores of Lake Cocha, eating pink trout with their fingers, drinking *aguardiente* from the bottle. They swam naked in the hot, green waters of Laguna Verde—they lost themselves there and were found—they went up and leaned fearlessly into the belching mouth of Galeras, and in just one day drove all the way to the ocean at Tumaco and back again. Nobody in Pasto could tell who was the drunker of the two, both of them going up and down the country in the Land Rover. That it never broke down, or crashed, was a miracle performed by Saint Aguardiente, witnesses said.

And they arranged to meet on Black Day, but they would never see each other again.

News of the doctor's adventures reached the ears of Primavera Pinzón—who could not and did not want to believe them. The pious Alcira Sarasti, Furibundo Pita's wife, heard about them too, and the thought nipped at her like a saucy pinch. Similarly, Zulia Iscuandé found out about his exploits: she had been laying siege to the doctor's house, waiting for him every morning for the past three days; she was after the deposit, an advance, at least, for the float, which was just about ready. She was worried that her doctor, so generous with words, might not be with money. And she was nearly right: Bolívar's carriage now mattered less to Doctor Justo Pastor Proceso López than reliving the memory of the widow Chila Chávez dancing naked *boleros* on her roof terrace—her face smeared with hand-spun local ice cream.

He had forgotten all about Bolívar, the carriage, the artisans, his pledge. For the first time in his life, all he was thinking about was the Black and White dance. If life was a vale of tears, as his grandparents had maintained, he did not want to live in it, and if life was a macabre circus enjoyed only by a few madmen—as they had also maintained—he intended to go mad for the years remaining to him, who knew how many there would be.

Impossible to imagine he had only three days left.

I couldn't care less about Bolívar, he said to himself: they make a god out of him, they go on making gods, I care only about my widow's honeypot.

But he was a man of his word, and that morning, when he recognized Zulia Iscuandé lying in wait for him at the door—Zulia Iscuandé no less, she who had said "Bolívar was a complete son of a bitch"—he acknowledged his recent past: he took her by the arm and led her into the consulting room and offered her a glass of sacramental wine.

"Don't worry," he said. "You'll have your money today."

Was he still drunk?

He seemed to be.

Zulia Iscuandé stayed waiting for him in the loneliness of the consulting room, while the doctor went out of his house and knocked on the door of his neighbour, Furibundo Pita, the only person in Pasto who could buy his *finca* outright, and pay for it that very day, the eve of carnival, in cash.

"Here you are, Doctor Justo," Furibundo Pita said, and held out a hessian bag containing the money.

He was in Furibundo's house, in his office with its high leather chairs. Furibundo was looking at him from behind his desk. They had already signed the sale papers.

"The bag is a gift," Furibundo went on. "You don't need to count the money. I already counted it the customary seven times. Now, if you don't mind me asking, what are you going to do with all that cash? Is there business on the boil? Any tasters going?"

"A lot of questions for a man in a hurry," the doctor said, getting to his feet.

He looked elated, with the bag over his shoulder. Taller, leaner, calmer. It was a stroke of luck that Furibundo Pita did not keep all his money in the bank; he had managed to sell the *finca* in the blink of an eye, the *finca* that had belonged to his grandparents and that by rights he should keep for his daughters, but all that mattered to him now was the joy of paying the artisans, his only joy, because he wasn't worried about his other delight, Bolívar's carriage.

"Doctor Justo," Furibundo Pita said, "I always knew I hadn't killed Maestro Abril: I knew it very well. But that old fool really deserved a drubbing, for poking fun. Don't throw away so much money on Bolívar's carriage; use your common sense: it would be money down the drain."

The doctor did not answer; now everyone in Pasto knew everything, he thought. He wanted to get out of the office as soon as possible, without staying for the coffee with little *achira* biscuits that Alcira Sarasti offered him, as soon as she heard of his unexpected visit:

"Another time, *señora*."

"What's the hurry, for goodness' sake?" she said. "Take it easy, it's not Innocents' Day and nobody's giving you poison. I baked these biscuits myself an hour ago." And she shook her head: "You've snubbed me."

"Never. I promise I'll see you on the sixth for White Day."

"If you can find me," the woman shot back.

That morning—in spite of her buttoned-up clothing, the veil for Mass on her head, her black lace blouse—the pious Sarasti struck the doctor as even more desirable than Chila Chávez. And he stole another look at the lace blouse, through which Sarasti's skin appeared, glowing like it was on fire; the doctor seemed to doubt his judgement, surprised at himself: "it must be because I'm seeing her with my heart for the first time," he said to himself, "and not as the idiotic doctor I've been up to now."

The pious Sarasti did not take her eyes off the walls. She clasped and unclasped her hands. Furibundo Pita picked up the conversation again:

"Does Primavera know anything about the sale?"

But the doctor could not hear him anymore; he had left.

And before Zulia Iscuandé's disbelieving eyes, he scattered the thick bundles over the consulting room's table: he counted out the money for the float and placed it on one side—three times the winner's prize money—then put it back in the bag. The rest he put away in his trouser pockets as best he could, like he was stuffing a guy for New Year's Eve—that's what Iscuandé said she thought of when she saw him doing it.

"Money," the doctor said. "Coffin and grave of the heart."

"Well if that's the case, my heart can die," Iscuandé replied.

They looked at one another without connecting: Doctor Proceso seemed not to hear her, and Zulia Iscuandé understood absolutely nothing. She had only gone there looking for the deposit, and she had received it all. And by the look of things, the doctor did not even want to know about the float.

"Don't you want to come and see it?" she asked, genuinely shocked. And she gripped the bag in her hands. "We've got it well hidden."

"Give my regards to the carriage," the doctor said oddly. "It can surprise me on January sixth. I'll be on some Pasto street corner waiting to see it."

That same January 4, Puelles was giving Enrique Quiroz his surveillance report, in the street, at the doors of the parish church.

From the corner they heard the combined voice of the crowd swell, cheering—the Carnavalito was being inaugurated for the first time, a preamble to the Black and White Carnival, a copy of the main event put on by children, with their little floats, marching bands and mini-parades: they wheeled their inventions along on bicycles and wagons. It was a procession of exalted little boys and girls: they sang while they danced; some carried *aguardiente* bottles full of lemonade, but stumbled about as they marched past, imitating the drunkenness of their elders in every detail; proud mothers applauded. A band of musicians went by, belting out the "Miranchurito." The secret poet strained to make out Quiroz's whispering, his rage interrupted by the celebration:

"So you haven't been able to track down the float."

"Hard to follow the doctor on this scooter," Puelles said, and pointed to the Vespa, battered and covered in mud, beside him. "The doctor went to Tumaco, to the Laguna Verde, up the volcano, he got to Las Lajas, and everywhere he went all he did was make love. This float you're on about doesn't exist."

"There's still time before tomorrow," Quiroz said. "Speak to the little doctor, make friends with him—you're smart, make him believe you think as he does, that you're on his side, and he'll tell you where the float's hidden. Meanwhile, we'll look for it on our own account too; we're all working to the same end, you know? We couldn't leave such a responsibility to you alone, you were never going to be up to the job on your own, we already knew that. Make friends with him, I tell you."

The poet got on the Vespa, he did not want to hear another word, far better to get away from the Carnavalito than have to swallow that lunatic's complaints. But suddenly he saw the lunatic right on top of him: it was as if the two of them were revealing their true colours for the first time. Quiroz confronted him, thrusting his face an inch away from him:

"This is serious stuff, Puelles. That little doctor is worse than the policeman. Do you understand me?"

Puelles did not.

And then he did not believe it.

It was as he supposed.

This isn't happening, he thought.

And then:

Not me.

"That doctor is a worthless bastard," he said. And now he could not hide his desperation. "But he's not worth a damn. The float is just a rumour. Think of the hassle—the doctor is an innocent little angel."

"He's poison, and the purest kind, the worst. An anti-Bolívarian, no less. An enemy of the people. Understand, chickenshit? This time we'll explain who we are, so there'll be no room for doubt. This time we'll leave our indelible signature. A new force is on the horizon. The future. Us. These people are my people, your people, our people. Are we going to defend them or not? Not one step back, not even to get a run-up—and down with the rich, dammit!"

Puelles nodded, as he switched on the Vespa and sped off without knowing where to go.

He fled.

*

He fled, zigzagging through the bodies lining the street, a row of blurs scattered in the Carnavalito: he saw two girls dressed in green, twins; a drunk man hugging a tree, talking to it; another drunk asleep on the pavement; three or four nuns holding hands—real nuns or fancy dress ones? And just then he spotted him: Doctor Justo Pastor Proceso López, his target—slouching, hands in pockets, tubby but tall, a huge black hat on, the kind an old hippie would wear—standing stock still. What was he staring at so attentively? The shuttered facade of Mandarina's big old townhouse, no less.

The secret poet shivered.

He braked and got off the scooter. And he joined the doctor, stood by his side, shared a silence for two—will he suspect me? No, it often happens during carnival that a random stranger follows your steps, Doctor, poor doctor, or rather happy doctor, as far as women were concerned. Even though it was only Carnavalito—Puelles thought— that parade of imps and monsters was just like the grown-up Black and White Carnival that was coming soon: the jaws were identical. A jubilant racket ran up and down the street: toy drums; goblins and clowns faced each other. The doctor turned his face towards him—no child's face could be more innocent or happy—and he drew a bottle of *aguardiente* from his pocket and deliberately poured half on the ground: the *aguardiente* seemed to boil on the paving stones.

"For the dead," he cried.

Puelles shivered again; such a greeting almost unhinged him.

"Here's to them," he answered.

The doctor held the bottle out to him; Puelles took a long swig. The doctor did not take his eyes off the townhouse:

"When will they open?"

"That house is a night-time business," the poet said.

"Well, love should be morning, noon and night, for the incurable. Now I'll have to wait." The doctor took back the bottle and looked at him attentively. "Would you like to have lunch with me?"

The poet Puelles stopped shivering.

The doctor's eyes scanned Mandarina's house again. He drank thirstily.

"The time will pass more quickly," he said.

They left the scooter safe in a garage, and did not have lunch: without agreeing it, without discovering who was leading who, they went from the illuminated street of the Carnavalito into a sort of subterranean labyrinth—like they jumped down into it—a bar near Mandarina's house, with neither name nor windows, just a metal door and a few steps resembling a descent into Hell, Puelles thought; they came out into a room half lit by ruddy candles, where music was pounding from rectangular black speakers hanging from the ceiling; in the space completely filled with bodies, shadows were dancing to "La Múcura" and singing along: a single voice, a single body, and one and the same sweat—the smell of hot, damp clothing—eyes like torches, hundreds of eyes glowing white in the gloom, because still further in there was no light, only that massed glow of eyesabove concealed bodies, linked together, sleeping bodies that danced.

And they walked in, feeling their way like blind men.

At the table they ordered *aguardiente.* Nearly all the tables were occupied by couples embracing, tightly clasped. What a place to talk, Puelles thought, but only if he was drinking could he talk to the doctor—*dare* to talk, he thought—and something similar might happen to the doctor: he might talk to his heart's content, even confirm once and for all that the float was a lie, and everyone would be happy. But what if the float exists? He said it out loud, as a waiter poured their *aguardiente*: "*What if the float exists?*"

"What did you say?" the unsuspecting doctor enquired from the other side of the table. With "La Múcura" blasting out it was hard to hear.

"Does the float exist or not?" the poet made up his mind to bellow, then drank the *aguardiente* down in one.

The doctor hesitated a moment. In the end he gave a shrug. He nodded silently—not as though responding, only as if talking to

himself—and drank his *aguardiente*, adjusted the ridiculous hat, put a
banknote on the table and stood up.

"Don't go, Doctor Proceso," Puelles held him back. "Doctor Justo
Pastor Proceso López. Sit down just for a minute, I have to tell you
something of interest to you. Afterwards you can go where you like. To
Mandarina's? I've had a visit pending too since I was fifteen, but listen
and the time will pass more quickly, as you want it to."

The doctor sat down again. Who was this ghost? Did he know him?
He had seen him somewhere before.

So they were going to kill him.

At least, that is what the kid shouted into his ear, in an exaggerated
whisper. What extraordinary news: according to the kid he should
make a "quick" visit to Mandarina's place, and then pack his bags
and skip the country "until it's all blown over," they don't call Pasto
Colombia's "Surprise City" for nothing.

"Are you having me on? You're making fun of me."

"No, Doctor, I'm not: Innocents' Day already came and went. I'm
just warning you, it's up to you. Remember the beating crazy Chivo
got? Who shook up Cangrejito Arbeláez, artist of the enemy? Now
things are going from bad to worse, Doctor, now they won't just do you
over, they'll send you to the other side. You'll see. Cheers."

"And all this over Bolívar's carriage?" the doctor puzzled. "Who
are you people?"

"We still don't know," Puelles said. Did he suddenly seem sad? "Or
they don't know," he said hurriedly. "I'm not with them anymore."

Doctor Proceso had another drink and remembered: this skinny
kid was the same one who had been reading outside his house, the
night of the thirty-first. So they had been following him since then.
He was a student—a pupil of Chivo's of course, one of those who had
kicked Chivo through the streets to the hospital—turned dissenter.
What was going on with the young? Not long ago Chivo himself had
told him they had "imported" a distinguished philosophy professor

from Italy; under his aegis, students not only started dressing in black and frowning like bitter old men, but many killed themselves and left suicide notes giving the same explanation: despair at existence, or something like that. Why were the kids bowing down? Why did they allow themselves to descend into idiocy? Because they were kids—he answered his own question—but these ones were different, faddish revolutionaries, and it seemed he was an enemy of the people, public enemy number one. What can I do?

"So my time's a bit tight for popping to Mandarina's?" he asked as a joke.

"You've got the time it takes a rooster with his hen," Puelles joked back. Quite a guy, this doctor—he thought—you have the courage to laugh, but you cannot imagine how serious the warning is, Doctor.

The music had changed: just as ear-splitting but, even so, they understood each other well enough as they drank outrageously. Puelles wanted to go to Mandarina's that very day, the day of the Carnavalito, when they opened—if they opened—and with or without the doctor— he wanted to visit that house as soon as possible—but the *why* of the doctor's visit piqued his curiosity: he knew of his wife, the famous Primavera Pinzón, eldest of the Pinzón girls, knew enough to dream about her, what a wild beast of a woman, what a magnificent drop of pure water:

"Why the hell do you need the whorehouse, Doctor?"

"I'm looking for a woman to take to a friend," the doctor said.

"A commendable service, *señor*. I'm just looking for my very first. Cheers."

From one moment to the next they found themselves walking through the streets of Pasto, far from the bar, how long had they been talking? Now it was night-time, minutes earlier Puelles had sat on the pavement to puke, now they were passing for the third time in front of Mandarina's "house of crossed legs," as Puelles put it. No doubt the girls aren't working during Carnavalito, the doctor said, they take their kids out to it too. Or they're in the procession themselves, Puelles said, and they went up steep narrow streets, they wanted to keep right on going till they got to the volcano, but their own talking stopped them on a corner, the doctor heard himself saying, from a people sunk in misery, with no industry, no hospitals, from a people without schools, without . . . from a . . . what can come of it? And Puelles's voice from somewhere: "They say revolution, *señor*." Yes, the doctor laughed in astonishment, but it lasts only a minute, because the people get drunk and go back to sleep, sleep for centuries, dream, as happened . . . when did it happen last? Even the dogs got drunk.

"Like us," Puelles said.

"What can come of it?" the doctor repeated.

"Dreams, you said it."

The last groups of children were dispersing now: kids with their costumes over their shoulders, almost asleep, some still singing, holding their parents' hands, others whistling, climbing trees, precariously balanced, rebellious birds, *we don't want to go home, it's Carnavalito*. Were they actually drunk? Very possibly, Rodolfo Puelles replied; the doctor said children were happy because they did not know about love. And above all they don't know about old age, the young Puelles added. They laughed over that for a minute, ludicrously, howling, choking, they could hardly manage to speak, saying in unison: "poor kids when they get old."

Another great swig steadied them.

A truck went by, full of young people protesting about the shoddy government, political slogans right in the middle of Carnavalito— against Yankee imperialism, against the bloodsucking oligarchy: "And the living and the dumb, kill them every one," they chorused, "And the donkey and the horse, one by one, of course." So the revolution comes from there, the doctor said. Did Puelles really believe in that? Revolution with those animals, no way, Puelles rebelled. Revolutionaries killing to left and right, the doctor went on, did you hear them? They included donkeys and horses on their list, with such a project in hand

I don't think they'll die in the attempt, they'll die old, still trying. I'm not involved in that anymore, Puelles said, exasperated. How to proclaim it to the four corners of the earth that he was a poet, that when he spoke, he was voicing his poetry? If I was up to it, I'd recite at the top of my voice all this humorous love that is springing from my pores, and sooner or later some girl would redeem me, he thought.

They were sitting very close together on one of the wooden benches in the children's park, a few blocks from the doctor's house, their clothes soggy with *aguardiente*; someone had stolen the doctor's hat—a hand stretching down from a balcony—Puelles's eyes were red, staring, as if he were hallucinating, his hands were shaking, they were each drinking from their own bottle; my problem, Puelles suddenly said as if renouncing life, isn't being alone, it's being with myself, Doctor, imagine a man who couldn't even be friend to a dog anymore. Want me to tell you something, *señor*? I've killed; do you realize what I just said? I'm a murderer; do you know what that means? It takes an enormous effort just for me to be with myself, and Puelles wondered if he was going to cry. Don't say that, the doctor said and tried to stand up, or are you going to murder me? Never—Puelles said in surprise—and the doctor countered: one death is enough? Better kill me off at once, don't keep me hanging about, and a shared fit of the giggles surfaced again, choking them, the doctor attempted to get up and did not manage it.

"I have to go home," he said, "Mandarina can wait till tomorrow."

"Doctor," Puelles asked, facing him, and clutching one of his arms, "why don't you leave Bolívar in peace? Put an end to this aggravation and everything will be alright." The doctor waved his hands about, drank:

"You can't leave the dead in peace if they won't leave the living in peace," he announced. "Well," he corrected himself, stunned, "I thought that once, now I don't know what I think. I'm at peace with the living and the dead: the, only, thing, I, want, is, to, love."

"Really?" Puelles said, reviving. "Go back to the merry widow? You're after fresh bread, how lovely she is, widows here are often almost girls, Doctor; pastures new for the old bull, eh?" Unlike the doctor, Puelles was able to get up and he opened his arms wide, flapped them, leapt up onto the bench, pulled himself erect—my freedom takes flight within me, he shouted without knowing why, still as a statue, the doctor sat looking up at him from below. Statues have mattered very little to me my whole life, but today I started to despise them; there are a great many statues in Pasto to pull down, we could do it—the doctor proposed excitedly—it always seemed outrageous to me that such a cretin of Liberty should have it his own way all these years, his great big lie rides through every village on horseback, every park, every town square, inside every brick—it should be buried in Pasto cemetery. What good does it do to broadcast that truth? I don't know, but I'm not going to stop my float from fulfilling its destiny: it is my hope, do you see? So—Puelles said, apropos of nothing, as if in response—you don't believe they torture our lot? Of course, the doctor said—it seemed they had been talking about torture for ages—and I'm sure, what's more, that you people torture the others, and torture comes and torture goes, and generations pass by. The doctor tried to get up again, a hand stopped him, he sat down—what was Professor Arcaín Chivo doing there? Since when?

So, Arcaín Chivo, emeritus educator, was sitting beside him, and his probable A-grade student was standing opposite them, swaying and listening, how much time had gone by? Am I imagining you, Chivo?— the doctor asked. You're not imagining me, Justo Pastor, I was passing by and stumbled upon you celebrating Carnavalito like any other child in the park, and you look happy, but I'm afraid I've got some bad news for you: it sometimes falls to us to be the bearers of bad tidings. Matías has left us—departed—our dear Matías Serrano died in his sleep, last night. What were you doing, Justo Pastor? We've looked all over Pasto for you. The doctor shrugged, as if it did not matter. Just from that, Professor Chivo was able to judge the extent of his drunkenness, he reproached him: And what'll we do when all our friends start dying, Justo Pastor, just shrug? The doctor shrugged again, but this time he spoke: We'll die too, what if we didn't? How would one go on living among strangers? The professor gave up, his eyes found the explanation in the empty bottles of *aguardiente* scattered around and the ghostly student swaying about listening to them, so he repeated his greeting: You look happy, Justo Pastor, and in the company of this disoriented soul, no less. Your name is Rodolfo Puelles, am I right? Thanks for reminding me, Puelles said, I needed the orientation, either I'm very young or you're very old. Don't mention it, Chivo replied, and became animated. Indignant? Well, yes, he said, the world is divided into young and old, would you like me to finish orienting you? I know very well who you are, you're one of Enrique Quiroz's merry band, am I right? More disoriented souls. What do you know about orientation? Puelles said, and spat. Chivo pounced: Would you like me to remind you of Kierkegaard?—he asked—disorientation ensues because one comes to speak highly of the opposite of what one would really like to, such as occurs when one moves abstractly within dialectic definitions, where not only does it happen that a person says one thing and refers to another, but one says the other: what one *thinks* one says, one does *not* say, but quite the opposite. Do you follow me? Do at least try to understand me, as you won't later. Oh, what a hassle it is to catch your drift—Puelles said—and the doctor added: Chivo my friend, you seem drunker than we are—he was trying in vain to stand up—did Matías really die in his sleep? What a very wise way to die—and once again he could not get up. Let me help you, I'll take you home, Chivo said. Leave him with me, I'll take him, Puelles said. Nobody need take me, I'll take myself—the doctor failed to get up—what was he dreaming about when he died? Either I get up or I'm done for, I must get back to the woman who doesn't love me, my wife.

"You're a good few bottles ahead of me," Chivo said. "I'm in the way here."

He left quickly, heading along the stone path. They no longer saw him; only his voice could be heard, in the night:

"See you tomorrow, Justo Pastor. It's Black Day, you'll have a sore head."

And, still shouting:

"Watch the company you keep."

Puelles and the doctor were hardly listening to one another anymore. Puelles was explaining to the doctor that death brought them together: it was death that was uniting them sooner or later, yes, Doctor, he repeated, if there's one thing bringing us together it's death, but were they talking about marriage or the deceased Matías Serrano? In marriage—the poet Puelles said, who had not known a woman—each partner thinks about the death of the other. I should say so—the doctor said—if you were to die, wife, I'd be the happiest man on earth, and then he did stand up, and he stayed that way with his index finger raised, in the pose of someone about to say something definitive— I wish you were my son, he said to Puelles in the end. Puelles burst out laughing: I don't wish you were my father; tomorrow or the day after I'd be an orphan. The doctor said he wanted to give him a hug, but he did not do it; Puelles did, he hugged him, you're a good bloke, he said, stressing each syllable as if telling off a surly child as he advised him: best fly to Singapore, stay there a century and only come back when the monsters disappear, you're like my granddad, another good bloke, he's stubborn, like you, the last thing we argued over was whether Pedro Infante had a purer voice than Javier Solís, a serious argument, two friends in Mexico settled it with pistols, my granddad said that to settle it in Colombia it would not be unusual for a grandfather to take it into his head to murder his grandson, funny, huh? One day he told me to take care: women's legs are actually scissors, you already know what it is they'll snip off, I really love that granddad of mine, I love you, what I'm telling you is a prophesy, I'm a seer, all I'm telling you is *get out*; and after he said that, the poet's face lit up with curiosity—as if a different Puelles was peeping out, the real one—Doctor, is it true you go to bed with all your patients? Now it was the doctor who burst out laughing: you're too skinny, you need to get more sleep, and he moved off towards the street—at last he could walk—Puelles stopped watching him: either I'm very young or he's very old, and he stayed on his feet, swaying about; if he sat back down on the bench, he would not get up again. He drank some more.

Alone. In the park. There was not even a passer-by to exchange a word with, a girl to offer this bouquet of words to, what great legs I saw today, what eager faces, what bums, and the day came back to him in flashes, events like a river passing before his eyes, fleeting voices, snapshots of fleeing girls with frightened faces, what did he say to them? Did he open his fly, did he show it to them? He had left Quiroz's Vespa in a Pasto garage. Which one? Tomorrow I'll go to Mandarina's place, Black Day is perfect for it, tomorrow Paris will burn when I paint my face black, maybe I'll bump into the doctor, happily surrounded by beauties. What else did we do for Carnavalito? We went past Santiago church, we drank a toast there, there the poet painted a sign in black on the white wall: *R.I.P, GOD*, and the doctor was not far behind: *GOD BLESS THIS BUSINESS*; he had his funny side, and they saw the little nuns go by, flirted with them, three or four nuns who did not kick up a fuss. Did we chase them? They're all wet between the legs, the doctor said, or was it him who said it? What a rotten memory: I've got gaps like black holes, I'll crash Quiroz's Vespa. Puelles's face clouded over: fuck, he cried in terror, why did we leave the bar? He suddenly remembered eyes like blue-black globes, Ilyich from Cali, his profile reminiscent of twisted wire, sitting on the next seat along, listening to them all that time, had he heard the denunciation? *Doctor they're going to kill you*, Ilyich had followed them into the furthest depths of the bar, Puelles greeted him with a wink, tried to explain: Enriquito ordered me to make friends with this good old doctor, let me introduce you, but Ilyich slipped away, without a word. Puelles let himself fall onto the grass, face up: "fuck," he roared, overhead the whole park grew dark, the lamps were switching off, fuck, he murmured something, and passed out, he looked like a corpse.

Doctor Justo Pastor Proceso still had one more Carnavalito surprise to go—other than the surprise of his imminent death, which he had already forgotten about.

The surprise revived him in the nick of time, because he was no longer finding it easy to walk: the devout Alcira Sarasti, who that very morning had offered him *achira* biscuits, was passing by—or was there, close to midnight, at his front door, waiting for him.

"This is sad, Doctor," he heard her say, "Arcángel won't come home tonight, he was seen very drunk at his new *finca* in Sandoná. Why did you sell it to him? He won't come home to sleep and I won't know what to do."

Neither will I, thought the doctor.

"Your wife and daughters aren't here," the pious woman continued, as if remarking on the day of the week. "They went to see street bands in El Tambo, with the servant and all. They told me they'd be back tomorrow, for Black Day."

Only then did Alcira Sarasti notice: he's completely drunk—and she wanted to go up the next street, run across the road to the other pavement, "all the men here go about drunk, they drink for one reason, they drink for another, Holy Mother of Mercy, Pasto is still sick and there's no cure," but it was already too late: the doctor stretched out a hand as if in greeting and pulled her to him hard and kissed her much harder still, crushing her. Then he just said "follow me" in her ear, and she did.

More than drunk, immoral—the pious woman thought, hearing him laugh; the doctor struggled to open the door, but when he managed it she went straight in, rather startled.

So they were going to kill him, the doctor remembered, and froze; he could remember it now he was inside, in the heart of his own home: some murderer might be lurking behind the walls. That fact shook him, waking him up, but the thought soon vanished; Primavera's absence grew more noticeable; so Primavera wasn't around, oh, how much her presence mattered to him—in spite of everything, he thought.

But he forgot about Primavera when he sensed, behind him, the perfumed shadow of the pious Sarasti silently encouraging him. She was a shadow aflame, burning the air, a red-hot apparition. He forgot his forthcoming death, forgot for ever that they were going to kill him and, amazed, observed the pious Sarasti in the pitch-black night: yes, he confirmed, the heat emanated from her, physically. He saw it as a sort of orange glow around her pale face. She had pressed her palms together as though praying, and her lips were moving in prayer, no doubt about it. What was she asking for? Strength? Protection? Which saint was she putting her faith in? The doctor saw light separate itself from the line of her stomach, another mouth, sinuous and floating. Or am I raving? The devout Sarasti was a living torch, levitating. "Not even modern science could explain you," he said. "What did you say?" the pious woman asked, but he was already dragging her by the hand, stumbling along. On the stairs, heading for the bed, the doctor tripped time and again, but the pious woman's hand appeared, to save him.

"Let us rest," she said, like a supplication. What a hallowed voice. She was praying. In the middle of the bed the doctor thought he could smell incense. She—the mystical voice—went on with utter sincerity: "I haven't experienced such excitement since my first communion; this is the first time I've been with a man other than my husband, and, I promise you, it is more terrible than the first time I was with him."

Doctor Proceso was struggling to pay attention to her, he did not know what had gone on or how, he did not remember. Before reality should hit him in the face it would be better to find another bottle of *aguardiente*, or reality will be worse, he thought. Was I rude with her in this bed? I threatened to nibble her biscuit, that's what he'd called it, and he'd nibbled away until he heard her cry out, and now he felt the devout woman's leg on top of his, rubbing it gratefully, he heard her

Mass-time voice, her voice of the Elevation. Dawn was not yet break-ing in the bedroom: Black Day was only lighting up the cracks in the window frames very slightly. One of the windows gave onto the gar-den, the other onto the street: the doctor did not know against which of the two Primavera Pinzón's face and silhouette were outlined.

Impossible, he thought.

"What a pair of rabbits," they heard. "You've been magnificent."

Yes, it was Primavera Pinzón's voice—like diamond because it seemed to cut through them in the gloom; a very different voice to Alcira Sarasti's sung Mass, a deep voice but deeply feminine, and in spite of that, a roar.

Neither of the two moved; they just listened, overwhelmed.

"I never imagined it," they heard, "such acrobatics, Doctor Don-key, what rubber doll bendiness, my God, what jumping, what jerking, what appetites, why did you never give me a bit of that?"

"Primavera," the doctor said.

"What?"

"We can talk later."

"Really? Painted black?" she asked.

Then:

"And in my own bed, with such a paragon of virtue: little Saint Alcira Sarasti."

The pious woman was heard to sob.

The doctor sat on the edge of the bed. In the incipient semi-dark he was casting about for Alcira Sarasti's clothes.

"There are no clothes," Primavera announced emphatically. "I threw them into the street."

Sarasti's exclamation of disbelief was audible.

"I threw out yours and your saint's," Primavera said.

The doctor wanted to look into her eyes: he made out her face with difficulty. Full of perversity, a woman possessed, he thought. And, nev-ertheless, inexplicably, he felt like laughing.

Primavera took a step towards him.

"If that Furibundo finds out," she said, "he'll leave no-one alive; aren't you worried? Are you very brave or very drunk?"

The voices of merrymakers leapt up from the street, quarrelsome cries. A rocket burst in the sky, its radiance lighting the room blue; the doctor discovered it was true: there was no clothing anywhere; bringing it in from the street would mean getting past the formidable obstacle of Primavera, in her white dressing gown—happy or unhappy?

"Now," the doctor said, getting up, "you'll have to lend her a dress, so she can leave."

Another sob from Sarasti.

Doctor Justo Pastor Proceso López, naked as found, and not trying to cover himself, went to the wide-open window. He leaned out and saw, by the light of the street lamps, Alcira Sarasti's clothes and his own scattered about; he even made out their shoes, here, there, upside down, on their sides, everything squalid and twisted like when there's a traffic accident, he thought, with fatalities.

He went up to Primavera, took her by the arm and, without effort, with just a hint of his anger, put her from the room. He closed the door.

"It doesn't end here," Primavera shouted from the other side.

Hearing her shout, the doctor realized she was drunk. He wondered whether his daughters were in the house, listening to it all. Furibundo Pita's wife was standing, waiting for him, covering her breasts with her hands.

"Has she really thrown out my clothes?" she asked in a thin voice.

"She may well have," the doctor said. "Pity she didn't throw herself out."

And he flung open the doors to the bedroom wardrobe.

"And dawn's already broken," the pious Sarasti moaned. And now she covered herself with the sheet, she was a frightened ghost. The doctor chose any old dress from a hanger.

"Not even my shoes are here," Alcira Sarasti said.

In her surprise, the sheet slipped off her body and she did not notice: her eyes were scanning the whole carpet. She knelt down and groped about under the bed; she did not care about bending over like a spectacle: the doctor positively applauded the fact.

"Put this on," he said, handing her the dress. "And don't worry, I'll come downstairs with you."

"What will they say at home?" the pious woman sobbed, "what will the maids think when they see me turn up in a different dress, and without shoes?"

"It's carnival," the doctor said.

Sarasti let out a deep sigh, as if she agreed.

"And in any case, pick up your things from the street, put your shoes on while you're there. See? No problem."

Sarasti finished dressing as well as she could, arranged her hair. She looked distressed, and was trembling so much the doctor felt sorry for her: after all, she was the only one who did not drink a single drop to relax; they had operated on her without anaesthetic. They opened the bedroom door: no-one. They went down the stairs; the doctor went first, naked, on the lookout for further surprises: Primavera might hurl herself at him, fingernails at his eyes, as had happened once before.

To Sarasti's relief, they found no sign of Primavera. Complete silence. But once at the front door they heard her sibylline voice anew:

"My clothes don't suit you, *señora*. You could hardly squeeze into my dress. In general, they say, thick calves mean a big bum."

"Primavera," the doctor said.

"And you, Doctor Donkey, you should see how you wobble along, with all that belly of yours. But no cow-fat mattress would have borne you better than she did."

"She's plump, but a real woman," the doctor said. It seemed incredible to him to be having such a conversation, and yet, it was true: there he was arguing over these details with two women. He gave way to laughter, albeit brief, bitter, like he was crying. And he concluded: "Every inch a woman."

"Watch out, little Alcira," Primavera went on, undaunted, "if your blessed husband sees you arriving without shoes he'll go into orbit."

"Oh, don't you worry," Alcira Sarasti said, startling them with her cathedral voice. "He's not there. He won't even notice. He doesn't want me, not like Doctor Justo Pastor wanted me here in his bed, God bless him."

And she left.

There they remained, frozen, looking into one another's eyes, Primavera Pinzón and her naked husband, the church voice still exerting its hold over them.

And the doctor had already embarked on his retreat to the consulting room, crossing the living room naked, when Primavera came towards him, tottering, bewildered, and knelt down, circling him with her arms, pressing her cheek to his sex, as if recognizing him for the first time. He put his hand on her hair and stroked it; she jumped as if she had been shot, leapt backwards:

"Don't touch me."

She really was drunk, worse than the widow Chila Chávez, worse than the student Puelles, worse than me, the doctor thought. He listened to her like he would a sleepwalker:

"Don't touch me. I only wanted to tease the hypocrite. To see how she cried, I bet she was praying. Did you hear how she said goodbye? You think it's funny? She pulled up her skirt at last, the holy little whore."

The doctor kept quiet. He still felt wrapped in his wife's ill-timed embrace. Primavera turned him upside down, pushed him to the point of insanity: he would never understand her, or only after death, he thought, when I kill her, if I kill her, best have another *aguardiente* and the sooner the better, go and sleep in the consulting room. Do I hate her? But what shamelessness, he thought—hating her—you come and humiliate me because of Sarasti, yet you open up your hidey-hole to generals and labourers even in your dreams; ah, but what a beautiful rosy bum you have, Primavera, after all is said and done any of your lovers would envy me, I worship you.

Primavera observed him, scrutinizing him; she did not manage to guess everything that was going through his mind. How could she?

It's very late for everything that might happen between us, the doctor carried on thinking: we'll never get back to what possibly never existed in the first place. But Mandarina would bring him back to life, this Black Day, black Mandarina would appear like the explanation of his life, a black solution, the blackest, and yet, a solution. No: the solution was in front of him, in Primavera's living flesh, he thought, in your eyes my darling, looking at me with love; he imagined her once more on her knees, embracing him, and now all he wanted was to fold her in his arms, do anything for a kiss, get her pregnant for the third time, multiply her; if they were both on board they would achieve it, he thought.

"Where did you leave the girls?" he asked as a show of concern, a truce.

"In their beds," she barked, and her voice descended into bitterness, "where they should be. I had to sleep with Floridita, your frightened daughter. Neither they nor I ever want to see you again, I want a divorce."

The doctor, who was coming to embrace her, stopped in his tracks; he pulled himself up to his full height; suddenly his face was stony, unfamiliar.

"It'll be after the sixth," he said.

Seeing him like that, as if teetering on the brink of rage, she thought he might take her by the arm again, open the front door, throw her out and close it. He was capable of it. Suddenly she thought he could kill her, above all he was capable of that, she believed she had discovered he actually wanted to kill her, and the dreadful thing about it all was that, right at that moment, sorry for everything she herself had done, she would have liked him to, she did not care, at the very least she would have liked him to throw her out on the street, pushing and shoving, so she could roar, laughing, "kill me if you want to," but suddenly she thought she would have preferred him to rape her, best of all would be if he raped her first and then killed her, but he would do nothing of the sort; when would you ever be capable of killing me, Doctor Donkey?— she wondered pityingly—pity for him, that he did not kill her, pity for herself that she wanted him to.

And she heard him say wearily:

"We're not going to spoil the carnival with a divorce. Nobody would take any notice of us anyway."

They looked at each other one last time before parting. But not as if sizing up their respective strengths: only with a sort of sadness; in the end, nothing they wished for had come to pass.

5

A dream woke him: he knew he was the only passenger on a train, and he knew it painfully, certain of his own loneliness. The landscape that flashed quickly past the window was lonely too: a single tree repeated itself ad infinitum on the horizon, the same tree bereft of leaves, dry, grey. But two more passengers arrived. Two passengers who blew his loneliness clean away with their impossible presence: he not only felt saved but freed from loneliness for ever. The passengers were a man and a woman, all in black, with black suitcases, and they sat down opposite him without saying anything; the woman's knees were almost touching his. The man had his eyes shut as if he had been sleeping for ages: despite the closed eyes he recognized his father's unmistakeable grey gaze, looking at him, and he discovered the woman at the man's side was his mother, also looking at him. And the limitless loneliness returned because he remembered at once they were both dead (in the dream and in real life). Astonished, he asked: "What are you doing here, if you're dead?" and his mother turned to face him, as natural as could be, almost as if she were congratulating him: "You are too."

*

He had not slept more than three hours; it was nine o'clock in the morning, Thursday, January 5, Black Day. He remembered his clothes had been thrown out of the window in the early hours of that day, but he also remembered his consulting room was a bedroom too, ever since things had started to go wrong in his marriage: he had bedclothes and pillows. He took a change of clothing from a drawer and got dressed, trying to make as much noise as possible to kill the lonely silence crushing him—and it was the same silence as in his dream. The consulting room's calendar clock sounded loud: the silence intensifying around its tick-tock. He touched his eight-day beard, and was grateful to hear Genoveva Sinfín's voice on the other side of the door:

"Doctor?"

He opened the door like it was his salvation.

"It's a miracle," Sinfín said, "that at this hour of the morning the poor of Pasto are sleeping, like you. They must have drunk from that river that turned into *aguardiente*, like you did. Here are your shoes and trousers, which I found in the street, Doctor; I was going out to buy salt for the corn parcels and what do I see, what can I be seeing? The doctor's shoes and trousers lying around, are those really the doctor's shoes and trousers? Yes they are, I've washed those trousers myself a thousand and one times, I know them like the back of my hand, there they were, Doctor, looking like a sleeping drunk, but they were your shoes and your trousers with the pockets well-filled, thank God I saw them first, no poor beggar came along, everyone already knows the rich have better luck than the poor, is that fair, Don Justo Pastor? Don't you think the time is coming to stop drinking? A nice shower would do you good, a vegetable broth, or do you fancy a roast guinea pig?"

She handed him the shoes and his trousers, the pockets bulging with banknotes.

"You don't just throw this stuff out the window, just like that," she went on, bitterly, and she left, before the doctor could reply.

The doctor put the money away again, into the trousers he had just put on. He pulled on his shoes, thinking that, far from calling a halt, he would have to drink more *aguardiente* if he wanted to get his head straight, to wake up, as he was not managing to emerge from his dream: he knew he was awake, but he was still suffering the same lone-liness—he just could not get out of his dream.

Genoveva Sinfín had not closed the consulting room door, which gave onto the living room. In the furthest corner, bathed in sunshine, little girls and bigger ones were painting their faces black. Standing around, dressed up as flowers, they were contemplating themselves in round hand mirrors, examining themselves with extraordinary attention, what were they looking at? He recognized his daughters, both rapt, in the midst of cousins and friends, the outlandish paper petals, the long quivering stamens did not hide them. What flowers were they dis-guised as? Now they all had black faces. Some of them had smeared their necks too, shoulders bare. The doctor was grateful for the crystal-clear voices, the garden of bright eyes, and the crowd of human flowers who freed him from the dream. Floridita was identifiable by her laugh, the tinkling but extravagant laughter that reminded him of Primavera: of Primavera herself there was not a whisper. What if I find her dressed as a flower?—he wondered.

Sinfín reappeared. She brought a tray of two steaming roast guinea pigs, which the doctor ate with his fingers, the way they should be eaten, and he polished off the whole lot, heads and all, but he ate standing up, entertained by the group of girls painting themselves; he did not want to sit at the table; he got Sinfín to pour him a glass of *aguardiente* and drank it—"to your health, Señora Genoveva Without Sin." She shook her head, disapprovingly. Sinfín always appeared where she had to, she saw and knew everything, she was an oracle, he thought. He asked her where he would find Primavera:

"She's having a shower now, Doctor. She had a cruel morning."

And then:

"That must be the reason she's going out, alone. She'll leave the house to celebrate Black Day, all on her own. The girls are staying here: it's their big flower party."

He headed for the stairs, followed by Sinfín at all times. He skirted the edge of the garden: not one of the flowers noticed him; Luz de Luna did not even glance at him out of the corner of her eye; she looked more beautiful black, he thought, her eyes were luminous. But didn't that flower appear to be sprouting a monster? Fur, tongue and fangs? Who thought up a carnivorous rose as a costume? Floridita, he discovered.

He got to their bedroom on the second floor, where water from the shower was hammering down in the en-suite bathroom. Hearing the water fall, he imagined Primavera's nakedness, vividly, as if she were before him. He trembled in spite of himself. Then he took the wads of notes from his pockets and scattered them over the bed. But he thought better of it and took one of the bundles back; he picked up another and gave it to Sinfín, who received it as though she had never been given it: she hid it in her bra and crossed herself.

They went down the stairs without hurrying, but it seemed like they were both running away. Only Sinfín's voice could be heard, sounding sympathetic, perhaps to occupy the doctor's mind with less solemn matters than Primavera:

"How lovely that carnival float you had made is, Doctor, but how sad too, eh? I saw it last night, they invited me over to see it, because I'm part of this household, your household. I know where they're hiding it, if you want to go by and correct any mistakes before the parade, they told me to tell you that your friends want you there, why don't you go along? You've got them all on tenterhooks waiting for you, go on, Doctor, go and have a look: a single one of Bolívar's hands is as big as the cathedral door; imagine the eyes like two wheels, they look up and down and shoot side to side, not just as if they're alive but crazy too, and they look at you like he's going to eat you up; what a tree stump of a nose, giant boots, giant spurs, the sword of a Goliath; they told me they had to take the whole head out through the roof, they had such trouble fixing it to the body, they say it weighs two tons altogether, there are loads of people working now to attach the carriage to the lorry, all will be well providing the engine works and Don Martín doesn't get drunk on us and instead of taking a turn around Pasto head off up the volcano and hurtle down inside with his Bolívar on his back. It's an absolutely immense Bolívar: his nose looks as though everything smells bad to him, lips as though he's about to curse, and how lovely and lively those girls are who pull him along, they look about to burst into song, that's how real they made them, Doctor, the smiles on their little mouths are very pretty, as gentle as kittens stretched out in the sun, but all those dead bodies around the edge, those unscreamed screams, that shower of blood, those hands tied up and so much pain, it scares you just to look at it. Was it true? Or did it only happen in a bad dream?"

"It happened in Pasto," the doctor said.

"Don't you want coffee? What do you want to do?"

"I'm going out."

"So it's true; don't you want to go see the carriage?"

"I'll go tomorrow."

And the doctor ventured out into Black Day.

He went along thinking about Black Day like the historian he was not: the celebration had been born out of jubilant amazement in 1607, when the slaves threw themselves into enjoying a "day off," the freedom of one day in the whole year granted by the Spanish king. In Pasto, this free day only got going in 1854: blacks went out to dance in the streets and their masters allowed them to come up and daub their white faces with charcoal, and the slaves must have done it with affectionate terror, or justifiably murderous intentions; but either way, certain that underneath it all they were still touching skin that was skin, with blood inside it just the same, the same shit from a different bum, he thought. The carnival began in 1926, always under that premise: one

day's freedom, its celebration; painting faces—hiding your face?—
hiding and becoming like everyone else; the silent one shouted, the
one who did not dance danced and the one who went without love
loved—exactly like me, he thought, in the thick of the crowd on a carnival corner; he did not need to paint his face: in less than a minute the
first revellers of the day painted him down to the neck, delighted to
take an unsuspecting fool with no paint on his cheeks by surprise, but
all the fool wanted was to be painted as soon as possible—Mandarina's
big yellow house was waiting for him ten steps away, open.

He went in without anyone noticing him. The rooms were small, dimly
lit, and unlike the streets of Pasto, which vibrated with light and whistles,
a smooth but despairing *bolero*—"Humo"—was all that could be heard
coming from the hidden speakers. Behind that *bolero*, the carnival faded
away: it had to be because of the eternal atmosphere holding sway in the
house—biblical, unassailable, be it carnival or Galeras erupting.

One girl after another appeared and disappeared.

He chose the table next to the staircase that the girls went up in
company, and came down later on, alone. Someone, a shadow, poured
him a double shot of *aguardiente*. There was a photograph on the wall,
above his table, a sepia shot, in a battered frame: Mandarina leapt out
of the picture in a long sequinned dress, smiling in the middle of a
group of happy men, obviously foreigners, explorers recently arrived
from the Amazon, hats and water bottles, boots and rifles, all raising
their glasses to the black woman's health. Beneath the photo he read:
*Mandarina opens her first establishment in Puerto Asís, Putumayo, 1916.
With her, from left to right: Wilson Fallón, Joel Schloss, Richard Cross,
James Reed, Hermann Price, David Dávoren, Alfred Wills and Félix
María Lindig, her most devoted admirers.* And the signatures of the
eight admirers lived on in the photograph, faded and looping, written
around the blades of a fan.

Not far away, on a carpeted dais, decorated with flowers, red curtains like a little theatre, a trio of musicians were smoking, sitting
down, their instruments lifeless between their knees. Old advertising

posters surrounded them: *FLANDES SWEETS, AMBALEMA CIGARS.* The doctor was grateful for a second drink: once again he could not see who served it. Around him there were dark red couches and mahogany tables, full-length mirrors, an upright piano, oil lamps, a clock with no hands; men drank in discreet corners, seated on leather chairs; girls, like shadows, waited standing up, leaning against the walls—and the student?—the doctor remembered, and looked around for Puelles: no Puelles anywhere.

Nothing had changed in that house since he had visited it for the first time: the whole place smelled of disinfectant. He needed to pee; in the entrance to the toilet he read the same notice that had frightened him as an adolescent: *BEWARE: HERE BE WITCHES.* But above the urinal he saw obscene drawings and posters that were new—one of them could very well have been written by any one of Chivo's students, he thought, or by Chivo himself: *Love constitutes the only universal principle of a complete synthesis.* Below that he read: *That's as good as saying love is the religion of humanity, arsehole.* Returning to his table he saw two men dressed up as monks, or two monks, fighting harmlessly in a corner; they were yanking each other around by their cassocks, shouting; one of them wanted to leave, the other did not. The first resigned himself to waiting "just a minute." The doctor sat down, and again a hand poured him more *aguardiente*, which he drank despondently. The three musicians were no longer smoking on the dais; the red curtains opened right up.

Mandarina emerged, dressed half in yellow, arms spread wide as if preparing to embrace the world. "Here you can only be happy," she cried, "there's no other way to be." Loud applause accompanied her words. What great strong teeth, they'll eat you alive, he thought, she's ageless, looks younger than me, she tended to me when I was a boy and yet she looks like a younger sister, it's impossible, but what a blazing woman.

"As you can see," Mandarina whispered, as if she were reading his thoughts and answering him, "I did not grow old: I went backwards," and with a tremendous shout: "The world ages around me, *señores*." Another burst of applause ensued. "Let every man seek out his other half," she cried, and disappeared as suddenly as she had appeared, into the cloud of pink smoke her girls were fanning towards her. The echo of her indomitable laughter remained, like a growl.

"You must do as she says," the doctor told himself.

"Whenever you like," a girl said at his side. At what point had she sat down with him? It was the woman who was pouring the *aguardiente*. All he could do was ask her name.

"Here, they call me Darkness," the girl said. "What will you get me to drink?"

She was all spirit: enormous liquid eyes, great violet shadows underneath, very fragile, but hands twice the size of the doctor's.

Then his attention was caught by the unusual names of the girls Mandarina was now calling, through a speaker, from the first floor, as if demanding they report in; she urged them to go up and do their duty.

"Density! Silence! Red Beard! Birdie! Poison Ivy! Baldy! Blame! Darkness!"

"That's me, as you may recall," the girl said.

But she sent a message with the girls going up to say she was sick.

"I'm a doctor, if I can be of any assistance."

"I'm not really sick. It's just that I know who's waiting for me up there, and I'm tired of that pig. He's got a thing like a donkey and I can't take it anymore; he really is an ass, more of a beast than any real one."

She was young, but the ravages of insomnia showed on her face.

"And you, *señor*, can I help you?"

"Not me, it's for a friend," the doctor said. The memory of Chila Chávez and the pious Alcira Sarasti, who were possibly waiting for him that Black Day, were a factor in his refusal, because he had been on the verge of taking her by the hand and leading her away, or letting her lead him away, until the last night of time.

And he explained to Darkness who Belencito Jojoa was.

"No kick left in him," she said. "He'll die on me."

She remained with her arms folded, deep in thought, assessing the picture the doctor was painting of Belencito Jojoa.

"Sick and old with it: impossible."

"Love works wonders," the doctor said.

"He must be a right bag of bones, or is he one of the fatties?"

"More the dried-up type."

"He'll crumble away to nothing."

"Don't be a pessimist."

"Fat or thin, I'd have to drive him."

"Drive him?"

"Hop aboard and steer."

The doctor imagined Belencito Jojoa receiving Darkness into his bed, his hands reaching out, and heard his voice, razor-sharp: "Drive me, drive me, kiss my soul."

"Grandpas cost double," Darkness went on, relentlessly, "it's more of an effort, though you wouldn't think so. It makes us think about death. Grubby old age. And, also, home visits are difficult, they're a risk, what if he's being nursed by Franciscan Sisters? That happened to me once before. And I don't know if Mandarina will let me out today, on Black Day, because tons of people are coming in with the carnival, not just men but women as well, who we lend beds to. Tricky, *señor.* You'd have to pay in pure gold."

"You will be paid in gold," the doctor said. "And you'll have to dress as a nurse, so they let us in. Me the doctor, you as the nurse."

"Costumes cost extra."

"But don't paint yourself black. Let him see you as you are."

Darkness made up her mind. "I'll go and speak to Mandarina. You wait for me outside, in the doorway. She'll tell me how much to charge you, and we can go. If Mandarina doesn't let me out, never mind, I'll escape: I was already keen to get away from this dump for ever."

"As you wish," the doctor said. And he went out of the house, into the confusion of the carnival.

A carnival troupe went by, and the revellers crushed in and around about: faces floated by, painted black—or black and white—there was a smell of bodies, alcohol, scented lotions. One of the merrymakers offered the doctor a cigarette, which he accepted. "So, are they worth it?" the man asked. The doctor nodded and the merrymaker went into Mandarina's townhouse.

He smoked with pleasure, streamers hung around his neck, confetti brightening up his eight-day beard with colour. They offered him *aguardiente* straight from the bottle, and he accepted. His face was painted, but even so, he thought, it was perfectly possible they recognized him; Pasto was a very small world: on any corner the whole population would find you. He imagined the faces the bishop and his learned friends would make if they discovered him right by the townhouse, as though about to go in or having recently come out. They'd be jealous, he thought, although the Wasp would excommunicate me anyway.

But what am I saying, he thought immediately, protect me, oh Matías, protect me, little brother of mine, wherever you are, whatever hell or paradise you're in, though I know very well you didn't believe in those places; you used to say: "The day you die you turn into a mosquito, and that's that."

None of his friends did surprise him that day. He never imagined who he would bump into.

"Well," Primavera said, "this is certainly a mistake."

She was dressed as an equestrian: black whip in hand, fitted jacket, her hair drawn back under a little round black cap. In her painted face her blue eyes distinguished her from the rest, as did her voice. Yes, it was Primavera; he was stunned. Her white riding outfit, blackened with handprints at her breasts and on her back, her bottom, gave a good idea of how much attention she had been paid that day, no doubt entirely to her liking, he thought. Her voice and the slight swaying of her body—she was speaking with her arms out as if preparing to fly away or as if already in flight—proclaimed her growing drunkenness, if she were not already completely inebriated:

"My Doctor Donkey emerges from a fine establishment, the most highly prized in Pasto, the most expensive, exclusive preserve of family men, civil servants and even undercover priests. In fact," Primavera carried on with her reprimand, but now her voice changed, became intimate, wistful, "one never stops admiring those girls, once I dreamed of joining them."

Her companions had already moved off: they were going along in a chain, men and women interspersed, holding on, one behind the other; at last they stopped to wait: they had guessed what the great mix-up was about and were enjoying it, furtively. Near to Primavera and the doctor, a nineteenth-century carriage, pulled by a mule bright with garlands, full of defiant girls as yet unpainted, was suddenly boarded by a mob of merrymakers: the shock absorbers creaked, springs popped one by one, the occupants of the carriage were thrown from side to side, and finally the excessive weight cracked the axles, which split, sending everyone crashing down, untold bodies on top, a heap underneath, tangling and untangling in dizzying fashion, so many arms and legs, so many faces slyly rubbing against each other like desperate kisses, greedy hands diving inside clothing, mouths and laughter and screaming, the whole street was erupting in howls, the mule collapsed, fell down in a dead faint, kicking out dangerously among the heads of girls and drunks, cries of panic rang out over cries of rejoicing. Primavera's companions, among whom General Aipe might very well be found—the doctor thought—ran to see the accident up-close. Primavera did not turn a hair: she stayed where she was.

"How was it, Doctor Donkey?" she asked.

"How was what?" the doctor asked. He genuinely did not understand her. They looked at one another closely, the same two enemies from that morning, confronting each other.

"With the girl, Doctor Donkey, or should I say *girls*? After shimmying about so nicely with that little saint, you're up to any miracle, aren't you?"

"What girl?"

Primavera burst out laughing.

"Oh," Doctor Proceso said, "the girl. I'm waiting for her, I'm going to present her to Belencito Jojoa."

Primavera Pinzón, who was already going back to her group of friends, stopped, frozen in her tracks. She turned to him, eyes glowing: surprise lit up her face, in spite of her having it blackened. It really was as though she had flushed, and the flush showed through in the astonishment in her voice:

"Can it be? You're finally taking Belencito his woman? What a great friend, what audacity, my hero."

She stood on tiptoe, briefly, up towards the doctor and, briefly, kissed him hard on the lips.

"Shall we go, Primavera?" her friends were calling. The people from the broken-down carriage had now got to their feet, bruised here and there, nothing major to report. Girls and drunks brushed off their clothing as if nothing had happened; even the mule came back to life: a bystander gave it *aguardiente* straight from the bottle; music and dancing took over again, playful shouting. But in the midst of the hubbub, there was a silence surrounding them.

"I'm staying here," Primavera said. "I'm staying with my lawfully wedded husband, as God requires."

No-one in the group objected. One behind the other, hanging on around the waist, playing choo-choos like children, they danced off again into the crowd.

Primavera dangled from the doctor's arm. He thought she was going to fall; he embraced her.

"We'll wait for your girl," he heard her say. Her voice sounded splendid: a happy ultimatum.

That very moment Darkness appeared in the doorway. She was carrying a small suitcase under her arm, no doubt containing the nurse costume, or was she leaving that dump for ever?

"How beautiful she is," Primavera said. "A real jungle flower for Belencito Jojoa, courtesy of his humble servant Doctor Donkey, my devoted husband."

Darkness could hear her. She approached them warily. She had to shake off a drunk who tried to anoint her cheek with the customary "lick of paint," and she did so with a shove, no hesitation about it: the drunk rolled about on the pavement, did not get up.

"Nobody paints me," Darkness yelled.

No-one else approached her.

And she stopped just inches from Primavera:

"Who's this?" she asked. "She seems drunk, or is she pretending? Is it a trick? Pay me right now, or I'm not going anywhere. Shall I tell you how much?"

"Pay her now, darling, just a little something," Primavera said. "Don't you see it's the most important thing to these girls? Pay her and let's go by ourselves, I'm going to replace her."

Without believing what he was hearing, the doctor held out various banknotes, which Darkness scorned: she shot a stream of green spit at Primavera's feet, and went back inside the townhouse.

So that was how Doctor Justo Pastor Proceso López and his wife Primavera Pinzón ended up alone again, in the street, towards the height of carnival. Neither of them seemed to remember the early hours of that morning now, with the pious Sarasti on board, the clothes in the street and the nakedness. Nor did Primavera mention the bundles of money found on the bed; another immediate future held theirs in abeyance: Belencito Jojoa lying in his bed, waiting—not expecting anything—for the carnival surprise they were preparing.

The doctor did not believe—or could not, or did not want to—that Primavera would go through with standing in for Darkness. But he started to believe it, watching her walk along at his side with the air of a determined teenager; then he desired her: surely he desired her for that very reason. What must be will be, he thought, although it'd be best to walk about a bit so she can think better of it—that is, if you do happen to think about it, Primavera.

It was getting dark, and the sun, which until that moment had been lighting up the most intimate workings of the celebration, its nooks and crannies, its guts, now lay swallowed up by storm clouds; a foggy sky smudged the horizon, was it going to rain? Primavera did not say a word. The doctor waited. They moved away from Nariño Square, which bubbled with revellers, and continued their walk blindly, without destination: she believed, or seemed to believe, they were going to Belencito's house, and he did nothing to dissuade her. They heard a fleeting conversation between two old men: "That bloke got bumped off ages ago," "Well, that's what happens if you go after married women." She seized his arm: "Let's have another drink," and they went into one of those improvised tents at the edge of the carnival where, apart from dancing to the *son* played for them, carnival-goers ate and recovered, returned to the game or were ruined for ever. There they got carried away by the Ronda Lírica; listening with mounting excitement to their "Sonsureño," "Agualongo," "Sandoná" and "Cachirí." The band members of the Lírica were vibrating along with the flutes and violins: they finished off with "La Guaneña." At the first notes, Primavera jumped up to dance in the heart of the crowd: she leapt like a deer, pulled off her jacket, got rid of the cap, her hair tumbling down rebelliously, she spun around like she was floating and carried on dancing madly, jumping and whirling, in wild spirals, breasts swinging, occasionally accompanied by other frenzied dancers: very soon they encircled her, applauding, while the doctor observed her, fascinated. "La Guaneña" finished and she came back triumphant, like a flame, splendid, teasing; "I'm exhausted," she said, but she did not seem so.

They bought more *aguardiente*—a bottle for us and another for Belencito—and carried on drifting through Pasto's carnival-filled neighbourhoods. The floats being created for January 6 remained hidden behind high walls, who knew which ones, awaiting the next day's parade. The doctor was still wondering whether his float might be nearby—it was possible, why not? How about a happy coincidence and finding the float's hiding place while he was with Primavera? Seeing the float with Primavera would be more thrilling than any frantic dance in the street, among a crowd of crazed revellers. Where in Pasto was his float installed? In which house, shed, patio or garage? Tomorrow was the hour of hours, the parade. Oh, Tulio Abril, Martín Umbría, Cangrejito Arbeláez and the rest of the artisans were not going to be slow in coming forward, they would make Bolívar's carriage count in their own fine way, warn of his dreadful legacy, they would not be scared off. The doctor did not worry that the artisans might end on bad terms with him: they were not going to end on bad terms with themselves, he shouted inwardly, they would face any consequences, in spite of Governor Cántaro, his General Aipe and the fanatics.

He repeated this to himself, following along behind Primavera, who was on her own, several feet ahead of him in the never-ending encounter with bodies flowing towards them, like a river. He caught up. Put his arms around her. They kissed there for an instant that felt like a century: no dark thing, no ill-omened thing had ever happened between the two of them; no widow, no general, no pious woman, no strapping youth, they had two daughters, my God.

The streets let them pass, respectfully.

But the carnival would not be long in shaking them up, snatching them from one ecstasy, or pushing them towards another, more extreme. In Pandiaco, they saw a man peeing under a tree, terribly intoxicated, with terrible timing; it was too late to avoid him; the man had to be drunk, he was swaying about; in fact, he was peeing on a woman stretched out on the grass, face up—drunker than the drunk who was urinating on her, the woman laughed dully, *shower me, tomcat, poison me.*

They kissed; it was as if everything was determined to push them together, entwine them, in spite of the squalor.

At the top of a street in the Tejar neighbourhood, people were crowding around: a huge ox, reddish in colour, too placid—had they got it drunk?—was being shown off by two proud little boys; a fluorescent fabric mask hung from its horns, over its face, the face of a lewd demon, tongue licking its lips; they had tied a tin trident with tinkling bells to the ox's tail. There in that street, captivated by Primavera's beauty, and with the ox in the background—like an idol looking on—three drunks knelt before her, their hands raised as if praying, each one giving his name and profession: "Paquito Insuasti, slaughterman," "Hortencio Villareal, saddler," "And I'm Rafico Recalde, goldsmith, we all die at your feet, blessed Virgin." The doctor was amazed that Primavera went along with her worshippers: she gave each of them a resounding kiss on the lips, and for each kiss the people cheered and the drums redoubled; Primavera did not stop there: she raised the ox's mask and kissed it on the snout; then music seemed to rain down from the skies and men and children and women threw themselves into dancing, with the ox in the middle. For the first time in years, Doctor Proceso—who boasted of never dancing—danced with Primavera until they had both had more than enough. The exercise saved them from the *aguardiente* they drank, as did all the spicy *empanadas* they ate.

So they danced on through many Pasto neighbourhoods: they were seen in El Churo and La Panadería, in San Andrés and San Ignacio and San Felipe, in El Niño Jesús de Praga, in Maridíaz, in Palermo and Morasurco. Up at Dos Puentes, when they were resting, sitting on a wall, heads together, holding hands, the carnival called for them again in the shape of a man who went by with his dog, tied to a rope. Primavera silently mocked the fact that both man and dog wore ridiculous black capes, and above all she smirked because the man talked to his dog, which seemed all ears and followed him along. He was talking to his dog for all the world to hear: "You know very well that I told her so,

I warned her, you heard me say it, you know I told her, I warned her, dear God let her not be dead, I pray to the Holy Souls in Purgatory, and if she is dead, don't you worry, she'll only be pretending, don't you pay her any attention, not when she opens the door, or when she comes to greet us, or when we find out she's not playing dead, oh, Holy Souls."

At this, Primavera lost her self-control:

"He's killed her," she said, retching.

"It's just an actor teasing us," the doctor said. He would never have imagined Primavera's reaction, fighting nausea, bent over the wall. But she was soon sound asleep for a long time in the doctor's arms—and he succumbed to sleep too, as night fell, to the beating of drums near and far, the carnivalesque *thump-thump*, deep, like an omnipresent heart.

The first drops of rain woke them. They drank a toast with more *aguardiente*, and then another.

Only in Mijitayo did they witness the finishing touches being put to a carnival float: although it was already night-time, the craftsmen were still working by the light of a string of lightbulbs. The gentle but steady rain was pattering on the zinc roofs. The tall garage doors, thrown wide open, allowed the curious to get a proper look at the float: at night, in the rain, it seemed all the more wondrous; it was a condor brought to life, on the highest nest in the Andes, and it stretched out its colossal wings as if it had just landed; in its claws lay a huge bull, black all over, in its death throes, bloodshot eyes imploring, mouth agape. Between its hooves was a sentence in Gothic script that the doctor did not have time to read. "Why aren't we going to Belencito's?" Primavera asked, impatiently, clutching his arm.

Ha made up his mind. "That is where we're going."

And they headed off there, by the half-light of the carnival. The last revellers were still up and about, the occasional *viva!* and other cries rang out; the crowd went up or down the puddled streets, on their way home. The pavements were littered with curled-up drunks, asleep or awake, who grunted at their passing. They went up through Santiago, adjacent to the Obrero neighbourhood, and the rain got heavier.

There was a spasm across the city: suddenly the electricity was cut off; people were using candles and kerosene lamps for light. In windows, candle flames guttered "like ghosts' eyes," Primavera said—her breath smelled of *aguardiente*, her speech was slurred—over-excited, my poor Primavera, the doctor thought, you want and fear what is to come. In Obrero, with its muddy streets, he pointed out Belencito Jojoa's house to Primavera from a dark street corner. Would she go? Would she dare?

"Let's get on with it," was all she said by way of an answer. And her impatience made the doctor uneasy.

But an instant after they knocked on the door, he saw her leap like a panther into the shadows of the front garden, far away from the candle lighting up the porch, she did not want them to see her.

I wasn't expecting that, Primavera, he thought.

"Belencito has just left us," Doña Benigna Villota announced solemnly from the doorway.

She held a candlestick beneath her face. Other yellow faces, of old, inquisitive women, accompanied her.

The doctor did not understand. He was going to ask where Belencito had gone to—thinking he might actually have gone off somewhere, like in his heyday—when the penny dropped. He understood it more fully when he heard Primavera's laughter from somewhere in the garden surrounding the house: she was laughing from nerves, but laughing, nonetheless, like at the circus.

"If you would like to, Doctor," Villota said, "come in and pray with us for our Belencito's soul. Fancy, he always did things his own way: now, for example, it occurred to him to go and die right in the middle of carnival, he made it hard on us, you can hardly find a priest, they're all off duty, but we got one, and now when Belencito's just passed away and we're starting his vigil, there's a power cut, isn't that another of Belencito's bright ideas? Maybe. Does Belencito want to tell us something? Maybe that too. Thank God that Father Bunch has the patience of Job, we'll begin in a minute, there'll be a lot of rosaries said tonight for the soul of a sinner: a great sinner, it's true, but one we loved and love still. All his children are here, that's what he left behind him, children and grandchildren by the dozen, who will follow his example, God willing."

And Benigna Villota's face disappeared, followed by the rest of the old women, silent, judgemental.

They had left the door open.

All this, which Primavera heard from behind the Capulin cherry tree, exactly in line with the half-illuminated window, inside which the vigil was taking place for Belencito Jojoa, gave her a fit of the giggles; so that they should not hear her, she covered her mouth with her hand, one knee on the ground, shaking like a woman possessed, among flowerpots and clumps of mint. She was, without knowing it, right beside the deceased's bedroom, lost in the insanity of her laughter, outside the room that must contain Father Bunch, the old women and the children and grandchildren; from the hazy window seemed to spring a silence that smelled of tallow; shadows passed back and forth. The doctor went there looking for her, underneath that window: he found her with her back to him, her knee on the ground, still in the grip of the muffled laugh that was making her curl up. And he seized her by the shoulders, he did not know whether from delight or exasperation, still not knowing what he was going to do, *what was he going to do with her?* Finally kill her?—he yelled to himself. Strangle her? Kiss her till he left bite marks? Bite her till she bled? Laugh with her? Laugh more, maddened, without end? Primavera's messy hair, the nape of her neck, the sort of perfume of sweated *aguardiente* on air redolent with mint disturbed him: "The man you wanted to make happy is dead," he said in her ear, she turned her head, her mouth open from laughing, her lips wet with rain, and he kissed her at last.

"So, Primavera, was this what we wanted?"

She was choking from laughing so much; she lowered her other knee to the ground and stayed on all fours in the garden, riotous with flowers; she was going to get up but he stopped her; effortlessly he slid Primavera's breeches down to the back of her knees:

"And let the whole world see your marvellous rear, eh?" And he gave it a resounding smack.

"What . . . ?" Primavera twisted around.

"Shout louder so everyone can hear," he yelled.

"What are you doing?" she cried.

The rain got heavier.

"So this was my fate?" the doctor said in her ear. "To have to subvert the order of things with my wife?" She said yes, after a rain-filled silence that unhinged them, arching her back beneath him, as he found her: from pure longing they fell on one side, he did not let go, and that was when Primavera looked up to the candlelit window, her eyes looked without seeing, transported, but she finally saw the faces of the children looking at them from behind a terrified silence. She was taken by surprise, but in the middle of her own apocalypse it no longer mattered to her, she did nothing, she could not. Let the children see her, she resigned herself happily, and said, without knowing what she was saying: "We could start again, a new life."

"Right now," he said.

"Until we die?"

"Until we burst."

"I like bursting best," Primavera said, and sought out the window again: more faces of astonished children. Witnesses.

The rain fell hot upon them, another body on top of their own; Primavera did not come back from her cataclysm; "kill me and get it over with"—her voice echoed in the downpour.

"Is that what you want?" he growled.

She slipped, face down in the wet grass, she thought she was falling from atop a speeding horse, she slipped down like a happy prayer, "my murderer," she said, and recalled the stallion she saw as a child covering the big yellow mare with lather and vigour, but a shriek that sounded like a bird returned her to reality from her calamity: there was the face of an old woman crossing herself in alarm, inside the window, where not long before there were only children.

Other women's faces were screaming behind the first, and other yellow faces took turns to look, all of them gathered together at the window. One of the old women rapped on the glass with her knuckles as though she wanted to break it.

The instant she heard them, Primavera was fully dressed once more.

The doctor, bewildered, heard shouting in the rain, without understanding it. In a second he saw that shadows of old women in mourning passed in front of him; they ran after Primavera, and ran on; among the most zealous was Benigna Villota, the one who hurled most insults, burning with rage, but the lithe panther had already bounded over the little wall surrounding the front garden.

Down that lonely street the old women ran in pursuit of Primavera; "whore bitch sinner," they shouted, "a thousand times profane, grab her, do her in."

It was the doctor's last sight of Primavera: she ran gracefully down the street full of yellow candles, sending her most inebriated peal of laughter heavenward, in the rain. Very soon she left the irate women far behind her.

The doctor took the street going in the opposite direction, feeling happy, completely happy: he was thinking about finding Primavera at home, in order to start living, all over again.

6

He thought it was getting dark, but it was dawn: a thin tracing of mist still eddied around the corner where the secret poet Rodolfo Puelles stood wondering whether it was getting dark or light. And just as he was hesitating, at that cold early morning hour of January 6, on that unfamiliar corner, he saw the ghostly Carriage of the Afterlife hurtling downhill from the streets furthest up—the one they say everyone sees, dreaming or otherwise—he saw it go by like a swirl of dust, cutting a great furrow through the mist, creaking and dark, full of witches from Sapuyes, El Loco and the Devil-in-Disguise, the Beggar, old man Carta-brava, the Mule Woman, the Faerie and weeping Turumama, crowded with all the monsters and ideas of this life and the next, he saw it turn corners without braking, carrying in its teeth the sorrows and ills of the body, as they say that at its passing all grow young, things and people, and even the dead cheer its fleeting appearance: there they go, there go the Spirits, Old Bombo, the Headless Priest, the Screamer, club-footed Tunda, the Taitapuro bonfire dummies, the Snoring Pig, the Mater Dolorosa, there we go: cheers!—Puelles greeted them, stretching out his arm with its empty bottle, but he heard no carnival whistles, no out-burst of astonished voices, nor the invisible heart of the drums. If the world is sleeping—he realized—it's because it is getting light, the celebration of the sixth has barely dawned, I haven't missed it, my blood is tickling me, and he threw the empty bottle against a tree, which received it, stretching out one of its branches; that is what he saw.

Puelles was not drunk: he was stunned.

The day before, at midday on January 5, in the midst of the carnival hullabaloo, he had taken the Vespa to Enrique Quiroz's house, and not found him at home: he was out having fun on Black Day, no-one was there, except his *servants*—he thought—maids and ranch hands from his estates who were not celebrating Black Day because they had to work. He left the Vespa with them, and a note written while drunk: *Rodolfo Puelles says goodbye. Don't count on Puelles for a thing.*

He would never know whether the servants delivered the note, but it was Enrique Quiroz who found him, hours later—or they found each other, somewhere neither of them had dreamed of: church.

A church open at the height of carnival—Puelles had thought, peering in. He was on his way from Mandarina's townhouse, but the open church on Black Day intrigued him. Not even an echo—no-one there? From the furthest reaches of the altar, Father Hoyos headed for the confessional, and shut himself in, what was Father Hoyos doing in this church? What was he doing shutting himself in the confession box? Whose confession was he planning to hear? Mine, he shouted to himself. And he moved towards the confessional, thinking: how did he find out? And the fact was that it had been a century—starting the day before, on the fourth, on Carnavalito—since the secret poet Rodolfo Puelles had remembered the man buying milk on the corner, the dead man, and the open church brought him right back, unassailably: *his dead man.* Father Hoyos had been his religious studies teacher when he was a boy, gave him the sacred host the day of his First Communion, heard his confession, why not confess again? A Jesuit priest had placed himself in his path to hear it—ah, he thought, he would say: "Father, save me from myself." He had tried to share the burden of the policeman with Doctor Proceso, and yet the doctor had not heard him, or maybe he had; he'd listened too closely and said: "If you're going to kill me get on with it, don't keep me hanging about."

Rodolfo Puelles set off resolutely for the confession box. He would say to Father Hoyos: "Forgive me Father, for I have sinned in not coming to Mass for years," and the priest would say to him: "You haven't come to confess that." And he would respond: "You already know what I would like to confess." And the father: "Everybody knows. Now God needs to."

"What are you going over there for, what are you up to?" came the urgent voice of Enrique Quiroz.

Enrique Quiroz was in the middle of one of the church pews, and he was praying on his knees. Praying? The church was not empty: Quiroz was there praying, on his knees. The puzzled Puelles saw Quiroz getting to his feet, summoning him with a look. And they left the church in complete silence, one behind the other.

Outside it no longer seemed like carnival: the meeting with Quiroz or Enriquito or Vladimir cast a shadow over the day and throttled joy—the secret poet thought—the sun hid itself, it was going to rain, how tedious, what a bore, how annoying that idiot is, and yet I obey him, why hold myself in such low regard? I could knock him down if I wanted to, I'm more than he is, practicing what he only preaches, I've already shown that.

Silent in the midst of the uproar, one behind the other at all times, they arrived at the parish church of Nuestro Señor de los Despojos, where they found Platter Ilyich and three strangers. Who were they? He had never seen them before, not in Pasto, not in Bogotá, and they were old fogies, he thought, about forty, in boiler suits, not in a party mood at all: they were unamused by the carnival, rather grim-faced, they did not look him in the eye when he greeted them. There were people from the neighbourhood celebrating Black Day in the corridors of the church, with the consent of Father Bunch—who must be tucked away in some nook surrounded by young men—but the secret poet Rodolfo Puelles did not share their feelings, it seemed to him that the happy faces and shouting accentuated his immeasurable sorrow, which was the same sorrow that ran through the parish and the whole world, all around.

Platter and the three strangers were in the most sacred corner of the parish church of Nuestro Señor de los Despojos, no less, behind the altar, near the sacristy door, and grouped around what looked like a carnival donkey. Puelles gathered that they were getting it ready for January 6. Two people would operate it: one at the front—arms pushed down inside the hollow forelegs, each one extended with a wooden stick like a cudgel, head and shoulders occupying the huge donkey head—and the other man behind, his own limbs down inside the hind legs, or cudgels, his back bent over, his body becoming the animal's rear end—he'll have a job to dance, Puelles thought.

The splendid disguise concealed them: the multicoloured flaps at the sides which brushed their shoes, the thick rope tail and the great head of a fairy-tale ass; Quiroz was at the front—he showed himself now—Platter at the back. When did they get into it? And they operated the legs like they belonged to a donkey gone berserk, banging into things, lurching from left to right, around in circles, zigzags, suddenly they launched themselves at the wall and pounded away, kicking: bits of pulverized brick went flying, so great was the rage they attacked with. Platter and Vladimir, draped with the magnificent covering, donkey tail swishing, donkey head laughing, took a turn around the altar, knelt before the cross, piously, and carried on trotting around deliberately. They galloped, pawed the ground, brayed. They are going to sweat buckets in there, Puelles thought: it was a donkey in all its dumbness, decorated with coloured cloth, stuffed with hay and hemp, and with four lethal wooden hooves, yet a genuine-looking donkey for all that, no-one would know whether it was real or pretend, all in all a donkey, the one that would kick Doctor Proceso, finally killing him with an almighty blow, the very next day—he thought—January 6, if they don't find him today, on the fifth.

Quiroz emerged from the donkey, and then Platter.

"I'm off to look for the swine," Platter said.

Puelles felt crushed: it was as if they held him responsible.

Platter Ilyich dried his sweaty hands on his knees; his face was painted black, but the orbs of his different-coloured eyes shone very white; he did not seek Puelles out on leaving, as though Puelles did not deserve the attention. He said goodbye only to Quiroz.

And Enrique Quiroz said to him, like an ultimatum:

"You will bring him to me."

The three strangers set about measuring and weighing up the donkey, going over it—Puelles thought—inside and out, worse than a gun.

"This donkey's for tomorrow, in case we don't find him today," Quiroz said. "We'll give him a good kicking, in disguise. Don't be scared, Puelles, don't say a word against us, we're not going to hassle your friend, although we ought to kill a sonofabitch from time to time for them to take us seriously, eh? But Ilyich will soon find him. The swine will come. We'll reason with him. He'll tell us where to go to destroy the float, and all will be well. And if Ilyich doesn't find him, better still: I will find him tomorrow. And let the float go out on parade, we'll blow it up on sight. I've even started to think it would be sweeter that way."

Just hearing him talk frightened Puelles: the crazy plan was true. Some Black Day this was: that morning he had woken up outdoors, in a corner of the children's park; at midday he had left a drunken note at Quiroz's house—fatal in its recklessness—but he never imagined this nightmare: him, in the church, witnessing the creation of the lethal donkey, what a black day, he thought, and devoted himself to listening to Quiroz's reasoning, without understanding it; the pale mouth moved before him, no sound came out, and Puelles nodded, Quiroz never blinks, he thought; one of the strangers asked where the urinals

were, I need a pee—me too, Puelles said, and led him to the toilets, but
did not go in, he left, fled the parish church, managed it. He got away.

He would make one last effort for the doctor, the definitive warning,
his charitable deed for Black Day. Am I really worried? It's his funeral.
And he set off for the doctor's house when it was already getting dark.
He did not find him, just as he would not find anyone this carnival
day. There was a "flower party" at the doctor's house, according to
the old cook who came to the door. Behind her he could make out the
mob of dressed-up children—not just flowers, but creepers, oaks and
myrtles—their faces painted. There were still *mamás* in Pasto who preferred their children not to go outside to play on Black Day, but to celebrate indoors, prisoners of security, he thought. He was about to leave,
wondering where he would find the doctor—possibly at Chivo's house
or the house of the seduced widow. He would try to warn him, his good
deed for January 5. Then he would migrate to his own home, to drink
and listen to the Ronda Lírica record with his grandfather.

"And I'll have a rest," he thought.

"The youngster doesn't look as though he's had lunch," Sinfín then
launched in. "Why do you drink? So you won't feel afraid? Wouldn't
you rather have some sweet pumpkin *empanadillas*? There's pork and
plantain soup and corn parcels. If you don't mind me saying so, you
look like a ghost. What is it with the youth of today that they don't eat?
They'll never drink like men at this rate."

Just then another guest arrived at the doctor's house—he must be
the last child to come to the party, the late one, Puelles thought. He had
a headdress on, a sort of crown of banana leaves. A *campesino* brought
him: it was old Seráfico, steward at the *finca* in Sandoná, with Toño, his
youngest. He brought him himself, amazed that his son should have
been invited to a party at the doctor's house.

Floridita came out to greet the guest. Beneath her disguise as a carnivorous plant, with teeth and fangs sprouting from the petals, her
hard, silent smile glittered:

"We'll bring him back to the *finca* tomorrow," she said to the steward, without more ado.

It seemed to Puelles that the recently arrived child was sweating in terror. What a shy boy, he thought. Behind them, the clamour of the other children rose to fever pitch. Floridita seized Toño's hand and led him away into the uproar, for ever.

Genoveva Sinfín repeated the invitation to the poet and the steward. Neither accepted: Puelles promised he would come back later, and Seráfico got on his high horse—as the doctor had sold the *finca* in Sandoná, he had no right to eat in his house, he said.

"Don't be silly," Sinfín told him. "Eat. There's more than enough food here, and it's a long way to Sandoná."

The steward went out into the teeming carnival without answering and disappeared.

Professor Arcaín Chivo was not at home either. Puelles found it amusing that he did not understand the Latin that presided over the professor's door, a wooden sign that read: *ALTERIUS NON SIT QUI SUUS ESSE POTEST*.

"It's spelled out right there," he thought, "another lost soul."

No-one came to the door at Chila Chávez's house either. Leaning against the willow tree that guarded the entry, Puelles felt faint; the old cook was right: the wanderings on January 4, added to the whirling about on Black Day, January 5, made his legs shake, now that it was getting dark. But he carried on sipping from the sea of *aguardiente* they offered him, and going from one toast to another, arrived home, transformed; he looked like he was made of wax. He listened to the family news: his grandfather was asleep.

What a terrible disappointment that his grandfather was sleeping.

His mother served him a cold guinea pig, cold wrinkled potatoes and icy plantain slices: "Eat it all up, like it or not," she told him. As soon as he finished, his father insisted he go to sleep; he wanted to carry him to bed: "You're very drunk, you oaf, you can't go round carnival like this, drunk yes, but not so drunk, do you understand?" Puelles was sorry his grandfather was sleeping; maybe his grandfather was the one who could save him from his death (he would finally tell his grandfather everything), but he did not feel up to waking him, and remembered his famous pronouncement: "If there's one thing that kills me it's people waking me up when I'm asleep. What if I'm dreaming of the one I love? I'd hate the person who woke me." "And what if I rescue you from a bad dream, Granddad, from someone just about to murder you?" Puelles imagined he might say, but he also thought his grandfather would reply: "Don't risk it."

No. He would not wake his grandfather.

Rodolfo Puelles said he would go to sleep, went to his room by himself and closed the door; he greeted the books surrounding his bed with a salute—too many books, he thought, an impregnable castle: at times, in the midst of so many books, he experienced the same feeling of desolation that had come over him the day he visited a hospital for the incurable.

Butting it with his forehead, he greeted the small wooden puppet hanging from the ceiling: a tormented Quixote. And he heard the lament of the familiar mouse that dwelled in the wardrobe and lived on those very books, and he stretched out full length, face down, fully dressed and with shoes on, hands linked behind his head: for a minute he made a concerted effort to sleep, yawned and closed his eyes—I'm sleeping now, he thought, I'm already asleep, already dreaming, but deep inside him, Mandarina's townhouse carried on nagging away: he did not care what happened to the doctor, the night outside his window was an invitation, there were stars in the sky. His parents dropped their guard: he got away.

Of what happened that night—and in the early morning of January 6 that he confused with dusk—Rodolfo Puelles the secret poet would remember absolutely nothing: he would not know whether he arrived at Mandarina's sleepwalking and sleeptalking, whether he got his girl—although you ought to remember such a cataclysm for ever, he thought—he would not know how he woke up on that isolated corner, with an empty bottle in his hand, he would not be sure whether or not he saw the Carriage of the Afterlife, he did not even remember who he was or what he was called—he panicked—what's my name? Tomorrow they'll call me the same as yesterday, but what's my name today?

"Cain," he cried.

And down the lonely road he went.

He was arriving in Unfamiliar Square—unfamiliar because he did not recognize it, he only made out a bell tower against the sky—when something landed at his feet: a stone; a dirty scrap of paper, tied with string, around a stone. He looked closely, saw lettering—a message, in the old style—he picked it up. There was no-one in the square, no window opened or closed, nothing to give away anyone who might have just thrown a message in the old-fashioned way. He untied the paper with a shaky hand and read: *im the gurl in the shop yu askt yestaday if ther woz lov and i sed no. Well see yu outsyd the chirch taday at ten.*

He stroked the paper, smoothing it out, and looked around him: no-one; doors and windows tight shut; the only movement on the street was Furibundo Pita's jeep, or was it the Carriage of the Afterlife? The fearsome milk dealer was making the most of the early morning to deliver his churns before the party began: the Carriage of the Afterlife cut across the empty square honking and disappeared. He realized he was beside one of those corner shops, with two stone steps outside and a big, green wooden door, all closed up: *The Spinning Top.* Its old window seemed sealed shut, did someone toss the stone from there? Was it in that shop he'd asked if there was love? Did he ask a girl yesterday? And was that very white church the one for the meeting? He put stone and all into his pocket, feeling hopeful. He made out the church clock: seven in the morning. His date was at ten, White Day would be in full swing, it wouldn't be long, oh, what to do, where to get another bottle—he fretted, and how cold he felt, how cold.

He stretched out across the pavement, next to the shop, his back against the wall, one leg on top of the other, and slept. He was woken by the enormous *marimba* some merrymakers from Tumaco were playing right beside him, rehearsing for the procession. He reached out and received the carnival bottle and drank without taking a breath—"here's to music," he shouted. A burst of applause comforted him. More people were beginning to circulate for White Day; the first volleys of talcum powder were thrown, streamers were spiralling from roof terraces, they coiled up and down like snakes in the air, menacing him; in the window opposite he saw the extraordinary face of a girl looking out: long black hair framing a white oval, eyes like water, he thought. From the way she was peering, hands clutching the curtains, covering herself from the neck down, he concluded she was naked; you have not disguised your nudity yet; are you my love? Someone at his side said: "It's as plain as the nose on your face," and he overheard: "I dreamed the cat was barking, can you believe it?" He felt those radiant eyes upon him: restless, bright with carnival passion, excited by the men passing at her feet—I've known some really beautiful girls, but a face with eyes like that, only in Pasto at carnival. "Was it you who threw me the love stone?" he shouted into the uproar of the dance, and knew she would never hear him, but she did because her eyes met his for an instant, and she smiled: was it her?

The door of the shop opened, interrupting them: an ancient woman, at least a hundred years old, whisked away the cobwebs around the door frame with her broom, and swayed rhythmically, to and fro, in time to the music spreading out around them—that can't be my girl, she's just a slip of a thing. Several green ostriches ran off down the street, "La Guaneña" was playing like there was no tomorrow; it seemed to him an eagle from the high plateau was flying over the rooftops, up into the carnival sky, a golden eagle, he mused—or a sparrowhawk?—a falcon with a white throat, would that he could open his eyes and fly, "Viva Pasto, Surprise City!" he shouted, I cannot see the volcano from here—he said to no-one, and no-one was listening, Galeras cannot see

me, the sacred Urcunina. Where does my girl live? Love's end: to forgive and be forgiven, all alone thinking of your unique naked voice,
this way we will save ourselves from ourselves. Who'll give me a bit of
bread? I'll laugh about this one day. He despised himself lying there,
dirty body across the pavement, time stood still or had passed by, the
secret poet Rodolfo Puelles just saw falling bones, bones raining down
before his eyes, never-ending, a shower of femurs, craniums, shoulder blades, getting soaked in a downpour of his own bones, he felt wet
with blood: it was the *aguardiente* other drunks were sprinkling in his
face. "Rise up, Lazarus," they said; he answered: "Fetch me Jesus."
He believed time was turning thick, unbreatheable, swarms of insect-
children buzzed at his side, who would ever think of bringing them
out flying? A puma-man said hello, he wondered whether dogs were
taking part in the carnival or if they had hidden them or if they ran
away frightened by the drums beating out *son* to all four points of the
compass; he sensed revellers somersaulting past his eyes one by one,
the clouds of talc, chests ragged with song, but he did not see a single
dog, since leaving home he did not recall seeing one dog, he laughed in
amazement, everything in the street turned white, whiter, as though
snow had fallen, he shouted—Pasto's snow, the carnival, Viva Pasto
dammit—and could not move.

If that old cook were to appear, one of those witches who no longer
appear, a wise woman in the ways of food, then a hearty *sancocho* would
be a miracle, he should eat meat, a poor animal, we even eat insects,
one of these days we will consume ourselves—we're already consum-
ing ourselves—you have to enjoy carnival, what am I waiting for? But
he did not manage to get to his feet, scrabbling, the window remained
without a face at it, without a girl, once more he wanted to get up in
search of the carnival, but it was no use: he fell again—like the Achaean
hero, he said—and, when he fell, the earth shook: "what makes
the hero weep," he quoted from memory, "what makes him appeal
to the forsaking sea, he is the strongest and fleetest of heroes, the one

who could have brought the war to an end, son of a goddess, condemned to a fleeting life, more fleet than he himself: he weeps for Briseis, she of the lovely cheeks, who the gods have taken away, the rancorous gods who do as they please in spite of the heroes," he kept quiet and waited for applause, heard it all around him, acknowledged it with a wave of the hand, "I love time," he shouted, and decided to wait, let the carnival come and find me, let the floats come here, let Simón Bolívar come like the punishment you deserve, oh horrible Quiroz, oh Platter you dog, but don't I have a romantic assignation at the church? He looked for the note he had kept in his pocket and recited it to the world, at the top of his voice; then said "that's what I call a love poem"—while hungrily eating the paper—now that girl will be mine, thanks to my binge, and she'll give me the love I asked for; she'll be the love of my life, she'll teach me her spelling, we'll make love three hundred and sixty-five times a day to mock death as it should be mocked, but he had to get to their date. How? He could not move—oh, let her come here, like the carnival. Who goes there? I see you, I'm watching you, why don't you say hello? Oh, old men, the street, walls, roofs coming down on top of him, numerous different-coloured noises, insatiable voices, unpronounceable faces, and yes, he rolled over, I see them going past. Or was he hallucinating? He saw those poets drunk on light pass by; there they went with their sonorous names: Helcías Martán Góngora and Guillermo Payán Archer, didn't one of them write that the world is a bitter bazaar of empty souls? Where to run to, where? Shivering, he saw the only great poet, Aurelio Arturo, on his own: dark suit, white hat. And a troop of friends followed; at what point did each of them turn to mist and vanish? He felt tremendous despair at himself, lying there, unable to move, a slave—worse than the whole mass of men who once received "a gift of a day" on which to be happy, far worse than all of them, what good did it do to greet the ghosts of poets passing by? Why all these spectres and Carriages of the Afterlife? When would he be capable of writing pure poetry? Or were the enchanted vaginas his poetry? Did he possess poetry, did poetry possess him? I must go, clear-headed, through the carnival for a minute, to see what's going on, nothing's going on, the carnival is pure intoxication, cheer up, but it laid him low to recall that he remembered absolutely nothing of the recent early morning, not one detail, a wink of memory's eye, nothing. What did he do? Kill?

He thought or dreamed he remembered walking through the outskirts of Pasto, lost; the carnival was thumping down below, but he carried on away from Pasto, stubbornly; he wanted to get as far as Tumaco, drinking. He crossed a bridge over a clear river, a spot he did not know, and saw a horse coming along the dusty highway, black head turned to the side, trotting hesitantly, and, behind it, stumbling along, an old woman, with a black hat and shawl, a lasso in her hands: she did not seem to be coming from any carnival, but there were talc marks on her skirt. From time to time she shouted "hey, hey," and stopped to catch her breath. He was watching her from the other side of the highway: her legs were swollen, she was barefoot, her feet the colour of soil, she must be sick, the skin on her face was ulcerated, peeling, like she was shedding it. She turned to look at him, for a second, and he was shocked to see her nose split down the middle, an old wound that looked like resin, the two eye teeth protruding over her lip greeted him silently, her eyes flashed ferociously, and she carried on running. She'll never catch it up, he thought, and, as though she had heard him, she turned her horrible face to look at him again. He closed his eyes, from pity, shame, disgust, panic, in order not to see her, but he carried on suffering that divided woman's face: he thought it was a face that hated, that hated him and that he hated, it was like revenge, he would dream of her, he thought, and he followed her, he followed them, in spite of himself, up to the highest point of the highway, and spotted them not far off, on a piece of flat level ground, she had managed to lasso the horse around its sweaty neck and was tugging on the slip knot, holding it tight. The horse reared up on its hind legs, surprised to be caught, and pawed the air. She approached, bent over, and continued calling out "hey, hey" until her voice became a triumphant whisper, and the horse stopped pawing, bent its black neck, allowed her to come near and almost touch it and then in a flash of hatred reared up and came down on top of the old woman, kicked her in the chest, knocked her to the ground and set off at a gallop, dragging the rope that snaked bloodily along through the dust on the highway, between curls of smoke. He ran to the old woman and leaned over her: the black hat on one side, white with dust, like she was; her hands fat-palmed and open on the ground, slashed by the rope; thick copper-coloured calves, tattooed with violet scars. He thought he should feel sorry for her, but the wound in the middle of her face stopped him: now it looked like a terrifying laugh, poking fun at him. "That horse is diabolical," he heard her say—what a sibylline voice, what a shiver-inducing voice—"but today I am more so," she said, "soon you'll know what I am," and he saw her get up as if nothing had happened; her skirt fell open; a bitter smell of burnt wood sprang from her body. Then he heard galloping again, coming closer all the time, thundering, he could not see the horse, where it came from, what place, what region it was galloping towards them from, and now the terror was too much, the whinnying sounded like a whirlwind, the galloping carried on getting closer, he heard it thump inside him, throb, heard his own heart thumping against the ground, Puelles had turned face down, on the paving stone, "the old woman will confront the horse," he said to passers-by, "the horse will kill her," he shouted, if his grandfather were to come to collect him, grandfather was up to the job, my saviour, he would be looking for him, he remembered his granddad dancing with a broom—more migratory bottles cut across the crowd from hand to hand, they came and went from one side of the city to the other, someone shouted "drink, dammit, the devil's at the party," the floating bottle appeared and Puelles drank, gratefully.

Doctor Justo Pastor Proceso López woke up on January 6 in his own bed, without Primavera at his side. It was the most important day of his life: the day of his death—as Enrique Quiroz would put it.

One day earlier, in the parish church, Quiroz himself had said: "I want him alive, so I can be the one to bury him." And, as Ilyich turned up with no news, he had burst out: "It's now or never." He issued orders: eight members of the group, led by Boris—Quiroz's brother—and Catiri from the plains, would pay a visit to a shed on the outskirts of Pasto that night where they believed—based on unreliable information—the float was to be found. Their mission had but one objective: blow up Bolívar's carriage, without further ado. Meanwhile, Ilyich and Vladimir would scour heaven and earth for the doctor. And yet, after receiving their orders, the group members did not move. A heavy silence pinned them in their places. It was not their own mission that seemed to shock them—the annihilation of the float—but the mission Quiroz and Platter took upon themselves, a mission they all, in their heart of hearts, considered a done deal, and which for that very reason scared them. Quite simply, they did not want to believe it. And there they stayed, surrounding their leader and Platter, as if waiting for an explanation: Was it all decided? Would they find Doctor Proceso? And then what? Would it really happen? Must it? They did not take their eyes off Quiroz and Platter—astonished, but still incredulous, you might say scared stiff. Quiroz and Platter let themselves be looked at, exalted. It was an oppressive situation, accompanied by a silence that, in spite of everything, was judgemental, and lasted only a few seconds. Quiroz and Platter had flushed; they were so different, but now they looked alike: their gaze was fixed, eyes wide open, as if they had both just been on the receiving end of an identical and terrible insult, and just the two of them, acting as one, were required to do something about it. Ultimately, their attitude and determination convinced the group: they displayed utter conviction that their action was justified; the whole world depended on the result; they were predestined to do this; they were going to kill.

"What are you waiting for?" Quiroz rebuked them. "Get a move on."

Immediately the group flew from the church, without a word. Their shadows moved resolutely through the night of wet streets. Quiroz and Platter were left alone.

"Shall we do it?" Quiroz yelled.

"Yes," Platter said, but in a hoarse, glad whisper.

"Yes," Quiroz repeated. And they both yelled it at once as they set off running into the rain, in search of Doctor Proceso.

And in fact they had looked for him the remainder of the night, fruitlessly: he was not to be found at his house or the houses of any of his abettors. In their frenzy, running from street to street in the rain of January 5, surrounded by the carnival on all sides, Ilyich and Vladimir imagined in despair that they crossed paths with the doctor on more than one occasion and did not recognize him—Pasto was like that, too. And still not knowing how the bombers had fared, when only a few hours remained for sleeping, they agreed to conclude their mission on January 6, during the parade of floats, the most important day of the doctor's life, the day of his death—Quiroz had said—on he would have to appear so he could be disappeared: it will be the fireworks of our carnival, the great test.

The morning of January 6, a noise like muffled thumping at the foot of his bed had woken the doctor. He discovered the thumps were coming from inside the chest where Primavera kept the sheets. He heard the defeated cry, the hopeless weeping of a child. He wanted to open the trunk, but it was locked; he had to break the catches. To his horror, an utterly terrified boy jumped from the chest and fled without saying a word. His head had been sheared and smeared with bird droppings. Who was it? He heard him go sobbing down the stairs, and out of the house with the distant slamming of a door.

"What's going on here?" the doctor asked himself.

His clothes from the night of the fifth lay scattered across the floor, still wet, muddy, testament to who knew what meetings and misses, where are you now Primavera, what are you up to? He put on his dressing gown and leaned out of the window overlooking the garden. He saw Sinfín, Floridita and the maid gathered round an ape—*the ape*—lying face up on the lawn, in the shape of a cross.

Homero.

"What's going on here?" the doctor asked.

"Nothing, *señor*, just that Homero got drunk and nobody can wake him up," Sinfín answered. "He's gone round scaring half of Pasto dressed up as a monkey, but it looks like he scared himself the most."

"Take off the costume, and let him breathe," the doctor said, "I'll come down." He was going to step back from the window but a burning question got the better of him: "Where's my wife?"

"She went to pick up Luz de Luna, who slept at her aunt Matilde's. She'll be back soon. She said for you to wait for her."

Sinfín was examining him from below; her eyes, accustomed to making things out in the distance, continued to scrutinize him inside and out; her sly face smiled indulgently:

"The *señora* woke up with you, Doctor, it's just that she woke up first, very early. She had to go for Luz de Luna: the girl stayed the night at her aunt's, without permission, you see? Wait for the *señora*, and don't despair, what else can you do?"

"The carriage," the doctor said. "Has the procession started yet?"

"It will in an hour. Just stand on Avenida de los Estudiantes and you'll see it go past sooner or later, but wouldn't you rather wait for the *señora*? Wait and see it with the *señora*, it'll be nicer."

The doctor did not reply. His whole life turned on a different question: where could Primavera have gone, with whom? The excuse about Luz de Luna sounded ridiculous to him—and he considered himself ridiculous too, for doubting. He did not want to remember the details of the night before, at the late Belencito's house, under the window with witnesses, he did not want to recall those details: their bittersweet aftertaste was embarrassing to him. He convinced himself to go out and find Primavera at the height of White Day: having her in front of him, face to face, he would know what to do, or they both would.

When he got down to the garden, Sinfín and the maid were pulling the costume from the gardener: they had just taken off the gorilla's head, exposing his reddened face, wrinkled and wet with *aguardiente*. Completely drunk, he was still in a stupor, he babbled incoherently, slapping himself, and all in front of Floridita, an observer of every gesture, every stutter, deliciously fascinated. Floridita's presence reminded him immediately of the locked-in, crying boy, a few minutes before. He was shocked observing her, so calm. He heard her say:

"He looks dead." And she nudged the gardener with the toe of her sandal.

"Leave him, girl," Sinfín said. "Let him sleep, he needs it."

The doctor picked up the disguise, and, just as he had done exactly ten days earlier, slung it over his shoulder. Then he turned to his daughter:

"There was a boy locked in the linen chest."

"So that's where he was," Floridita sounded surprised. "We were playing hide-and-seek yesterday. Nobody could find him, he beat us all."

"Oh, Floridita," Sinfín butted in, and shook her head. "It's a wicked, wicked, wicked world."

And she said no more.

"He ran off, that boy," the doctor said. "Who is he?"

"Seráfico's son," Sinfín told him. "I thought he had already escaped, yesterday. But he's a sharp one, he'll know how to get to Sandoná."

"You invited him to the flower party?" The doctor was amazed.

"He's a good boy," was all Sinfín said by way of an answer. "He can't read or write, but he likes singing. Thank God he's still alive."

Floridita and the maid burst out laughing. Sinfín showed her disapproval with a shake of the head.

"It's a wicked, wicked, wicked world," she said again.

Sinfín had her eyes half-closed, sorrowing, on the verge of tears—the doctor thought—and she remained engrossed, as if she were glimpsing, on the narrow horizon of the garden, everything to come, the next few years, and years far into the future, and found them grey, unchanging, really identical, but ominous too: she gave herself little pats on the forehead while saying, like a complaint to no-one in particular, "it's a wicked, wicked, wicked world."

The doctor ordered Floridita to go to her room:

"No carnival for you today. Shut yourself in there, till tomorrow."

Floridita shrugged.

"I don't care," she said. "I can play on my own."

And off she went.

Then they heard a groan from the gardener, as if he were waking up.

"The poor thing's lovesick," Sinfín said, "and doesn't learn; he suffers without learning a thing, suffers right in his guts."

"Oh, my darling," Homero said, "where am I? What did they do to me? It's so hot, what bastards, where are they? I want my revenge."

He opened his eyes and looked around him; he did not seem to recognize anyone, but he did seem to remember something, very far off:

"Take me to that bandit girl, she killed me, bring her to me, living without her is impossible."

The maid, all ears, burst out laughing again; she sought the doctor's eyes—as though summoning his approval, but the doctor did not share in the joke.

"Love is made of glass, my friend," Sinfín said, leaning in towards the gardener's ear, "sooner or later it shatters. Don't let it get you down, take my advice, a good lunch and plenty of sleep, that's all you need."

"So feed him up," the doctor said, "and let him sleep. You're always right, Genoveva. Bring him back to life."

"Doctor, dear doctor," Homero said, recognizing him and stretching out his arms. "Give me back the monkey costume. It's unlucky. I'll burn it."

But the doctor had already left the garden.

"What are you dressing up as, Papá?"

The doctor was in his room, about to put on the great ape head. Floridita was watching him from the doorway, without emotion. If that was his daughter, he thought, she was unrecognizable. Anyway, shouldn't she be shut in her room? Why did she ask that question if she already knew what he was dressing up as? Or did she want to initiate a conversation, be forgiven? But what was that about, locking a little boy in a chest all night? And the shorn head and bird muck? How would he punish her? And yet, a kind of tenderness took hold of him: she was his baby girl.

"As an orangutan," he said.

There was a strange silence; the doctor thought it was the first time he and Floridita had looked each other in the eye.

"Do you want me to tell you why I'm dressing up?"

He thought that he finally had the chance for a chat with his daughter. He had already thought of his answer—when she asked him why— "All the better to frighten you," he would say, imitating the wolf in the story. Then he would give her a hug.

However, Floridita did not oblige:

"No," she said, "I don't want to know why."

She said it as if she were winning a game.

She was leaning up against the door frame, looking at him with glinting eyes; at that moment she looked as though she was either going to cry or insult him; she turned and fled. He finished putting on the giant ape head: the mechanism in the throat did not work; he heard his voice just like normal. "What's going on here?" he had said. He had his daughter's glinting eyes engraved on his memory. "She's another Primavera," he thought, "she's more like her than she is me: she hates; she's stronger than me."

Minutes after Doctor Justo Pastor Proceso López left his house dressed as an orangutan, a carnival donkey arrived at his door looking for him.

Floridita, Genoveva Sinfín, the maid and the revived gardener were leaning over the balcony. Maltilde Pinzón, recently arrived in the company of her two sons and Luz de Luna, was presiding: they were all waiting for Primavera so they could go out and watch the parade; where on earth was she? Maltilde was getting impatient: Primavera had them all used to her ways. And what a surprise; suddenly a participant in the parade itself appeared in their street, under the balcony: a gleaming carnival donkey no less, capering about in front of them, among the happy people. They even saw that the multicoloured donkey stopped by the house, bowed as if in greeting, and kicked softly at the door, like it was knocking. The music around them got louder: an explosion of tambourines and drums. They saw the man who was inside the donkey's head emerge: his painted face was a grimace of delight, he had his hair streaked red and blue; he drew a bottle from inside his jacket and waved it about.

"And the good doctor?" he shouted up to the gathering on the balcony. "I want to drink a toast with him."

Sinfín yelled that the doctor was not at home:

"Wait for him, he'll be back."

"We'll look for him," shouted the smiling Quiroz. He was going to get back inside the donkey head, when the little girl on the balcony caught his attention:

"Are you looking for Papá?"

"Of course," Quiroz said.

"Well you won't find him," the girl hollered back. "He's dressed up."

Quiroz paused in suspense; the girl's face glowed, as if she were saying: "Aren't you going to ask me what Papá dressed up as?" At that moment Platter Ilyich came out from inside the donkey; he wiped the sweat from his forehead, his painted face was running, his hair a yellow clump.

"And what is he dressed up as?" he hollered.

The girl did not hesitate:

"An orangutan," she told them.

And, not yet knowing why, Genoveva Sinfín felt as if the air were actually growing dim, the feeling of ill omen that was running through her that morning solidified, and she crossed herself as she heard Floridita's reply.

*

And why an orangutan? Why this costume? Suffocation. Do I imagine discovering her without her discovering me, following her without her knowing who I am? How pathetic.

No-one pointed at him, his costume lacked soul: the ape was just one more participant in the carnival; Homero had really made him hate it now. He was skirting the street full of hands and heads stretching towards the avenue like branches; at least the disguise meant they did not recognize him. No floats were visible from the Obelisk; the carnival was growing apace; any arm, any hand could stretch out towards him from anywhere, stroke him, squeeze him or strangle him, he thought. At that moment he was assailed by a trio of formidable pigs, yoked together as horses from the crusades: the red crosses glowed from silk cloths covering their flanks, they squealed madly, he had to jump out the way; a dwarf couple were driving them along; very close by, a knot of black women were dancing with lit candles in their hands; one of them started to dance in front of the gorilla: her silhouette blazed amid beads of sweat; he heard horses' hooves clattering on the pavements, heard their whinnying; he smelled the pungent smoke of marijuana; beardless young men were smoking it beside him, sucking eagerly on the joints; someone yelled that they could see the first float of the carnival coming, elbows and knees shoved him; a little girl was crying, lost, she ran without direction through the carnival, not a puff of talc on her dress—as if protected under an invisible glass dome—in her hand she was carrying a sunflower bigger than herself. A finger sank itself into his hairy chest, three, four, five times; a voice:

"I know who's in there."

It was Matilde Pinzón. Alone. Without Primavera.

"I still don't," the doctor replied.

"Can't you find her?" she asked. Her tongue glistened very red; she seemed about to burst out laughing.

"Find who?"

"Go home and wait for her," Matilde said, pitying him, "I'll look for her for you."

The doctor did not know what to reply. Matilde Pinzón looked just like Primavera, but something repulsive set her apart, she was a sad woman, her expression a perpetual sneer. It felt inexplicable to him to be discovered in his ape costume by none other than Matilde Pinzón; how did she find out?

"Justo Pastor," she went on, "do your bit and everything will work out, you and Primavera are the ideal couple, you understand each other, you hear one another without speaking."

"Yes," the doctor told her, he and Primavera understood each other so well that he was forever losing things and she found them all:

"Now, for example, I'm out looking for her."

Matilde Pinzón started to laugh.

"Then first you'll have to find her," she said, "so she can tell you where she is. What a sense of humour you have, Justo Pastor, at least you still have that."

And she moved off: an older man, who was not her husband, was waiting for her cagily, one arm open; the doctor recognized him, the fabulously wealthy but now decrepit Luisito Cetina, owner of the Luz del Pacífico hotel chain. He saw them slink furtively into the crowd. The sun grew stronger; the ape got further towards the edge of the avenue, not just pushing, but pushing people right over, and no-one complained; it was the fiesta.

He did not want to find out what or who was parading, he wanted to lose himself as soon as possible; an orchestra was announced; he felt as though they had turned some incredibly powerful lights on the day, out of nowhere; the ear-splitting orchestra began to rock the pavement to its core, the crowd thundered applause, bodies swayed desperately to and fro as one, faces daubed with powder and paint rubbed up against one another, a surge of multicoloured skirts dazzled him, two girls who were dancing—streamers and sawdust like glue in their hair—kissed greedily, far gone, happy; he craned his hairy ape head into the cleavages of celebrating women, one or another hung on to his arm a few seconds, a drunk span around crazily on one leg and did not fall, the women seemed to want him to, but the drunk did not fall, he did not fall; a bald man rubbed his eyes, bawling that they had thrown flour and lemon juice at him, the tarmac smelled of urine, dung, he forced a way through and reached the side of the avenue and leaned out; a troupe of old people were dancing a waltz: seven or nine columns of geriatrics enduring the morning sun, daintily dancing the waltz played for them by the San Pablo band, made up of musicians older than the dancers themselves. The bodies, their outer trappings—he thought, feeling sorry for them—they do what they can manage for us, what they can manage, should I get drunk? They were all at least ninety years old, he reckoned, from the Don Ezekiel Home for the Elderly— according to the banner—and some of them pretty senile, more in the next world than this one, he thought, it's well worth dying while dancing without knowing we just died. Pushed by the crowd, a girl squashed her face against the orangutan's hairy chest, and flapped her arms in distress; the ape embraced her and let her go, as if moved to pity, with tender little taps on her cheeks: those nearest laughed; the old people's strange waltz started to twirl right in front of him; he heard someone asking: "Are they really old folk, or are they wearing corpse masks?" And someone answered: "Of course they're old folk, but they dance like children; they're made of stern stuff." And a woman's voice: "There are real nuns parading too, three blocks from here, and real luna-tics, a lot further behind, the mad from San Rafael, the genuine article." Another voice chipped in: "They say that in the prisoners' troupe, the prisoners dressed as prisoners are real prisoners, and they swore to go back to jail when the carnival's over." "If I was a prisoner, I wouldn't go back," somebody said, and someone else: "I would, your word is your word, and your word is sacred."

At that point Doctor Justo Pastor Proceso López did not know which he would prefer, to find Bolívar's carriage or to find Primavera in the crowd. Primavera would be best, he thought, to give her a fright, to cover her eyes with his great mitts and ask, throatily: "Guess who?" Frighten her in order to kiss her, or the other way around, he thought.

One of the ancient couples waltzing, she and he exactly alike, siblings in decrepitude, saintly smiles on toothless mouths, turning very slowly, came to an ill-timed halt beside him. In the old lady's eyes was the look of someone about to pass out. He heard her say: "I can't go on," and her partner: "We'll have a rest," and she replied: "It's not the dance I can't go on with, it's life," and they separated themselves from the procession, hand in hand, heartbroken. No-one came to their aid. The doctor took off the great ape head: "Go and get some fresh air and no more dancing," he ordered, like the doctor he was. Someone offered them a bottle of *aguardiente*, which he turned down; he took the old people by the arm and led them to a nearby tent, where the different soloists and trios were taking turns to play. He sought, found and fought over two chairs for them. Just then, Pasto's most glorious musicians greeted the audience from the stage: Maestro Nieto, on the *requinto*, and Chato Guerrero on guitar. They were announcing the already legendary "Viejo Dolor," to be played as a foxtrot, which made the old lady swoon with emotion: "Don't let me die without hearing it." The public uttered cries of "*viva!*" for Maestro Nieto, famous not only for his "Viejo Dolor," but the phrase he once used to describe his musical abilities: *I can't read a note, but nobody notices.* The doctor listened to the opening cadenzas of the foxtrot for a magical minute and moved away. He had the ape head in his hands, undecided whether or not to put it back on: he was dripping with sweat; he decided to plunge into the broad current of the crowd and strike out in the opposite direction to the way the parade was going in order to finally encounter the floats, one by one. There, astonished, he heard a woman shouting, calling him by name. He froze. The shout came again, from a nearby balcony. He moved forward until he was underneath it, beside an unfamiliar house: the doorway teemed with bodies going in and coming out with considerable difficulty. In the middle of

that balcony brimming with women, the pious Alcira Sarasti laughed
and stretched her bare arms towards him:

"Come up, Doctor, what are you doing with that ape head? Come
up and we'll watch the floats from here."

"I don't think I can come up," the doctor shouted. "There's an absolute forest of people."

And he put the big ape head on again—she recognized me, he
thought, what if I bump into the widow? What'll I do with two lovers
at once?

"Then I'll come down," Alcira shouted, and disappeared from the
balcony.

He waited for her a good long time, under a crushing sun, but she
did not come. At one point he thought he saw her head float past on a
sea of heads, going under and coming up again, and then he saw her no
more: it was as if the crowd had swallowed her up. The sea of heads was
crashing on the shore of the avenue; at last the first carnival float
was seen approaching. He did not need to move: the entire mass of merrymakers, like a river, dragged him along to the foot of the float. And
still he did not manage to make out the theme, the spirit of the float; he
was at its feet, but he could not guess what it was about, it presented
such a vast spectacle to his eyes, an edifice; to take it on board in its
full enormity you had to be on the balcony where Sarasti had shouted
from. And he read the notice on it, a banner suspended between the
feet of an unidentifiable animal: WHEN THE POPPIES FLOWER. It
was not his Bolívar float. In a sort of royal box, stuck halfway up, he
saw four girls dancing: the sequins on their miniscule costumes flashed
in the sun; clouds of talcum powder swirled out around their ankles,
streamers flew through the air; "It's the House of the Sun," the crowd
guessed, and the titanic animal seemed to agree—half fish, half lion;
huge seahorses swam about, a resounding jeer was heard on all sides,
the doctor wondered who the crowd was laughing at—is it me?—
and he looked himself up and down: he was an ape, white with powder, but no-one seemed to see him. He continued to overhear absurd

comments: "My bitch and my grandma are going there," "They're the governor's canaries," and he raised his eyes higher, as the orchestra exploded over his head; then he discovered the queen of the carnival, beauty of beauties, almost naked, jiggling about at the very top of the float, shimmying on a narrow beam; she held a small sign against the triangle of her crotch which read: *TROY WAS HERE.*

The ape allowed the destination of the crowd to pull him along. He thought that sooner or later, by chance in all the commotion, he would come across Primavera or Bolívar's carriage, whichever cropped up first. He would receive them gratefully, as one might receive infinite repose, but he would abandon Bolívar's carriage to the mercy of the world, and Primavera he would take home, to bed, and into his arms, he thought. And yet, after an hour adrift he lost hope: corner followed corner with-out a sighting, the carnival soon smothered him: Primavera was nowhere to be found, better to return home as soon as possible and wait for her—as the world seemed to be advising him. But immediately after coming to this decision it became impossible for him to go towards any destination other than where the crowd was heading. He made out a carnival donkey on the other side of the avenue, a donkey separate from the group of weavers who were parading along: the donkey was spinning rapidly around among the revellers. Me and that donkey are the only animals here, he thought, and he examined himself again, inside his ape suit—what was it for? Wouldn't it be better to drink to the point of oblivion, turn into smoke blown away on the wind? Then the mob seemed to push him towards the spinning donkey, and, funnily enough, from the other pavement the crowd seemed push the donkey towards him. The multitude lapped around them, like dark waters opening up to the point of devouring them—like one more carnival game.

A few metres away, General Lorenzo Aipe and Primavera Pinzón observed him for the last time. They had discovered him long before, when he took off his ape head to speak to the old people, but under the balcony where he shouted to Sarasti "there's an absolute forest of people" was where they properly recognized him, and it was where Primavera did not know what to do: she did not know herself, her life and her daughters, she did not know whether to run to him, embrace him or lose him again—she thought—for all eternity. When she realized she did not love him, she felt a tremendous sorrow for him, to the point of tears, but composed herself in time: General Lorenzo Aipe did not notice her emotional state. The general was sweating, dressed as Bolívar: he could think of no better costume to taunt Doctor Proceso with, a Simón Bolívar in civilian clothing: tall straw hat, with red-and-blue poncho, woollen jacket and breeches, and long leather boots.

That morning General Lorenzo Aipe had personally taken charge of Bolívar's carriage. His soldiers located the float a day earlier, but he chose the dawn of the sixth to surprise the artisans and confiscate it. None of them put up any resistance: some were in nightclothes, others in their underwear; they were frightened men, women and children, of all ages. They had hidden the float in a shed on the outskirts of Pasto, on one side of the cold highway leading to Lake Cocha, and now it had been found: soaring up like a ship in full sail, it seemed to touch the sky; he was a monster, this Bolívar pulled along by girls, Emperor of the Andes. But that early morning, Arbeláez the sculptor, Martín Umbría and Maestro Abril, makers of the float, lost heart: the soldiers spread out around the inside of the shed, pointing guns at them.

On the night of the fifth they had resisted an attempt by hooded men to blow up the float, who besieged them without order or agreement, and who—following their strange engagement—took flight, in the rain. They threatened them with blowing the float sky high in the procession—"and you're responsible for putting the citizens of Pasto at risk"—but nothing more, only words; they fled, the gun that one of them was holding went off in his hand, which made the women laugh. Two more fired without consequence: one hit the ceiling, above his own head, and a cascade of falling plaster turned him white, and the other struck Boozy, Maestro Abril's dog, and did not even hurt him, it was just a graze, but they heard him yelp, which inflamed the children. "It's not the dog's fault," they cried, and the fight began. The youngest artisans easily took care of those in hoods, who outnumbered them. When the makers entered the fray, genuinely determined to defend the float from the destroyers, the hooded ones were already "scampering away like guinea pigs"—according to Maestro Abril. And, yet, the winds of victory did not stay the course: now it was not a matter of hooded men—more amusing than dangerous—but the army itself. "Sonofabitch," they said, this is serious: the army was pointing guns at their chests; they were surrounded.

They confiscated the float, along with the truck carrying it and everything: Martín Umbría's truck.

General Lorenzo Aipe considered the mission accomplished. He regretted the military deployment, and that was what upset him most; he ordered the soldiers to return to base, "quietly," and climbed into the jeep waiting for him; a cinch, the only tricky bit had been finding out where the float was hidden. Now all he thought about was his Simón Bolívar costume, and blonde Primavera Pinzón, naked. He retired, leaving an officer and seven soldiers in charge of transporting the float; he did not even want to look at it in any detail, but he did order it to be covered up as soon as possible: "Don't let anybody see it," he said, "that's the main thing."

The soldiers proceeded to cover it up immediately, even though it was early and all Pasto was sleeping. Shrouded, the float looked like who knows what kind of folly-surprise, advancing through the streets of Pasto in the early morning of the sixth.

They were taking it to the barracks to dismantle it.

There were seven soldiers and their officer—later people would say there were twenty, fifty, a hundred and many more. They were not far from the barracks when Martín Umbría, Tulio Abril, Cangrejito Arbeláez and the rest of the artisans caught them up—backed up by their wives and children. The soldiers did not suspect the attack. They thought it was a parade group arriving in Pasto to join in White Day: they were dancing, throwing streamers and drinking. Perhaps the only peculiar thing was the time: too early in the morning for such larks. But anything was possible at carnival.

It was the same early hour that in another part of the city the secret poet Rodolfo Puelles confused with dusk.

Now it really was getting dark, but the carnival was still in full swing, and it danced in front of the Spinning Top, in that Pasto street where Rodolfo Puelles still lay, not moving.

"Okay, Puelles, wake up," a voice said. "We've been looking for you." And a different voice:

"The moment of truth has arrived, Puelles. Get up. They're here, and they want to meet you; on your feet, Puelles. The time has come to walk."

He opened his eyes. Suddenly he saw Quiroz: his head. Quiroz moved to the side to allow Ilyich's head to appear.

They had both shaved off their hair.

Platter Ilyich laughed, his mouth very wide open.

"They want to meet the chosen ones, and you are a chosen one, of course."

He bent down and placed a hand like a bird's talon on Puelles's shoulder:

"Let's go. It's getting late."

Quiroz looked at his watch:

"They're not far away."

Puelles started to get up: the bird's talon weighed his shoulder down, rather than helped him. It must be five o'clock; it was getting dark. Puelles panted, gulped down air. He still felt exultant:

"And where did you leave the donkey?"

Quiroz did not miss a beat:

"We showed off the donkey this morning," he said. "We got delayed by a monkey."

It was the only time they ever laughed, all together. In his delirium, the secret poet did not imagine what monkey they were referring to; Rodolfo Puelles did not imagine anything at all.

The carnival blazed up more brightly, right across the street. The music strolling past got louder: a group of revellers were dancing a step away from them. All of a sudden, as if obeying the impulse for one last burst of joy, or because a suspicion of the sacrifice entered his head for the first time and he wanted to run away, Rodolfo Puelles threw himself into the centre of the human wheel and began to dance, transfigured, pop-eyed, shouting *"viva!"*

Quiroz and Platter stayed at the edge, looking at him in astonishment: they had not expected him to do that. Platter took a step forward, to catch hold of Puelles.

"Leave him," Quiroz said. "Let him finish dancing."

The little carnival band was playing "La Danza de la Chiva": it finished with a clatter of cymbals, the trumpet bade farewell, and a sea of applause came crashing down. The people dancing offered Puelles a bottle, and Puelles drank, he drank and went on drinking, down to the last drop.

"That's it, that's it," Platter told him, "have one for the road, because we're taking you to paradise now."

"Follow us," Quiroz said.

And Puelles followed them.

He thought that he did not mind.

The light from the sun became reddish, a cold red light, eerie at this hour of explosions. They made their way quickly through the streets, despite the crowds.

They left the carnival, which meant, in effect, leaving Pasto.

It had been Zulia Iscuandé who called on the artisans to put up a fight— they had already given the float up for lost. "We can't end on bad terms with the doctor," she said, "and it's not about his money; the fact is that we made the carriage ourselves and those heartless bastards are going to wreck it." Cangrejito Arbeláez had no illusions: even if they did get the float back it would be difficult to exhibit it, with the army in the way plus the balaclava boys, who would soon surround them, pop up where they might; the Pastusos were the only hope, he thought, the people of Pasto might defend the carriage, but how? It was unlikely they could count on this defence: this was a fiesta, people went out to dance, how does one arrange a battle overnight for the sake of a carnival float? A float that only seemed like a bit of fun at the outset. The urgent thing was to hide the carriage from obliteration, it would have to bide its time for all Pasto to come to its defence.

He heard the artisans shouting "*viva!*" for the doctor. "Thanks to him, on behalf of the float-makers," he heard: "We're not going to abandon him, dammit," "Let's get a move on," "Here we go." The sculptor observed the makers' large, deeply lined hands, which looked carved from stone; they had painted their faces; they got out bottles of *aguardiente* and pretended to start the January 6 binge, but they were off to recover the carriage from the hands of the army, no less. And they set off at a run through the sleeping streets, in pursuit of the stolen float.

It was also Zulia Iscuandé who started the battle. She offered a swig of *aguardiente* to the soldier nearest her, who was perched up on the shrouded carriage, holding the bottle out to him, and when the soldier went to take it, he got smacked around the face with it instead. In minutes the soldiers were disarmed and hurled from the carriage as if by an unstoppable whirlwind—with the same rage and courage as in the days of Agustín Agualongo, Cangrejito reflected while he fought. It was a silent and speedy battle. Just one shot was fired, which got lost in the cries of "*viva!*" from the assailants: the officer fired; he was driving the truck the float was embedded on, and his shot hit Maestro Umbría in the arm, up on the running board alongside him; in spite of the burning bullet, the maestro stretched out his other arm and took the officer by the throat, pulling him out through the little window by brute force. The few inquisitive onlookers who caught a glimpse did not understand what was going on, just a "dressed" float, as they put it, and a few soldiers chatting with some early birds. They were not chatting, they were grateful to still be alive: the attackers occupied the cab of the truck, the various vantage points on the carriage, and made off.

In the isolated neighbourhood, which Puelles was struggling to recognize—wasn't it here I played spinning tops, as a kid, and won?—the dirty, narrow streets of unfinished cement houses, looking like black, upside-down skeletons as night fell, started to oppress him, but he was crushed altogether by the shock he got on the last corner, in the dusk, when the houses were already petering out: three or four boys were playing war, they fell and died, came back to life, killed again.

Now Puelles saw wheat fields, not far away, behind the last house.

"And what have you got in your pocket, Puelles, a stone?"

Platter had slipped a hand into his trouser pocket and went on, amazed:

"Yes, it is a stone, for pity's sake. For killing wood pigeons? Self-defence?"

"And that cross?" Puelles said to Platter, pointing to the gold crucifix dangling from his neck. "Did Father Bunch give it to you?"

Platter stopped walking.

"Christ was the first of us," Quiroz said. "Don't sneer, Puelles. We have a religion too."

He signalled to Platter for him to keep on walking with them.

"Ah, religion," Puelles said, and once more the hidden poet peeped out. "Mankind's worst and most perfect intolerance."

"Yeah right," Platter said. "Now you've taken it into your head to talk like that crazy Chivo, you philosophizing prick. Who do you think you are? You want to have it out with me?" And he broke into a string of rapid insults, which Puelles ignored; but he could not help laughing on hearing the last: *revolting revisionist.*

I can laugh, Puelles thought, it's still possible.

"Steady, Ilyich," Quiroz said. "There's time."

They had left the neighbourhood of grey houses behind them now. Everything was green in the failing light. Now they were treading on soft, lush grass, the damp earth. Around him Puelles saw rolling hills knitted together, the ruddy sky. They carried on towards the fields of high yellow wheat, swaying just a little further on, ruffled by the wind. Puelles no longer felt the desire to talk, to ask anything. Much less to flee. It was as if a great lethargy towards everything and everyone, including himself, were stored up in his limbs, in his intelligence. He remembered the dead policeman again, like so many times before, and now he could not go on, he could not go on. He could not go on. And he smiled dumbly; he wondered whether, when he died, as had happened when he killed, he was going to piss himself with fright. Neither Platter nor Quiroz paid him any attention.

Now they were crossing the field sown with wheat. The stalks were tall, they brushed Puelles's chest.

"Ah, Puelles," Quiroz said. "Why did you have to talk so much?"

Puelles did not answer.

"Relax, Puelles, we're not going to do anything to you," Quiroz went on. His voice had gone hoarse; he seemed to want for air. "We're just going to execute you."

Puelles felt an immense tiredness: when I die I'll think of Grandfather, or will I think of Toña Noria's enchanted vagina, enchanted because she never gave it to me?

The tremendous fatigue befuddled him. He thought it was not just a fatigue of his bones, but reached far beyond him, to the entire universe.

"Here, here," he told them.

He wanted to rest in that place, hidden in the middle of yellow wheat, at dusk, looking at the sky. He felt exhausted, and yet, surprising himself, remembered he had often run the marathon at school and won, the hundred-metre dash too, a hare, and, as if dreaming, he broke into a run, and believed he ran faster than a hare, turned to look, they were close, deranged faces, arms stretched out, they could touch him, but he would get home and carry on to Bogotá and then Singapore, he thought, and thought on, managing to have time to think—they'll say Puelles got away.

The shot rang out and a flock of pigeons flew up over the wheat fields.

They fled with the float, they fled.

When General Lorenzo Aipe found out, he did not order the reprisal his men were expecting: this time he would not play cat and mouse; he would wait until the carriage materialized and impound it immediately, "They'll have to appear sooner or later," he said, and ordered the official starting point of the floats to be monitored, as well as the route, in case they had to intercept it. He was worrying needlessly, because after that morning Bolívar's carriage vanished; nothing more was ever heard of it: few early risers saw it cross Pasto, wrapped in canvas, and go up the highway to Lake Cocha. And in that jungle chasm, in the solitude of the plains, the makers hid it—in a cave?—underground, they say, waiting for next year's carnival.

EVELIO ROSERO is the author of seven novels and two collections of short stories. In Colombia his work has been recognized by the National Literature Award. He won both the *Independent* Foreign Fiction Prize and the Tusquets International Novel Prize for *The Armies*.

ANNE McLEAN is a translator of Latin American and Spanish literature by authors including Julio Cortázar, Javier Cercas and Enrique Vila-Matas. Her translation of Juan Gabriel Vásquez's *The Sound of Things Falling* won the 2014 International Impac Dublin Literary Award.

ANNA MILSOM is an academic and translator currently living in Ecuador. This is her second co-translation with Anne MacLean.

ABOUT THE TYPE

Typeset in Cycles Eleven at 11.5/15 pt.

Designed by Sumner Stone and published by
Stone Type Foundry, Cycles has different versions
that are optimized for setting at specific point sizes
for use in publications with complex typography.

Typeset by Scribe Inc., Philadelphia, Pennsylvania.